THE COIN AND THE KEY

Fergus P Egan

THE COIN AND THE KEY

Author and Publisher: Fergus P Egan

ISBN: 978-1-9993941-4-1 (Electronic Book Edition)
ISBN: 978-1-9993941-5-8 (Hardcover Edition)
ISBN: 978-1-9993941-3-4 (Paperback Edition)

Email: FergusEganPublishing@gmail.com

Editor: Andrew Niall Egan
Cover design and photographs: Andrew Niall Egan

ISBN: 978-1-9993941-3-4

On Wednesday 02 August 1950, Canon Paul Anthony MacMorrow is discovered lying injured inside St. Bawn's Church. He speaks a few words – 'a coin' and 'a key'. Are these clues that will lead to his assailant? He falls unconscious and dies within minutes.

Why would anyone kill a harmless old priest in a quiet rural haven in the west of Ireland? Detective Inspector John Patrick Murphy, 'Murf', searches for evidence and motives in the parish and the town. Later he learns of a related incident many miles away at the border. When a foreign connection is uncovered, the Royal Ulster Constabulary becomes interested, and so does 'London'. Has the Cold War arrived at the doorsteps of a quiet country church in remote County Mayo?

This story is for my sister, Emer, with whom I spent my childhood in Ireland. It is a work of fiction. The location and setting of each crime are purely imaginary. Otherwise, the descriptions of the towns and countryside are fairly accurate.

It is because of Emer's encouragement that I was motivated to write and finish this story. If she alone enjoys it, then it will have been a worthwhile endeavour.

TABLE OF CONTENTS

PART 3 – THE QUEST IS PUT TO REST

LIST OF CHARACTERS

<u>Detective Inspector John Patrick Murphy (Murf)</u>:
Police detective in rural Ireland

<u>The Ward Clan of Itinerant Travellers</u>:
<u>Paddy More Ward</u> – Ganger of a work crew
<u>Paddy Lamp Ward</u> – Junk recycler and mender of lamps and clocks
<u>Francie Clé Ward a.k.a. Paddy Clé Ward</u> – Street entertainer and psychic
<u>Collie Tricks Ward a.k.a. Paddy Tricks Ward</u> – Street entertainer and con artist

<u>Secret Service Agents</u>:
<u>Piper's Son a.k.a. Patrick Piperson</u> – British Foreign Office
<u>Andrews</u> – MI6 agent assigned to 'Code White'
<u>Brady</u> – MI6 agent assigned to 'Code White'
<u>Cody</u> – MI6 agent assigned to 'Code White'

<u>Constable Manus McCann</u>:
Member of Cheshire County Police assisting in the search for John Cross

<u>Garda Seamus O'Reilly</u>:
Member of Killbawn police and assistant to Detective Inspector Murphy

<u>Thomas 'Farouk' Gilban</u>:
Accountant at St. Bawn's Church, previously with the British Foreign Office

<u>Jack Gilban</u>:
Sacristan at St. Bawn's Church

<u>Malachy Gilban:</u>
Senior Security Officer at Shannon Airport, previously a member of an IRA splinter group with Soviet Russian connections after the Irish Civil War

<u>Bélyy and 'Code White':</u>
Bélyy (White) – Cryptonym of entity engaged in Soviet intelligence gathering, active from 1943 to 1948 in Canada, U.S.A. and in the Middle East.
Bélyy reactivated in 1950 and is the subject of the 'Code White' investigation by the British Secret Service

<u>John Cross:</u>
British research scientist engaged at High Explosive Research in Royal Ordnance Factory, Risley, Cheshire, England – (a.k.a. Peter Oldthorpe)

<u>Peter Oldthorpe a.k.a. Pyotr Staryygorodsky:</u>
Cryptonym of John Cross, under investigation in 'Code White' – Soviet spy and British defector to USSR

<u>Sally 'Granny' McGrath:</u>
Elderly widow, previously in splinter IRA. The McGrath family and the Gilban family were active IRA-Soviet collaborators in the post-civil war period

<u>St. Bawn's Church Members:</u>
<u>Rev. Andrew MacNamara</u> – Parish curate
<u>Maggie Friel</u> – Parochial housekeeper
<u>Eamon Currie</u> – Canon MacMorrow's driver
<u>Doctor Marie Antoinette McBratt</u> – Killbawn district doctor
<u>Danny (the Divil) Begley</u> – Doctor McBratt's driver and local inebriate
<u>Patrick Joseph Casey</u> – Killbawn merchant and parish benefactor

PROLOGUE

ST. BAWN'S CHURCH
COUNTY MAYO, IRELAND

Wednesday 02 August 1950

Two minutes before 8:00am, Jack Gilban parks his bicycle at the side of the church and walks to the main door. Jack is the church sacristan, as was his father before him, a position originally bestowed on his grandfather in 1880 when the present St. Bawn's Church was built. Hanging from his trousers' belt is a chain. It is like a watch chain but heavier and stouter. Attached to the chain is a six-inch iron key, similar to a gaoler's key. He inserts the key in the main door of the church, unlocks it and swings it to a fully open position. The porch is large. It serves as the narthex and contains the entrance to the nave and to the tower. From the narthex, one enters the nave of the church through glass-panelled swing doors.

Jack, however, does not enter the nave. Instead, he approaches the tower. A small heavy wooden door gives access to the tower. Jack puts his hand to the top rail above the door and locates the hidden key. He unlocks the tower door and returns the key to its hiding place on the top rail. He enters the tower. This area gives access down to basement storage, and up the winding staircase to the choir loft, and higher still to more storage compartments, and eventually ending in the belfry. Jack recognises the familiar smells in here. This is where he keeps his tools, oils, candles, cleaners and polishes. The smells from his polishing rags, hanging on hooks, are ever present – furniture polish, silver polish and brass polish. It is dark inside the tower.

Electricity was installed in St. Bawn's two years earlier, but this area is still illuminated by oil lamps. It is too troublesome to light a lamp. If Jack needs a light he reaches for one of the many candles stored on the shelf inside the doorway alongside matches, lighters and snuffers. Jack does not descend the stairs or ascend the stairs. Jack does not even strike a match for light. He is so familiar with his daily routine that he strides unerringly to the space behind the circular staircase. He reaches up and makes contact with the bell rope. From the time he parks his bicycle to reaching the bell rope, two minutes have elapsed. Jack is sure of his routine. It is unnecessary to check the time. At 8:00am he sounds the Angelus bell – three rings of three, followed by nine rings. The Angelus bell is heard throughout Killbawn. Many people rely on it for their morning wake-up. It also informs the citizens that Mass will start in half an hour.

Jack now prepares the altar for Mass. First he checks that there is enough oil in the red sacristy lamp to last until 8:00am the following morning. This is a much easier task since Canon MacMorrow replaced the elaborate hanging lamp with a wall-mounted fixture. Previously, the lamp was suspended from the ceiling over the transept in front of the sanctuary on a series of chains and weights. Jack would require a pole with a hook to snag the bottom of the lamp and pull it down to replenish the oil. The entire lamp with chains and weights was hefty and cumbersome. It was impressive and ornate, but it was in danger of falling down. Rather than repair it, Canon MacMorrow decided on something much safer. Now there is a bracket projecting from the apse wall from which hangs a lamp suspended in front of the tabernacle. The lamp is accessible from the ambulatory space behind the altar in which Jack has placed a chair to assist him in this duty. Jack stands on the chair and checks the oil level. He is satisfied with the amount remaining. Next he checks the Mass candles. There is a ledge at the back of the altar which serves as a step to check the Mass candles. Mass candles are made from beeswax, and they are not as tall as they appear. There are three candles on the Epistle side of the altar, and three on the Gospel side of the altar. The wax candles are concealed inside white cylinders that have the appearance of candles. The real candles are inside these resting on springs. As each candle burns down, the spring pushes it up. When ignited, Mass candles always appear to be of equal height and size. Jack elevates the cylindrical sleeve of each fake candle to check the actual candle inside. He is satisfied with the amount of candle still remaining in each location.

Jack's next duty is to check the candle stand at the side altar. As he approaches, he is aware that something is amiss, but cannot identify what. He will need to replenish the stock of penny candles for the votive lights. About 20 to 30 are burned each day. Then he notices what is amiss. The coin box for the penny offerings is missing. It should be there beside the candle stand. Jack rushes over to investigate. He sees the box, still attached to its iron stand, lying in the aisle. Jack wonders how it could have been knocked over. It is a sturdy stand. The people who come here to pray are unlikely to knock it over. Maybe some children came in last night after 6:00pm and were running around in the shadowy aisle while their mother was at prayer? Jack rights the stand and shakes the box. He is satisfied that the box is intact and was not robbed, not that anyone would rob a petition box of a few bob in pennies. Jack positions the stand back in place and is thankful that no harm was done.

Jack walks along the aisle, back towards the narthex and to the tower room, to obtain a supply of penny candles. Alerted by the coin box, he looks around to see if anything else is out of place. Everything appears to be in order in the nave, in the transept and in the sanctuary. He exits through the glass-panelled swing doors into the porch and attentively casts his eye around the narthex. How could he have missed it when he first entered? Muddy boot prints. He looks back into the nave. No boot prints in the nave, only in the porch. He follows the prints from the entrance to the tower door and thence inside to his supply room. This time, Jack takes a candle from the shelf and lights it and secures it in a candlestick. He follows the boot prints to the basement stairs. So someone with muddy boots went down to the lower level storage room. It could only have been after 6:00pm last night, after the six o'clock Angelus. That was when Jack finished at the church and went home. Jack decides to ask Canon MacMorrow when he comes to say Mass in a few minutes time. Just now, he has insufficient time to investigate the boot prints any farther or to mop the floor before the start of Mass. He needs to complete the preparation of the altar. He grabs two fistfuls of penny candles. He extinguishes the lighted candle with a blast of his breath and goes back to the side altar where he replenishes the supply of penny candles. Two more tasks and the altar will be ready for Mass – fill the cruets with water and wine and place them with the finger bowl and cloth on the side table beside the altar, and light the Mass candles.

Jack considers it unusual that the sacristy is quiet. It is the canon's habit to say Mass before he eats breakfast, so if he rises when he hears the Angelus bell, he should be here by now. Jack decides to fill the cruets with the required amounts of water and wine. Then, if the canon has not arrived, he will enquire in the parochial house.

From the sanctuary, in the apse of the building, Jack enters the sacristy. The sacristy is windowless, and the light switch is at the other end beside the exit door. This does not deter Jack. He ensures that the door from the apse is fully open in order to permit the light from the nave to illuminate the interior of the room. The tray with the cruets and finger bowl are on the counter inside the door. The wine is stored in the cupboard underneath. Jack brings the two empty cruets to the sink to wash and rinse them. That is when he unexpectedly encounters the canon.

Jack drops both cruets, shattering them on the floor. Canon MacMorrow is lying on the floor in a pool of blood at the exit door. Jack cries, "Canon MacMorrow, are you hurt?"

The canon opens his eyes, looks at Jack for a second, and closes his eyes again. In panic, Jack runs for help. The parochial house is only 15 feet away via the interconnecting passageway, but Jack runs via his familiar route through the apse, into the nave and out through the narthex. Running along the sidewalk to the parochial house, Jack sees Eamon Curry, the canon's driver, sitting in his car reading his morning newspaper.

Jack slaps the side window shouting, "Eamon, go get the doctor! The canon has fallen and is badly hurt. Hurry, for God's sake!"

Eamon starts the car and shouts back, "Where?"

"In the sacristy. He is lying on the floor and is bleeding."

Eamon hears 'In the sacristy' before he drives out of earshot.

Breathless, Jack reaches the front door of the parochial house, and then decides to run around to the back where the kitchen is located. This is where Mrs. Friel would be, and perhaps Father MacNamara too. Jack is shouting loudly as he approaches the door. Alerted by the shouting, Mrs. Friel opens the back door before Jack reaches it. "Canon MacMorrow is hurt! Come quickly! He has fallen and is hurt!"

Father MacNamara rushes out from the breakfast room. All three now run along the passageway to the sacristy. "The key!" shouts Father MacNamara upon realising that Jack hadn't come this way and the sacristy door is still closed and locked. Father MacNamara makes a quick U-turn and runs back to the house. He retrieves his bunch of keys from the hall table and runs with greater urgency to the sacristy. Because he is much younger than the others, he reaches the sacristy door at the same time. He quickly inserts the key and turns the lock. The door opens inward and stops upon hitting an obstruction.

Jack shouts, "Be careful. The canon is lying on the floor right inside the door."

Gingerly, Father MacNamara squeezes through the space of the partly-open door, followed by Mrs. Friel and Jack.

Canon MacMorrow opens his eyes.

Mrs. Friel cries, "Lord have mercy! Let's move him to a more comfortable position."

"And get the doctor!" shouts Father MacNamara.

"She's already on her way," responds Jack.

"Right. Let's see if we can move him and place a cushion under his head."

The three of them attempt to move the canon by the upper arms. He moans in pain at their attempt.

"Stop!" cries Father MacNamara. "He is in pain. A broken bone perhaps? Don't move him. We'll only make it worse."

Mrs. Friel is weeping and crying, "Canon, can you hear me? Can you talk?"

The canon opens his eyes again and moves his lips. "Cross...Cross..." he murmurs faintly.

"Oh, he wants the crucifix." She takes the crucifix from the counter and places it on the canon's chest. She bends low to place an ear close to the canon's mouth. "Is there anything else? Water?"

The canon's lips move feebly. "The mirror...in the mirror...."

Mrs. Friel urgently instructs Jack. "Jack, cover the mirror. Quickly, before his soul passes."

Jack is familiar with the sacristy. The only mirror here is the full-length mirror attached to the back of the door to the apse, the mirror in which the priest checks his vestments before entering the sanctuary. He quickly covers it with an alb.

The canon is still attempting to speak. Mrs. Friel strains to hear. "What's that? I didn't catch that. 'The fecking British something'?"

'Feck' is not a word that Mrs. Friel would use. But she knows that the canon, when upset, could utter it. She moves closer in an attempt to hear the canon's weakening voice.

They all hear the canon's feeble words, "...a key – a coi..." and exhausted, he closes his eyes again.

Mrs. Friel turns to the others. "Why does he want a key? What key?"

Before they can speculate, Doctor Marie Antoinette McBratt enters the sacristy from the apse followed by Eamon. "Turn on the light and move back." She sees at a glance that the canon, whose bones are as brittle as a stick of chalk, has suffered a broken leg. And he has a bloody bruise to the head. "Send for the ambulance. The canon must get to the hospital immediately. Eamon. Run to the guards. They'll arrange it." Eamon goes off in great urgency to drive to the Garda station.

The bruise is weeping blood. Doctor McBratt stitches it. But is the wound deep? Is there a concussion? Elevate the wound; stop the bleeding; the leg should be stretched and straightened. She accomplishes this with the help of Father MacNamara. If only the guards would come. They are all trained in first aid. She needs to move the canon, but he is too heavy, and the present company is not sufficiently skilled. She administers a painkiller and is attentive to the effects of shock. The canon is an old man. He is not likely to survive. But she keeps this opinion to herself.

The canon is breathing evenly. The altered leg position has alleviated some of the pain, and the painkiller is kicking in. All four look at the canon and at the surrounding area. On the floor is a small pool of blood. Close by, there is the shattered glass from the broken cruets. A brass acolyte's candlestick is lying on the floor beside the canon. The candlestick is smudged with blood. Did the canon knock it off the counter when he fell, and did it roll on the bloodstained floor when Father MacNamara opened the door? Or maybe it rolled when they moved the canon? How did the canon fall? His legs are unsteady, of course. Did he slip and fall? Did he fall against the counter and bruise his head against one of the candlesticks on the counter, knocking it to the ground?

Doctor McBratt is anxious. How long before the guards come? The guards know how to make a makeshift stretcher. Then we will be able to move him to a bed and wait for the ambulance. Castlebar hospital is an hour away, then one-hour return journey. The canon may not make it. Father

MacNamara hurriedly puts on his confessional stole and administers last rites.

Doctor McBratt continues to check the vital signs. The canon's pulse is weakening. His breathing is shallow. Then the rhythm of breathing is replaced by the slow exhalation of failing lungs. They hear the unmistakable gurgling and rattling of the lungs collapsing.

The silence is broken by the sound of running feet. The guards arrive – Garda Seamus O'Reilly, Station Sergeant Kevin Hughes and Inspector John Patrick Murphy. Instantly, they size up the situation. Canon Paul Anthony MacMorrow is dead. They wait for the ambulance. Only now, instead of a patient for hospitalisation, they have a body to be delivered to the county medical examiner for a forensic autopsy.

Sergeant Hughes informs Father MacNamara, "The church is filled with people waiting for the 8:30 Mass. It's now almost a quarter to nine. I think we should ask them to leave. We don't want a crowd of the curious around when the ambulance arrives."

"Yes, Sergeant. Do that. And inform them that Mass is postponed until twelve noon." And to Jack, "Jack, lock the main door and stay there. Let the ambulance medics in, but not anyone else. We will reopen the church when we are..." He was about to say 'back to normal', but Jack understands.

"And what will I tell people if they ask? Well, they WILL ask."

"Just tell them the truth. The canon was old and feeble, and he collapsed and died in the sacristy."

Jack, Sergeant Hughes and Garda O'Reilly organise the evacuation of the church, gently revealing the reason to the parishioners, and informing them that Mass is postponed and will be celebrated at twelve noon.

Back in the sacristy, Doctor McBratt draws Murf aside. "Murf, I don't like the look of this. I have seen the result of a fall numerous times, but this doesn't look right." Doctor McBratt is required to issue a death certificate. 'Accidental death due to a fall?' She decides to delay issuing the certificate until the coroner's report confirms the cause of death. This is the protocol in the case of an unexplained or violent death. The county medical examiner, who is the coroner, is required to investigate in order to permit a death certificate to be issued.

Murf is scanning his expert eye over the scene. "Mrs. Friel. Did the canon return from his night prayers last night? I'd like to check his room."

Mrs. Friel takes Murf to the canon's room. Murf sees that the bed there was unslept in.

"Guard Murphy, I don't think the canon came back from the church last night. At least I did not hear him."

"Is that unusual?"

"Oh, he usually falls asleep while praying. I sometimes hear him return from the church after midnight."

"But last night you did not hear him return?"

"No. I assumed he came back while I was sound asleep."

Murf quickly scans the room. Everything is in order. And there on the mantel is the canon's new clock. On his bedside table is a stack of English newspapers. Murf recognises the top paper, 'The Sunday Mirror', dated 16 July 1950. "Mrs. Friel, does the canon read English papers?"

"The canon? Lord, no. I get the English Sunday papers from Casey's, but the canon does not approve. He makes me hand them over. 'They are only fit for lighting the fire.' That's what he says. He stuffs them into the turf box by the fireplace so I can use them for kindling."

"But these are on his bedside table."

"Oh, that's from last night when Doctor McBratt was waiting here for him. I saw her thumbing through them when I went to get her a glass of port."

"Oh, yes. I was here then." And to himself, "But his bedside table was cleared to accommodate Mrs. Friel's tray of cocoa." The only thing out of place is the bundle of English newspapers that should be in the turf box.

Mrs. Friel notices Murf hesitating. "If you want those rag papers, Murf, take them. They are only going to be burned anyway."

Murf takes the newspapers and says, "Okay. Let's go back to the sacristy."

Back in the sacristy, Murf places the bundle of English newspapers on the side counter and studies the location of the candlestick. Where did it fall? Was it moved? The location is consistent with an accidental fall if the canon knocked against it. The canon was feeble and unsteady on his legs, so a fall is not surprising. There is a burned-out match on the floor. Why would there be a burned-out match at the exit door? The canon, if he needed light upon entering from outside, would have switched on the light; or, if he was leaving by the exit door, he would have no need to light a match. If the canon needed light in the sacristy as he entered from the sanctuary, he would have struck a match and lit a candle at the sanctuary door. Why is the burned-out match on the wrong side of the room?

The sink is near the door. Was the floor wet last night? Perhaps he slipped on a wet spot. If it was wet last night it would have dried by now anyway.

There is no sign of a break-in. No one has access except a key holder. Of course, an intruder could hide in the church before it closes, and wait until later to commit a robbery. But there is no sign of robbery or vandalism.

Murf walks slowly through the interior of the church surveying the nave. At the main door he encounters Jack Gilban. "Jack? When you opened the church this morning did you notice anything out of place?"

"Well, yes. But not at first, like."

"Like what?"

"Come. I'll show you." Jack leads him to the side altar and points out the coin box for the penny offerings. "This morning this box and stand were lying in the aisle."

"And what could be the reason for that?"

"Childer. That's what I think. Some mother here, saying her rosary after six, and her childer playing hide-and-seek in the shadows."

"Are you sure that's what happened?"

"No, I'm not sure. It's just that it happened before."

Murf thinks to himself, "Or could it have been knocked over by the canon experiencing faintness, stumbling his way to the sacristy before he finally collapses?"

"Anything else, Jack?"

"One other thing. The muddy boot prints. Here, I'll show you."

Jack leads the way to the porch and into the tower. Murf sees the footprints. He bends down and inspects the dirt with spittle and finger, smearing a spot of dirt in a circle. "Ah," he says knowingly. "Let's see where they lead, Jack."

Jack is anticipating this. He has a candlestick ready in his hand. He applies a flaming match to the candle and leads Murf down the basement steps.

"Aha! Look at this," exclaims Jack. "Here's where they stop."

"Or just fade out," says Murf.

"Well, would you look at this?" Jack is looking at an empty spot in the midst of an assortment of jumble.

"It's an empty space, Jack. Is something missing from there?"

"Yes. The old sacristy lamp."

"Ah, now. That makes sense. Last night the canon was showing us his new mantle clock. He got it from Paddy the Lamp that afternoon. Paddy would not accept payment, so the canon told him, in lieu of payment, to choose a lamp from the disused items stored in the basement."

"Ah well, that's all right then." Jack would like to say that it's NOT all right. Now he has extra mopping to do.

Murf is tabulating in his mind all who were in the church last night. Not that there is reason to investigate. Murf just likes to have the complete picture.

"Okay, Jack. Let's go back up."

In Jack's supply room, Jack takes a candlestick from a shelf. Not any candlestick, but one identical to the acolyte's candlestick that is lying on the sacristy floor. "A replacement for the one that got knocked over. It's likely dinged. And it will need cleaning."

Murf selects one of Jack's polishing cloths, a clean one, and takes it. "Good thinking there, Jack. And, if you don't mind, I'll take the damaged one until the results of the autopsy come in. I'll wrap it up carefully in this."

Murf is not sure why he is doing this other than an uneasy feeling. Doctor McBratt is also questioning the state of the accident. Just in case he needs to look at things more closely, he needs to keep the candlestick uncontaminated. He is unsure if the candlestick was knocked before the fall when the canon was stumbling, or during the fall when the canon could have fallen against it. Or did it tumble off the counter after the canon had fallen? By examining the candlestick he might be able to obtain an answer. Does it matter? Maybe not. But to alleviate his unease, Murf wants to get an understanding of the details surrounding the canon's tragic death, and how it actually occurred.

The ambulance arrives. Doctor McBratt and Sergeant Hughes direct the medics to the sacristy where they remove the body of Canon MacMorrow. They place the body in the ambulance and they drive off to deliver it to the county medical examiner.

Murf returns to the Garda station with the bundle of English newspapers and the blood-stained candlestick. Sitting at his desk, he ponders the circumstances surrounding the canon's death. There is no reason to suspect foul play. Yet, he cannot shake the feeling of unease. Murf himself was at the church last night to attend the Planning Committee meeting. And he knows all who were at the church when it was locked for the night. Murf scribbles on sheets of paper and sticks nine of them to the wall. There is a sheet of paper for everyone who was at St. Bawn's last night, the people associated with the canon's last known movements.

Maggie Friel, parochial housekeeper, widow. Access to the church – anytime.

Andrew MacNamara, C.C. curate, ex-Royal Navy. Access to the church – anytime.

Eamon Curry, the canon's driver. Access to the church – daily, but not a key holder.

Paddy the Lamp Ward, itinerant. No access to church, but he delivered a new clock to the parochial house and went into the church basement last night.

<u>Marie Antoinette McBratt</u>, medical doctor. No access to church, but made a professional visit to the canon last night, and spent time at prayer. She gets cooperation to access the church after hours.

<u>Thomas Gilban</u>, parish treasurer/accountant, Spent time abroad. Doing what though? Find out more. Access to church – anytime.

<u>Jack Gilban</u>, parish sacristan. Access to church – anytime.

<u>Patrick Joseph Casey</u>, merchant. Access to church – no. But he supplied the locks.

<u>Sally McGrath</u>, widow. Access to church – no. But she is a frequent late-night visitor and was there last night.

Murf knows a great deal about all nine. No, not quite. There is a large gap in his knowledge of Thomas Gilban. Thomas 'Farouk' Gilban served overseas with the British, so that would have been with the Foreign Office. Who would know? Who could fill in the gap? If Thomas Gilban served with the Foreign Office, Nobbie would know, or at the very least he would know someone who knows.

Nobbie is Sir Robert Norton, Inspector-General of the Royal Ulster Constabulary, previously with the British Colonial Police, and originally with the Royal Irish Constabulary prior to the 'Troubles'. Murf has the phone number of the RUC on Waring Street, Belfast. He lifts the phone and requests the front desk to place the call. A few minutes later he is connected to RUC HQ. As expected, when he requests to be transferred to Sir Robert, the operator at RUC HQ takes his contact information and tells him to wait for a return call. Murf knows that the Chief Constable in Northern Ireland has all his calls screened. Few, if any, go through to him. Instead, they are redirected to appropriate departments. Nobbie might phone him back today, or tomorrow, or sometime later.

PART 1 – THE QUEST FOR 'X'

CHAPTER ONE

ST. BAWN'S PLANNING COMMITTEE
KILLBAWN, COUNTY MAYO, IRELAND

Three Weeks Earlier
Wednesday 12 July 1950

1950 is a Holy Year. Pope Pius XII is expected to proclaim the Dogma of the Assumption into Heaven of Mary, the Mother of Jesus. Preparations are underway and many pilgrims are planning to attend St. Peter's in Rome for the proclamation on 01 November. Here, in Killbawn, as in many parishes throughout the country, preparations are being made to celebrate locally.

It is 7:30pm. Canon Paul Anthony MacMorrow, Parish Priest of Killbawn, has called on his trusted parish advisors to form a planning committee to make preparations for an outdoor procession to be held on 15 August, the feast of the Assumption. Rosary and Benediction could be celebrated at the 'The Home', the sports field located by the Blackwater River. 'The Home' is a pleasant walk from St. Bawn's Church by way of the pedestrian trail along the riverbank.

The meeting is taking place in the parochial house, the priests' residence and parish administrative office, situated next to the church. Canon MacMorrow looks in on the meeting just long enough to make it clear that he wants a great procession, with children dressed up as for First Communion, a choir, incense, and a covered altar erected at the goalposts; and with a police escort.

Eamon Curry, the canon's driver, remarks that mounted police would be nice – mounted on horseback, not on the usual big black bicycles. "Isn't that right, Canon? Big black horses." And turning to where Inspector John Patrick Murphy is seated, "C'mon, Murf. Wouldn't you look great up on a big black horse?"

Canon MacMorrow ignores Eamon. He leaves the room, closely followed by Eamon who pulls a face at the committee members before he shuts the door.

Canon MacMorrow is a crusty old priest with a heart of gold. He is eighty years old and should have retired. He is cranky and humourless and suffers from rheumatism. His large frame is permanently stooped from a combination of his ailment and old age. He wears his black hat indoors so that his head will not get cold. He is accompanied, most of the time, by his driver, fifty-seven-year-old Eamon Curry who, by contrast, is diminutive, talkative and active, and who is given to leg-pulling. Eamon quite frequently pulls the canon's leg. This is something no one else would dare do. Not only does the canon accept it, he secretly enjoys it. It gives him some relief from the tediousness of his day.

Notwithstanding his frail health, Canon MacMorrow conducts a busy daily schedule. Eamon Curry is on hand every day to drive the canon to various appointments and events. Killbawn is not a large town, but Killbawn Parish covers a large rural area. There are five primary schools and two chapels of ease located in the parish. Today, the canon said Mass at 8:30am in the parish church; Father Andrew MacNamara attended to the two remote chapels. Later, the canon visited one of the rural schools to check up on the progress of the floor repairs. The work needs to be finished in time for the resumption of classes at the end of August. And he subsequently brought Communion to elderly shut-in parishioners in Ballycorry.

His usual daily duties end at 6:00pm. He likes to be home in time for the Angelus. The final part of the day, from 6:00pm to 9:00pm is his private time. High tea is always served at 6:01pm, after the Angelus. He meets with his curate after tea to discuss the administration of the parish. The curate is free to run the parish his own way, so long as he does what he is told. Tonight, Father MacNamara is chairing the Planning Committee meeting. Canon MacMorrow customarily goes to his room at 8:00pm.

As per his usual routine, the old priest goes to his room assisted by his driver, Eamon. His room is actually the living room. A bed is installed there for the old priest. He has difficulty going upstairs, so the living room doubles as his private reception room and bedroom. The house is large, constructed of impressive stone walls, but it is cold and draughty, even in summer. Eamon helps him to his bed. The old priest kicks off his shoes and lies on his bed, propped up with an abundance of pillows and cushions and still wearing his black hat. There is a pleasant welcoming fire burning in the grate, even though it is the middle of July. This is his preferred state of comfort at this time of day. Mrs. Maggie Friel, his loyal and devoted housekeeper, knows his schedule quite well. There is always a welcoming fire for the old priest when he enters his room.

At 8:00pm, on the dot, Mrs. Friel knocks and enters. She has the priest's usual supper tray, hot cocoa and ginger snap biscuits, which she places on the side table beside the bed.

"There you are, Canon. And how was your day then?" And she pats the pillows and cushions to a better shape to accommodate the priest's posture. She removes his hat, which he grabs back.

"Aw, me head is cold and me nose is running, and me legs are heavy...."

"There ye are now." she interrupts "Some hot cocoa to warm ye up. That's what ye need."

Eamon, who is never left out, addresses Mrs. Friel. "What's this, Maggie? Cocoa? And it's the 12th of July and all. Where's the whiskey? And not that Catholic Murphy's stuff – 'Paddy'. We need some Black Bush to toast King Billy. Have you no Protestant stuff at all, at all?"

"Ah, go on w'yourself, Eamon. The divil a bit o' whiskey tonight. Cocoa is what the canon needs. Lord, you'd be puttin' him in the grave if you had your way."

Both Mrs. Friel and Eamon exchange a twinkle. This is the usual friendly banter they engage in. Mrs. Friel leaves the room smiling, and gently closes the door.

"The cupboard (cough, cough)..." The priest is waving his hand and pointing.

This is unnecessary. Eamon knows him too well. He goes to the cupboard and finds the bottle of Black Bush. He removes the cork, sniffs the contents, and pours a liberal amount into the priest's cocoa. The old priest sighs in contentment. The room is filled with the aroma of burning turf, hot cocoa and whiskey fumes.

Then Mrs. Friel knocks and re-enters. "Canon, the doctor is here to see you."

Canon MacMorrow swings his arm away from Mrs. Friel lest she removes the cup from his hand. "Doctor Antoinette? Well, show her in."

Eamon is innocently admiring a picture of 'The Agony in the Garden' on the far wall, his back to Mrs. Friel.

Doctor Marie Antoinette McBratt is a frequent visitor. She enters immediately. "So, Canon. How are we all the day?"

Eamon turns around to face her. "Lord Almighty!" says Eamon admiringly. "If it isn't Claudette Colbert herself, all the way from Hollywood, come to visit us here in little Killbawn."

Doctor Antoinette McBratt is from Pluck, in north-east Donegal, where the lingua franca is Ulster Scots. Sometimes it slips out as in 'the day' rather than 'today'. She is noted for her elegant and fashionable attire. She is 34 or maybe 21, depending on who is asking. Today she is dressed in slacks, not appropriate for church, at least not by Killbawn conventional standards.

The priest ignores Eamon's interruption. "Oh, I'm grand now that I'm resting."

Without being asked, Eamon goes to the cupboard and pours a glass of port which he hands to the doctor. She takes the glass and sips.

"Lord, Eamon, can you not put something into the port for me?"

"Right you be, doctor. What would you like?"

"Brandy." And to the old priest, "I'm on my way to do my stations before you lock up the church at nine. Just checking on you."

"Well, you still have plenty of time. Sit down and enjoy your drink."

Doctor McBratt sits in one of the armchairs at the fireplace, the one facing towards the bed. Eamon remains standing with hands thrust in his trouser pockets. He prefers to stand while others sit: it is the only time he feels tall.

Doctor McBratt takes a sip of port & brandy and asks, "And how can you tell how much time I have? Your clock is stopped."

They all look at the mantle clock.

"Sure that old clock hasn't run in years," says the canon with displeasure.

Eamon jumps in with advice. "You know, Canon, it's time to get a new clock. Time? Get it?"

Neither the priest nor the doctor laughs at the joke, and Eamon feels deflated.

"Tell you what, Canon," says Doctor McBratt. "I'll get you a proper mantle clock. Just leave it to me."

And so it is as with most evenings. Mrs. Friel mothers the canon, the canon discusses his travel plans for the next day with Eamon, Doctor McBratt checks up on the old priest before visiting the church for her private devotions of the 'Way of the Cross'. And they all down a dram of friendship – except Mrs. Friel, of course, who only 'nips' in private.

Doctor McBratt leaves the canon and Eamon to finish their business and makes her way to the back door. En route, she pops into the meeting room, curious to see who is there. The committee members are sitting around a table. Father MacNamara is there, of course. He was previously a chaplain with the Royal Navy during the war, now reassigned back to his diocese. He has a penchant for military precision and order, two qualities underappreciated in Killbawn.

"Good evening, Father MacNamara."

And there is Inspector John Patrick Murphy, who regards it as his duty to know everything that is going on in Killbawn.

"Good evening, Murf."

And it is no surprise to see Casey (does Casey have a first name?), the owner of the general store. Casey never misses an opportunity to make a sale, and this event, now being planned, should encourage people to dress up, for which Casey's General Store can supply shoes, ribbons, hats etc.

"Good evening, Casey."

And there he is – the final member of the committee. The local lad recently returned after serving 30 years in... What WAS it that he did? Police? Military? Something very important and secret by all accounts. Yes, there he is in a perfectly tailored lightweight suit from some exotic place, a perfectly groomed moustache and brylcreemed hair, sporting tinted glasses, as if he were King Farouk of Egypt himself. This is Thomas Gilban, the recently appointed parish accountant.

"Good evening, Farouk."

They all chime back, "Good evening, Doctor McBratt," except for Thomas Gilban who humorously plays the game of apparel association. "Bonsoir, Claudette."

"And could one of you kind gentlemen permit me access to the church by way of the sacristy, rather than have me walk down to the street and around the corner to the main door?"

Thomas Gilban immediately springs to his feet and gallantly offers his arm to escort the doctor. He extracts a Yale key from his waistcoat pocket and tosses it in the air. He turns and catches the key behind his back without even looking to see where it is falling. "Permit me to escort you, Mademoiselle."

The parochial house and the church are two separate buildings. Originally, the priest would exit the house by the back door and walk the 15 feet to the sacristy of the church. A few years ago, Canon MacMorrow had a covered passageway built, to connect the side of the house to the sacristy. Now he is able to walk from house to church in comfort, regardless of the weather.

"So, Thomas, YOU don't think it improper for a lady to enter the house of God in slacks? Do you?"

They exit the back door into the porch. They could continue on through the porch to the yard outside. But as intended, they turn into the passageway and proceed towards the church.

"You know, Doctor, I have seen strange attire in many places. This is actually quite restrained compared to a...."

"What places? You have been to many strange places? Doing what?"

"Mostly boring police stuff."

McBratt is inquisitive and presses to know more. "People around here joke that you were doing a lot of secretive stuff during the war. Perhaps you were a spy."

Gilban throws his head back and laughs loudly. He settles down but maintains an amused smile. "No, I was on bodyguard detail for diplomats and international delegates during the war." He lowers his eyebrows to appear ominous and whispers jokingly, "Now some of THEM may have been spies. Ah, here we are. I'll let you into the sacristy," turning the key in the Yale lock and pushing the door open, "and you'll find your way to the sanctuary from there."

"Thanks, Thomas. I know my way from here."

"Well, good night, Doctor. I must get back to the meeting." And off he goes, retracing his steps through the interconnecting passageway.

It is gloomy inside the sacristy. The door swings shut behind the doctor and the Yale lock auto-engages. With familiar ease, Doctor McBratt makes her way through the dim sacristy with confidence. Electricity was installed in the church two years earlier, but McBratt chooses not to switch on the light. Firstly, the light switch is at the exit door. She would need to return at some point to switch off the light and walk through the shadowy sacristy in any case. Secondly, electricity is supplied by the local saw-mill. The power is weak and intermittent, and the miller turns off the power when he goes to bed at midnight. The electric light emanating from the bulbs is so dim that candlelight is still the preferred lighting, and is more reliable. Doctor McBratt makes her way from the sacristy to the apse, and then to the nave. She lifts her scarf, which is draped stylishly on her shoulders, to reverently cover her head.

She sweeps her eyes around the interior of the church. The red glow from the sacristy lamp illuminates the nave area but is unable to penetrate the shadowy aisles. She notices one figure in the church. Old Granny McGrath is at the side altar. She is kneeling at the communion rail next to the candle stand. It is difficult to see her clearly. She is dressed all in black with a black headscarf knotted at the chin and is motionless except for her lips moving silently in prayer.

The side altar is dedicated to 'The Sacred Heart of Jesus'. Carved into the front of the altar is a depiction of a heart encircled with thorns, a small cross on top of the heart, and flames spurting out of the heart to envelop the cross. It is a depiction of 'God's burning love for us'. Appropriately, the candle stand for prayer petitions is situated at this spot. There is a penny candle burning as Granny McGrath prays. Her husband, Brendan, died last week. And now she spends every evening praying in church for the duration of her burning votive candle. It is an effort for her to come here. She is old, over eighty. And she cycles all the way from Lough Corry. It must take her almost two hours of pushing uphill to the mountain glen to return home.

Doctor McBratt feels a pang of pity for Granny McGrath. She is taking the death of her husband very hard. Brendan was bedridden for a year and his death came as no surprise. Now she has no one. There is no member of her family left alive in Ireland. They are all dead or emigrated many years ago.

Doctor McBratt commences the Way of the Cross. The journey starts at the main altar, then along the interior wall of the nave, encircling the church to end back at the main altar after the fourteenth station. And so she progresses,

"The First Station. Jesus is condemned to death....

The Second Station. Jesus is made to carry his cross....

...because of your Holy Cross you have redeemed the world...."

She reaches the Eighth Station. "The Eighth Station. Jesus comforts the women of Jerusalem."

Doctor McBratt hesitates. She ponders the picture on the wall. It has a small wooden cross on top, just like the other 13 pictures encircling the inner wall of the church. Each picture is a stop, or station, on the journey to Calvary and to the tomb of the Redeemer. She turns her head slightly in order to get a view of Granny McGrath in her peripheral vision. She repeats the title of the Eighth Station with a modification, "Jesus, comfort the women of Lough Corry."

She notices the flicker of the dying candle. Granny McGrath's votive candle expires. Old Granny gets up from her kneeling position slowly and painfully. Her joints have locked from the lack of motion in the past hour. It takes her some moments to get mobile.

"The Ninth Station. Jesus falls for the third time."

Granny McGrath makes her way along the side aisle next to the wall. She passes close to Doctor McBratt at the Ninth Station located at the exit door. The two women nod to each other in greeting. They do not speak. They refrain from speaking in order to observe devotional silence in the house of God. Instead, Doctor McBratt extends her hand to make contact with Granny's arm as she passes. Unexpectedly,

Granny McGrath does not break her stride. She continues walking and the doctor's hand fails to make contact.

Of course, they know each other very well. Doctor McBratt was a frequent visitor to the ailing Brendan McGrath throughout his period of infirmity. And Granny McGrath is included in her weekly professional rounds. Once upon a time, she was Sally McGrath, but no one remembers that. She is only known as 'Granny McGrath', even though she has no grandchildren. Granny McGrath pushes open the big wooden door. There is a momentary flood of light washing through the dark nave before the door swings shut behind her.

Doctor McBratt is worried about Granny McGrath. Since Brendan's death she has become remote. Her face has assumed a distraught mien. At one time she was talkative; now she only talks to God. Doctor McBratt pushes her forefinger against her brow to calculate the number of minutes left in the day. It stays bright in July well into the evening, long after sunset at 10:00pm. Night will fall at 11:00pm. So Granny McGrath should get home before dark. Still, it is uphill all the way from Ballycorry to Lough Corry. And in her feeble condition, cycling the 14 miles must be a painful struggle for the old woman.

Doctor McBratt interrupts her Stations. She is standing at the Ninth Station, next to the main door. She dips her finger in the holy water fount, crosses herself, and departs from the church. She looks for Granny McGrath and is surprised to see her in the distance cycling speedily with the steady rhythm of one accustomed to such activity. Satisfied that the old woman appears to be well able for the journey home, Doctor McBratt turns to re-enter the church to conclude her interrupted devotions.

Just then, she sees Murf on his way from the parochial house. The meeting must be over. Taking her scarf from her head she waves it to get his attention. "Inspector Murphy!" she calls.

He sees her and approaches.

"Murf, be a gentleman and walk me home."

"I can do better. I can drive you home."

Doctor McBratt is quite able to walk home on her own. But she wants to get information from Murf.

Murf continues, "My car is right here at the sidewalk," indicating to a black 10hp Ford Prefect. "It's the same car as yours. Isn't it?"

Doctor McBratt, indeed, has a similar car. But she does not drive. Her driver is 'Danny the Divil', the local inebriate whom she has employed. He only drives when moderately drunk. When totally drunk, he is prevented from driving. When sober, he has the shakes and sees rats – he cannot drive then either. He is able to function only on a 'maintenance dose' of alcohol. His level of equilibrium is at 'moderately drunk'. Tonight, as on most nights, he is too drunk to be of service. Tomorrow morning he will consume the 'hair of the dog'. And when he reaches his level of equilibrium he will be able to function again for a few hours.

Murf opens the passenger door of the car. Doctor McBratt seats herself sideways with both feet still on the sidewalk. Then she swivels like a dancer, feet together, knees slightly raised, and gracefully positions herself in the seat. Murf is impressed. He gets in on the driver side, one leg at a time like most people. He turns the ignition key and pulls the choke followed by the starter. He knows where the doctor lives. There is no need to ask. He waits for the anticipated question as he pulls away from the sidewalk. Everyone wants to know something in a rural town.

"Murf, there is something not right about Farouk."

"Why do you say that, Ant?"

"He laughs too easily. But do you notice his hard eyes? There is something else going on inside his head."

"Is that a fact? How do you make that out?"

"So why is it such a big secret – what he did in the war? People with secrets cannot be trusted. Do you think he was a spy?"

"Secrets? Don't you have secrets?"

"Of course. But I'm a doctor. I'm supposed to protect my patients' confidences."

"And I have secrets...."

"Yes, Murf. But you're a policeman. That's to be expected."

"And Canon MacMorrow...."

"Yes! Yes! But with Farouk it's different. Do YOU think he was a spy, Murf?"

"He was with the British Foreign Office. More likely he CAUGHT spies."

"Ah! Maybe he interrogated spies. And tortured them to get information."

"Ant, don't get carried away. Foreign Office police work is not as intriguing as in 'Casablanca'. And here we are. You're home safe and sound."

Murf pulls in to the side of the street and goes around to open the passenger door. Doctor McBratt does her elegant reverse swivel and holds Murf's arm to stand erect. She holds on a moment longer to impart a warning.

"You know that Farouk has radio stuff up in St. Bawn's bell tower. He is up there at night when honest people should be in bed. God only knows what secret stuff is going on up there. Mark my words, Murf, before the year is out you'll be dealing with some unsavoury business there. Keep your eyes on Farouk."

"Okay, Ant. I will."

She releases Murf's arm, and he returns to the driver side. Before he can drive off, Doctor McBratt comes to his driver door and knocks on the window. He rolls down the window.

"One more thing, Murf. I'm a bit worried about old Granny McGrath. Could you follow her and see if she needs help? She is cycling to Lough Corry, on her way home from her private devotions in St. Bawn's. She's not gone more than five minutes."

"No problem, Ant. I'll see to her." And off he drives.

Driving on the Ballycorry road, Murf has time to consider Doctor McBratt's opinion of Thomas 'Farouk' Gilban. Her instincts are good. She is adept at eliciting information from patients to diagnose their condition. She reads body language well. She reads between the lines and can see below the surface. But this is different than diagnosing a case of appendicitis. Or is it? Murf himself finds Farouk Gilban strange. But surely it was his time with His Majesty's Foreign Office Service that made him so. But, now that a second person expressed this same opinion, his policeman's curiosity is aroused. To satisfy himself, he resolves to enquire through non-official friendly contacts to ascertain if Gilban is as neat and clean as he appears to be. There is nothing much else to do in Killbawn at the present time – except plan a religious procession.

Where is old Granny McGrath? He has already passed by the creamery and is almost at the straight mile. He should have seen her a while back. He must have missed her, distracted by his thoughts of Farouk Gilban. The road is narrow here. He decides to go as far as the old RIC barracks to make a U-turn and go back to find her. Then he sees her.

She is travelling at a steady pace, quite fast. She is bent forward, concentrating on her progress. He draws up alongside, but she doesn't alter her speed. Murf leans over and rolls down the passenger-side window.

He shouts out, "Granny! Granny McGrath! I've come to drive you home. Can you hear me, Granny? I can put your bike in the boot and drive you home."

Granny McGrath slows her pace just a little, and peers in through the window. "Who is it?" she shouts in.

"It's Murf. I've come to take you home."

"Murf? Guard Murphy is it?" And with that she waves him away and cycles with greater speed as if she had seen the devil himself.

What a tough and independent old bird, Murf thinks in admiration. He slows down and makes the U-turn at the abandoned RIC barracks.

Now his mind is off Farouk and is bothered by Granny McGrath. Why didn't she say a few friendly words of greeting? It's not like her to be so dismissive. It must be part of the grieving she is going through. Murf drives home. Granny McGrath is on his mind. Now Farouk Gilban is on his mind again. By the time he reaches home he cannot get either of them out of his head and is agitated by both.

9:30pm. Things are quiet in St. Bawn's. The church is locked for the night. Canon MacMorrow is sitting in the darkened church saying his night prayers and, as usual, falls asleep. He awakens, continues his prayers, and nods off again. In the meeting room in the parochial house next door, Farouk Gilban and Father MacNamara are sharing light-hearted conversation over a glass of port.

"It's past 9:30, Thomas. Let's make our way to the radio room in the tower."

"Sure. We should get a strong reception shortly. Let's go."

Thomas Farouk Gilban and Father Andrew MacNamara proceed to the church via the interconnecting passageway to the sacristy. Farouk takes a key from his pocket and unlocks the sacristy door. They are careful not to disturb the canon at his prayers, or disturb his sleep. They make their way through the apse to the narthex and to the tower. The canon opens his eyes as he hears the two men walk through the church and to the tower. He hears them climb the stairs and the footsteps fade away. At night in a quiet church, even a mouse's pitter-pattering feet could be heard.

Farouk and Father Mac climb the tower stairs by the light of a candle. They climb up past the choir loft and stop below the belfry at the door to the radio room. Farther Mac looks at Farouk, and Farouk looks at Father Mac. Both wait.

"Aren't you going to open the door, Thomas?"

"No. I thought you had the key."

"I left my key in my jacket in the meeting room."

"And I left mine in the glove compartment of the car. I don't like to carry a lot of keys. They misshape my pockets."

"Not to worry. I'll go back to the parochial house...."

"No. There is no need to do that. You may disturb the canon. I'm parked just outside. Open the main church door and I'll nip out quickly and quietly to get the key."

They retrace their steps back down the stairs to the narthex and Thomas Farouk Gilban slips out through the main door. Momentarily he returns with the key, and Father Mac ensures that the church doors are made secure again. As they ascend the stairs a second time, they decide to obtain a duplicate key and to hide it on the rail above the radio-room door, a variation of the 'key under the mat'.

"Tomorrow I'll get the original key from Mrs. Friel...."

"Why bother Mrs. Friel, Thomas?"

"A duplicate of a duplicate is not prudent. I should use the original."

"Okay, Thomas. I trust you and Mrs. Friel to get a duplicate key cut in Casey's."

"Consider it done."

10:30pm in St. Bawn's. The canon is asleep somewhere in the middle of his night prayers, and the two radio hams are comparing weather situations with a ham in Germany. And all appears to be right with the world.

Or is it?

CHAPTER TWO

SHANNON, IRELAND

Thursday 13 July 1950 6:00am

"Rinneanna. The Bird Marsh. That's what you are looking at. Shannon Airport is just a small section of the marsh." Malachy Gilban, Senior Security Officer of Shannon Airport, is sitting in his Land Rover at the perimeter of the airport, parked in a narrow access track to the adjacent bird sanctuary. The early morning sea mist is lying heavily on the marsh. A hundred yards behind is the end of the actual roadway at Barley Harbour. And from Barley Harbour there is a road access to Shannon Airport. That's not quite true. The road from Barley Harbour passes within 50 yards of the termination of the airport perimeter road. Malachy's Land Rover has no trouble traversing the gap by way of a dirt track. It is Malachy's 'backdoor' to and from the airport facility, passing the fuel storage tanks and the airport's marine dock.

Sitting beside him is his cousin, Thomas Gilban, treasurer (unpaid) of St. Bawn's Church – Thomas Gilban who, until recently, was in the service of the British Foreign Office. Malachy often comes to this place, not to view birds, but to view the approach and departure of product tankers engaged in bringing aviation fuel to the airport by sea. The merchant ships travel slowly, very slowly. Their average speed is 12 knots but, in the Shannon Estuary, their speed is reduced to four knots. A pilot from The Shannon Foynes Port Company is required to navigate ships in navigable lanes through the shallow waters and sloblands of the estuary to and from the airport's marine dock.

A Russian merchant ship is slowly departing the airport in the direction of the Atlantic. She sails a distance of 1,650 nautical miles through the North Sea, the Skagerrak, the Kattegat and the Baltic to the port of Ventspils, and returns again. Over the course of a year she delivers 4,500 tons of aviation fuel to refuel Aeroflot and Soviet military transports. The Soviets have a shortage of hard currency and are unable to pay for Western aviation fuel. So they ship in their own fuel. And Shannon, the most westerly place in Europe that is non-NATO, is their choice for refuelling trans-Atlantic flights to Central and South America. Both Warsaw Pact and NATO unarmed military transports are serviced and refuelled at Shannon.

"And there she goes, СВОБОДА." He pronounces it perfectly 'Svahbohdah'

"'Freedom'. That's pretty good Malachy. You haven't forgotten your Russian, I see."

"Three months in Russia...well, you know..."

Thomas knows quite well how Malachy learned Russian. He is not as fluent as Thomas himself but is adequately versed nevertheless.

In the summer of 1925, a mere year after the end of the civil war, the anti-treaty IRA sent a delegation to the Soviet Union for a personal meeting with Joseph Stalin, in the hopes of gaining Soviet finance and weaponry. Malachy Gilban was a member of this delegation headed by Pa Murray. In exchange, the IRA agreed to spy on the United States and the United Kingdom and pass information to the Red Army intelligence in New York and London. The secret IRA-Soviet espionage relationship collapsed in 1931 with the breakup of the IRA into factions.

The chief faction, and the only successful split, was Fianna Fáil – the new Republican Party. Relationships between the IRA and Fianna Fáil were initially friendly. After Fianna Fáil won the 1932 election, the Fianna Fáil government legalised the IRA and freed all those imprisoned by the previous government. IRA membership grew from 1,800 to over 10,000. However, by 1935 relations had soured. Thereafter, IRA enmity against the Free State government resurfaced. A landlord's agent was murdered in a land dispute, shots were fired at police during a strike of Dublin tramway workers, and the IRA commenced bank robberies to obtain funds. The government reacted with force. In 1936 the IRA was officially banned. By then, most Irish people disagreed with the IRA's claims that it remained the legitimate army of the Republic. Later, when the government introduced a republican constitution in 1937 abolishing the Oath of Allegiance to the British monarchy and introducing an elected head of state, most of the IRA members were reconciled to the Free State. Thus, Fianna Fáil support increased at the expense of the IRA.

Malachy Gilban made the transition from IRA to model responsible citizen. But like many North Mayo anti-treaty proponents, Malachy's relationship with the anti-treaty IRA was never completely severed.

Thomas Gilban knows this. There is no need to dwell on it, or to consider it. He just knows it. "Which brings me to the purpose of my visit."

"A visit that must occur at a bird sanctuary?"

Thomas Gilban knows his cousin too well to misunderstand the question. Malachy is acknowledging that secrecy is required.

Thomas explains. "I got a message last night."

"Oh, yes?" 'Message' with an ominous tone.

"From a Russian contact."

"I thought you were retired from all that since Cairo in 1948."

"Cairo, 1948. A bad scene."

"Right. When you all trashed the American staffer's apartment and were hauled back to Britain."

"I'm still puzzled by it all. It was McLean that led the drinking and brawling. And then it was his wife Melinda that requested 'medical leave' for him from the ambassador. He and a few of us were whisked back to England very quickly."

"And before that, you were busy couriering messages to and from the Russians?"

"Me? Cairo was the busiest time ever for me. But I couriered one-way only, always to the Russian contact, never from a Russian contact. But you are right, Mal, I have had no assignments since then. I have maintained constant contact; the channel of radio communication is kept active. But no messages have been delivered since Cairo."

"And now?"

"I have been requested to make a delivery to the Russians at Shannon."

"What Russians at Shannon? And what kind of delivery? And..."

"I don't know anything. That's how it works. All I know is that a delivery is scheduled for Shannon Airport to the attention of Aeroflot for the 1st of August. Can it be done?"

"Is it illegal, this delivery?"

"Not illegal. It is authorised by an unidentified top-level official in the Service. It IS a SECRET Service, Mal. The delivery is unorthodox, and is secret."

"If it's a secret and being delivered to the Russians, then it's unlawful as per the Official Secrets Act.

'Communication with, or attempted to communicate with, a foreign agent, whether within or without the United Kingdom, shall be evidence that he has, for a purpose prejudicial to the safety or interests of the State, obtained or attempted to obtain information which is calculated to be or might be or is intended to be directly or indirectly useful to an enemy'."

Malachy reams off a section of the act. Other than to make a point, this is unnecessary. Thomas knows the act by heart.

"Wow! Malachy. You are very cognisant of His Majesty's statutes. This is not Britain, and we are not British subjects."

"Says one who has accepted the 'King's shilling'. And have you considered our obligation to a 'friendly nation', Thomas?"

"Since when have you regarded Britain as a 'friendly nation', Óglach MacGiolla Bháin?" responds Thomas, addressing Malachy as an IRA member. He waits for the rejoinder. Malachy needs to digest the import of the request.

"A secret delivery to Aeroflot at Shannon Airport, you say?"

"Yes. Can you arrange access?"

"Why Shannon?"

"I can only guess that the previous channels in Britain are being watched...."

"After what was learned from Klaus Fuchs."

"Yes. He was code-named 'Charles' and 'Rest'. They knew about him since 1945. But it wasn't until last year that they succeeded in linking the code-names to Fuchs."

"And what is your code-name, Cousin Thomas?"

"I don't have a code-name," lied Thomas. "I am just a courier. I know nothing. I am of no interest to anyone. I don't know if what I deliver is sanctioned by the Service, or if it is a mole's leak, or even if it is deliberate misinformation. I don't know. There is safety in not knowing. And that is how I prefer it. Anyway, I'm retired from all that. This delivery is a one-off."

Malachy rolls down his side window, takes out his pack of Players Navy Cut from his tunic breast pocket, strikes a match and lights up a cigarette. He flicks the spent match out the window and into the marsh. Some clegs fly into the Land Rover from the marsh. Malachy is too deep in thought to notice them. After two puffs and a cleg bite on his wrist, he flicks the cigarette out the open window and into the marsh. He closes the window against the waft of moist malodorous air. Three clegs are trapped inside the Land Rover and are trying to fly out through the closed window. They fly in a circle and hit against the glass. Then they crawl up and down the window and start the process all over again – flying, circling, crawling. Malachy appears to be concentrating on the clegs' futile attempts to exit the Land Rover. Suddenly, he slaps the window and crushes all three clegs with the flat of his hand. He watches the bloodied squashed clegs slide down the glass, streaking it with three red lines.

"Thomas, here is what will happen. I will give you access to Aeroflot. It will be after midnight. The Russians have a four-hour slot with a half-hour grace period either side. The limit is 4:30am. At 5:30am the Americans start to arrive. Both Warsaw Pact and NATO planes are serviced here, but not at the same time. During the allocated Russian time there is nothing illegal in permitting you access to Aeroflot. You could fly off to somewhere with them if you like. If you have a delivery for Aeroflot and they accept it...well, okay. But a warning. If anything, and I mean ANYTHING smacks of trouble..."

"No trouble. Just a secret delivery. Confidential, like a postal delivery by registered post."

They sit in silence for a moment. "Okay, Thomas."

Thomas Gilban knew that Malachy could be relied upon to cooperate. There was never any doubt. Malachy needed time to play 'devil's advocate' to assess the risk and to play it out in his mind. Malachy, of course, is no stranger to passing information to the Soviets, albeit in a former time before the war. Today there is a Cold War. The participants engage in one-upmanship, and employ espionage and counter-espionage to gain an advantage. Even allies, the British and the Americans, don't trust each other. No one trusts anyone, and no one tells the truth.

Ironically, spies are more likely to conduct their clandestine affairs with greater integrity than their respective governments, governments that engage in the fabrication of misinformation, denials and propaganda.

"Good. Now drive me back to my car. I haven't slept since the night before last. And I still need to send a reply to, to..."

"To your contact."

"Yes. And then some sleep."

Malachy starts the Land Rover. He puts it in reverse, kicks up a lot of dirt and spins around to face the roadway. The geese and marine birds screech in protest, take flight, and after circling once in fright, return to a slow calm lazy flapping to glide down and settle again in their marsh nests. A few minutes later, after a bumpy ride over a dirt track, Malachy is on the airport perimeter road. He waves at the security guard in passing the fuel storage tanks and the marine dock and continues onward to where Thomas has parked his car.

Thomas and Malachy exchange looks to acknowledge each other's thoughts. Not another word is spoken. Thomas steps out of the Land Rover with familiar ease while it is still in motion, and Malachy continues to the facility administrative building. Thus, they part company in silence. Thomas exits the airport by the approved route and returns to Mayo.

The 'СВОБОДА' clears the shallow waters of the Shannon. The pilot from The Shannon Foynes Port Company departs and she enters the Atlantic. She had been docked at Shannon since Tuesday 11 July. That is the normal routine: two days to unload the cargo and to check the ship's condition and, if necessary, to do a bit of cleaning. Then she is off again to repeat the same voyage, six days to her home port, and proceed to execute another delivery. On 26 July, she is scheduled to depart Ventspils and arrive back at Shannon on 01 August, Lammas Day.

CHAPTER THREE

KILLBAWN
COUNTY MAYO, IRELAND

Tuesday 01 August 1950
Lá Lúnasa, Lammas Day
The First Day of Autumn

Killbawn Garda Station is busy from early morning. Casey came in, and so did a half-dozen farmers, to complain about the presence of 'tinkers'. Garda Seamus O'Reilly is at great pains to point out that the correct term is 'travelling people' or just 'travellers'. 'Tinker' has its origin in 'tinsmith', but the term has lost its original meaning and is now used only in a derogatory manner against itinerant travellers. Secondly, Garda O'Reilly points out that unless the travellers have committed an offence there are no grounds for a complaint.

Garda O'Reilly has heard it all before. Every year on Lammas Day the Ward clan of travellers set up camp on the outskirts of Killbawn, out by the creamery at the edge of the wood on the Ballycorry Road. They collect junk, mend it and attempt to resell it – items such as pots and pans, lamps and clocks and other items of such ilk. Garda O'Reilly hears things like 'I don't care what you call them. Get rid of them!' and 'So you'll wait until they steal the eyes out of your head before you do something?' and variations on this theme. The denizens of Killbawn take opposing sides in the matter – expel the travellers or accommodate them. On one hand the travellers are accused of thievery, of being frequently drunk and belligerent and dirty; and on the other hand they are considered deserving of charity due to their unfortunate circumstances – victims of the Irish past when they were forced to wander, unwelcomed, from town to town. Casey is a strong adherent of the former view; Doctor McBratt is a strong proponent of the latter view.

Inspector John Patrick Murphy comes to the relief of Garda O'Reilly. "Ah, Seamus. The Ward clan is back. You're going to have a busy day. Tell you what. I'll go out to Paddy the Lamp Ward and see how he's doing. I'll remind him of the code of conduct in Killbawn, and I'll check to make sure he's not being pestered by confrontational farmers."

"Oh, thanks, Murf. I appreciate it."

"And tell the next lot of complainers that we have things under control."

Murf has sympathy for the travellers. Nonetheless, they need to be kept in check. Paddy Ward and his clan are unable to grasp the concept of 'ownership'. They understand 'possession', but one only 'owns' something while holding it. Once you let go, it's up for grabs. And lots of things cannot be 'owned' – the air, the water, the grass. And so there is conflict. Farmers object to the presence of travellers who attempt to graze their horses on farmland. There is no doubt that the incidence of theft rises during the travellers' sojourn in town. Murf is convinced that most of the theft is committed not by travellers but by locals who shift the blame.

Murf drives from Killbawn through the farmland and to the edge of the wood, and then onward to the location of the creamery, actually a milk collection station. He drives slowly. His side window is open and his elbow protrudes to catch the breeze. He looks for signs of litter or rubbish on the roadside, grounds for one of the many complaints that are levied against the travellers.

The area between the farmland and the bogland, the section where woodland becomes gorseland, is where the Ward family has set up camp. It is the closest place to town where their presence is least likely to give rise to protest. Murf slows as he approaches the site. He admires the whins (gorse or furze) that grow here at the edge of the bog. The newly-opened autumn blossoms, beautiful deep yellow flowers, are already in abundance, imparting a pleasant odour. The blossoms are medicinal, but Murf cannot remember for what ailment. Maybe it's like tea?

Whins are a curse and a blessing. They are invasive to farmland and must be burned and slashed periodically to keep them at bay. The plant grows rapidly and is highly flammable. The exterior of the plant burns so fast that the sap-rich stump remains undamaged. Unless the plants are slashed directly after burning, they sprout new growth within a week. On the beneficial side, whins form a barrier against encroaching bog, halting the creeping progress of sphagnum moss. And whins, in turn, are halted by the presence of trees. And so the order – farmland, woodland, whins, bogland. Whins also afford a nesting site and shelter for many species of birds. Whins can thrive in rocky soil and in poor growing areas, and over time their nitrogen-fixing capacity helps other plants establish. They are therefore frequently employed as a first stage in land reclamation.

Murf continues slowly in the direction of the travellers' camp. Paddy the Lamp and the Ward clan have a close relationship with whins, one from which they cannot be rid – a condition that distinctively marks the traveller. Because whins are abundant and are readily available, and since no one bemoans their loss, travellers rely on them for their primary source of fuel. They use whins for heat, to dry clothes and to cook. Flaming whins produce a lot of smoke.

And the smoke is oily-moist and heavy. It is reluctant to rise. It drifts along the ground clinging to all it encounters. Its strong unmistakable pungent odour permeates the clothes and hair and the entire body of every traveller in the camp. On a Sunday, when the Ward clan attends Mass, no one is brave enough to venture closer than two pews' distance from them. The smell of whin smoke and the smell of a traveller are indistinguishable. Murf chuckles to himself as he pictures the front pews in the church – the Ward clan in the first two pews, and no one else until the fifth pew.

Murf brings the car to a halt when he encounters three hobbled horses grazing on the roadside grass, the 'long acre'. The roadside grass is lush, the result of a few hundred years of fertilisation from horse-and-donkey traffic. The horses are loosely hobbled in the typical fashion of the travellers. They are able to walk unhindered and in comfort, but they cannot gallop or trot or run at any speed. So, when it is time to be harnessed to a cart, they are caught with little effort. Murf is satisfied that the hobbling cords are humanely employed. He is not surprised. Paddy Ward treats his horses well. Horses and dogs and domestic animals 'belong'. Murf has never heard of a traveller stealing any of these. It's funny, though – it is 'stealing' to take a hen from a farm, but not the hen's eggs.

Murf parks his car at the roadside. He goes to the boot, opens it and takes out a pair of wellington boots. He changes from his favoured rubber-soled farm boots into these. Up ahead he sees Paddy the Lamp's wares lined up along the roadside opposite the creamery, the place where the road is double the width to accommodate the creamery activity.

Paddy's business is not exclusively in lamps, but in anything to which he can employ his tinsmith skills. There are a few clocks, pots and pans on display, but mostly lamps.

As electricity is being introduced throughout the country, the urban population has less need of Tilley lamps – popular pressure lamps fueled by paraffin oil. Paddy collects their discarded Tilley lamps. He mends them and cleans them, and he adds them to his stock of wares. The not-so-well-off, hitherto relying on oil lamps, are then able to purchase Tilley lamps from Paddy at a very reasonable price. They, in turn, dispose of their old wick-and-oil lamps which Paddy thus obtains. Paddy mends and cleans the old oil lamps. He sells these lamps in turn to the well-to-do as antique lamps, the same people from whom he obtained the discarded Tilley lamps in the first place.

There is no sign of Paddy the Lamp at his roadside display. This is no surprise. Paddy would be alert as to the identity of the visitor. Just as Murf can smell a traveller from a distance, Paddy can smell a guard. A thirteen-year-old girl is in charge of the wares.

"Hello, Maura. And is Paddy not about?"

"Ah, no, Me Honour sir. Sure I don't know where he could be."

"No trouble, Maura. I'll just make my way to Paddy's tent. You never know, he might be in there."

"All right, Me Honour sir."

What is really being said within the figures of speech –

"Hello, Maura. I know that Paddy is here."

"I know you know, and I see that you are wearing wellingtons, so I know where you are going."

"If Paddy is not visible, he can only be in his tent. And since you noticed my wellingtons, you know that this is where I'm going."

"Good. You are going to the tent. Now we can hide the cart from your snooping."

Each is perfectly aware of each other's understanding of the conversation. It is the diplomatic language of police/traveller euphemisms.

Murf jumps over the sheugh, the drainage ditch at the roadside, through the scraggy hedge, and across the rushy moist ground to Paddy's tent. As Murf is thus progressing, three of Paddy's cub gossoons wheel the cart to the opposite side of the road, into the creamery yard and out of sight, ensuring that the canvas tarpaulin remains firmly in place.

Murf reaches the tent. Paddy has gouged out a depression at the entrance which holds a pool of water. The tent entrance is small. To enter the tent dry-foot is almost impossible, unless one is small or can walk like a spider. Paddy's children enter the tent barefoot and don't mind the water. Paddy is short and well practiced at walking through the entrance crouched low with knees together and feet apart. Entering the tent with dignity is problematic for a large policeman. Murf, however, knows Paddy's tricks. The obstacle at the tent entrance is there to deter snooping guards from entering the abode. Murf splashes his way through in his wellington boots. "Hello, Paddy. Nice to see you again."

Inside the tent, there is a flap partition at the halfway point. Two rows of beds/shelves flank the area. Are they for storage or sleeping? Probably both. Paddy appears from behind the flap before Murf can reach it and snoop behind it. Paddy has long black hair which he usually keeps in place with his paddy cap, the Irish soft cap. He wears his cap with the peak clasp open, so that he can pull it well down on his head. Just now, Paddy is not wearing his familiar cap. His black hair is hanging down completely hiding his face. With a flick of his head, he flings his hair back over his head, like a horse flicking its tail. It is as though he has his hair the wrong way around. The hair at the back of his head is cut short with a fringe; the front has a long horse-tail that he wears flung back along his head and falling down to his neck.

"Oh, Me Honour Murf, is it?"

"Lord, Paddy, it's nice that you still call me 'Me Honour'."

"Murf, it's a hard habit to break. And are ye lookin' for something? Maybe a nice lamp. Eh?"

"No, Paddy. I'm just checking that you are all right."

"Oh, I am that."

"Anyone causing you trouble?"

"Divil the one."

"Well, let's keep it that way. I've had a complaint or two. So, you know, keep it quiet, and we'll all get along."

"Oh, Murf, y'know me..."

"That's right, Paddy, I certainly do know you. And where's the good woman, Maggie-Anne?"

"She's in town with the wain. She's gone to see Doctor McBratt."

"And what's behind the flap that you don't want me to see?"

"It's Maechael. He's not well at all, at all. That's why Maggie-Anne is gone to the doctor."

Paddy pulls a corner of the flap aside. Murf sees a boy, about three years old, with a runny nose and tired eyes, staring at him from an upper-level bed. Paddy shuts the flap quickly and squeezes past Murf to the tent entrance. He reaches under a 'bed' and extracts a plank of wood which he places through the entrance – Paddy's invitation to depart the tent. "There ye go, Murf. A pontoon bridge for ye, to keep yer feet dry."

"Thanks, Paddy." Murf appreciates the courteous gesture, even though the plank is unable to support his weight. Murf splashes his way out of the tent and returns to the roadside accompanied by Paddy.

At the roadside, Murf strolls along Paddy's display of goods. The workmanship of his repairs is very good. Murf's inspection of the wares is interrupted by the arrival of Doctor McBratt. She is on her professional rounds driven by Danny the Divil. Sitting in front, beside the Divil, is Maggie-Anne and the wain. When the car comes to a complete stop they alight from the car. Two of the Ward cubs run up to the car carrying plywood boards. They place one board at the rear door of the car. When Doctor McBratt steps out, she steps onto clean plywood rather than place her stylish shoes in roadside mud. The children address her as 'Mammo'. Murf is greatly intrigued by this. 'Mammo' is a matriarchal title, reserved for female elders of the clan. Why would the Ward children address her as a clan member? Doctor McBratt waves an envelope as she addresses Paddy.

"Paddy, is there just the one letter? The one for Paddy Ward c/o The Crumlin Road Gaol?"

"Ay, Mammo. Just one the day."

Murf understands. The Wards are illiterate. The doctor has written a letter on their behalf to be sent to a clan member in the gaol in Belfast. Being of 'no fixed abode', the only permanent address a clan member is likely to have is a prison address.

Doctor McBratt is walking slowly along Paddy's display of wares. "Maggie-Anne tells me that Wee Michael is sick."

As she is walking, the Ward cubs place a sheet of plywood ahead of her. There are two sheets of plywood which they place in turn, alternating one and then the other. Doctor McBratt continues to walk on a clean surface.

"Paddy, the canon needs a fine mantle clock."

"With chimes?"

"Of course, 'with chimes'. It's for Canon MacMorrow."

"Oh yes, Mammo, I have just the thing. And it keeps great time too. Fit for a king it is."

"Good. Can you bring it to St. Bawn's parochial house before the day is out?"

"Och, aye, Mammo. Before the Angelus bell stops ringing."

Murf is very attentive to the dialogue. Paddy the Lamp Ward and clan, although they don't have fixed addresses, have a home turf to which they gravitate and assemble. It is in North Donegal, where the greater part of the related clan has actually settled. Maybe not quite settled. They engage in seasonal work in Scotland and England, and return home periodically throughout the year. As the dialogue progresses, Murf detects that both Paddy Ward and Doctor McBratt are drifting into a vernacular familiar to each other.

"That's great, Paddy. Now take me to your cub, Maechael."

Murf is about to leave. But he wheels around at hearing this. Doctor McBratt is going to enter Paddy the Lamp Ward's tent? Quick as a flash, two young lads appear with a chair. They place the chair on the plywood. Doctor McBratt sits in the chair, totally familiar with this arrangement. The lads push two poles through slots in the seat of the chair and lift it, doctor and all, and carry it to the tent. They do not carry it high up on their shoulders like carrying the Pope, but carry it low like stretcher-bearers, so that all three are at head level together. At the tent entrance, two cubs hold the flaps aside, and the two chair-bearers, without breaking stride, glide like dancers into the interior of the tent.

Murf shakes his head in disbelief and walks back to his car. He passes Danny the Divil, still sitting in the driver's seat of the doctor's car. He asks the Divil if this is usual.

"Ah, Murf, you haven't seen the half of what she does, or the places she goes."

The Divil takes a small swig of his Baby Power. The slender bottle's neck-band sports three swallows on the wing, an indication of its liquid capacity. For Danny the Divil, it is more likely one swallow, but Doctor McBratt regards it as 'three hours' of whiskey. So the Divil takes small sips. This is all the doctor permits him while on her rounds. It is important that he carefully paces his intake of whiskey. He needs to maintain his level of functioning efficiency for the duration of the doctor's calls, hopefully no more than another two hours. Danny the Divil falls apart when sober, and he falls apart when drunk. While functioning on his maintenance dose, the Divil cleans and maintains the doctor's car, a responsibility Doctor McBratt affords him. This gives him a degree of dignity, the only buffer he has from slipping over the abyss into oblivion.

Murf's work is done here. He changes back into his rubber-soled boots, gets into his 10hp Ford Prefect, and sets off back to town. He is still picturing the morning events as he enters the Garda station, Doctor McBratt with the travellers and with the Divil. What an interesting morning.

Back at the Ward camp, Doctor McBratt is leaving to continue on her professional rounds. "Paddy, don't forget the canon's clock. And keep an eye on that sick cub. Make sure he is warm and dry. If there's no improvement on the morrow, he's coming with me to be put in a cot in the dispensary."

"Oh, aye, Mammo." And shouting across to the camp, "Do ye hear th'on Maggie-Anne? Wee Maechael's to be kept dry and warm!"

Doctor McBratt returns to her car, walking on her personal clean plywood walkway. Paddy Lamp opens the rear door of the car and Doctor McBratt enters in her distinctive sitting-pirouette movement, swivelling in with knees together and legs slightly raised to clear the running-board.

"And Paddy, I know that Mrs. Rodney Maguire has an old hen that's stopped laying. I'll see if I can get it for you. It's too tough to eat, but if you simmer it for a day or two it will make great soup. And Wee Willoughby-in-the-middle-of-the-woods always has a hare or a rabbit or a pigeon in the larder. I should be able to get you something from him to make a stew."

"God bless you, Mammo!"

Doctor McBratt departs the camp, driven by her faithful divil, and waved off by barefooted children with running noses.

CHAPTER FOUR

ST. BAWNS CHURCH
COUNTY MAYO, IRELAND

Tuesday Evening, 01 August 1950

It is 6:00pm. The Angelus bell is echoing throughout the town of Killbawn. Jack Gilban, St. Bawn's sacristan, is tugging at the bell rope, his last duty for the day. At one minute past six, he will cycle home. Inside the parochial house, Eamon Curry, the canon's driver, is seated at the kitchen table. He will join Mrs. Friel for tea after the priests are served. Canon MacMorrow and Father MacNamara are seated at the dining table praying the Angelus. At the conclusion of the Angelus, they anticipate the usual high tea to be served by Mrs. Friel. Mrs. Friel enters at the expected time, only she is not carrying her customary tray.

"Canon, Paddy the Lamp is here and insists on seeing you. He won't take 'no' for an answer."

"Well, I'm not getting up from the table. Show him in here."

"You want me to bring a tinker into...?

"He's NOT a tinker. He is one of 'God's gentry', Mrs. Friel. Now show him in!"

"Yes, Canon."

Mrs. Friel admires the canon's charity, but fears that it is misplaced betimes, times like this when it accommodates muddy boots in the house. Presently, Mrs. Friel ushers Paddy the Lamp into the dining room.

"So, Paddy. What's the big urgent matter you've come about?"

"Your clock, Canon." Paddy is carrying a shiny black mantle clock, which he places on the dining table. "The doctor told me to get you a mantle clock that chimes. Now, this is the best clock you'll ever see, or hear."

The old canon brightens up. This is a pleasant surprise. He is so taken with the clock that he forgets about high tea. "Well, Paddy, let's set it up on the mantle in the parlour." The canon gets up from the table and shuffles to his room followed by Paddy with the clock.

"It's a great-looking clock, Paddy. Is it English? And does it chime?"

"It's English on the outside. See the little brass line with the name 'Sessions Clock Co – *Castle*'. And look here at the clock face, '*L Charvet ainé & Cie*'."

"French?"

"And inside it's 'Johann Worle'."

"English, French and German?"

"And it chimes the hour, and the half-hour and the quarter-hour. Here, I'll show ye."

Paddy places the clock on the mantle, facing backwards. He opens the little door and reveals the inside. There is a pendulum constructed from a plumbing pipe washer, suspended from a piece of bent wire. Looped through the wire are a number of small washers and some metal links from a bracelet chain.

"See here, Canon, there are three switches which ye slide 'on' or 'off'. When you slide to 'off' the little hammer misses the chime and just strikes air. This way ye can choose – hour, half-hour or quarter-hour. When all the switches are 'on', all the hammers strike the chimes every quarter hour. And see, ye can adjust the clock to faster or slower by sliding off, or adding on, some of the little weights. I put a few extra there in the corner beside the pendulum."

The old canon is delighted with the clock. "Paddy, this is a great clock. And what is it going to cost me?"

"Nothin'. Not a hate. It's a gift, like. But I'll take the old one, if that's all right." Paddy positions the clock in the centre of the mantle and removes the old one.

The canon stands back to admire it. "And you say that Doctor McBratt arranged this?"

"Aye, Canon."

"Tell you what, Paddy. Why don't you go to the church basement and choose an old lamp in exchange."

Canon MacMorrow has forgotten about his meal. He shouts for Father MacNamara to come. "Father MacNamara. Take Paddy here to the basement to choose a nice lamp in exchange for this fine clock here."

Father MacNamara, who has been taken away from his meal, hurriedly admires the clock to be polite. He escorts Paddy the Lamp to the church, and down to the basement.

Mrs. Friel enters the canon's room. "Well, Canon. Will you be coming in for your tea now?"

"Oh, yes, Mrs. Friel."

With the mention of 'tea', the canon's appetite returns. He happily shuffles back to the dining room. Mrs. Friel goes to the scullery and gets the bucket and mop, and proceeds to mop up Paddy the Lamp's muddy boot prints. How is he able to trek in so much dirt on his boots? From the back door to the dining room, and thence to the canon's room, and back up the hallway again. There will be mud in the church too, but Jack Gilban will attend to that.

Shortly thereafter, Father MacNamara returns and the meal proceeds in peace. Father MacNamara consults his watch. He calculates that he has enough time for another cup of tea and a fig roll biscuit before the half-seven-o'clock meeting with the planning committee.

"There's a meeting tonight?"

"Yes, Canon. Planning for the events of August the 15th, the final touches."

"You know, Father MacNamara, I think I'll join the meeting tonight. I'm feeling quite energetic." And he is thinking of showing off his new clock to the committee members when they arrive.

"Of course, Canon. It'll be great having you there."

At 7:30pm, the meeting convenes in the parochial house's meeting room. Canon Paul Anthony MacMorrow is seated nearest to the door. Father Andrew MacNamara, being the chairman, is seated at the head. Beside him on his left is Patrick Joseph Casey, known simply as 'Casey', the local small-town big shot and entrepreneur. Next to Father MacNamara, on his right, is Thomas Gilban, known by everyone as 'Farouk', but not to his face (except for Doctor McBratt), Parish Treasurer (unpaid position) and recording secretary of the meeting, a first cousin of Jack Gilban, the sacristan. And next to him is Inspector John Patrick Murphy, known as 'Murf', who is seated sans boots in his favourite dotty woollen socks, a situation which resulted from the look he got from Mrs. Friel when she admitted him into the house. Eamon Curry, the Canon's driver, not a member of the committee, is seated next to the canon.

Father MacNamara brings the meeting up to speed on the arrangements. "Canon MacMorrow, it is suggested that due to the unpredictable weather here in Killbawn, we should forego celebrating Benediction in the sports field. It would be tragic if the wind blew the canopy off the platform, or could even blow out all the candles..."

"...or blow the whole of the clergy clear into the Blackwater..." interrupts Eamon unceremoniously.

"...so it is proposed that the procession should proceed on the route as previously planned, carrying the statue of 'Our Lady of Fatima'. Hymns will be sung during the procession. In the sports field, at the erected platform at the goalposts, I will lead the recitation of the rosary. Thereafter, we will return to St. Bawn's along the riverbank with more hymns. And at St. Bawn's you, Canon, will meet the procession; you will be prepared for benediction, already vested, with candles lighting, and burning incense prepared. Are you in agreement with that, Canon?"

Canon MacMorrow would like all the trappings of an outdoor procession like in the Holy Land or in Rome, but now he has visions of himself tripping on the steps of the elevated platform, or even tripping on his long vestments in the breeze, or slipping in the rain.

"Good planning, Father MacNamara. I believe your recommendation to be a sensible one."

Father MacNamara checks off the remaining items on the agenda. "Inspector Murphy? Garda escort and traffic control?"

"All arranged."

"Casey? Ribbons and baskets with petals?"

"All arranged. Sure half the shop is working overtime on it."

"Thomas?"

"Mistress Connolly has the children's choir rehearsed and ready. And the carpenters are working with the GAA to have the sports field ready on the day before. Casey has generously donated the timber."

Casey interjects, "Can you not write on the platform that it is donated by me?"

"Don't worry, Casey. You will get the appropriate recognition."

The canon is impatient to conclude the meeting and show off his clock. "Well, are we all done now?" He is shifting his weight off the chair to stand up. Eamon comes to assist him.

"One more thing." Casey is speaking. "What are we going to do about the tinkers...?"

"God's gentry," the canon interrupts loudly.

"...roaming about looking to steal stuff from my provisions yard," continues Casey. "Murf, you're a guard. Why aren't you guards doing your job and moving these tinker-travellers or whatever...."

"They are God's gentry!" the canon shouts loudly.

"Casey, beware the canon's roar!" gibes Eamon.

Murf settles the question with a standard "We're on top of it. We have things well in hand."

Casey waves his hand in frustration and drops the matter.

"Come," says the canon. "I have something to show you all."

The canon shuffles out of the meeting room towards his private room, assisted by Eamon. Eamon turns to the company following in procession, and with hand gesture and mime, he forewarns them to be cooperative to the canon and express delight at whatever he has to show them.

Murf is coming up the rear, still bootless, following behind Casey. He understands Casey's displeasure with the travellers. Two years ago, Casey built a row of houses for the travellers. It was one row divided into four separate units, four one-story two-room abodes with running water and bathrooms. Casey wanted a grand name for the project. He asked the schoolmaster for the name of a grand building. There was 'Áras', of course, but Casey feared that 'Casey's Áras' would be lampooned. He considered 'Mansion' and

'Manor'. But these were too 'English'. The master suggested something continental – 'Chalet'. And it is not ostentatious. That was it. Casey's (non-ostentatious) Chalets. The locals, being unfamiliar with the word 'chalet', referred to the project as 'Casey's Shalleys'. So, out by the woodlands, 'Casey's Shalleys' were constructed. They received great publicity. They were officially opened with a ribbon-cutting ceremony by the bishop, whereupon a family of travellers took up their abode.

A week later Casey went to visit the new occupants to see how they had settled in. He was surprised to find it quiet at the site. He expected to hear the sounds of children playing. Approaching closer, Casey observed that the doors and windows were missing. Inside, the floorboards were gone. So too were the fixtures, the plumbing, the bath and toilet, the cooker. Other than the shell of the outer walls and the roof, there was nothing left of 'Casey's Shalleys'. Thereafter, they were referred to as the 'Silly Shalleys'. Enraged and embarrassed, Casey had the entire lot levelled. For a year after that, Casey would slow down and inspect the wares sold by travellers at the roadside in the hope of identifying some of his donated house fixtures. But in vain. Casey still holds a grudge against any traveller that comes within ten miles of Killbawn.

The canon's room is at the front of the house. Although it is the canon's bedroom, it is also his receiving room. Its original purpose is the parlour. Doctor Marie Antoinette McBratt has arrived on her weekly visit to the canon. And since the canon was delayed by the meeting, Mrs. Friel, according to etiquette, correctly directed the doctor to the parlour. And further, Mrs. Friel invited the doctor to sit by the fire in her preferred easy chair, and served her a glass of port from the canon's 'hidden' stock. When the canon enters,

Doctor McBratt is idly leafing through the English Sunday newspapers, the papers the canon had confiscated from Mrs. Friel as 'only fit for lighting the fire'.

Doctor McBratt says, "Good evening, Canon." And to Eamon, "And Eamon, could you put something in the port for me, please."

"Brandy," directs the canon.

Doctor McBratt addresses by name all who enter the canon's room, one after the other, except for Thomas Gilban who is dressed in his foreign light-coloured clothes and tinted glasses. She addresses him as 'Farouk'. He in turn notices that she is dressed in a stylish dark-blue Peblum two-piece, with pinched waist and flowing skirt. He addresses her as 'Claudette'.

Unlike his usual routine of resting upon the bed, the canon sits in the second easy chair at the other side of the fireplace facing Doctor McBratt. Eamon is too slow to dissuade him. Eamon knows that later the canon will have difficulty removing himself from the low soft seat. The canon is still wearing his hat. He is jovial and talkative and is pointing out the attributes and features of his new clock. But his head is still cold. His head is always cold. He directs Eamon to get drinks for all assembled in his room. But the doctor signals Eamon and the company that it is time to leave. They all understand. The canon will over-tire himself. They take their leave, not forgetting to praise the acquisition of such a fine clock, and permit Mrs. Friel to continue with the canon's order of the day. It is 8:15 when she enters with the canon's hot cocoa and biscuits. That is 15 minutes later than usual. Eamon helps the canon up and out of the easy chair with a bit of a struggle and positions him on his bed. Mrs. Friel does her usual thumping and patting of pillows and cushions to ensure that the canon is comfortable, and places the tray within his reach on the bedside table.

Things are back to normal, almost. The doctor assesses the canon's state of health, and goes off to do her stations. Eamon ascertains the canon's schedule for the following day, and having established this, goes off, promising to be at the parochial house at 8:00am the following morning. The canon consumes the remainder of his hot cocoa, liberally laced with Black Bush by Eamon and, when suitably revived, he gets off his bed and shuffles to the church to say his night prayers.

En route to the back door and the passageway to the church, Canon MacMorrow passes by the meeting room. He hears voices and laughter. Curious, he enters. Father MacNamara and Thomas Gilban are in the room.

"It's nine o'clock. Are you still here?"

"Oh, we're waiting for ten o'clock, Canon."

"And what's happening at ten o'clock, then?"

"There's a better reception at night time."

The canon understands. These two are heavily into ham radio. Father MacNamara took an interest in it while in the Royal Navy. And Thomas Gilban appears to know all the ins and outs of it. When Gilban arrived back in Killbawn, about six months ago, he and Father MacNamara installed four radio receivers and transmitters in the tower of the church, high up near the belfry. The aerial antenna, which needs a high structure, usually a mast, is located very successfully on a projection atop the belfry.

"Canon, you should hear Thomas. His call name is 'White Dog' and mine is 'Black Dog' on account of our clothes. You should hear him talk. He knows every language – German, French, Arabic, Russian."

And turning to Thomas Gilban, "And what others?"

"I worked as a translator and interpreter in these languages during the war. But I also have an understanding of Polish, Swedish, Italian, and Spanish."

"That's right, Canon. Thomas here spent most of the war with diplomats and delegates at international meetings."

"Boys-oh-boys. Is that a fact?" The canon is only mildly interested. "I'm off to say my prayers. Father MacNamara, will you check that the church door is locked for the night when you go to the tower?"

"Of course, Canon. We'll be there shortly."

The canon makes his way to the church via the connecting passageway. He opens the sacristy door with his Yale key and shuffles the familiar route through the sacristy to the sanctuary and into the nave. There is still some light in the church coming in through the windows. At nine o'clock, there is still an hour of daylight.

The sacristy lamp illuminates the nave. But the side aisles are in shadow. The aisles are always dark, even on a bright day. He sees Doctor McBratt complete the 14th Station. Then, just the concluding prayer at the main altar, and a prayer for the pope's intention, and she is finished. Kneeling at the side altar, the altar to the Sacred Heart of Jesus, he sees old Granny McGrath. Her votive candle, the sole light in the side aisle, is spluttering. It extinguishes, thus throwing the side aisle into darkness. Granny McGrath gets up off her knees slowly and stiffly. She has been kneeling for an hour and her knees are locked. It takes her a while to get mobile. Then she leaves, walking close to the wall in the darkness of the aisle. She swings open the door and a brief surge of daylight enters the nave for one second. Following her, almost immediately, Doctor McBratt exits the church and another brief wave of daylight swings through the nave like a marine lighthouse light – it's there – and then it's gone. There was no indication that either woman saw the canon. It is usual that all three would be in the church at nine o'clock. When things are usual they go unnoticed. Should one of the three not be here at nine o'clock, now that would be noticed. Tonight, the canon chooses to pray before the altar of the Sacred Heart.

The canon enters into the rhythm of his familiar prayers. He is interrupted momentarily by the sound of Thomas Gilban and Father MacNamara locking the church door, and then the sound of the key unlocking the tower door, followed by the sound of striking a match to light a candle in the tower room, and the ebbing tramping sound as they ascend the tower steps. Now complete silence. The canon resumes his prayers, but the rhythm lulls him to sleep.

Sometime later, the canon awakes. What time is it? It is totally dark. He is unable to distinguish the location of the windows. Did he hear a sound? Maybe the two radio hams are still in the tower. He strains his ears. No sound. It is totally silent. The canon attempts to rise. He has difficulty moving and fails to get up. He remains seated and tries moving his legs to get some feeling back in them. To be this stiff, the canon must have been sitting like this for hours. He attempts to rise one more time and leans on the offering box for support. This time he succeeds in rising, albeit lop-sided. He leans heavily on the offering box. It wobbles on its stand and shifts and is in danger of tilting over. The canon regains feeling in both legs and manages to grab hold of the altar rail, leaving the coin box and stand protruding some six inches into the aisle. Using the altar rail for support he moves slowly to the main altar, and to the opening in the rail. In front of the main altar, the sanctuary lamp affords him sufficient light to see his way. The canon enters the sanctuary and ascends the three steps of the altar. Each step is painful. From here he hobbles to the sacristy and, with great effort, he reaches the chair by the exit door. He sits heavily in the chair. He waits to regain his strength. He stretches out his legs and moves them, rolling his heels and pressing his thighs to encourage circulation. He is sitting in total darkness, but he knows the sacristy intimately without the need of light. He can make out the outline of the door to the apse in the faint light of the sanctuary lamp reflected from the nave. He is grateful for the Yale lock on the exit door here. He needs the key to enter, but not to exit. He can reach up and locate the latch and open the door with his eyes shut, and the door will lock behind him when he departs.

But first he must be sure that his legs are strong enough for the walk through the passageway back to the parochial house. A few more deep breaths and he will be ready. Was that a sound in the nave? Mice? No, it's quiet. Yes, he heard it again. It must be mice. A loud noise echoes through the nave. The coin box and stand are knocked to the ground. This is not mice. Ah, it must be Father MacNamara, the radio ham. He has knocked over the coin box. The canon thinks to himself, "Silly me, I moved the coin box when I stumbled, and now Father MacNamara has knocked it over in the dark. So why isn't he using the lamp from the tower? Or one of the many candles from the tower storeroom?" The canon is worried. He pulls his feet in under the chair to ready himself to rise.

A silent figure enters the doorway of the sacristy from the apse. Canon MacMorrow sees it silhouetted against the dull glow of the sanctuary lamp reflected off the walls of the nave. It is a man's shadow, slighter than either Father MacNamara or Thomas Gilban. It is not the shape and size of anyone he can identify. Whoever it is, he walks stealthily and confidently into the dark sanctuary. This is someone who is sufficiently familiar with the place that he moves unerringly through the dark room to the exit door. He is unaware of the canon sitting by the door. The intruder is about to disengage the latch to open the door when the canon raises his hand. The canon's hand bumps against the intruder's arm. This unexpected encounter causes the intruder to drop two objects into the canon's cassock. The old priest chokes back a shout of surprise.

"Bélyy?" the intruder cries out in alarm.

In a reflex action, the canon grabs the objects on his cassock lest they fall to the ground. This is an instinctive action he executes frequently whenever he drops his rosary or prayer book on his lap. His fingers instantly identify the objects. A coin, could be a penny or a half-crown, and a key of the same size and shape as his own Yale key. But these items are an intruder's things, so he flings them away with all his strength. The coin and the key fly out through the open door to the apse, noisily striking stone, rolling and bouncing. The sound echoes back and forth throughout the nave long after the two objects have come to rest, but because of the multiplicity of sounds, where exactly the objects stopped is indeterminable.

Concurrent with the canon's action, the intruder shoves out his hand blindly in the direction of the sound of the canon's movement. It is a defensive movement. He is fearful that the person in the dark may attack him. The intruder's hand makes contact with the canon's shoulder and knocks him out of the chair and onto the floor. The canon's left leg is caught under the chair, and he falls twisted. There is an audible 'snap' of a bone breaking. The canon cries out in pain and then lies moaning on the ground. The intruder, in an attempt to see what is happening, takes his match-box from his pocket and strikes a match. In the flare of the match, he sees the old canon lying on the ground in a semi-prone position against the door. Too late, the intruder realises that the light which illuminates the fallen person also shines on himself. The canon turns to look at the intruder and opens his eyes wide in recognition. He lifts his finger and points, and groans audibly and convincingly.

"You. You. I know you. I've seen you…"

The intruder lifts the closest object at hand, a candlestick from the counter. He swings it, hitting the canon on the side of the head, thus silencing him. His action extinguishes his match. He drops the spent match and the candlestick on the floor and reaches for the door. He hears the sound of the canon's breathing. He finds the latch. He opens the door, pushing it against the weight of the canon's semi-prone body, and exits into the passageway; the door behind him swings shut self-locking. He runs thence to the parochial house porch, and from there out into the backyard and away into the night.

The intruder knows his way around St. Bawn's.

CHAPTER FIVE

KILLBAWN GARDA STATION
COUNTY MAYO, IRELAND

Wednesday Afternoon, 02 August 1950

Murf checks the time. It is 12:50pm. By now all Killbawn knows of the canon's death. How long before the county medical examiner will be able to confirm the cause of death? It shouldn't take long. Murf can see that the cause of death is TBI, Traumatic Brain Injury. But can the autopsy show whether it is accidental or suspicious? Doctor McBratt is uneasy about it. So is Murf. He can't really devote his time and energy to a non-case. So Murf decides to make a pot of tea and to consider what to do next.

Before the kettle boils, Murf receives a call from RUC, Belfast. It's Nobbie. Murf can tell from Nobbie's tone that he is busy. No time for Mayo small-talk. He goes right to the point. "Nobbie, Thomas Gilban, early fifties, former Foreign Office? Do you know him?"

"No, can't say I do. Working on a case?"

"No, filling in dots. Depending on how they connect, there may be a case, or there may not be a case."

"Not much happening in Mayo, then? Sorry. No can help. I must run. Cheers." And a click as he disconnects.

Murf raises an eyebrow and addresses the mute phone. "That was short." He hangs up the phone. Ah well, back to the kettle. Blast. The kettle has gone off the boil. The water must be boiling to make proper tea, so he waits for the kettle to boil a second time.

"Inspector Murphy, a call from London!" Murf lifts the phone.

"Hello. This is Inspector Murphy. How may I be of assistance?"

"Murf."

Just one word, but Murf recognises 'Piper's Son', the man with no name from British Intelligence.

Murf addresses him with the name he previously used. "Patrick? Do I call you 'Patrick'?"

"Of course, 'Patrick' is fine. So I hear that you are on a case and Thomas Gilban's name comes up."

Why is London phoning? And why so soon after his phone call from Nobbie? Murf's hairs are standing up in high alert. "No case, Patrick. Just filling in my white dots."

Silence. One second, two seconds, three..., four..., five.... Murf coughs to check for a reaction. Did Piper's Son hang up?

"Don't hold out, Murf. What do you know?"

This is unsettling to Murf. What IS there to know about Gilban? That's his dilemma. Murf doesn't know anything of significance about Gilban. And if Patrick is phoning, then what does HE know?

"Actually, Patrick, I'm asking you. What do YOU know about Thomas Gilban?"

"Same as you, Murf. Nothing."

Patrick's 'nothing' sounds a lot like 'a lot'

"If I tell you what I have...?"

"So tell me."

"He spends most evenings, no, most nights after 10:00pm, on his ham radio."

"After 10:00pm? That's a..., well, of some interest. After 10:00pm, you say?"

"Yes. Is there some significance in that?"

"Murf, we need to connect OUR dots too. I'll be in touch. If you learn anything else contact me."

"How...?"

"Through Nobbie. Reference 'Code White'." 'Click' He hangs up.

Now Murf is convinced that something big is going down. It even has its own code-name. But what? Is there a connection to St. Bawn's and, if so, to the canon's death? Damn, there IS a case to be investigated. But what am I investigating? Murf notices that the kettle is off the boil again. But this time his mind is off tea. Doctor McBratt's suspicion that Farouk was a spy may have some foundation, or perhaps he was in counter-intelligence. Intelligence and counter-intelligence and counter-counter-intelligence. "Stop it, Murf," he says to himself. "Deal in facts. Connect the dots. But first, I must assemble all the dots, collect information, collect evidence. Back to the sheets on the wall. Let me complete the profile of each player."

Completing profiles on each player is not to establish guilt or innocence on any one of them. It is to establish a picture of the playing area, which in turn may point to something relevant or reveal what is out of place. Like 'what's wrong with this picture?' Murf already has mental profiles on all the players, except for the missing part on Farouk Gilban. Now to jot it down on paper and study how they interconnect. This may take a few hours. Of the nine players posted on the wall, none have motive to kill Canon MacMorrow. They all have means. All had opportunity between 9:00pm yesterday and 7:30am today. It is unlikely that any of the nine killed the canon. But could one of the nine, knowingly or unwittingly, lead to the answer? "Murf, you're ahead of yourself. First, establish that a crime has been committed. And, if so, then look for clues, conduct forensic examination, interview witnesses.... In other words, conduct a standard police investigation."

Murf lifts the phone and spins the handle. "Get me the County M.E. Thanks." The phone connects. "Finbar? It's Murf. Have you worked on Canon MacMorrow yet?"

"Not yet, Murf. Is there a hurry? Are you suspicious of foul play?"

"Finbar, I'm not happy with how it looks. I need to be satisfied that the death was due to an accidental fall."

"Murf, I may be able to tell you a lot, but 'deliberate' or 'accidental' is more in your area. Anyway, I'll have a report tomorrow."

"Okay, Finbar. But can you put a time frame on when the injuries occurred?"

"'Yes', to the broken leg. 'Not yet' to the TBI, the actual cause of death."

"But wouldn't they have occurred at about the same time?"

"Not necessarily. As I say, I'll know tomorrow."

"No, wait, Finbar. A time for the broken leg?"

"Between midnight and 12:30am."

"And the bruise to the head could be earlier or later than that?"

"The lesion and swelling to the head could not have occurred prior to the broken leg. Look, Murf. I really can't say anything with accuracy until I conduct the post-mortem. I'll contact you tomorrow."

"Okay. Thanks, Finbar."

Murf hangs up. "I really can't do much until I learn something of substance." Murf doodles and squiggles and makes notes on the posted sheets, and gets the coloured threads to map the connecting data.

Murf decides to call it a day when he hears the Angelus bell at 6:00pm. A half hour later, Murf is resting at home. His rubber-soled boots are out on the porch, and he is sitting on a couch with his feet up on a chair. His trouser ends are tucked into his dotty woollen work socks, and he is too comfortable to get up and pour a Powers Gold Label. He decides to leaf through the bundle of English newspapers from the canon's room. Did the canon find something of interest in English papers? Associated football or sport? Horoscopes? Gardening tips? No, it couldn't be any of those. The remainder is all gossip and speculation – not any real news. Loath to disturb his comfort, he changes his mind and decides to go through them later.

His rest is disrupted by the arrival of Suey McBride who bursts into his house without knocking or a 'how-are-ye'. Murf and Suey live next door to each other in adjoining semi-detached cottages. They enjoy an unusual relationship. Each has a key to the other's house and they walk in on each other as the humour hits.

"Well, Murf. Have you had your tea yet?"

"No, Suey. I forgot."

"And have you anything in the house? Food, like?"

"I forgot that too."

"I knew it. Well, come next door. I have two nice lamb chops, all done up nice and ready for the eating."

This is not an unusual invitation. Murf is not sufficiently disciplined to stock up on provisions for his own well-being. Suey, on the other hand, takes care of her larder. She is also very pretty and very moody. When the mood hits, she can get suicidal. So there is an understanding – each looks after the other's well-being. The relationship is a lot more than that. Murf got Suey a job in Casey's Accounts Department, well away from customers who might be distracted by her prettiness or her moodiness. The routine of the job is good for Suey's self-esteem. And Mrs. Casey, the controller of the Casey finances, is unconcerned about Suey's prettiness or moodiness so long as the accounting is done efficiently and accurately.

Mrs. Casey prides herself on being the most informed person in town. Some information she suppresses, and some she broadcasts. A lot of information passes through Casey's. Murf needs an intelligence agent on the inside to keep him informed. Suey McBride is a first-class and willing espionage agent.

Murf jumps to his feet. Suey points to the English newspapers on the couch beside him.

"Murf, which papers are they? Do you have 'The Mirror'?"

Murf lifts the bundle and fans them. "Empire News, Sunday Telegraph and The Weekend Mirror."

"Oh, do you mind if I look in 'The Mirror'? They have a great horoscope page."

"Here, I'll take them next door with me."

"Great."

Suey bounces off and Murf follows her to next door, not bothering to put on his boots. Suey is either fishing for news, or she has a report.

"Suey, you are spending a lot of money on food here, are you not?"

"Don't worry, Murf. This all comes from Casey's, and your share is put on your account."

"You remember that I get the 5% Garda discount?"

"Murf, you get a lot more than that."

"Suey, I hope you're not fecking stuff from Casey."

"No chance of that. Mrs. Casey has every penny accounted for."

"...and every lamb chop."

Murf and Suey go to the kitchen table, where the meal is already served – lamb chops with fried tomatoes, and tea with bread and butter. Murf and Suey dig into the food with relish.

"So, Murf. What's the story on Canon MacMorrow?"

"C'mon, Suey. You know I can't comment during an investigation."

"An investigation? I thought he just fell and cracked his head."

"We are waiting for the medical examiner's pathology report before commenting. It is standard procedure in deaths of this nature – violent deaths and sudden deaths. An 'investigation' does not imply a criminal investigation.... Oh, never mind. This is normal 'police stuff', Suey. Anyway, I thought you might have a report today?"

"Well, yes. Mrs. Friel was in with Mrs. Casey today."

"Mrs. Friel the housekeeper at the parochial house?"

"Yes. What other Mrs. Friel is there?"

"Two others," thinks Murf, but he continues eating.

"Mrs. Friel gave a full account of the canon's passing. I heard it with my own eyes."

"Ears. You heard it.... Oh, go on, Suey."

Suey shifts in her chair and assumes the posture and voice of Mrs. Friel.

"Well, there I was. Holding the dear canon's head against my chest. And him holding the blessed crucifix to his heart. He'd asked me for it, you know. He said 'Cross. Cross'. He was too weak to finish the sentence, but I knew what he wanted. And I knew that he knew that he was dying. He told us to cover the mirror. He said 'Look in the mirror.' That's how I knew he knew. You couldn't have a soul depart the body and be confused by a mirror. Oh, I've heard tell of souls that were so confused that they entered into the mirror and could never find their way to heaven, and now they'll wander lost for all eternity. Well, that didn't happen to the blessed canon. Jack Gilban covered the mirror in the sacristy. And then the canon said something strange. He said that the British are all a lot of feckers. That's what he called them – 'fecking British'. Well, we all know that, of course. But it was odd for him to say that and him dying. But here's the best part. He said 'key'. At first I couldn't fathom the significance of 'key'. So I closed my eyes and do you know what? I could see what the canon saw. We were standing at the gates of Heaven, we were. And there was St. Peter himself. The canon said 'key', and St. Peter takes this big key from his belt and puts it into the keyhole of the heavenly gate. He turns it with one twist of the wrist and the gates swing open, and I could see right into Heaven itself."

Here, Suey adopts another pose, presumably of Mrs. Casey.

"You saw into Heaven itself, Mrs. Friel? And what did it look like?"

"Sure the light of Heaven was too bright for my earthly eyes. I was blinded by it. But I DID see the blessed canon walk through the gates and into Heaven. Then the gates shut with a great big 'clang', and I opened my eyes, and there I was in the sacristy. But this much I can tell you, Mrs. Casey, Canon MacMorrow went straight to heaven, so he did. Lord, what a blessed man."

Suey assumes her normal voice. "Is that how it was, Murf? You were there. Right?"

"Suey, when I reached the canon, he had just passed away a few minutes earlier."

"So you missed it then?"

"From what you tell me, I sure missed a lot. But I'm not convinced that Mrs. Friel heard correctly. Now why, Suey, would Canon MacMorrow, knowing that he was about to enter Heaven, say that the British are 'feckers'?"

"But sure, they ARE feckers, the way they took every..."

"Yes, Suey. But why would Canon MacMorrow need to tell us that with his dying breath?"

"Yeah.... You know what, Murf? Maybe Mrs. Friel didn't hear rightly, what with the canon being so weak and all."

"Perhaps."

Murf is thinking that a lot went on in the Canon's dying moments. He resolves to have the events reported to him firsthand, before the parties outdo each other in embellishing the account. He thinks to himself, "Father MacNamara and Jack Gilban were there. I must talk to them first thing tomorrow."

Suey is already engrossed in a copy of 'The Mirror'. "This is great, Murf. Look, there are three Mirrors, the Sunday Mirror for 16 July, 23 July and 30 July. That's three horoscopes to read. And look here, Murf. In this one it says that I will cross water soon."

"Suey, you cross the river every morning on your way to work."

CHAPTER SIX

KILLBAWN
COUNTY MAYO, IRELAND

Thursday Morning, 03 August 1950

Murf enters St. Bawn's Church at eight o'clock coinciding with the arrival of Jack Gilban. Murf helps Jack set up the church for Mass. He is familiar with the routine having done so himself a number of times, and falls into step with Jack. Jack is recounting to Murf the routine of the previous morning and how he encountered the injured priest. When it comes to the events surrounding the canon's death, Jack is confused. He remembers covering the mirror. Beyond that, his memory is befuddled by Mrs. Friel's account.

"Jack, I don't want to know what Mrs. Friel said or saw. I'll ask her myself for that. What I need to know is what YOU saw, Jack. And what did YOU hear?"

It is pointless. Jack's responses are all coloured by what Mrs. Friel said she saw. "Well, Murf, Mrs. Friel said that she saw Heaven and angels...."

During Mass, Murf speaks with Mrs. Friel. Her accounts of the events are becoming more fanciful. She saw Canon MacMorrow transported to Heaven by Michael the Archangel himself. And she heard angels singing. The narrative she gave to Mrs. Casey just yesterday has already grown into a description of a miraculous encounter.

Murf goes into the sacristy and waits for Father MacNamara to finish Mass. At the conclusion of Mass, Father MacNamara enters the sacristy and goes through his exercise of disrobing while Jack Gilban assists with storing the sacred vessels.

"I thought I'd find you here, Murf. You have been asking questions this morning about the canon's death?"

"That's right."

"And now it's my turn."

"I need an accurate account of what transpired during the time you were with the canon before he passed away."

"An account without the angels and Heaven's gate and Mrs. Friel's visions?"

"If you don't mind."

Father MacNamara removes the alb, the final large vestment, and passes it to Jack Gilban. He reaches for his jacket hanging in the wardrobe and puts it on. He views himself in the mirror to check and straighten his clerical collar.

"Is there a reason to be asking questions? Will it not give rise to unnecessary speculation and gossip?"

Father MacNamara sits down in a chair. He looks tired from the events of the past day. Jack Gilban is clearing up after Mass, and is delaying with ears cocked in the hope of hearing something of interest. From his jacket pocket, MacNamara extracts a pack of Churchman's No.1. He places one of the fat cigarettes in his mouth and hunts in his pockets for his lighter. Jack Gilban passes him a box of matches from the supply cupboard.

Murf chooses not to answer. He waits for Father MacNamara to settle.

"I suppose you would not be asking questions unless you consider it necessary." He takes a drag on the cigarette, inhales deeply, and blows out the smoke. This settles him. "Murf, there is not much to tell you."

"What did he say to you?"

"He was mostly incoherent. Just a few broken words in incomplete sentences."

"Can you repeat them?"

"Yes, if it will do any good."

He takes another drag on his cigarette, not so deep this time, and concentrates on recalling the canon's last words.

"'Cross. In the mirror. Defecting British s...' unintelligible word, 'A key. A coin.' Not sure of the last word. It could have been 'a coy', but there's no such noun."

"And that's all he said?"

"No, Murf. That's all I HEARD him say."

"If he spoke with great effort, then there was an important message in what he said. Don't you agree?"

"Murf, I hadn't put any store in what he said until now. I see what you mean about the circumstances of his death. Maybe some questions are indeed in order."

"One more thing. When did you see him last, prior to the accident?"

"At nine o'clock the previous evening. He looked in at Thomas and me in the meeting room on his way to the church to say his night prayers."

"And that's the last time you saw him until the following morning?"

"Not quite. Thomas and I went up the tower to our radio transmitters/receivers after that. It was a little after nine, and we locked the church doors on our way. We could see the canon sitting in front of the side altar, at the altar to the Sacred Heart."

"And did you see him when you returned?"

"We left, Thomas and I, sometime before eleven. I know that because I listened to the eleven o'clock news in the parochial house. But we did not see the canon then."

"He wasn't in the church then?"

"No. We didn't see him. He could have left, or might very well have been there. If he was still in the same pew, he would not have been visible to us in the dark."

"And Thomas Gilban left at the same time?"

"Yes. We left together. I heard his car drive off while I was waiting for the news to start."

"And did you see or hear anything unusual – anything out of the ordinary?"

"No. It was just another night in St. Bawn's."

"Okay, Father Mac. That's all I need for now. I'll be off. I still have a few more people on my list."

"Oh, Murf, before you go."

"Yes?"

"And Jack here too. Give me a hand to remove the flagstone from behind the altar."

"What? The access to the crypt under the altar?"

"Yes. The canon will be interred under the altar. I want Jack to check it out and prepare the area."

A few minutes later Jack has a coil of rope. They know the location of the flagstone, the one with the brass rings. Jack threads the rope through the rings, and the three of them pull on the rope and lift the stone, sliding it to the side. They hear the unmistakable 'ping-ping-ping' of a small metal object falling through the opening and striking the stone floor of the crypt. Without any prompting, Jack fetches a candle and lights it. All three peer down into the crypt floor. Reflected in the candle's light is a shining newly-cut Yale key.

Father MacNamara and Jack simultaneously exclaim "A key!" And in how they intone the words 'a key', it is clear that they are mindful of the canon's final words. Jack prepares to crawl into the crypt with urgent haste.

"Stop!" shouts Murf, and grabs Jack's sleeve to haul him back. "Don't touch it. I need to retrieve it with a gloved hand or with a hanky...."

"To check for fingerprints," adds Father MacNamara.

Jack supplies one more of his cloths, a clean one, to serve as a retrieval cloth and pouch for the key. Murf lowers himself into the crypt and lifts the key delicately with the cloth. He wraps the key within the cloth, which he folds and places in his pocket.

Back on the sanctuary floor, Murf stands up and brushes the dust and cobwebs off his shoulders. He instructs the two men to keep quiet about the key. Father Mac and Jack are still kneeling, looking down into the crypt.

"Yes," says Father MacNamara, staring at Jack. "Let's keep this quiet."

Jack, who has been silent up to now, mutters, "It sure isn't the key to the gates of Heaven."

All three, in their silent thoughts, agree that the canon's death has an element of mystery. It may not have been an accidental fall that killed him after all. Jack visibly shivers as he considers all the dark areas of the church that he walks through day after day in the course of his duties.

Murf breaks through their thoughts. "Gentlemen, I must go. I have some things to check out...." and hurries off without finishing the sentence.

Father MacNamara and Jack Gilban remain staring down into the crypt. This one little key has thrown an entirely different light on the circumstances of the canon's death. Both men are rethinking and reinterpreting what they witnessed in the sacristy on the previous morning.

Murf hurries back to the Garda station. He is planning his next step. The accidental death of the canon is now a 'suspicious death'. An official police investigation is undoubtedly warranted. Murf considers it fortuitous that he preserved the candlestick uncontaminated. He also has a shiny new Yale key that mysteriously turned up at the entrance to the crypt under the altar. Could this be the key that the canon referred to before he died? Both of these items need to be examined for fingerprints. And that means fingerprinting all who were in or near the sacristy and sanctuary since the evening of Lammas Day. Also fortuitous, Murf's list of 'interested parties' is already posted on the wall of his office. He can undertake collecting fingerprint samples from the names on the list right away. But first things first, he must inform the forensic team to conduct an examination of the accident site and inspect the two items of evidence.

Reaching the Garda station, Murf bursts in and makes for the closest phone to contact Castlebar. Panting from exertion, he leans on the front counter momentarily to catch his breath. But before he can reach over and lift the telephone receiver from behind the counter, Garda Seamus O'Reilly waves two telephone message slips in his face.

"Murf, the medical examiner phoned twice for you in the past hour. 'Urgent'. That's what he said."

"The M.E.? Urgent?"

"Yes. Urgent."

O'Reilly is already spinning the handle to alert the operator. "County Medical Examiner, please." He pauses while awaiting the M.E. to answer. The M.E. picks up on the first ring.

"Killbawn Garda Station." O'Reilly identifies himself to the M.E. "I'm putting you through to Inspector Murphy."

O'Reilly looks at Murf to indicate that he will transfer the call to his office. But Murf is impatient and stretches to take the receiver from O'Reilly. O'Reilly hands it over, "There y'are, Murf."

"Finbar? It's Murf. What do you have for me?"

"Murf. The canon's death, Canon MacMorrow. The blow to his head could NOT have been caused by him falling against a candlestick. The incision is too deep, and the angle of the cut is wrong."

"You sure?"

"Murf, do you have the candlestick there? I need to study it to match it to the injury."

"Yes, I have it. But I also need to have it examined for fingerprints and other possible evidence, skin, hair etc."

"Of course. I understand. I know how to work with the forensic team. There WILL be a team working on this now, Murf. Right?"

"You bet. It's my next phone call."

"Wait, Murf. Tell me the dimensions of the candlestick. I need weight, height and circumference."

"Give me a minute. I'll phone you back."

Murf hangs up without a 'goodbye' and rushes into his office. The candlestick is on his desk, still wrapped up securely. He takes a tape measure from his desk drawer and determines that the candlestick is 2′ 6″ tall; the circumference of the candleholder is 10″; the midsection is 6″; and the base is 12″. But the weight? Murf runs with the candlestick to the butcher shop around the corner.

"Quick, Marty. Weigh this."

Marty McGettigan, the butcher, removes a porterhouse steak from his scales and replaces it with the candlestick. "Exactly 2lbs...."

Before Marty can finish his sentence, or obtain an explanation for the unusual request, Murf grabs the candlestick and is out of the shop, running back to the Garda station.

Garda Seamus O'Reilly is waiting for Murf's return. As Murf runs into the Garda station, O'Reilly commences a telephone connection to the M.E. Murf reaches the front counter and leans on it panting, and delicately places the piece of evidence on top.

O'Reilly hands him the telephone receiver. "The M.E. is on the line."

"Finbar, the candlestick..." (pant, pant) "...is two pounds. Two feet six inches in height; twelve inches at the base, ten inches at the top, and six inches at the middle."

"Murf, that's the instrument that caused the injury? Then it must have been propelled with considerable force, or forcibly wielded horizontally like a club to have caused the injury."

"Homicide?"

"That would be consistent with my findings. Murf, I still need to examine the candlestick to match it to the contusion and confirm that it is the instrument that caused the canon's death. But that will not take long."

"Finbar, you'll have it within the hour." Murf hangs up.

"O'Reilly, you heard all that?"

"I sure did, Murf."

"Okay. You know the protocol. Get on to the district office in Castlebar and inform them. We need forensics. And get Foxy for me. I'll be in the sergeant's office."

"Right you be, Murf. Regional Chief Superintendent David Fox? And you'll be in Sergeant Kevin Hughes' office?"

Murf is already running down the hallway and up the stairs. He shouts back to O'Reilly in acknowledgement, "Yes, yes!"

Sergeant Kevin Hughes is reading the morning newspaper, the Irish Independent, accompanied by his morning cuppa, when Murf bursts in. Murf goes to the sergeant's desk and, uninvited, opens the bottom left drawer and removes a Jameson Crested Ten and one glass. He pours a half-glass measure and downs it in one gulp. The sergeant raises one eyebrow and glances at Murf askew. Murf's eccentric behaviour is tolerated, but this is out of the ordinary.

"Kevin, we have a homicide."

This is reason to put the newspaper aside, and the cup of tea. "Homicide? Who?"

"Canon MacMorrow."

"The old canon? Are you sure? I thought he just fell over and hit his head."

"No. It's no accident. Finbar confirms it. And Castlebar is informed. Expect a call from Foxy any moment."

And, as if on cue, the sergeant's phone rings. He lifts the receiver. "The Chief? For Murf? Put him through." Hughes hands the receiver to Murf.

"The Chief?"

Hughes nods in affirmation.

Murf speaks into the phone. "Foxy?"

"Chief Superintendent Fox" is the reply. Fox is touchy about the form of address since his promotion. That is the main reason that Murf, who is actually on staff in Castlebar, has an office in Killbawn. Fox does not want Murf's casual manner and his choice of 'plain clothes' rubbing off on the well-polished officers in the regional office. "So you have a homicide in Killbawn, Inspector Murphy?"

"Here's the lowdown, Foxy."

And over the next ten minutes, Murf gives a concise account of the incident and of his recent findings for the benefit of Fox and Hughes.

"Okay, Murf." Fox, cognisant of the serious nature of the case, addresses Murf in the familiar parlance he once enjoyed prior to his promotion to Regional Chief Superintendent. "I believe you are the best detective for this case. Proceed as you see fit. Sergeant Hughes will give you all the local assistance you need."

Within minutes, Sergeant Hughes undertakes to have Garda O'Reilly deliver the candlestick to the medical examiner and obtain fingerprint samples of the canon (clear prints are obtainable up to four days after death) and to return back with both, post-haste to Killbawn. He puts in place the protocols to accommodate the forensic team and to have uniformed officers at their disposal. He arranges to obtain fingerprint samples from all the interested parties in Killbawn. He checks off the list with Murf –

Mrs. Maggie Friel, the housekeeper;

Father Andrew MacNamara;

Jack Gilban, the sacristan;

Doctor Antoinette McBratt;

Patrick Joseph Casey, general merchant;

Eamon Curry, the canon's driver;

Thomas Gilban, parish treasurer-accountant;

Paddy 'Lamp' Ward, itinerant;

Sally 'Granny' McGrath;

And Murf.

Paddy Lamp and Granny McGrath are not local within the town of Killbawn. Murf decides to visit them both to obtain sample prints.

And he still needs to question six more of the nine names. One or more of these may have seen something suspicious or may have significant information to report. Something to add to the 'dots' that Murf accumulates to form a picture.

Casey's is the only place in town that cuts keys. Casey may have a record of a newly-cut Yale key. He is also the only supplier of Yale locks in town. Casey would know everyone in Killbawn who has a Yale lock installed. That would be a start in matching the new-found key to its respective lock, hence to its door, and ultimately to its owner.

Murf considers Paddy Lamp Ward. Paddy Lamp is very canny. He is always on the lookout for valuable junk and for anything not nailed down. Could he have seen something of interest?

And why is Doctor McBratt addressed as 'Mammo' by the Ward clan? Is this of any significance or relevance?

And Granny McGrath. She is acting strangely. What is bothering her? Did she knock over the coin box for the votive lights as she struggled to get to her feet on the night prior to the canon's demise? Or was it intact when she left the church? She came to St. Bawn's again last night. She said her prayers and spoke to no one.

And then there is the mysterious Thomas 'Farouk' Gilban. Farouk is too clean. And that is suspicious. He is secretive, playing his cards close to his chest. There are blank spaces in Farouk's profile. Murf is suspicious of blank spaces. And why did his name spook 'Piper's Son'? They both once worked together in the British Foreign Office. Is there a secret in Gilban's previous life that is protected by the 'Official Secrets Act'? And if so, is it relevant to this inquiry?

Murf considers all the strange people associated with the case. There is something secretive about many of them. Casey has under-the-counter transactions. The Gilban clan has an IRA past that is kept hushed up. But being strange isn't a crime. And being secretive? Well, what family doesn't have a skeleton hidden in the closet? And none of them, despite their idiosyncrasies, have any reason or motive to harm Canon MacMorrow.

Murf has a lot of digging to do. He cautions himself not to dig in the wrong places.

Focus on the facts of the case, not on the personalities.

Where does the candlestick lead?

Where does the key lead?

Murf leaves the key with Sergeant Hughes to give to the forensic team for examination. It is still morning. He leaves the station, intent on visiting Paddy Lamp and Granny McGrath. He is hopeful that by the end of the day a clear picture will emerge.

At Paddy's camp, Murf performs his customary change of footwear. As it turns out, it is not necessary. Uncharacteristically, Paddy walks up to Murf who is still at his car. Murf shuts the boot and is surprised that Paddy actually seeks him out. This is a change. Perhaps Paddy doesn't want Murf snooping around the tent like last time?

Paddy addresses him. "So, Murf, Me Honour, why the visit the day?"

"Actually, Paddy, I need your help."

"Hah! The guards need the help of a travelling man?"

"Paddy, it's about the canon."

"What, Canon MacMorrow? I heard he fell and hit his head. Then he died and went to Heaven. I know about that. A good and holy man, the canon. May God rest his soul. Is there a problem with his clock?"

"Paddy, there may very well be a problem – no, it's not the clock. And you can help us."

Murf places his hand on Paddy's shoulder. Paddy is wary lest this is the hand of an arrest. But Murf slides his hand down to Paddy's shoulder blade in a gesture of comradeship. Murf continues, standing side-by-side rather than face-to-face, speaking low into Paddy's ear. "Paddy, the canon's death may not have been an accident."

"What? You mean someone kilt him?"

"'Unusual circumstances', that's our suspicion."

"Murf, you know I wouldn't harm the canon."

"No, Paddy. I know YOU would not harm the canon. But someone did."

"And I can help you? How?"

"A few ways. Number one. I know you are very observant, Paddy. You see a lot and know a lot, even though you pretend otherwise. But I know you, Paddy. Now, you were at St. Bawn's on Lammas Day. Did you see any strangers around the place? Or did you see anything unusual – something not right?"

"Like when?"

"Lammas Day. In particular, the evening of Lammas Day, when you delivered the clock to Canon MacMorrow."

"That's when it happened?"

"Sometime between then and the Angelus next morning."

Paddy rubs his stubbly chin. He pushes his cap back on his head and scratches his crown. With his cap removed, Paddy's hair falls down in front of his face. He throws it back with a flick of his head and jams it back in place with his cap. From these actions, Murf feels sure that Paddy knows something, but he is weighing the advantages of disclosing or concealing what he knows. Or is he considering some editing to make his story credible?

"Weeeell now, Murf," drawing the words out slowly to make it sound like he is in deep mental deliberation. "I'll think about it. If I come up with something, I'll let you know."

"Paddy. It's not for me. It's for Canon MacMorrow."

"Ah, so it is. So Murf, what's your 'number two'?"

"Yes, Paddy. We are dusting the church for fingerprints. We hope to find the fingerprints of the person responsible for the canon's death. I need your prints so that I can eliminate you...."

"Eliminate me? Like the way IRA eliminates people...?"

"No, Paddy. Not that kind of 'eliminate'. I need to separate the innocent from the guilty."

"And which am I?"

"In this instance, Paddy, you are innocent. But I need to isolate your prints from the guilty person's." Murf realises that it is improper to use the term 'guilty' in referring to a suspect. But he uses a language that Paddy clearly understands.

"So you want to take my fingerprints?"

"That's right, Paddy. I'd like you to provide them voluntarily."

"Or..."

"C'mon, Paddy. The alternative is to take you into the station and..."

"You're right, Murf. I'll help you. We'll get the divil what killed the canon. Don't you fear, Murf."

They go to Murf's car, to the fingerprinting kit. Murf is pondering the significance of Paddy's enthusiasm. He was hesitant at first: now he is keen. 'We'll get the divil what killed the canon' is stuck in his mind. Murf wonders if there is a deeper meaning to Paddy's statement, something more determined than mere cooperation with the police. With the fingerprinting completed, Murf is ready to leave for his next meeting.

"Paddy, I'll come back to call on you in about an hour's time. If you remember anything by then, you can let me know."

"Oh, right you be, Murf. In an hour's time."

Fifteen minutes later, Murf's car is bumping along the rough surface of the road to Lough Corry. It's not a road, Murf thinks, as his head bumps against the roof. He shifts down to a cautious second gear. It's hardly a track. Who would want to live up here in the wilds of Lough Corry?

Lough Corry is located in Glen Corry, a mountain glen. The glen is so-called because of its shape. 'Coire' is a cauldron. It is a cauldron-shaped valley carved out of the mountains by glacial erosion during the ice age. The hollow of the glen, the bottom of the pot, contains a lough – hence, Glen Corry, Lough Corry, and lower down in the farmland, Ballycorry.

In answer to his question, 'who lives here?' Granny McGrath. That's who. No one else has reason to be here, not since the anti-treaty IRA used it for training and hiding during 'The Troubles'. There hasn't been IRA activity here since the early thirties. And since Brendan McGrath's death last month, old Sally McGrath is the sole inhabitant of the isolated mountain glen.

As the car climbs higher towards the mountain glen, Murf is aware of the barren windswept bogland, dark, forbidding and treeless. Here and there the bleak landscape is punctuated by a copse of trees. These are the windbreaks that are planted around houses to shelter them from the incessant wind. But most of the houses here are just stone roofless shells. This was once the community of Lough Corry Lower during the Penal times. Then the Great Famine came and wiped it out, devastating Glen Corry and Lough Corry Lower and much of the county. It's over one hundred years since the Great Famine. But the traces of the ridges and furrows of the failed potato crop are still discernible stretching away from the boreen and up the slopes. No spade or hoe has pierced the sod of Glen Corry since 1847.

Murf refocuses on the road ahead. How much further to Granny McGrath's cottage? Looming before him is Lough Corry Upper, the mountain range that drains into the glen. It is not a high range. It is hard to judge. Murf has never seen the top of the range. It is perpetually cloaked in cloud from the air blowing in from the Atlantic that condenses as it rises, becoming cloud, mist and drizzle. Today is a soft day, dry by Lough Corry standards, but moist and windy nonetheless. On a wet day the entire glen is shrouded in precipitation.

It is precarious driving on such a narrow track. The edges are soft, and if he skids off the road he will get stuck in the bog. How on earth does the inebriated Danny the Divil drive the doctor here every week? And worse, how does Granny McGrath cycle this every day to St. Bawn's?

The boreen bends with the contours of the land and swings along the bank of the Corry River. He is close to the lough now. Rhododendrons grow wild on the bank of the river. They thrive in the acidic soil and rainy climate but require good drainage. Hence, they are abundant along riverbanks and on lough shorelines, but not in the stagnant saturated bog.

With relief, Murf sees a copse of fir trees surrounded by a circle of rhododendron. This can only be Granny McGrath's windbreak. The cottage will be tucked comfortably inside. Yes, there is the turf smoke rising from within the grove. The smoke rises lazily until it reaches the treetops, where it is snatched by the wind, disappearing before it reaches the low-flying cloud. Here the road is edged with rhododendron in a straight line, clearly planted as a hedgerow some years ago. It is very pretty, but it forces the road to narrow. The broad green leaves brush against both sides of the car. Murf slows down even more and proceeds with caution.

Suddenly, Murf is in a clearing. And there it is, a fresh-looking white-washed thatched cottage, hens running away from the car, a collie barking, and the half-door closed to prevent the animals from entering the cottage through the otherwise open doorway. Murf is taken aback. What was he expecting? A hovel? This is picture-perfect. Was this how it was before the Great Famine?

Murf brings the car to a halt, exits, and walks slowly towards the doorway. Granny McGrath appears momentarily, peering over the half-door, and disappears again. Murf wonders if he should knock or just announce himself.

"Come in, Guard Murphy," says Granny's voice from inside. "So you've come to arrest me, is it?"

Murf leans his hand inside the half-door and lifts the wooden latch. The door swings open. He enters and secures the door against the curious dog and foraging hens. The dog lies down at the doorstep, and the hens resume their scratching and pecking.

Turning around to enter into the house, Murf observes that the doorway is like a shallow tunnel. The outer walls of the cottage are six feet thick, eight feet at the base and tapering to three feet at the roof. Are the walls actually this thick, or are they constructed as double walls? Murf cannot tell. In any event, there is an abundance of stone in the glen. It is common to see thick stone walls in the Irish countryside, not that thick walls are a requirement, but the land needs to be cleared of stone to accommodate tillage. The stones need to go somewhere. Murf walks through the brief tunnel and past the coat pegs on the wall. His silent rubber-soled boots squeak on the stone flags of the floor. It is like entering a monastery chapel. Granny McGrath is kneeling at the other side of the room, busy with her duties at the fireplace. She turns halfway to catch a glimpse of Murf, and turns back to resume her tasks.

Murf has not replied to Granny's question. Perhaps it is meant as a humorous greeting. He pauses to take in the quaint surroundings. A holy-water fount is by the door; and inside, on the wall, a clock with weights and chains and pendulum swinging up and down; and further in, a dresser filled with shining delph, speckled with white and blue and brown; and at the far end, the heaped-up sods upon the fire; the pile of turf against the wall; the hearth, and stool, and all.... Murf stops himself as he realises that he is mentally reciting a poem by Padraic Colum. This is what the poet pictured. Is this how it once was? He peers up at the ceiling, at the underneath of the thatch. Instead of straight angular beams, there are tree trunks and branches at crazy angles serving as rafters. The entire ceiling is painted black, or is it a tar?

"Turf smoke." Granny, still kneeling with her back to Murf, is reading his thoughts. "After the thatching, the thatch is smoked to drive out insects and to prevent seeds and things from growing there."

Murf continues his visual tour of the room. There are two small windows recessed in one wall, the same wall as the doorway. They could not be more than 18″ square. One window is directing light onto the area of Granny's current attention. Wooden slats of bog oak form a panelling on all the walls to a height of 4′, and above that, the inside white-washed stones give an unexpected brightness and cheeriness to the room. The interior stones are smoother than the exterior stones and are fitted together to a flat surface. The whitewash here is heavily layered into a lime plaster generating a fresh clean smell. Beside the dresser there is a box with a back, not unlike a small church pew. During the day this serves as a seat. From the hinges on it, Murf deduces that this is Granny's box bed. At night she sleeps in it, next to the fire.

At intervals along the walls, on the ledge of the panelling, are candles inserted into small saucer-shaped candleholders of delicate white porcelain. And each one has a handle, like a cup handle, so that the candleholder can be easily carried and placed on a table or shelf. And there are one or more lucifer matches in the hollow of each candleholder. Higher up, on the wall facing the windows, are two paraffin oil lamps set in brackets in the stone, their glass globes polished to a gleaming sparkling translucence.

Dominating the wall next to the entrance, and beside the clock, is a picture of the 'Immaculate Heart of Mary', below which, on the ledge, is a small burning oil lamp with a blue glass globe. Murf turns to face the opposite wall, the wall above the fireplace. As expected, he sees above the mantle a picture of the 'Sacred Heart of Jesus' with its own little burning oil lamp, but with the appropriate red glass globe. This is the same 'Sacred Heart' that Granny visits nightly in St. Bawn's. The mantle is lined with tin boxes. From the pictures and writing on them, it is clear that these once contained tea. What do they contain now? Recipes? Prayer leaflets? Photographs? Little treasures?

There are framed photographs lining the wall between, which is the wall facing the windows. Patrick H. Pearce is there in profile, next to a miniature green-white-orange flag of the Republic. Pearce, the president of the Provisional Government of the Republic of Ireland in 1916, never permitted a full-face photograph because of the turn in his lazy eye. Beside Pearce is a photograph of James Connolly, the de-facto commander-in-chief of the Easter Rising. And next to Connolly is the blue 'Plough-and-Stars' flag of the Socialist Republic of Ireland. To the left of Pearce and

Connolly is a framed copy of the Proclamation of the Republic of Ireland – '...We declare the right of the people of Ireland to the ownership of Ireland...'

Granny McGrath rocks back off her knees onto a low three-legged stool while still maintaining her crooked bent posture. She swivels the stool on one leg, turning to observe Murf as he slowly makes his way along the wall viewing one exhibit after another. There are numerous pictures of men dressed in civilian country clothes laden heavily with rifles and bandoliers and sidearms.

"That's Brendan with Seán Mac Eoin. Ay, Mac Eoin, 'The Blacksmith of Ballinalee'. He's the one in uniform. They were comrades back then. And then they were enemies, after the English (she spits into the fire) gave us the rag they call 'the Treaty'. What? It's not for the English (spit) to give us anything except suffering. They called us a 'Free State', but those what fought the most for freedom were gaoled. Brendan was in gaol for six years until De Valera freed the Republican prisoners in, in..."

"...in 1932."

"Ah yes. Do you mind it?"

Murf moves on to the next picture and Granny continues her commentary. "And that's Brendan with Fenian Gilban. Fenian's the old one. He was Brendan's mentor, and introduced him to the Republican Brotherhood. Sure the two of them ran together for years as anti-treaty IRA."

Murf peers at the older man's image in the picture. 'Fenian'? So he was from the earlier era of republicanism, before Sinn Fein.

Granny is still talking. "Fenian didn't go to gaol back then. They thought he was too old and past being active, so they let him be. And, by jaypers, if he didn't lead the raid on the Ulster Bank in...I can't mind exactly..."

"The IRA raided the Ulster Bank in Westport in 1931, making off with £10,000. It was later recovered. And in the ensuing struggle to apprehend them, three IRA men were shot and killed."

"Lord, Guard Murphy, you seem to know a lot about it. Were you there?"

Murf doesn't enlighten her. He realises that Granny McGrath is suffering from false memories. She has trouble putting things into chronological sequence, and she remembers things she couldn't have experienced. Fact and fantasy, story and myth, have been shuffled and misfiled in her memory banks.

"And that's me two sons, Mick and Joe. They were shot dead by the guards too. All three kilt: Fenian, and Mick and Joe, after the bank job back in...I can't mind when. But afore Dev got in. You weren't one of the guards what shot them? Were you, Guard Murphy?"

"Lord, Granny, that was almost twenty years ago. I was still in school back then, in short trousers."

"Oh, aye. Twenty year ago, you say?" She sighs and continues. "All the rest of the lads escaped with guns and all, and they are still hunted."

Murf is familiar with the account. After the robbery, three IRA men were shot and killed in an engagement with the police. The others were never apprehended. They escaped with their guns and ammunition. The guns were never surrendered, and are considered to be in the hands of the IRA to this day. Granny is correct to say that they are still hunted. Firing on the police is a serious offence. The case is still officially open and will remain so until the 20-year limitation expires. The bank recovered the £10,000. The bank acknowledged that the amount recovered was the actual amount stolen. But the guards were suspicious that the bank did not disclose the true amount stolen.

"And what about the rest of the family?"

"Mary Ellen went off to Amerikey after that. She never came back. Got kilt in a car accident she did. When Brendan returned from gaol they were all gone. All dead. And now Brendan. All dead."

Granny swivels the stool back to face the fire and resumes her tasks. Murf walks closer on the stone flags to admire the most interesting part of the room. The entire floor is flagstoned, except for one large area in front of, and slightly to the right of, the immense fireplace. Instead of a flagstone, a thick wooden slab like a butcher's block is embedded in the floor. This is Granny's kitchen table. At hand are her kitchen tools, knives and ladles. Everything she is working on is within reach of her kneeling or sitting position. She moves around on her three-legged stool as if it has wheels, rocking it from side to side, balancing it on one leg and alternating on all three.

The fireplace occupies the entire wall. It narrows to a chimney, but down here at Granny's work area it is divided into sections. To the left and right are brick hobs about 12″ high – the warming area. The hearth is in the centre. There is no grate. The centre of the hearth is raised so that ash can be shoved to the side. Granny controls the heat by moving a desired amount of ash onto or off the fire, and by feeding it with sods of turf. There are two black iron bars running horizontally above the fire. Both are attached to upright iron posts that swivel. Thus, the horizontal bars can be swung outwards from the fire to suspend over the wooden block on the floor. On each horizontal bar are a number of flat iron bars of varying lengths hanging down over the fire. Granny can slide these flat bars left and right to hang over the fire or over the hobs. The hanging flat bars are pierced through with a series of vertical holes to accommodate hooks. The hooks can be moved up or down to engage a selected hole, thus moving them farther from the heat or closer to the fire. The hooks, in turn, accommodate pots, kettles and pot ovens with appropriate swinging handles that latch onto the hooks. From her single position, Granny can tend the fire and control her cooking – up, down, left and right, in and out – with tongs and poker.

Using a poker, Granny raises the height of one hook over the fire. From within the ash and embers, a pot oven appears rising up out of the smouldering fire. Three chains are hooked on to its three ears which in turn are joined to the hook suspended over the fire. Granny takes a goose feather and brushes the ash and embers off the lid. Then she raises the pot a few more inches and slides it to hang over the hob. With poker, she lifts the lid and peers inside the pot. Satisfied with her inspection, she removes the lid and swings the pot out over the wooden slab and tips out the contents. A scone of soda bread rolls out.

"Here, Guard Murphy. Put this in the windy to cool."

Murf understands. He takes the hot scone, tossing it from hand to hand, and places it on a metal cooling rack on the window ledge. Turning back to Granny, he sees her slide the black kettle to the centre of the horizontal bar. She lowers it one rung and it sings and boils in seconds. The lid is jumping up and resettling. Granny leans over to the hob and slides a brick in the wall to reveal a dry warm cubby-hole. She takes out a tea caddy and measures three spoons of tea into the black teapot on the hob. Next she slides the boiling kettle towards the hob and tips it. The boiling water pours into the teapot, and not a drop of water is spilled.

"Guard Murphy. Me knees are locked and I can't straighten me back for a few minutes. Can you refill the kettle for me?"

Murf fetches the white enamelled water-bucket from the raised stone ledge by the dresser. Granny holds the kettle lid aloft with the tongs and Murf refills it. She then repositions the kettle to its simmering spot in preparation for the next tea wetting.

"Granny, the water bucket is empty now."

"So go to the well and fill it."

Murf takes the bucket and walks to the door. He stops and turns back to Granny. "I'm sorry, Granny, but where is your well located?"

"Open the door at the base of the cófra," pointing to the two doors at the base of the dresser.

Murf is puzzled, but does as he is bidden. Upon opening the doors, he is surprised to see a spring well in the floor about six inches below the floor level. He dips the bucket and fills it, and places it back on its ledge. By now, Granny has limbered up. She gets milk and butter from a hole in the wall next to the windows, and before Murf can register all her actions, he is seated on the box bed. Beside him is a thick slice of warm scone on a plate, the butter melting on it, and a mug of strong tea.

Granny has made herself comfortable in her rocking chair on the other side of the fireplace, the non-working side. From her sitting position, she stretches her hand back towards the pile of turf against the wall beside the hob. She selects a sod and lobs it into the fire. And then repeats the exercise with a second sod. Murf notices that the sods of turf have the distinctive markings of a breast-slane. Granny's fuel is not 'shop-bought turf' or 'machine-cut turf'. This turf was cut horizontally from the bog in distinctive County Mayo fashion, an exhausting and demanding task, well beyond Granny's ability. Murf deduces that someone local supplies her with turf.

The hob at Granny's side serves as her side table. She stretches out her hand to the hob cubby-hole, where she stores her tea, and withdraws a small snuff-box. She places a pinch of snuff on the back of her left hand. She carefully places the snuff-box on the hob and, thus satisfied, she holds the small pile of snuff against her nose. First the left nostril, 'sniff', and then the right nostril, 'sniff'. She slaps her hand over the fire to clear any residue and leans back staring up at the ceiling.

"Granny, how do you happen to have country butter and fresh milk? I didn't see a cow or a byre here."

"I get it from Mickey Travers' milking shed. As much as I want. I bring him eggs in exchange."

"Mickey Travers? That's four miles away."

"Is it now? I don't know. I cycle it in 15 minutes."

Maybe Mickey Travers also supplies the turf. Murf eats the bread and drinks the strong tea. He remembers that he is working on a case. But, sitting here with Granny McGrath, he is transported to another world.

Granny is speaking again. Murf is not sure to whom. She appears to be addressing the black ceiling. "This house was built in 1750. It was illegal for us to have a house back then. It was illegal to own a horse, to carry a weapon, go to school, to own land, to speak in Irish, to go to Mass – it was illegal for the Irish to be Irish. The English (spit) didn't want us dead. They wanted unpaid labour, and to see us humiliated and made suffer. But they were afeard to venture into Glen Corry. Back then, there was a community here.

"One time the horse soldiers came. The horses sank in the bog and they had to kill them – the horses, that is. The horse soldiers then left on foot. Later, foot soldiers came.

They found it slow-going walking over the bog. They didn't have the knack for it – sinking into bog holes and the like. The mist came down and they got lost. Then night fell and they wandered into the lough. Many of them drownded. What was left of them walked along the shoreline to the river, and then walked in the riverbed until they got out of the glen. They never came back.

"After that, we got 'Emancipation' in 1829, thanks to Dan O'Connell and Archbishop McHale, the 'Lion of Connacht'. Then in the 'black 47' the famine wiped out the whole of the community, except for this house, and there was no reason to live in the boglands anymore. But we stayed."

"Granny, the reason for my visit..."

"Oh, yes. You've come for me."

"No, Granny. The canon's death. You know that Canon MacMorrow died yesterday morning."

"Ah, yes. Died, he did."

"Granny, I need your fingerprints...."

"Of course. That's usual when you arrest someone."

Murf takes the kit from his pocket and proceeds to take samples of Granny's fingerprints.

Granny is cooperative and continues to talk. "Ah, you know I done it. And there he was with his eyes bulging and staring at me, and his nose pointing at me like a hen's beak. So now I go to gaol. I die there. And then I'll burn in Hell forever."

Murf realises that Granny's grip on reality is tenuous. How is she going to manage on her own out here in the lonely glen?

"One question, Granny. At St. Bawn's on the night before last night, did you notice the coin box at the penny candles when you were there? Was it moved? Did you knock against it or anything?"

"What are you talking about, Guard Murphy? Sure the coin box is where it always is. It's never moved."

Murf sees that Granny can't tell him anything reliable. But Murf has the sample prints he came for and prepares to leave.

"Guard Murphy, are you leaving and not taking me into custody?"

"Well, Granny, there is a lot of paperwork to do, and I need to get a warrant. And that can take days, or weeks, or even years. I won't be able to arrest you today."

"Not today? What day is it, anyway? And what time is it at all, at all?"

The clock begins to chime 12:00 noon.

"Ah. Now I know. It's time for my noonday rosary. And I must remember to pray for the conversion of Russia and for the damnation of England."

Murf hurries off. Granny is still talking. Talking to herself or to God or to the ceiling or to who knows what. He is loath to leave, but he has fallen behind schedule. Murf had hoped to be back at the station by 11:00am. He resolves to contact Doctor McBratt to discuss Granny McGrath's state of mind. Murf exits the cottage, pausing to secure the half-door. He sees that it is raining now. He bids goodbye to Granny, to the yawning collie and to the scattering hens, and drives back to Ballycorry.

Upon leaving Glen Corry and entering Lough Corry Lower, he looks about, peering through the rain, to locate Mickey Travers' place. Off the road, two furlongs away, he sees a grove of trees. That would be it. And next to it is a solitary red-and-white Friesian cow, a hardy breed, grazing in a small green patch reclaimed from the bog. Granny's supplier of milk and butter.

Murf continues. He has one more call to make en route to Killbawn. To stop at the travellers' camp and speak once more to Paddy Lamp. Murf suspects that Paddy is keeping something back. It could be important to Murf in solving the case. He hopes to coax it out of Paddy.

Fifteen minutes later, Murf leaves the Glen Road. He turns right onto the Ballycorry road, past the old RIC Barracks, along the long mile, and around the bend to the creamery. He slows down in anticipation of stopping at the encampment. Murf is taken aback. The camp is cleared. Gone. No sign of travellers or tents, or carts or horses. He drives into the creamery yard. This too is empty. He parks his car in the yard and walks across to the vacant campsite. The rain is falling heavier now. He conducts a quick inspection of the entire area. He identifies the water-filled depression where the tent entrance had been. And not much else. Down near the sheugh, amongst the rushes, he sees a few pieces of shredded tin, some bits of rope and wire, and a bent-up Tilley lamp. In frustration Murf kicks the beaten-up Tilley lamp. It sails through the air, over the salley bushes, and lands with a splash, sinking into the murky water of the sheugh bordering the field.

Why did Paddy Lamp Ward suddenly disappear? And to where? Which road did he take? And why travel in the rain? Murf is well aware that Paddy Ward knows all the hidden roads and laneways in the county. If Paddy chooses to be unseen, then Paddy will not be found.

What a morning this is turning out to be. Murf, now saturated by the rain, returns to his car. He thumps the steering wheel in frustration. Granny McGrath confessing to a murder she did not commit; Paddy Lamp Ward withholding information that is likely pertinent to the investigation. What next? Murf continues to Killbawn in the hope that there is good news awaiting him back at the Garda station.

CHAPTER SEVEN

THE WARDS' MEMORY PORTAL
COUNTY MAYO, IRELAND

Thursday 03 August 1950

11:00am. The Blackwater flows dark and deep past the creamery on the Ballycorry Road, a mile outside Killbawn. Today, like most days in north Mayo, it is raining.

A small Ward boy in bare feet and with a running nose comes to the riverbank and speaks with Francie Clé Ward. Francie, who is sheltering under a tree, signals to his brother Collie Tricks Ward who is some distance downstream with an outsider, an 'English divil' named Peter Oldthorpe. "Paddy wants us all back in the camp."

Back in the camp, Paddy Lamp's merchandise is being wrapped up in canvas, and the horse is hitched to the cart. The women and children are busy packing and assembling their effects. This is no easy task to perform in the rain. Paddy has finished restoring a Tilley lamp which he is buffing to a shine. He holds it aloft by the handle and casts his eye up and down to admire his handiwork.

He shouts to the gossoons, "Tether the two relief horses to the back of the cart. But not too tight. A cart length is the right distance."

Francie looks around at the campsite. It is almost completely cleared. "You're not leaving in the rain, are you?"

"After what I learned from Guard Murphy, I want to be cleared out and gone before he returns. He'll be sticking his nose into every tent and cart in the camp. And we don't want that, do we? He said that he would be back here in an hour –

we'll be gone by then. But don't you worry none about that, Francie. Your work here is done and I have things well in hand. I'll look after things from here on. You get on with your pilgrimage. Don't you fret yourself with my going. You should be off to the Reek, you know."

"Aye, too true, Paddy. To the Reek we go, the fourth and final portal. Then we're done 'til next year."

Francie and Collie turn and walk away in the direction of the straight mile, leaving the outsider, the English divil Peter Oldthorpe, with Paddy Lamp Ward. They have nothing to pack. They wear greatcoats with deep inside pockets that contain all their earthly belongings. They reach the bend in the road and take one last look back at the campsite before disappearing from sight. The camp is already totally cleared and the cart is loaded. The rest of the clan is lined up on the roadside ready to commence walking. They round the bend. Ahead is the straight mile and bogland. They leave the shelter of the woodland with its border of whins, and set a steady pace.

Two itinerant travellers, dressed in oversized ankle-length greatcoats, wearing unclasped soft paddy caps, tramp, tramp, tramp, in a rhythm inherent to all travellers. Their greatcoats are unfastened. They billow and flap in the incessant wind that blows across the treeless bog. The pair strides onward to the Reek, impervious to wind and weather.

Francie has made the pilgrimage ten times in his life. This is his eleventh, but it is his first without Shanwar. Her name is 'Sean-Mhathair', which means 'old-mother'. She is Francie's grandmother. Shanwar is a respected and revered elder member of the clan. Shanwar is too old to make the pilgrimage this year. She may never make it ever again. Shanwar is revered because she holds the clan's sacred and treasured memory. Francie is the only other member of the clan to display the gift of memory. Shanwar recognised it in the left-handed boy. She undertook Francie's apprenticeship ten years ago and taught him how to reach through the portals and draw forth the memories.

Collie's skills are different. He is known as 'Tricks' for good reason. He earns money by performing tricks as a street entertainer, but his greatest tricks are in the art of survival. His skills include, but are not limited to, snaring rabbits using boot whangs, catching fish with his hands, and making fire from wet wood.

Francie and Tricks are the past and the future of the semi-nomadic Ward clan. They support each other in a satisfactory relationship of interdependence, and so they stick together.

It is incumbent upon Francie to perform the memory pilgrimage each year. The memory weakens if it is not refreshed and revived annually at the portals. At each portal he recites and relives the events pertaining to each respective portal. The designated clan memory-keeper has been doing this since the origin of the clan, long before the Éireannach came to Ireland, and long before the Sassenach came to England. Collie is not convinced that the memory-keeper actually experiences or witnesses the events, but rather, has memorised the folklore knowledge that has been passed down from ancient times. There is no doubt that the memory-keeper undergoes a trance-like experience during each 'memory' experience.

Since the July new moon they have visited 'Dara', the sacred oak in Cheshire; Drumceatt in Derry; and Drumskinny in Fermanagh. Tomorrow they will climb the 'Reek', Cruach Phádraig, Ireland's Holy Mountain in Mayo.

Friday 04 August, Croagh Patrick, Mayo, Ireland. It is late in the day when Collie and Francie climb the Reek. Observing their customary ritual, they circumambulate the summit of the Reek seven times sunwise, walking clockwise around the chapel. Francie then stands westward facing towards the setting sun.

Other than Francie and Tricks, the only other visitors are the gulls wheeling in the updraft from the ocean. Three days ago, on the last Sunday in July, the Reek was crowded with pilgrims. The few pilgrims that had climbed earlier today had returned home by mid-afternoon.

Francie removes his cap and leans forward against the ocean wind, his greatcoat flapping like a wild sheet on a loose clothesline. His long black hair whips about like a horse's tail. He raises his arms and points them horizontally at the setting sun.

Tricks has seen the memory encounter many times. He goes around to the sheltered side of the chapel and sits on his hunkers with his back against the chapel wall. He draws his arms and head inside his greatcoat like a snail entering its shell. Inside the tent of the coat Tricks removes a bottle of porter from one of the inside pockets. Using his multi-purpose pocketknife, he extracts the cork and consumes the contents of the bottle. Having thus satisfied his thirst, he carefully replaces the bottle back into the pocket. He will later sell it for one penny. The mountain is relieved at his consideration. Pilgrims frequently dispose of empty bottles by throwing them unceremoniously off the summit to shatter on the rocks of the holy mountain, despoiling it with shards of black glass. Tricks is out of earshot, but he knows every word that Francie utters. The entire ceremony is embedded in his memory from last year and every year for the past ten years.

Francie undergoes a trance-like experience. With eyes shut, he describes the holy site as he sees it in its ancient pagan origin.

Then St. Patrick comes to the mountain and shatters the idol Crom Cruach. Francie speaks the words of the saint, followed by the cries of the defeated god. Crom Cruach disintegrates to a powdery dust and is dispersed by the wind. But 'that which is, cannot not be', so Crom Cruagh, the god of slaughter, is still close by. He is a god no longer. The One True God does not permit other gods, so Crom Cruagh is relegated down to the level of malevolent spirit. And there he bides his time, waiting for the opportunity to return with devastating vengeance to ravage the country.

The Normans come to Connacht. Shortly after the arrival of the Normans, Francie's branch of the clan leaves the west and moves to Northern O'Neill. Thereafter, the Wards of the north become itinerant bards, serving the Gaelic lords of the north.

Having thus experienced the 'memory', Francie is exhausted. He sits down to recover his strength. He flicks his hair back from his face and jams his soft cap on his head to keep his hair in place. Tricks goes to him and offers him a bottle of porter. Neither speaks. Francie accepts the bottle and consumes the black liquid thirstily. Thus revived, they return down the mountainside in the post-sunset waning light and, like their forebears of six hundred years before, they embark on their journey from the west to the north, from Connacht to Northern O'Neill.

Their first stop is Murrisk, two hours' walk down the mountain and thence on Reek Road.

Saturday 05 August. Murrisk has little to offer Collie and Tricks. They proceed to Westport, a two-hour walk from Murrisk. Westport is more promising. Francie and Tricks engage in street entertainment. They earn enough money to purchase food.

It will take three days to walk from Westport to Kimmid in Donegal. Francie and Tricks need to stock up on money and food for the journey. They set their sights on Castlebar, a three-and-a-half-hour walk from Westport. They reach Castlebar on Saturday evening.

Sunday 06 August 1950. It is the August bank-holiday weekend. Castlebar is hosting the annual horse jumping and dog trial events in the convent grounds. Bands and floats parade up Market Street to Ellison Street and around the Mall to the convent grounds. This is a profitable venue for street entertainers. Francie engages in singing. Tricks sets up a table, an upturned cardboard box, and proceeds with his card tricks in the Mall. He fascinates the crowds with his card tricks. And once he has an audience, he progresses to 'find-the-lady', a lucrative con game. The victim, the 'mark', is tricked into betting on the assumption that in the three cards on the table he can find the Queen of Hearts. The mark has no chance whatsoever of winning. For a while, this goes well for Tricks until a mark feels cheated and a row ensues. The guards arrive on the scene. Francie and Tricks and two belligerents are taken into custody. Francie and Collie's journey to Donegal is thus rudely interrupted.

CHAPTER EIGHT

KILLBAWN
COUNTY MAYO, IRELAND

Thursday Afternoon, 03 August 1950

Murf enters Killbawn Garda Station at 1:35pm. He is not in a good mood. He is wet, and he is disappointed at the lack of progress in the investigation.

Garda Seamus O'Reilly greets him. "Murf, guess what? I'm assigned as your assistant in the investigation."

"You are, are you, Seamus? Well, here's your first task. Deliver these fingerprint samples of Paddy Lamp Ward and Granny McGrath to the forensic team for comparison. I'm off to change into dry clothes and to grab a bite. When I return, I want to know the results."

"The results of the fingerprints, or t'other?"

"Everything the team has to offer. And the M.E.'s report. I'll be back in a jiffy."

1:53pm, Murf is back. "Seamus, what do you have for me? I sure need a lot of good news after the morning I had." Hardly hesitating, Murf hurries past the front desk.

Garda O'Reilly follows Murf up the stairs and into his office. Murf grabs a pencil off the desk and goes to his paper-bedecked wall where he makes marks and squiggles on the sheets of paper stuck thereon. Without interrupting his wall notating, he speaks to O'Reilly. "So what do you have for me, Seamus? I'm waiting."

Garda O'Reilly gathers from this that Murf multitasks. He wants to hear O'Reilly's report while drawing lines and repositioning the coloured threads on the wall. O'Reilly coughs to clear his throat.

"Spit it out, Seamus. No time for dawdling."

"Oh, yeah. Well, first, the medical examiner confirms the cause of death – blunt force trauma. There is no doubt that the candlestick you provided is the instrument of injury, delivered or propelled with force to the head."

"No doubt?"

"No doubt. The full written report will be delivered tomorrow."

"And did the team examine it for fingerprints?"

"A perfect set of prints."

"Matching any of the samples?"

"No, Murf. No match."

This appears to fuel more note-making on the wall. "Is anyone missing? You have the list, Seamus. Did we get sample prints from everyone?"

"Yes, Murf, from everyone on your list."

Murf stops arranging his wall-notes. He takes a blank sheet of paper from his desktop and pins it to the wall. He marks on the top of the page '10' and draws a big 'X' in blue pencil and makes a marginal note 'connects to?' He stands back to view the wall-notes as a whole. He appears to be calculating in his head. "Go on, Seamus."

"Is this good news or bad news, Murf?"

"It's good news for the people connected to St. Bawn's, but it's not good news for the investigation. Now we are looking for 'X', the unidentified perpetrator of the crime. And what about the key? Any results on that? And where are they – the key and the candlestick? I need them here in my office with all my notes and strings and all. They are an essential part of the picture."

"They are with the forensic team next door to us in the records room."

Murf thumps loudly on the wall. He thumps again. A grumpy man with a pot belly and glasses slipping off his nose comes into Murf's office.

He asks sarcastically, "You called, sir?"

"Divers, you ray of sunshine. I might have known that you would come. So tell me. What did you find on the Yale key?"

"Ah, the key. Well, Murf, it is smudged. There could be a number of overlapping prints on it. It's hard to tell."

"Any match to the sample prints?"

"There is a partial match to the prints on the candlestick, and a partial to the canon's prints. We're only about 50% sure. But Murf, the interesting thing is, it is a newly-cut key and it may not have been used. Or if used, only once or twice. The sharp edge from the cutting is still attached. It usually flakes off in the first few insertions into the lock."

"Hmm." Murf regards this as significant. He taps his pencil against his brow. "Tell me, Divers, you are unable to say with certainty if the assailant's prints are on the key. But can you rule him out either?"

"I am 50% sure of his prints on the key. He most certainly is NOT ruled out. And considering the proximity..."

"...proximity in location and time, it is a fair indication that the key was handled by the assailant."

"But 50% match is not acceptable as conclusive."

"True. But it is part of the whole and a lead worth following. The key could lead us to the lock. And when we locate the lock..."

"We're finished examining the candlestick and the key. You can have them back now." Divers says this with a mixture of courtesy and sarcasm. One never knows with Divers.

Murf goes to the records room/forensic room and retrieves the candlestick and the key. The key is in a small evidence bag, one with a pocket and flap so that the object may be examined while avoiding contaminating contact. Murf remembers that he has four more interviews to conduct. And he has yet to read through the English papers. He places the key in his pocket and grabs the bundle of newspapers. Tonight he will read through them.

"C'mon, Seamus. We have a lot of locks to inspect in Killbawn."

"Where are we off to, Murf?"

"Casey's"

At Casey's General Store, Murf and O'Reilly walk through the shop to the office in the back. They enter the office. Mrs. Casey and Sucy are hard at work totting figures and sticking work orders on sharp spikes.

"Mrs. Casey, is himself in?"

"Casey's in his inner sanctum. Go right in." She turns her head and shouts in the direction of a frosted glass door. "Casey. The guards are here to see you," and she goes back to adding figures in hope of squeezing a five out of two-plus-two.

Murf is amused that even Mrs. Casey calls her husband 'Casey'. And Casey, in turn, addresses her as 'Mrs. Casey'. Murf hurries into Casey's inner office. He hopes to surprise Casey and catch him in the act of an under-the-counter transaction. But Casey is studying the horse-racing page of the 'Irish Press'.

"Hello, Murf. You're making inquiries, so I hear tell. So you think that there has been foul play in the canon's death? Eh? So what brings you to me?"

"Just checking all angles, Casey – to get an accurate picture of what occurred."

"So why don't you arrest the tinkers. If there is anything afoul, it's to do with the tinkers."

Murf ignores his reference to 'tinkers'. There is no need to get sidetracked onto Casey's prejudices. "On Lammas day, in the evening, you were in St. Bawn's. Did you see or notice anything unusual, or anything out of place. Strangers perhaps? Anyone loitering?"

"Yes. Paddy Lamp Ward. That's who I saw. Other than that, everything was Killbawn normal."

Murf goes over the evening step by step from when the meeting in the parochial house terminated. Casey left immediately after that and is unable to add any more helpful information.

"One more thing, Casey." Murf shows him the key. "Do you know what this is?"

"Of course. It's a newly-cut Yale key."

"Could it have come from here?"

"Probably. We're the only hardware merchant in town to stock them. Come, let's check with Sammy Walsh, the hardware manager."

Casey leads Murf to the hardware department, followed by O'Reilly.

"Sammy, let's have a look at your daybook to see who last got a Yale key cut." Casey runs his finger down the book. Sammy is looking at the key.

"That key? It looks like the key I cut for Canon MacMorrow just over a week ago."

"Well, there's no record of it here."

"Of course not. I don't charge the canon."

"Sammy, how many times do I need to tell you? For the Church it's free, but you still need to record the transaction as 'complimentary'."

"I know that, Mr. Casey. But I don't know how to spell 'complimentary'."

"So write 'comp'."

"Mr. Casey, I can't do that. Then people will think I can't spell 'complimentary'."

"For Pete's sake, Sammy, you CAN'T spell 'complimentary'."

"I know that. But no one else needs to know. Then how do you spell it, Mr. Casey?"

"It's 'c-o-m-p-l-e-m-i-n-t-r-y'."

"Is it not 'i' before 'e'? So you would spell it –
'c-o-m-p-l-i-m-e-n-t-r-y'?"

"No. It's 'i' before 'e', except after 'c'. The word starts with a 'c'."

"I don't know, Mr. Casey. It doesn't look right."

Murf digs O'Reilly in the ribs to stop him laughing. He interrupts Casey to bring him back to the inquiry. "Casey, how many Yale locks are in Killbawn? Do you know?"

"I certainly do, Murf. Sure am I not trying to install these secure locks all over town? I can name every single house that has a Yale lock. Let me see now. There are 20 in all. I can count them on me fingers here."

Casey holds up a finger on his right hand and starts naming houses in sequence, street by street. When he reaches 'five', he holds up a finger in his left hand and starts again on his right hand. O'Reilly is busy recording all the names and addresses in his notepad. The list includes St. Bawn's, the Garda station, the dispensary, Doctor McBratt's house, Chief Superintendent Fox's house, the Church of Ireland rectory, and on and on.

Murf turns to Sammy. "Sammy, one question before I leave. Did Canon MacMorrow say why he needed an extra key cut?"

"Well, I wouldn't rightly know, would I? He wasn't even here."

"Didn't you say that you cut a key for Canon MacMorrow?"

"That's right. But the canon himself didn't come here."

"No? Then who did?"

"Mrs. Friel. She said it was for Gilban."

"For Gilban the sacristan?"

"No, the other Gilban, the Farouk Gilban. I remember the original key though; it had a label stuck to it with a big 'B' on it."

"Thanks, Sammy. And thanks, Casey. That's all for now."

Murf rushes off with O'Reilly in tow. "O'Reilly, let's check out this key at St. Bawn's."

Murf and O'Reilly go to the back door of the parochial house. There, they speak with Mrs. Friel. "Mrs. Friel, you keep a copy of the keys here?"

"There is a drawer in the hallstand with all the keys properly labelled."

"How many Yale locks are there here in St. Bawn's?"

"Three. Here, I'll show ye."

They follow Mrs. Friel to the hallstand. She opens the drawer. Inside is a tin box containing over twenty keys. "See. There are three Yale keys, labelled 'F', 'S' and 'B'."

"We need to check a key in the locks to see if it fits. Is that all right?"

"Go ahead. Sure you know your way around."

Murf tries the evidence key in the back door. If the key Sammy cut for Farouk was for the back door of St. Bawn's parochial house, and if the evidence key Murf is holding is that same key, then it should fit the lock. Murf inserts the evidence key, but it resists and refuses to turn. Then he tries it in the front door, and in the sacristy door. No luck. Three Yale locks, back door, front door and sacristy door; and the evidence key doesn't fit in any one of them.

"O'Reilly, it's important to find the lock that this key fits. You have the list of Yale locks in town. Here's the key. Go find which lock it fits. I have more interviews to conduct. I'll meet up with you at the station later."

Murf has three more interviews to conduct: Eamon Currie, Farouk Gilban and Doctor McBratt.

First, he goes to visit Eamon Currie. Eamon Currie has a bicycle shop that is never open. There is no reason for it to be open since Eamon lives there. If anyone needs the shop, he simply knocks at Currie's front door and a member of the Currie family will take him to the shop via the hallway. Murf sees Eamon's taxi car parked at the kerb. As usual, the hall door of the house is wide open. Murf shouts to announce his arrival.

Mrs. Currie shouts from the kitchen, "Come on in!"

Murf is familiar with the Currie home. Upon entering the kitchen, he sees Mrs. Currie busy kneading dough and Eamon sitting at the same table working on a wireless radio that he has taken apart. Bits of the radio and screws and washers are in danger of getting caught up in the bread dough.

"So what is it, Murf?" Eamon asks. "Do you need a ride to somewhere?" Canon MacMorrow was Eamon's biggest customer. Since the canon's death, Eamon has a lot of free time on his hands.

"Ah, no, Eamon. It's about the recent tragic event at St. Bawn's. I need to fill in all the details to complete the investigation."

"There's an investigation? So what can I tell you?" Eamon puts down the screwdriver and leans both elbows on the table.

Eamon gives his account and answers Murf's questions, but he is unable to add any more to what Murf already knows. Still, confirmation of other witnesses' accounts is valuable.

Next, Murf visits Thomas 'Farouk' Gilban. Farouk lives up a laneway at the edge of town behind a big house. At the rear of the house is a remise – a modified carriage house. It is a suitable dwelling for a small family or a single person. There are two cars parked there. Murf recognises both, Farouk's and Father MacNamara's. Murf walks up to the door. He observes that the keyhole in the door is to accommodate an old-fashioned coach-house key. It is not a modern secure lock, and certainly not a Yale lock. Farouk opens the door for him before he reaches it.

"Hello, Murf. I heard your car drive up. Come in."

Inside is one large spacious room, open up to the rafters, around which are upper-level lofts along the walls. Vertical ladders, rather than stairs, give access to these loft rooms. This area once housed horse-drawn carriages and related tack. Now it is the kitchen, living room and sitting room, all in one big room, defined only by the furniture settings. Father MacNamara rises from sitting at the kitchen table (or is it the dining table?) and proceeds to exit the house.

"Hello, Murf," he says in passing him by. "We were just going over the funeral service arrangements for Canon

MacMorrow." As he brushes past Murf, he whispers, "He doesn't know."

Murf interprets this to mean that Farouk Gilban knows about the canon's death, but not about the suspicious circumstances. Father MacNamara leaves and Farouk shuts the door.

Turning back to Murf he says, "Sit down, Murf. I'll make more tea."

Murf sits in the chair that Father MacNamara vacated, and pushes his empty cup aside. "No thanks, Thomas." He chooses to address him by his proper name rather than by his nickname. "No tea for me."

Murf notices that Farouk is uncharacteristically dressed in shirtsleeves and is not wearing a tie. He has never seen Farouk dressed in anything other than in his distinctive Mediterranean-style dapper suit and tinted glasses – a style of dress he adopted while serving in Egypt, the style favoured by King Farouk of Egypt and Sudan. Farouk Gilban has not shaved today either. Has he just recently arisen from bed? Murf continues. He informs him of the purpose of his visit. "I'm conducting an investigation into Canon MacMorrow's death."

"Really? But isn't it 'natural causes'?"

"Well, you know, Thomas, in cases of violent death, even accidental death, we must conduct a forensic autopsy to determine the cause and manner of death and render a coroner's report of the incident."

"Yes. I suppose you do. And what does the coroner's report tell you?"

"I'll have that tomorrow from the county medical examiner. In the meantime I need to fill in some details."

"Sure. Okay, Murf. Fire away." Farouk Gilban sits down in the chair facing Murf.

"Now, on Lammas Day, in the evening, you were at St. Bawn's."

"Of course. You and I both, and the whole committee."

"When did you leave the church?"

"Let's see. I was up in the bell tower to half-past ten or so – Father MacNamara and I. We left via the sacristy as usual."

"And did you see the canon at that time?"

"Well, he certainly was not lying on the sacristy floor. I'm sure of that."

"But could he have been in the church?"

"I don't think so. At least we did not see him."

"But he could have been sitting in a dark area of the church?"

"Yes, I suppose. But he would have addressed us, if he was there."

"Unless he was asleep."

"I don't know, Murf. I don't think he was there. For sure, I did not see him."

"So you left St. Bawn's sometime after 10:30pm? And you drove home?"

"No. I left St. Bawn's, but I did not drive home."

"No?"

"No, I went to Shannon."

"You went to Shannon in the middle of the night?"

"That's right. I went to visit my cousin, Malachy. He's in security at Shannon Airport. I went to discuss some business with him. Malachy works shifts. He was working the Russian shift that night."

"What's the 'Russian shift'?"

"That's when the Russians use the airport. It's different to when the Americans use it. We can't have both of them using it at the same time."

"Russians AND Americans use Shannon?"

"Yes. To refuel planes. Shannon services diplomatic and unarmed military planes crossing the Atlantic, both NATO and Warsaw Pact."

"I didn't know that."

"That's not surprising. None of the parties want it publicised."

"So after your business with your cousin, you returned to Killbawn?"

"Yes. I arrived back here in mid-afternoon. That's when I learned of the canon's accident. I went to the church, to the parochial house actually, to catch up on some bookkeeping, and Mrs. Friel told me all about it. I was tired then, anyway, so I came back home and went to bed."

"And when did you get out of bed?"

"Oh, about an hour ago. I still haven't shaved or dressed. Oh, I see you wondering why I slept so long. Well, it's something I picked up in Africa. It's not serious. But I suffer mild flu-like symptoms every so often. I sleep a lot when I am like this. It passes in a few days."

"One last thing. Did you lose a key?"

"I don't think so. Let me check. I have my keys and wallet next to my bed."

Farouk climbs up one of the ladders to a loft room and returns with his wallet and keys in his pockets. He dumps all onto the table. Murf sees three Yale keys amongst the assortment. Scratched on the Yale keys are the letters, 'B' on one, and 'S' on another, and 'F' on the third. "All keys accounted for. Why do you ask?"

"I found a key."

"May I see it?"

"No. Garda O'Reilly has it and is looking for the owner."

"Ah, lost-and-found duties."

"Okay. Thanks, Thomas. I'll be off now."

"Oh, Murf. You're listed as an usher for the canon's funeral Mass. Is that okay?"

"I didn't know that. When is it?"

"Saturday morning at ten o'clock."

Murf is about to object on the grounds of being too busy with the case, but immediately realises that this could be of benefit. He would get to look into everyone's face. That could be revealing. And he will determine who is absent from the Mass. That, too, could be revealing. All this information will add more 'dots' to the picture on his evidence wall. "Of course. I would be honoured."

Last on his list is Doctor McBratt. Driving to the dispensary, Murf assesses Farouk's statements. Farouk Gilban may have secrets – family secrets and leftovers from his previous job. The former due to anti-treaty republican sentiments, and the latter from serving in the British Foreign Office during the war. But what about now? Farouk answered Murf's questions without evasiveness, and he cooperated fully. He has nothing to hide. Or, he covers up skillfully. Murf probes his own mind for an answer to a niggling question "Why don't I trust Farouk Gilban?" No answer is forthcoming.

It is close to 4:30pm when Murf enters the dispensary. Three mothers with small children are sitting in a row of chairs in the waiting room.

The social worker at the reception desk greets him. "Inspector Murphy? Are you here to visit the doctor?"

"Yes. If you don't mind, inform Doctor McBratt that I would like a word with her."

"Very well. I'll check with her in surgery. Please have a seat."

Murf sits beside the three young mothers. He chooses the fourth chair, given that all three of the waiting patients looked at it and looked at Murf. Clearly, there is an order in the waiting room that should not be overturned. Murf is number four. He better not expect to jump the queue to number one.

The receptionist returns. "Inspector Murphy, the doctor says that, unless you are Jesus Christ, you will wait your turn; or if you ARE Jesus Christ, come in and do some healing."

Murf is both amused and annoyed. He had hoped to be back at the Garda station by 5:00pm to meet with O'Reilly. This will not likely happen now. He will meet with O'Reilly tomorrow at 8:00am.

The receptionist is talking to him. "Please feel free to read the information pamphlets while you wait."

There are pamphlets in racks all around the walls. He reads the titles 'Pregnancy', 'Free Spectacle Glasses for Children', 'Whooping Cough'. These are the same government-issued information pamphlets they have at the Garda station, but more prominently displayed here in the dispensary. At the Garda station these health pamphlets take second place to the 'Wanted' notices, and warnings about the fines pertaining to offences such as illicit liquor distilling. Murf decides that his waiting period in the dispensary should not be wasted. He runs out to his car and fetches the English newspapers that require his perusal. Back in chair number four, Murf busies himself leafing through the newspapers. The three mothers look at him with disapproval. English newspapers are known to have pictures of women indecently clad. English newspapers and children do not belong in the same place together. The receptionist coughs to get his attention. She signals to him the inappropriateness of English smut newspapers in this environment. Murf understands and relocates to chair number eighteen. This appears to be acceptable.

Murf leafs through the 'Sunday Express', the 'Empire News' and the 'Weekend Mirror'. He ponders, "What could have interested the canon in English 'smut' newspapers?" This is probably a waste of time. Two of the mothers have already been and gone, and the final mother and child are in with the doctor. He decides to continue leafing through the pages, at least until the doctor is free to see him.

'Cross'. Murf stops leafing through the newspaper. He momentarily saw the word 'Cross'. He turns back the page to find the word that flashed by. The canon must have seen a news article pertaining to a church or to a religious event, or maybe 'crossword'. He continues to leaf back slowly, scanning the pages carefully.

"What on earth are you doing, Murf?"

He hadn't noticed Doctor McBratt come from the surgery and approach him. "Right now I'm looking for the word 'Cross'."

"You're looking in the 'Mirror' for 'cross'?"

Murf suddenly stands up and spills all the newspapers from his lap onto the floor, except for the one he is clutching.

Doctor McBratt is concerned that Murf is working too hard. Here he is now, requesting a visit and spilling newspapers all over the floor.

Murf, still clutching the newspaper, points at Doctor McBratt with his free hand. "You said 'looking in the mirror for cross'." Murf repeats it, "You said 'looking in the mirror for cross'."

"Come into the surgery, Murf. Let me take a look at you."

"You said exactly what the canon said before he died. Don't you remember? You were there."

"When I attended to the canon, he groaned a few times in pain. But he did not speak. Are you sure, Murf?"

"Father MacNamara related it to me. I'm certain."

"Related what?"

"What he heard the canon say – 'Cross. In the mirror. Defecting British s...' unintelligible word, 'A key. A coin.' Not sure of the last word.' That's how Father MacNamara remembered it."

"Oh, he must be referring to the news item, not really news, more likely some kind of gossip or gutter-press speculation about a British scientist that disappeared. Here, give me the paper. I'll find it for you."

Doctor McBratt snatches the newspaper from Murf and finds the appropriate page. "Here, read this." She folds the paper so that the chosen page is on top and thrusts it back at Murf.

Murf sees at a glance the words of significant relevance:

'The Mirror followed up on a crime scene, with no crime in evidence, in Cheshire on Saturday morning. Interviewing staff and patrons of the Crowing Cock...disappearance of John Cross who works at Risley. Could we be looking at a defecting British scientist in the aftermath of Klaus Fuchs's arrest and sentencing for spying? The Fuchs case revealed that Soviet espionage agents are active in Britain.'

Doctor McBratt is not finished. She is flipping through another newspaper. "You have the Mirror of Sunday the 16th of July? Right? Here is the Mirror of the following week, Sunday the 23rd of July, with a follow-up story."

She hands him this paper too, open at the appropriate page. Murf sees that in the middle of the column is a picture of John Cross. The newspaper reports –

'Police in Cheshire issued a statement on Monday morning concerning the disappearance of John Cross, one of Britain's leading scientists. Police are treating Cross's disappearance as a 'missing person' case. They declined to comment.... Cross works at Royal Ordnance in Risley. We have learned that Cross and Klaus Fuchs, a convicted spy, were colleagues for a number of years. Questions are being raised about whether Fuchs has contaminated other British scientists with his Soviet sympathies....'

"Ant, do you know what this means?"

"That the Brits lost a spy-scientist to the Russians? So what!"

Murf is tempted to explain that it may have a connection to his current investigation, but decides against it. He needs to keep the ongoing investigation confidential. During this discourse, Doctor McBratt has steered Murf to the medical bed where he is now seated.

She pulls down Murf's lower left eyelid. Then she says "Stick out your tongue and say 'ah'."

"Forget the tongue, Ant. I'm here to ask about the night of the canon's death."

"Relax. Let your legs hang down." She hits him on the knees with a little mallet to check his reflexes, and continues speaking, "Granny McGrath was acting strangely that night. The canon was himself though, a bit excited about his new clock but health-wise as good as could be expected."

"And next morning?"

"Ah, the canon's death. I don't believe his injury was accidental, Murf. I declined to issue the death certificate until I could confirm the cause of death. So, Murf, when am I going to get the coroner's report?"

"The report has been dispatched. We'll have it tomorrow. And Ant, your suspicion is correct. Death was the result of blunt force trauma to the head. The candlestick is identified conclusively as the instrument of execution, executed either by propulsion or clubbing with force."

"And..."

"That's all I can tell you at this point. And THIS is confidential."

Doctor McBratt opens the surgery door and speaks to the receptionist. "Agnes, go on home. I'll lock up here. And don't worry about the mess of papers on the floor."

She returns to the surgery. "Murf, that's all you can tell me? I don't think so. You and I need a confidential talk."

"About?"

"Well, the canon's death; Farouk Gilban; Granny McGrath; Paddy Lamp. How about that for a start?"

Doctor McBratt locks the front door of the dispensary and returns to the surgery. She sits at her desk and scribbles a note, which she passes to Murf.

"What's this for?" enquires Murf.

"Iron. You're anemic."

Then she slides open one of the desk drawers and removes a bottle of Hennessy XO and a pack of Craven 'A' cork-tipped cigarettes. Doctor McBratt has a lot to share with Murf, and Murf has things to share with Ant. They compare notes on Granny McGrath. They agree that follow-up visits are required to check on her state of mind.

Doctor McBratt recalls, "She is suffering loss from the death of her husband, Brendan. I can still see her in my mind's eye as I recollect when I last went to visit Brendan. He was already dead when I arrived. Brendan's sickroom was a wee room off the kitchen, the only other room in the cottage. There she was, standing motionless at his doorway staring at him. And him staring upwards with eyes wide open, clearly dead. His face was severely shrunken from his long-suffering sickness, except for his nose. His nose projected pointedly out from his withered face. God, what a shock for her to see him like that." She pulls on her cigarette and blows out smoke without inhaling. She sips her brandy and says, "But enough. Let's consider Farouk Gilban."

They agree that Farouk Gilban has a hidden past. Farouk comes across as acting a role rather than as authentically sincere. Neither is able to read him.

They do not agree on Paddy Lamp Ward, however. Murf feels that he is hiding something and has flitted for fear of arrest. Doctor McBratt is critical of the police attention given to the travelling Wards. The Gardaí, and particularly Murf, have frightened him off. Paddy Ward flitted in the rain with a sick child that needs medical care. Doctor McBratt is of the opinion that the Wards are due to be in Kimmid in two weeks hence. But could they have headed there early? Murf doesn't ask, but he is intrigued that Doctor McBratt knows the travellers' schedule. And where the hell is 'Kimmid'? All along, he believed that travellers move around by random chance, dictated mostly by the tolerance or intolerance of the towns they pass through.

Canon MacMorrow is discussed. Murf enquires of Doctor McBratt if, in her professional work, she has ever encountered an unstable person capable of motiveless murder? Doctor McBratt is unable to think of anyone. So far, the identity of the assailant remains a mystery, and there is no likely suspect.

It is 7:20pm when Murf leaves the dispensary. He is pleased that Doctor McBratt and he are in agreement in their opinion of Farouk, and that both sensed from the outset that the canon's death was suspicious, and that the emotional and mental state of Granny McGrath should be addressed. They are in agreement, but not necessarily for the same reasons. Paddy Lamp Ward is a different matter. How is Doctor McBratt so familiar with the travelling Wards?

7:30pm. Murf decides to call into the Garda station and pick up his messages. The night-duty officer informs him that Garda O'Reilly was unsuccessful in locating any lock in Killbawn to fit with the key – and he tried them all. The key is back in his office. The forensic team will be in tomorrow morning to wrap up their work and report their findings. They would like Murf to be present. There was a phone call from England, a 'Mr. Piperson', no message left.

He feels like sitting down, but he knows that if he does so, he will be loath to rise again. He decides to go home.

Driving home, he passes by St. Bawn's church. He stops the car, makes a U-turn back to the church. He parks at the kerb and goes up the steps and into the building. It is quiet inside. He needs some quiet time, and he needs to immerse himself in the interior environment of the church – in the setting of the crime. He imagines himself as the assailant. What would he do here in the church? Why would he even be here in the church? What purpose? Motive? Not theft. Profit? Revenge? "No, Murf. Stop thinking for a while, clear your mind and just sense and see." He sits and permits his mind to wander. Granny McGrath has not yet arrived for her nightly ritual, and neither has Doctor McBratt. Murf is alone in the dim nave of the church.

Murf understands how the canon could have fallen asleep sitting alone in a quiet church. Murf stares sleepily at nothing in particular and permits his eyes to drift out of focus. He is aware of the sacristy lamp's red light, now spiking like a star as he observes it through unfocused half-shut eyes. In his peripheral vision he sees to his left, low down at floor level, a small red glittering reflection of the lamp. Curiously, he turns his head to see what is causing the light to reflect. When he does so, and bringing his eyes back into focus, the reflection disappears. He dismisses it as a trick of the light hitting the lashes of his half-closed eyes. He resumes his relaxed position and sees the reflection again. This time his eyes are wide open and alert. But like the last time, when he turns his head, the reflection disappears once more. He resumes his previous position, and for a third time he sees the small red reflection in his peripheral vision. Murf is annoyed as it disappears a third time.

For Murf this has become a challenge. The next time he sees the reflection, he attempts to pinpoint its location in his peripheral vision. Satisfied that he has located it, he points to it, moving his finger to where it appears and disappears. Then he turns his head and looks to where his finger is pointing. His finger is pointing to a pew, to a place on the ground where the pew is pushed up against a pillar.

Murf examines the spot. It is a narrow space between the leg of the pew and the pillar. In the narrow space he sees a coin standing upright where it must have rolled and then jammed in an upright position. He takes a pencil from his inner breast pocket and pries the coin loose. It rolls back and spins a few times and comes to rest. It is a Saorstát Éireann leath coróin, dated 1929. Murf, careful not to touch it, flips it over with the pencil and sees the familiar Irish Hunter stallion on the obverse side. It is an Irish silver half-crown. Saorstát Éireann coins were issued in December 1928 shortly after the establishment of the Irish Free State. They were withdrawn from circulation in 1938 and 'Saorstát Éireann' was replaced with 'Éire' in subsequent issues. Saorstát Éireann coins are seldom encountered today in 1950. This coin warrants closer examination. Murf picks it up using his handkerchief and places it in his pocket. The canon said 'key' and 'coin'. They found the key. Could this be the coin? If so, all the canon's dying words have been identified. But will this help solve the case?

Murf feels that the investigation is at last progressing. Now it is time to go home. Murf has a list of things to do on the morrow:

-Check the coin for fingerprints;

-Contact 'Patrick Piperson' and try to get some background on Farouk Gilban;

-And the Cross defection, if it is a defection – is there a connection?

CHAPTER NINE

KILLBAWN
COUNTY MAYO, IRELAND

Friday Morning, 04 August 1950

Murf is busy at work in his office from 6:00am. He is scribbling notes and 'connecting dots' and stringing threads from the sheets of paper attached to his wall.

At 8:00am he hears Garda O'Reilly arrive. "O'Reilly!" he shouts, loud enough to be heard all the way down the stairs to the front desk.

Garda O'Reilly enters Murf's office, panting and sweating. Garda O'Reilly is on the county team and likes to keep fit. He walks briskly to work every morning. "Yes, Murf. What is it?"

"O'Reilly, did you check all the Yale locks in Killbawn yesterday?"

"Of course, everyone on the list."

"And how many did you check in Casey's store?"

"One. The shop door."

"And did you notice the office door?"

"Ah..."

"O'Reilly, check ALL Yale locks in Killbawn. That includes exterior doors and interior doors. Here's the key. Go back and check the ones you missed." O'Reilly rushes off to carry out the orders.

Divers, the forensic expert, enters Murf's office. "Hmm. I thought I heard someone here. Ah, there y'are, Murf." He sits down in Murf's own chair, the only chair not laden with papers and strings and all sorts of aids in Murf's investigation. Divers' glasses slip down his nose, and he slaps a file down on Murf's desk.

Murf leans back against his wall of papers and threads and looks at Divers. "So what's the report?"

"There was very little of any use in the church. Gilban did an excellent cleaning job before we got to the sacristy. And in the nave, well, there was a lot of activity for a whole day before we even arrived. Even so, you have an excellent set of prints on the candlestick, and a moderately good set on the key. But not much else from me, alas. Here is the report."

"Don't get up yet, Divers. On the desk, there, is a handkerchief. Inside it is a half-crown. Take a look at it and see what prints you can lift from it."

"A half-crown? Where did it come from?"

"I found it last night, wedged in between a pew and a pillar, standing upright."

"And which was standing upright? You or the pew or the pillar?"

Murf knows that Divers is just taking the mickey with him, so he declines to rise to the bait. Divers takes the handkerchief and his file, repositions his glasses on his nose, and goes back to his temporary forensic room.

"Give me a minute or two," he says as he manoeuvres his portly body through the doorway.

"Piper's Son," Murf says aloud to himself. "He telephoned yesterday. I wonder...O'Reilly!" he shouts down the hallway.

Garda Caldwell comes to his office. "Inspector Murphy, you sent Garda O'Reilly out. I'm manning the front desk this morning."

"Very well. Put a call through to RUC HQ on Waring Street, Belfast."

"To whom, or to which department?"

"Just get me the internal telephone operator, and I'll take it from there."

Sergeant Kevin Hughes pops into Murf's office. "The post was delivered. This should interest you; it's the coroner's report on the canon. You may want to put it with the file."

Murf takes the report from Hughes. "I hope Finbar typed it in duplicate."

"It's in triplicate, Murf."

"Good. I need a copy for Doctor McBratt."

"Oh, okay. And how is your investigation going?"

"I'm still collecting data."

"Okay. I'll let you get back to it."

Sergeant Hughes leaves and Divers comes back in. "Murf, you have an excellent print of the canon's on the horse (obverse), and you have an excellent print of the assailant's on the harp (reverse). There are older smudged prints there too, but these two are prominent. 85% to 90% match. You know that these coins were withdrawn from circulation over ten years ago. The only person with these coins today would be someone who hasn't cleared out his mattress bank account in a long time. I included a footnote in the report. Here y'are, Murf."

This time Divers remains standing. He places the report file and the coin on Murf's desk and shuffles out through the doorway. From the hallway he shouts back, "You know how to get hold of me, Murf, if you are unable to read my writing."

Murf appreciates the additional piece of evidence; but, before he can reply, his telephone rings. He picks it up. Caldwell has connected him to RUC HQ. "Hello. RUC HQ? This is Inspector Murphy of An Garda Síochána. Put me through to Sir Robert. Just say these two words 'Murf' and 'Code White'."

"That's three words, sir. Please hold."

Almost instantly, Sir Robert Norton, Inspector-General of the RUC, speaks on the phone. "Murf?"

"Hello, Nobbie. Like you, I'm busy right now. I'm returning a call to 'Piper's Son'. He tried to get hold of me yesterday. I'm in all day today. Can you send him word?"

"Sure thing. So you have something of interest?"

"Nobbie, you can't tell with Patrick what is of interest and what isn't. He seems to think that I...oh, I don't know what he thinks. But yes, I have something." Murf still refers to 'Piper's Son' as 'Patrick' although he knows that this is not his name. It sounds better than referring to him by his code-name.

"Okay, Murf. Sit tight. You'll hear from him."

'Click'. He disconnects.

Murf looks at the dead phone. "Things move a bit faster in Belfast." He hangs up the receiver. The conversation was so short, Murf remained standing. Murf stretches over his desk, opens the top drawer and takes out a retractable penknife. He selects a blade and busies himself in sharpening his pencils. When done, he sits on his desk pondering the relationship of all the data stuck up on his festooned wall. He checks his squiggles and threads by cross-referring to the two reports he just received. Satisfied that his wall-notes are accurate, he twirls a pencil through his fingers while in thought.

The telephone rings. "Inspector Murphy. I have a Piperson on the line for you."

"That was fast. Right. Put him through, Caldwell.

"Hello, Patrick."

"Hello, Murf. I don't have time for small talk. I'll come right to the point. Thomas Gilban."

"Yes. Thomas Gilban what?"

"Murf, I'm assimilating information and cross-checking for relevance, or as you would put it, 'connecting dots to form a picture'. A case I am following up on has developed an Irish connection."

"And the connection leads to Gilban?"

"I don't know yet. So tell me. The name 'Gilban' – how would you render that in English?"

"It's from the Irish 'Mac Giolla Bháin'"

"The 'mac' I get, and the 'gillie' – 'son of the servant'. What about the rest?"

"'Bán' is 'white'. In this case the name means 'son of the devotee of the white-haired saint'."

"'White'."

"Yes. You could render his name in English as 'White'. Hey, Patrick, has this something to do with 'Code White'?"

"For years, we have been trying to identify someone with the code-name 'Белый, Bélyy'."

"Belly?"

"It is 'Белый'. That is 'White' in Russian. It could refer to the colour white, or to a fair-skinned person, or to a Caucasian...."

"...or to 'Gilban'."

"So, Murf. Is there any 'Bélyy' connection to Gilban?"

"Perhaps. Gilban has been to Shannon, at least once, during the 'Russian Shift'."

"The 'Russian Shift'?"

"That's when Russian planes stop over in Shannon. They are serviced and refuelled. Some are passenger planes, but most are diplomatic planes and unarmed military aircraft."

"Murf, you have given me a lot more dots than I expected."

"Hold on there, Patrick. You may be able to help me in my case which has a Gilban connection too. You worked with Gilban once?"

"Not directly. But I certainly know him."

"The local canon was killed here early on the morning of August the 2nd. He was violently struck either late on Tuesday night, or early Wednesday morning. He died from his injuries at 8:30am. Thomas Gilban is one of two people who left the building around the time of the assault. Patrick, from your knowledge of Gilban, do you think it possible for him to be involved in a murder?"

"What I know of Gilban and the work he did in the Service, he is not a murderer. On the other hand, he would not hesitate to kill if it were deemed necessary in the line of duty. But that was the Gilban before Cairo."

"Before Cairo?"

"Yes. After Cairo 1948 he suffered a nervous breakdown and was relegated to a desk job. A year later he retired from service in the Foreign Office."

"And the significance of Cairo?"

"Very briefly this is the significance of Cairo. After Cairo, Bélyy went silent. We understood this to mean that Bélyy changed his code-name. Then on July 12 this year, we intercepted a coded transmission either to or from Bélyy. We believe that after sleeping for two years, Bélyy has become active again. Exactly three weeks later, two days ago on the 2nd of August, you contacted me inquiring about Gilban. Like you, Murf, I am assimilating information with possible connections to one of our operations."

"And what of Gilban now? Has he recovered from his breakdown?"

"I cannot vouch for his present state of mind. Sorry, Murf, I cannot give you a straight 'yes' or 'no' answer to your question."

"Oh, I see...." Murf ponders the significance of this piece of information.

Piper's Son regards Murf's silence as the end of the conversation and says "If that's all, Murf, I must get on with things. Cheerio!" and hangs up.

"Blast, I wanted to ask him about Cross. Now I'll need to phone back via RUC HQ to send a message for him to contact me. Blast the Brits and their secure telephone lines and undercover phoney names. It's impossible to telephone anyone there." Murf places another call to RUC.

This time the response is "Sir Robert is not in his office at the minute. I'll leave a message to have him contact you. Please give me your number for the return call...."

"Blast again. Now I must wait for Nobbie, and then wait for Piper's Son." Murf looks from his desk to the wall. The candlestick and coin are on his desk. The key is missing, at least until O'Reilly returns with it. Murf addresses his desk. "The candlestick undoubtedly identifies the murderer 'X' by his fingerprints; the coin should lead me to him; the key should lead me to him. X's fingerprints are certainly not Thomas Gilban's, so he cannot be the murderer. But is the mysterious Farouk Gilban a link in some way? I need to speak with Farouk again."

11:35am, Thomas Farouk Gilban's house. "Come in, Murf. Is it about the funeral tomorrow?"

"No, Thomas. It's about my inquiry."

"I just made tea. Would you like to join me?" Farouk Gilban is dressed properly this time. He is even wearing his tinted glasses and light-coloured tropical suit.

Murf sits down at the dining/kitchen table. "Sure, Thomas, I'll join you in a cuppa. You know, I got confirmation from the coroner's report that the canon was killed by a blow to the head, not from falling down."

"That's the story that's going around. Now who in Killbawn would kill the canon? It makes no sense." Farouk goes to the kitchen cupboard to fetch an extra cup for Murf. "And what is it you want to know this time? I'm not a suspect, surely."

"Tell me about Cairo."

Farouk fumbles the cup which falls from the cupboard and smashes on the kitchen floor. Farouk's hand is frozen in the spot where the cup had been. He slowly lowers his arm and turns around to face Murf. "Cairo? That's a long story. Why do you want to know about Cairo? It has nothing to do with the canon's tragic death. Is it part of your inquiry? Or another unrelated inquiry?"

"No. I'm establishing a link to everyone who was with the canon on the night before he died. Not suspects, but..."

"...but peripheral. I understand. To put the events into perspective."

"That's right, Thomas. I was compiling a profile...."

"Checking up on me."

"Yes. I reached out to the British Foreign Office. Not officially, of course, but in the interests of joint cooperation in a related case. They mentioned 'Cairo' more than once. I would rather hear your version."

Farouk does not question what 'cooperation' or what 'related case' it may be. Murf notes the absence of the query. Gilban knows something that he wants to keep hidden, he reasons. Farouk Gilban walks slowly to the table and sits down in a chair. He has forgotten all about the tea or the need for a second teacup. He removes his glasses and rubs his eyes.

"I was twenty when I joined the RIC. Then in 1919 the troubles started. Our whole family was, and still is, fiercely republican. The choice I faced was to work for the IRA from inside the RIC, or turn my back on the IRA. There was no neutral ground. Either way, my career as a police officer was over if I stayed in Ireland. So I arranged a transfer to the colonial police. I served mostly in Africa and in the Middle East. I very quickly learned languages: Arabic and French in Egypt, and Russian and German in Jerusalem. Once I started, I expanded my language skills. When war broke out, I was reassigned to interpreter duties. Actually, my real job was to police delegates at international meetings and work with German agents. 'Interpreter' was my cover to give me access to some very sensitive meetings.

"My duties took a turn when I was responsible for cleaning up after meetings to ensure that paper notes and paper trash did not fall into Russian or American hands. We and the Russians and the Americans all rushed to these cleaning duties for the same reason. Except that sometimes I was instructed to 'leave' a piece of paper trash for the Russians to find. Never for the Americans, though. I see you raise your eyebrows, Murf. Why would we do this? Germany was going to win the war, or so it looked at the time. America was not yet an active participant, only a passive participant. Our only hope for success lay in the Eastern Front. It wasn't D-Day or any of that that won the War. It was the Russians. However, Russia could not win in the Eastern Front without substantial aid from the West. This was Churchill's solemn promise. We and the Americans supplied weaponry and support vehicles and technology to the Russians, but we held back a lot too. Information was leaked to the Russians to bypass the slow red-taped official channels. I never knew what was passed on to them, only that it came from high up and I was to comply.

"After the war, information continued to be passed to the Russians to a greater extent than before. And Cairo was the preferred gateway."

"AFTER the war?"

"Yes, you heard correctly. In 1948 there was a party in an American embassy staffer's apartment. There was a drunken episode that resulted in the wrecking of the apartment. The entire team, me included, was immediately called back to London. So you see, Murf, there was disgrace at being recalled from duties because of a drunken brawl. But that wasn't it, at all." Farouk stops and attempts to drink from his cup. Finding it empty, he goes to the kitchen tap and fills it. "Murf, this will knock you down." Farouk resumes his seat and continues. "Later I learned that American intelligence had uncovered the existence of a mole in the British Embassy in Cairo. They had set up a sting operation to entrap him. This trap was set and ready to be sprung, and they expected to expose the mole in less than a week. But then the fracas in the apartment occurred and, with the team recalled to London, the entrapment could not be executed. The mole was never exposed. You think that was bad, Murf? It gets worse. This was a top-secret American operation. Yet someone in American intelligence tipped off the mole so that he could stage a drunken brawl so severe that the entire team was pulled out of Cairo. This operation did not come to light until some months later. The Americans were livid at the Brits. And the Brits pointed back at them that the failure of the entrapment was due to their own mole's tip-off."

"There was a high-ranking mole in the British embassy, and a high-ranking mole in U.S. intelligence? Wow!" Murf leans back in his chair. "And you accommodated theses intelligence leaks?"

"I was played, Murf. All those years. I still don't know if I was serving the Foreign Office or if I was working for a mole. Or both at the same time."

"And were any of them caught?"

"No. And that's when I left 'interpreter duties'."

"And have you?"

"Have I what?"

"Have you left 'interpreter duties' completely?"

"I still keep in touch with my international friends."

"Your 'friends'? And what about your relationship with the Foreign Office? Are you still in touch with your contacts there?"

"Murf, you know I cannot answer that."

"Which means?"

"The past lives in the present, until death do us part."

Murf considers this new revelation. Does it have a bearing on the canon's death? As for the British Foreign Office and their secrets and moles, Murf cares not one whit. But if the Foreign Office still has their hooks into Gilban, what could they make him do 'in the line of duty'? Murf adds Farouk to his 'to be watched' list. "Okay, Thomas. I'll see you at the funeral Mass tomorrow." Murf sees himself to the door. He glances back at Thomas Farouk Gilban who is holding his cup to his lips and is staring blankly ahead.

Murf returns to his office. O'Reilly is in the station and goes to Murf to report. "I have tried every Yale lock in Killbawn, front doors, back doors, interior doors. This key does not fit any lock in Killbawn."

"Okay, O'Reilly. Leave it on the desk. Thank you." Murf looks from the desk to the wall. The key and the coin must surely reveal some significant clue. He looks at his watch. It is 2:50pm. "I have time to run to the bank across the street before it closes at 3:00pm." Murf grabs the coin and goes across to the bank.

Jim Woods, the head teller is counting his cash in anticipation of the close of business. "Hello, Jim. Ever see much of these anymore?" Murf shows him the Saorstát Éireann leath coróin dated 1929.

"Yes. So what?"

"A lot?"

"One or two each week. Sometimes four."

"You seem very sure."

Jim stops counting his stack of £1 notes and lifts a paper coin bag marked 'silver' and dumps out the contents in front of Murf. "Take a look. Saorstát Éireann leath coróin coins that I am obliged to withdraw from circulation and remit to the Central Bank. What a pain. When the bag reaches £5, I send it off by registered post. Yes, I am sure of the number of these coins that come in."

"So, where do they come from?"

"St. Bawn's. All these coins came from St. Bawn's. Every week, for months and months, Saorstát Éireann leath coróin coins arrive from St. Bawn's every Monday morning."

"Thanks, Jim. That's interesting."

Back at the Garda station, Murf peruses the 'Wanted Posters' on the wall. He searches for a poster on John Cross. He sees it. A seemingly unimportant 'Missing Person' poster dated 20 July lists John Cross as missing from Cheshire, England. It suggests that he may be in Ireland and requests that any confirmed sighting should be reported immediately to the Special Detective Unit (SDU). No reason or explanation is given. His picture, which could be a passport picture, is displayed at the top of the poster, a similar picture to the one in the 'Mirror'. Normally, English missing persons are treated with disinterest in North Mayo. In Killbawn Garda Station, the John Cross poster is hidden behind a notice on the need for sheep-dipping to protect sheep from infestation against external parasites such as itch mite (Psoroptes ovis), blowfly, ticks and lice.

Murf did not notice it before, but now he sees that the information on John Cross should be reported to the SDU. This is unusual. The SDU is an elite arm of the Gardaí, and is known to liaise with its British intelligence counterparts. It appears that the speculative news in the 'Mirror' is correct. The Brits have lost a spy who is defecting, and he might be in Ireland. Publicly, the Brits are treating it as a missing-person case rather than a defection.

Back in his office, Murf considers the significance of this new piece of information. He telephones the SDU. When he identifies his location as North Mayo, he is asked if he can actually confirm a sighting of John Cross. "No. Not yet," he answers.

"Well, phone back when you have confirmation. We have unconfirmed and unfounded sightings from all four corners of the country."

"Well, how about that?" he says to the disconnected phone, and hangs up. Murf places the Saorstát Éireann coin back on his desk and gives it his attention. He considers that it must be a parishioner, a regular churchgoer, who is putting these half-crowns into the Sunday collection.

Murf is an usher at the Mass, and he sees who puts money into the collection box. Casey always puts in a half-crown, making sure that everyone sees him. Murf cannot recall any other person putting in a coin of this value. Most people put in a penny. Murf puts a pencil notation on the Casey information sheet on the wall, and resolves to pay special attention to the next church collection, including volunteering to help with the counting. But the murderer cannot be Casey. Casey always holds his donation coin firmly between thumb and two fingers, waving it high before dropping it in the collection box as it slides past him. His fingerprints would be firmly imprinted on the coin. No, it's someone else. So who in St. Bawn's is putting old half-crowns into the collection box? The killer? And it could not be John Cross from way over in Cheshire.

Murf looks from the coin to the key. "The answer lies in those two objects. If only they could talk. But what about Cross? What possible link could there be between two local objects and a defector in England? Piper's Son said that his case has developed an Irish connection. Is there a link?" Murf considers the key to be a 'local object' although he has not yet located its respective lock.

Murf has been working since 6:00am. It is close to 5:00pm. He calls it a day. One more call on his way home, to deliver a copy of the coroner's report to Doctor McBratt. At the doctor's house, Murf refrains from knocking on the door. He pushes the report through the letterbox quietly and departs from the house unobserved.

Driving from Doctor McBratt's house, Murf passes by St. Bawn's. He notices activity there and remembers that tonight is the vigil wake for Canon MacMorrow. Murf parks his car and walks back to the church. The canon's coffin is resting before the main altar. The Legion of Mary is reciting the rosary; designated leaders are selected to lead their respective decades. The townspeople lead the prayers in English, the country people and the republicans choose Irish. And so the five decades alternate, Irish, English, and so on.

Murf looks around and notices Maura Rua O'Hara. Maura Rua is still called 'Rua' even though her hair is no longer red. She was a hot spark in the republican movement during the 'Troubles', and is still looked upon as the matriarch of the local anti-treaty adherents. He waits to intercept her leaving the church.

"Dia dhuit, a Mháire." Murf addresses her in Irish to get her attention.

"Dia 's Muire dhuit, a Sheán," she replies.

Murf switches to English. Maura Rua is so proficient in Irish that she always manages to confuse him with conundrums and figures of speech. "Maura, a word, if you don't mind."

"Mas maith leat. Cad é d'fhiosrúchán?"

Murf sees that this is going to be a bilingual discourse. He speaks in English, and Maura Rua responds in Irish. Nevertheless, Murf presses on and enquires about Russian-IRA relationships and how it may have involved the Gilban family. Maura's answers are all in the form of questions. 'Is that a fact?' or 'Is that what you heard?' Maura Rua does not enlighten him. She walks away. Then she turns back and enquires about Granny McGrath. She concludes with "Féach ar na pictiúir ar an mballa." 'Look at the pictures on the wall'. This time she strides off without turning back.

Murf understands that having enquired about the Gilban family's links to the IRA and Russia, Maura instructs him to look at the pictures on Granny McGrath's wall. She managed to land another conundrum on Murf.

Murf drives home at last. He puts Granny McGrath on his 'to do' list for multiple reasons, and calls it a day. Murf calls to mind the wording of the British Official Secrets Act.

If any person knowingly harbours any person whom he knows, or has reasonable grounds for supposing, to be a person who is about to commit or who has committed an offence under this Act, or knowingly permits to meet or assemble in any premises in his occupation or under his control any such persons, or if any person having harboured any such person, or permitted to meet or assemble in any premises in his occupation or under his control any such persons, wilfully omits or refuses to disclose to a superintendent of police any information which it is in his power to give in relation to any such person he shall be guilty of a misdemeanour....

It also **applies to British subjects anywhere else in the world.**

CHAPTER TEN

KILLBAWN
COUNTY MAYO, IRELAND

Saturday Morning, 05 August 1950

Murf forewarns Father MacNamara that he will be paying close attention to the attendees at the funeral this morning. He requests that as part of his ushering duties he be assigned as scrutineer of the collection. Father Mac does not enquire as to the reason. He understands that Murf is conducting an investigation. Doing it within his ushering duties is less intrusive than questioning people after Mass.

The Requiem Mass is attended by most of the parish. Five priests and the diocesan Vicar General are present to assist at the Mass. After the Requiem Mass, Jack Gilban brings a small folding table to the transept of the church. The coffin is in the centre of the transept, in front of the main altar, and the writing table is placed upright before it. Thomas Gilban follows behind Jack carrying a chair, a ledger and a ruler. Thomas sits behind the table facing the people. He takes a gold fountain pen from his pocket slowly and deliberately as if in a religious ceremonial rite and holds it poised in a writing position. Murf assumes a standing position to Thomas's right.

Father MacNamara walks from the sanctuary and stands behind Thomas and announces, "There will now be a silver collection for Canon MacMorrow's funeral." There is a murmur from the congregation. A 'silver collection' is rare. People who had dug into their pockets and purses to find a penny now search for a silver thruppence, or failing that, they'll need to tender a sixpence. There is a reluctance to be first up to set the collection in motion. The first person up, in estimating the appropriate donation amount, sets the bar. This is a difficult decision to make. If the bar is set low, Father MacNamara will be displeased. On the other hand, if the bar is set high, parishioners will be expected to match their donations accordingly. A miscalculation by the first contributor could provoke the displeasure of either party.

J. J. McPhee, the publican, is sitting in the first pew. Father Mac signals to him to come forward. J. J. calculates – thruppence is the minimum donation, so that is for the poor people; sixpence would then be for regular people; but a prosperous publican shopkeeper like himself should put in more. J.J. places a shilling on the table very quietly. He keeps his finger on it and looks at Father MacNamara for approval. Father MacNamara shouts in a loud voice and announces to the assembled congregation, "J. J. McPhee, two shillings!"

Thomas Farouk Gilban, the parish treasurer, writes in the ledger 'J.J. McPhee, 1/-' (one shilling), the actual amount tendered. Murf, the scrutineer, slides the coin into the coin box before the coin is observed by anyone else. Murf suppresses a smile at Father Mac's ploy to raise the bar.

Now that the first person has come forward, a queue quickly forms. The second person to approach the table is the schoolmaster Sean McGinnelly. Master McGinnelly already has his shilling poised to place on the table. He frantically digs in his pockets for another shilling but finds only a sixpence. "Master McGinnelly, one shilling and sixpence!" announces Father Mac. There is a murmur of disapproval from the congregation. Master McGinnelly returns to his pew where his wife argues with him and shoves him back into the aisle. He walks past the queue to the top of the line and places on the table the sixpence his wife gave him. "There is a correction. Master McGinnelly, two shillings!" Nods and murmurs of approval.

Next in line is Casey. Casey holds his half-crown high and drops it on the table spinning it loudly. Murf notices that it is an 'Éire' coin. "P.J. Casey, two shillings and sixpence!" Well, that's to be expected. The rest of the well-to-do are at the front of the line.

Doctor McBratt approaches the table. This should be interesting. As a professional person, she ought to tender two shillings. But as a single woman she is expected to put in half. The congregation holds its collective breath. "Doctor McBratt, one shilling and sixpence!" Murmurs of approval. This is a very tactful compromise.

The queue progresses down through the one shilling donors, to the sixpenny donors, and to the thruppenny donors. A few people, too poor to put in a thruppence, are too embarrassed to put in a copper donation. They sit quietly at the back hoping that no one notices.

Once the collection is complete, the coffin will be interred in the vault beneath the altar. Father MacNamara scans the assembly and waits to give ample time for all donors to come forward before proceeding.

One final person shuffles forward. The last to come forward to the table is Granny McGrath. People whisper. Granny McGrath surely doesn't have enough wealth to put in a penny. What is she doing, going up to the collection table? "Sally McGrath, two shillings and sixpence!" The congregation is stunned to silence, and then buzzes with loud whispers. Murf slides Granny's half-crown into the coin box and observes that it is a Saorstát Éireann leath coróin dated 1929, in mint condition. Thomas Gilban shuts the ledger. Murf lifts the coin box and they both move to the side aisle.

Jack Gilban removes the table and chairs and the internment begins.

Father MacNamara sprinkles holy water and incenses the coffin. Then he gives the signal to the pallbearers. They carry the coffin to the rear of the altar and struggle to pass it down through the opening in the floor. In the space below the floor, the pallbearers slide the coffin onto the vault beneath the altar. The scraping of the coffin is heard throughout the church as it is pushed into position. After a moment of silence, the attendants reappear from under the floor. They place the flagstone back in position in the floor. There is a clang as it slams into position, sealing the entrance to the vault. The ceremony is over. The reverend gentlemen of the clergy stand up and troop from the sanctuary to the sacristy. The congregation vacates the church, commenting to each other in respectful whispers on how appropriate the ceremony was for the dear departed Canon MacMorrow.

After disrobing, the clergy go to the parochial house to partake of Mrs. Friel's bountiful board. Murf and Thomas follow behind, not to join in the meal, but to finalise their duties with the donation money. They go into the meeting room next to the dining room. Murf, as scrutineer, counts the money, noting the break-down of coin denominations. He confirms that the total agrees with Thomas Gilban's ledger. Both are satisfied. Thomas uses his gold fountain pen and ruler to square off the ledger and they both sign it. Next, Thomas prepares the bank lodgement docket for the agreed total, £7-16-9 (seven pounds, sixteen shillings and nine pence).

Thomas remarks, "That's the first time I've seen a collection exceed £5. I'll get it into the bank first thing on Monday morning. No – on Tuesday morning. This Monday is a bank holiday." He places his pen and ruler on the table and packs the lodgement docket and the money into a canvas moneybag, ties the loop to close it, and places the bag in the corner safe.

Murf is sure of the count, and he intends to confirm it later with Jim Woods in the bank on Tuesday. Will Jim Woods notice the one old-issue leath coróin?

Now that the count is confirmed and the ledger is squared off, Murf is impatient to visit Granny McGrath. Granny McGrath is turning out to be a surprise in many ways. He and Farouk Gilban decide to exit the parochial house by way of the back door so as to avoid the dining room. Murf is in a hurry and has no wish to delay in talking with priests and the Vicar General. Farouk Gilban appears to be in a hurry too.

Upon passing through the back door, Farouk pats his breast pocket searching for his gold fountain pen. "Rats. I left my pen in the meeting room. Murf, I'm going back for my pen. Goodbye. I'll see you tomorrow."

He takes three Yale keys from his pocket and selects the one marked 'F'. Murf is about to comment that he has selected the wrong key for the back door, but Farouk turns the key with practiced ease and opens the door.

On the journey to Glen Corry, Murf passes the vacant itinerant camp across the road from the creamery. "Blast Paddy Lamp. He is holding back on something. I wonder what it is. Only God knows where he is now."

Murf turns his thoughts to Granny McGrath. She has a peculiar life. It is orderly in a quaint way. Not orderly like Farouk. Farouk is neat and precise. Except that his parochial house back-door key is marked with an 'F' instead of a 'B'. It is not like Farouk to slip up like this. What if 'F', 'B' and 'S' mean something other than 'Front', 'Back' and 'Sacristy'? Maybe it's in Irish. 'Tosaigh'? No. There's no 'T' on any key.

Murf decides to confirm the key-markings after Mass on the next day.

Murf parks his car in Granny's front yard, or as Granny refers to it, 'the street'. The old collie rises from the doorstep, stretches and yawns, and approaches Murf's car wagging his tail. Murf lingers in the driver's seat to admire the cottage, an inhabited relic from 1750. The moist mountain air swirls in a lazy mist behind the house. Murf, if he ignores the car, imagines this scene two centuries ago. Granny McGrath appears at the half-door and looks out at Murf, curious as to why he drove up here and is now just sitting in his car. Murf sees her and comes back to the present.

Granny disappears from the half-door. So Murf leaves the car, walks to the cottage, and lets himself in.

"Come in, Guard Murphy."

Murf carefully closes the half-door lest the dog or hens enter the house. Unlike last time, Granny is not active in any task. She is sitting in her rocking chair within reach of her turf pile, her snuff-box and the poker & tongs.

"Hello, Granny."

Granny appears tired and looks frailer than on Thursday. But of course she must be exhausted, having cycled from the canon's funeral at St. Bawn's.

"Guard Murphy, I knew you would come back. And now you will arrest me. That's why you're here." She rocks her chair gently and stretches for her snuff-box. "He was a good man, you know. But he was old. And I kilt him, I did."

Granny repeats the description of the staring eyes and hen-beaked nose. And she rambles off where Murf's logic cannot follow.

To distract her from her confession Murf strolls along the wall from picture to picture, eliciting Granny's explanation on each of them in turn. He is looking for an answer to Maura Rua's clue from last night. "I see that the McGraths and the Gilbans were active together."

"Yes. That's a picture of them all, taken before the raid on the Ulster Bank in, in..."

"...in 1931."

"Yes, in 1931. Me two boys, Mick and Joe, were shot dead after that. Twenty-six and twenty-four they were then. Shot dead, they were, along with Fenian Gilban. Were you there, Guard Murphy?"

"And this picture here? It's very grainy. This looks like James Connolly, but it can't be. Mick and Joe are in their late teens in it. Connolly would have been dead for ten years at that time."

"Oh, that's Mick and Joe, all right. And that's Malachy Gilban with them. And that other one beside them is Pa Murray...."

Murf's brain clicks in recognition of the name 'Pa Murray', the leader of a delegation to the Soviet Union to obtain support for the IRA in 1926.

"...and t'other one is not IRA at all. I can't mind rightly what his name is. Joseph Horse or something, I think. Yes. Joseph Stallion."

Murf is quick-filing the information in his brain:

Soviet delegation; Malachy Gilban with Joseph Stalin; Malachy Gilban now head of security at Shannon; Malachy Gilban, with whom Farouk Gilban met in Shannon during the Russian shift in the early morning of 02 August at, or shortly after, the time the canon was attacked. The 'dots' are spilling rapidly and Murf needs to return to his festooned wall with its sheets of paper and coloured threads. A picture is forming. And Murf feels that he is on the brink of a significant revelation in the case.

"Granny. The half-crown."

"What about it?"

What connection has she with the Gilbans? Back in the thirties the IRA conducted clandestine activities from here. Is someone using Granny's place again, only this time for running spies? Without pausing, Murf continues speaking to Granny. "Where did you get it?"

"From there." She points to the tea caddies lining the mantle over the fireplace.

"From the tea caddies?" So Granny has a few coins hidden in with her mementos and recipes?

"Take a look."

Murf removes a tea caddy from the mantle. It is much heavier than he expected. He prises off the lid and discovers that the tin is crammed to the top with mint-condition leath coróin, all dated 1929. He takes down a second tin and discovers a similar hoard. Ten tea caddies, and all crammed with 1929 half-crowns. "Granny, where did these come from?"

"I found them in a bag."

"Where?"

"In Brendan's bed. When he was took away, I turned the mattress in his bed. And below the boards underneath was a bag."

"And all this was in the bag?"

"No, not all this. I put one coin in the collection at the funeral."

"Can you show me the bag now?"

"No, I can't, Guard Murphy."

"Why not, Granny?"

"Because I cut it up and made myself something out of it."

"What?"

"I can't tell you, except that I'm wearing it."

"Was there any writing on the bag?"

"There was. It said £100 SILVER. And there was a string and a label."

"And you have the string and label?"

"Yes, in the drawer in the box bed."

"May I take a look at it?"

"Well..."

"Granny. I'm a policeman. I'm used to seeing things that people don't want me to see."

She points to the drawer. Inside are Granny's undergarments all neatly folded. And there is the label and string. Still attached is the lead seal with 'UB' impressed on it. The label identifies the bag as the property of the Ulster Bank, dated and initialled by the teller on 17 December 1930.

So, how did Canon MacMorrow's killer come to have one of Granny's coins? Is she telling the truth and is she involved in some way in the canon's death after all? Her house was an IRA hide-out once. In her confused state of mind, is she reliving the 'Troubles' and is she being manipulated? Murf struggles with the realisation of this possibility. He argues silently with himself. "Follow the evidence. No, Granny is feeble and senile, incapable of aiding or abetting." And aloud, "Granny. Tomorrow is Sunday. On Monday I will return. Don't spend any more of the money while I'm gone." He almost added, "And don't leave the area until I return."

"So you're off then, Guard Murphy? You forgot your papers again? And you'll be bringing them on Monday to arrest me? All right then. I think I'll go to sleep now."

Sure enough. Granny falls asleep in her chair. Murf leaves the tea caddies on the box bed. There is no need to disturb her. He lets himself out and drives back to Killbawn. He knows that he should feel elated that important information is coming to light, information that could lead him to the canon's killer. But this development with Granny McGrath disturbs him.

Sunday 06 August 1950, 11:00am Mass, St. Bawn's Church. Murf is ushering. He assists with the collection. Unlike the funeral collection, the Sunday collection is conducted by sliding a wooden box on a long handle across the front of each pew. 1p is the preferred offering on a Sunday. Casey puts in his customary half-crown. Murf notices that Granny McGrath is absent from Mass. Her spot is vacant for the first time in over 50 years.

After Mass, Murf counts the money with Farouk. The total is £2-1-7, and contains one half-crown and two sixpences. The rest is pennies. Murf notes the total and the break-down. The customary procedure is followed and Murf leaves when Farouk places the money and its accompanying bank lodgement slip in the safe.

Murf enters the kitchen where Mrs. Friel is preparing the mid-day dinner. "Mrs. Friel, do you mind getting the keys again. There is something I'd like to check."

"Lord, Murf, I'm way too busy. You know where they are kept. Go and fetch them yourself."

Murf goes to the box in the hallstand and removes the three Yale keys. He successfully tries the 'F' key in the front door. The 'B' key fails to work in the back door. The 'S' key works in the sacristy door. What if he tries the 'F' key in the back door just like Farouk did? He tries it, and it works. "Mrs. Friel, why does the 'F' key work in the back door, but the 'B' key doesn't?"

Mrs. Friel is teeming the potatoes. The steam is wafting past her face. "Good God, Murf, you have me demented. The front door and the back door is the same lock, so the one key fits."

That would be the 'F' key, Murf deduces. "So what is the 'B' key then?"

"Well, for the belfry, of course. Murf, you are in my way. Go off to the belfry and try it there."

Murf walks down the passageway and opens the sacristy door and enters the church. He knows Jack Gilban's routine with the bell-tower door. Are not the bell-tower door and the belfry door one and the same? Could there be a second door inside the tower? Murf opens the bell-tower door using the big iron key from the upper rail of the door. Inside Jack's supply room he finds the candle and matches. Lighting the candle, he makes his way up the winding stairs. Is there another door higher up? The belfry proper is at the top of the stairs. Sure enough, Murf encounters a locked door with a Yale lock. He tries the 'B' key. It turns smoothly and the door swings open. Murf steps inside. In the room he observes radio receivers and transmitters. This is the radio room where Father MacNamara and Farouk Gilban engage in their ham-radio hobby. It is no surprise that they would want a secure lock to protect this equipment and restrict access to it.

Murf hurries back down the stairs and into the nave of the church. A few women are still here from the Mass. They are praying the Rosary or performing the Way of the Cross. One of the women waves to Murf to halt. It is Doctor McBratt.

"Murf," she whispers. "Have some respect. You are clomping loudly, disturbing the respectful quiet of the church."

"I'm sorry, Ant. I needed to check something and I got distracted."

"What? That Granny McGrath did not come to Mass today? And that she failed to arrive for her nightly devotions last night?"

"Granny McGrath? I went to see her yesterday. She insisted that I arrest her for killing the canon. I can't do that. There is no way she could have struck him with her own hands."

"What all did she say?"

Murf repeats to Doctor McBratt how Granny described it.

Doctor McBratt repeats a few things for Murf's confirmation. "Staring eyes?"

"Yes."

"A nose like a hen's beak?"

"Yes."

"Murf, she is not describing the canon. She is describing Brendan McGrath. She is confessing to euthanizing her invalid husband."

"Good God. And did you know?"

"Of course not, but it's always a possibility. Look here, Murf, euthanasia is not a rarity in rural Ireland. Some people cannot deal with a nonresponsive bedridden relative. If someone is dying, well, they just hurry it along. If an invalid is expected to live a few weeks, but dies within a few days, well, how can you tell? You can only speculate. And judging from what you tell me about Granny McGrath, this appears to be the case with Brendan's death."

"And that is why she has been coming to the church."

"It's not the police she needs. It's the priest."

"Tell you what, Ant. Let's go to visit her. I have something to finish up here. It will take me half an hour...."

"Off you go, Murf. I'll go to Father MacNamara and tell him. Perhaps all three of us can go to Granny today."

Murf returns the keys to the box in the hallstand.

"Did you find what you were looking for?" Mrs. Friel shouts from the kitchen.

Murf returns a quick "yes" and runs out the back door.

Ten minutes later, Murf is back in the church. This time, he has the evidence-key from the Garda station. Now at the belfry door again, he holds his breath as he tries the key in the lock. The key slides in, but with a scraping sound. It's a newly-cut key and is still rough at the edges. It turns without resistance and the door swings open. Who would have a key to the radio room? Father MacNamara and Thomas Farouk Gilban are the two names that first come to mind. Farouk's name keeps popping up. Did he obtain a key via Mrs. Friel as Sammy said? And is that his sole key? If so, he still has possession of that key. Could he have obtained an extra key? Or did Mrs. Friel? She has access to the original key. Sammy at the hardware department could have cut an additional key for himself and made it available to Casey. Some more probing questions are in order. How many keys are there in total? Are they all accounted for?

1:30pm. Murf knocks at the back door of the parochial house. Mrs. Friel opens the door and invites him in. "Guard Murphy, are you still here?"

"I was up in the belfry."

"So have you sorted out the keys?"

"Almost. Could I have a word with Father Mac? Or is he still at dinner?"

"Father Mac is having his after-dinner coffee. He's waiting for Doctor McBratt. I believe they will be going to visit Granny McGrath. Aren't you going with them, Murf?"

"Well, yes. That is one of the reasons I'm here."

"Murf, I suppose you haven't eaten. Come into the kitchen. I'll fix something for you. And I'll let Father Mac know you're here."

Murf hurriedly consumes roast beef and carrots with boiled potatoes. Mrs. Friel sneaks him a glass of wine from the deceased canon's stock.

Father MacNamara enters the kitchen and sits beside him. "So Murf, Mrs. Friel says you've been playing with the keys. Have you found anything of interest?"

"Actually, there is something. I hope you can enlighten me."

Murf rises from the table and signals to Father Mac to follow him into the meeting room. Out of earshot of Mrs. Friel, Murf takes the evidence key from his pocket and shows it to Father Mac. "You remember this key?"

"The one we found at the entrance to the vault behind the altar? Yes. What of it?"

"It bears the same fingerprints as the bloodied candlestick."

"That's very significant."

"Hold on. There's more. This key fits the door to the radio room."

"The radio room in the belfry? Sure there are only three keys – mine, which I have on my key ring with my car keys; the original key in the box in the hallstand; and there is the one with Thomas Gilban. Has Thomas lost his key?"

"No, Thomas showed me his key. I understand that a duplicate key was cut only recently."

"Hmm. Let me check that."

Father MacNamara returns to the kitchen and speaks with Mrs. Friel. "Mrs. Friel, do you know if we got a new key cut for the belfry?"

"Yes. And I told you that, two weeks ago. And Thomas Gilban says to tell you that he put it in the agreed-upon place; and that you would know what that means. Don't you remember?"

Father MacNamara re-enters the meeting room. "Yes. You are correct, Murf. I told Thomas to have an extra key cut in the event of us going to the belfry without one. That happened a few weeks ago when both of us were at the radio-room door and neither of us had a key with us."

"And where is that key now?"

"Hidden in the belfry. It should be in our agreed hiding-place. Come, I'll show you."

Father MacNamara and Murf go to the belfry. They stop at the radio-room door.

"Watch this," Father Mac says as he slides his hand along the rail above the door. Having slid his hand the length of the rail, he repeats the action in reverse pressing his hand father back into the rail. "That's funny. The key is missing from its hiding place."

"So this key, the evidence key, must be the missing key." Murf inserts it in the lock to demonstrate its effectiveness.

"That's right, Murf. It must be."

"And who knew of this key and its hiding place?"

"Just Thomas and I."

"Just you two?"

"Yes. And I didn't move it. Or disclose its existence or location to anyone else. You should ask Thomas about it."

"I intend to."

"And when did you discover this? Just now?"

"That's right. Just a short time ago when Mrs. Friel gave me the original keys to check the locks."

"Surely Thomas isn't..."

"Don't jump to conclusions. I am following the evidence. This key bears fingerprints of Canon MacMorrow and of 'X the unknown assailant. Not clear fingerprints I grant you, but about a 50% match to both. There are no clear fingerprints matching Thomas Gilban on the key."

"Which means he never handled it."

"Which means he wasn't the last, or even second last, to handle it. There are older smudged prints that might be his."

"Or even Sammy at the hardware counter; or Mrs. Friel who obtained the key from Casey's"

"Precisely."

"So..."

"Don't ask me anything more. I cannot comment on an ongoing case. Just keep this information to yourself. The case is progressing well, but I have more questions to ask people before they are forewarned of what new evidence has come to light."

"I understand perfectly. Let's go back to the house and wait for Doctor McBratt. And you may have another glass of the canon's wine."

2:30pm. Doctor McBratt arrives, driven to St. Bawn's by her faithful divil.

Father Mac asks, "So whose car should we go in to visit Sally McGrath? My car is the biggest."

"Oh no," says Murf. "A big car is not suitable for Glen Corry. You'd slide off the bumpy road and land us the bog. No, let's go in the Garda car."

"Nonsense," says Doctor McBratt. "Danny the Divil will drive us. Sure he could get us there with his eyes shut."

Father Mac mouths to Murf, 'blind'.

They enter Doctor McBratt's car. McBratt enters with her signature swivel and sits in her usual place, the left side of the rear passenger seat. Murf sits beside her. Father MacNamara and the Divil sit in front.

Throughout the journey to the glen, Doctor McBratt maintains a running commentary on every point of interest on the road. She has a comment on every family in every house they pass by. There are very few houses in Lough Corry Lower, so she switches to recognising each pothole and bump in the road. The Divil certainly knows the way. He avoids potholes and slows done in anticipation of a bump and speeds up where he can. Father Mac attempts to light a cigarette. The ride is so bumpy that he is unable to apply his lighter. He gives up, and then finds that he is unable to place the cigarette back in its pack. They continue on through Lough Corry Lower to Glen Corry and they eventually reach Lough Corry.

They arrive safely, albeit rumpled, at Granny McGrath's humble house. The Divil remains in the car. The others step out and approach the front door. As usual, it is open except for the lower half-door.

"Do you get the smell?" Murf asks.

"What smell?" asks Doctor McBratt.

"The smell of turf smoke."

The priest remarks, "Well, I don't get the smell of smoke."

"It's absent."

"There is no smoke," says Doctor McBratt hurrying to the half-door, "because there is no turf burning."

Murf rushes after her and they enter the cottage together. They both know that the fire in this house has burned continually for 200 years. They see Granny McGrath sitting in her rocking chair beside the expired fire. Her pile of turf is completely depleted. Her tea caddies are still on her box bed from yesterday.

She opens her eyes and addresses Murf in a weak voice. "Guard Murphy, I knew that you would not forget me. Did you bring your papers for the arrest? And I see you brought the doctor along with you."

"Murf!" orders the doctor. "Get the fire going, and put the kettle on. And find some food in the larder."

From his previous visit, Murf is familiar with the house and sets about his tasks. The doctor takes a mug from the dresser and bends down to the dresser's lower door to access the spring well underneath. She dips the mug in the water and brings it to Granny.

Father MacNamara enters and sizes up the situation.

Granny speaks feebly, "And did you bring the priest too, Guard Murphy? Sure that's great."

Murf cannot hear Granny. He is out at the turf stack filling the turf bucket.

Exhausted, Granny continues to speak. Her voice is not much above a whisper. "So did Guard Murphy tell you that I kilt him? And now he is here to arrest me. Isn't that so, Guard Murphy?"

"Shush, Granny. Guard Murphy is getting the fire going. We'll soon have hot soup for you. And you know Granny, Guard Murphy says that he will not arrest you. He says that you need the priest, not the police. And here is Father MacNamara. Why don't you tell him all that you told Guard Murphy?"

"Yes. Why don't you Granny?" says Father MacNamara. "You have been talking to God every night for the past few months. Sure, you can tell me now. There is nothing that God doesn't already know."

"So I won't go to gaol?"

"No, Granny."

"Nor to Hell?"

"Nor to Hell, Granny. Just tell God, and tell him you're sorry."

"Oh yes. I'll tell God. Take down the 'Sacred Heart' and I'll tell him face-to-face."

Father MacNamara nods to Murf, who is lighting the fire, and points to the picture of the 'Sacred Heart' on the mantle above the fireplace. Murf takes down the picture and sets it upright, supported by sods of turf, in front of Granny. Father MacNamara dons his confessional stole and Doctor McBratt and Murf retreat to a respectful distance.

An hour later Granny is much revived. The fire is blazing brightly. Murf has stacked a pile of turf within reach of her arm, enough to last a week. There is an adequate supply of food in the pantry. Granny stretches to her cubby-hole at the hob and locates her snuff-box. Even Danny the Divil comes in and offers to share his meagre supply of whiskey. Satisfied that Granny is revived, the party leaves her.

Doctor McBratt has the final word. "No more cycling to Killbawn. It's much too far for you, Granny. I'll call in to see you tomorrow. Goodbye until then."

On the drive back to Killbawn, Doctor McBratt addresses Father MacNamara. "You should prepare for another funeral soon. I believe Granny McGrath is about to be reunited with Brendan."

CHAPTER ELEVEN

KILLBAWN
COUNTY MAYO, IRELAND

Monday Morning, 07 August 1950

Murf is in his office. He is joined by Garda Seamus O'Reilly. Murf addresses him. "O'Reilly, it may be a quiet day in Killbawn, this being the August Bank Holiday and all, but for us it's another day."

"A policeman's lot."

Murf leans back against his desk, not quite sitting on it, and studies his wall. "O'Reilly. Look at the wall. There are three strings for every name on the incident wall, all strung in the direction of the centre."

"Yes, I see that. And in the centre is Canon MacMorrow."

"Red, black and white; for motive, means and opportunity."

"I see that the means and opportunity strings are linked to everyone on the wall, but the motive string falls far short."

"Except for 'X' the unknown assailant, whose fingerprints we have on the murder weapon. He is our prime suspect, the one we need to catch. But who is he? Where is he? Is he the British defector, Cross? Why would a Brit, defecting to Russia, come all the way to North Mayo? And what reason would a British defector have to murder Canon MacMorrow?"

"Well, if we find Cross, we can ask him."

"Don't be funny, O'Reilly. Nevertheless, you are correct. We must find the assailant – Cross, or whoever it is."

Murf addresses the wall, or maybe himself, "Someone on this wall knows. Cross could not have parachuted into St. Bawn's from nowhere. If indeed 'X' is Cross, we need to confirm that the fingerprints on the candlestick are his."

Murf walks slowly to the wall. He removes the 'X' paper and reattaches it, joining it to Thomas Gilban. He commences connecting strings from the combined Thomas Gilban/'X' and attaches all three strings to the victim.

"Murf, do you realise what you are doing?"

"The only one with links to the Brits is Farouk Gilban. If Farouk is connected to Cross, then we have the picture complete."

"Are you saying...?"

"O'Reilly, this is where the investigation will focus."

"Do we bring him in? Farouk Gilban?"

"No, not yet. We do not have sufficient grounds. We can only ask for his help and cooperation in assembling data relevant to the investigation. To question him probingly in a fishing exercise would be futile at this point. He is too experienced to disclose anything he chooses to conceal. He may even attempt to manipulate us to deflect our suspicions elsewhere. No, O'Reilly. When we question Farouk as a suspect, we will have sufficient grounds. And we will ask questions for which we already know the answers, not necessarily all the answers, but enough to trip him up if he attempts to mislead us."

"So what now?"

"As I say, establish the identity of the assailant, and establish a connection to Farouk."

"How?"

"With the help of His Majesty's Intelligence Service. They urgently need to apprehend Cross before he succeeds in getting to Russia. The pieces of evidence in our murder investigation may lead to Cross's whereabouts. I expect the Intelligence Service of the Foreign Office will quickly confirm that the fingerprints on the candlestick are indeed John Cross's, or are definitely NOT John Cross's."

"And if they are his, Farouk may lead us to him?"

"That's where we are headed."

"And if these are NOT his fingerprints?"

"We refocus."

"Murf, have you contacted the British Foreign Office?"

"Yes. I have a contact through a third party. I've been in touch a few times already. And I sent a message on Friday. I'm surprised he hasn't responded to it by now. I'll give him until noon, and if there is no communication by then, I'll phone the RUC in Belfast."

"The RUC?"

"Yes. The RUC is my third-party contact medium."

Murf positions the candlestick close to the key and the coin on the desk, so that he can view them together in the context of the case notes on the incident wall. "Yes, O'Reilly, I think it's time we had Farouk Gilban in here for a talk. Not quite yet, but very soon."

10:44am, the phone rings. The front desk puts through the call to Murf. The call is connected and Murf speaks, "Patrick? I thought you had deserted me." Murf dislikes the code-name 'Piper's Son' and address him as 'Patrick'. It is a good telephone connection. O'Reilly hears the other party clearly.

"So, Murf what is it? Tell me you have something for me."

"John Cross. What can you tell me about him?"

"He is one of our top research scientists. He appears to have disappeared."

"You mean 'defected'."

"That is very likely."

"Do you know where he is now?"

"We had information that he went to Ireland. However, there have been no confirmed sightings of him in Ireland. There were a few unconfirmed sightings, yes. But they are unsubstantiated and without any credible basis, so we dismissed them. One report actually came from Mayo on Friday."

"I contacted the SDU on Friday, but they cut me short. They told me to call back when I have a confirmed sighting."

"Regardless, we have come to the conclusion that the reported sightings of Cross in Ireland were unfounded, and that the Irish lead was a false lead. John Cross didn't just simply vanish. His disappearance has the hallmark of a sophisticated organisation adept at spiriting things into and out of the country – like a smuggling ring. With all points of exit being closely watched, Russian agents would need to smuggle John Cross out of the country through one of the smuggling channels. Our focus is now in the Liverpool area and in the south of England. Personally, I do not rule out Ireland. Is this what you want to know?"

"Listen to me, Patrick, I have a homicide case. The victim is an elderly priest. Before he died, he said a few disjointed words – 'Cross', 'in the mirror', and 'the fecking British'."

"When was that?"

"On the morning of August the 2nd. The assault occurred in St. Bawn's Church either very late on the night of August the 1st, or in the early hours of August the 2nd; five days ago. The most likely interpretation of what was said is this –

"'Cross' refers to John Cross;

"'In the mirror' may refer to an article that appeared in the Sunday Mirror a short time before;

"And 'the fecking British' may actually have been 'defecting British'."

"Hmm. I see."

"Patrick, we have a perfect set of fingerprints on the murder weapon, a brass candlestick found at the scene. Can you provide us with a set of Cross's fingerprints for comparison?"

"Yes."

"How long will it take for us to receive it?"

"I'll deliver a set personally. I will leave today and I should be in Killbawn tomorrow morning. Murf, this might be the first solid lead on Cross since his disappearance from Cheshire on the 15th of July. And Murf, the information you have, coupled with the information I have, may bring both investigations to a close. Which is your closest airport?"

"There is no airport close to us. Shannon is 2½ hours; Dublin is 3½ hours, and Belfast is 4 hours from here."

"I will come via Belfast. I have reason to connect up with the RUC en route."

"Thanks, Patrick. I await your arrival. Killbawn is a small town. Just come to the Garda station on the Main Street next to the Market Square."

"Okay. Cheers," and he hangs up.

In London, Piper's Son lifts his phone and makes another telephone call. Piper's Son into the phone, "When did Cody last report?

"Saturday?

"And you say he went to Mayo on Friday night?

"The next time he phones, transfer his call to me before he disconnects. I need to speak with him."

Piper's Son hangs up the phone. He regards this as interesting information on Cody. Cody would have connected Londonderry – from MI6's last reported lead – to the Russian presence in Shannon and drawn a line. Of all the unconfirmed sightings of John Cross in Ireland, only one coincides with this line – the one reported from North Mayo. Cody, a crafty undercover operative, has reasoned that Cross is in Mayo en route to Shannon. This is a judicious move on his part. If Cody succeeds in catching up with Cross, he will execute a swift and tidy conclusion to the entire matter.

Garda O'Reilly is impatient to act on Murf's theory and bring in Thomas Farouk Gilban for questioning. Murf decides to wait for Piper's Son's arrival on the morrow. The combined forces of the Killbawn Gardaí and H. M. intelligence services will be a formidable force for Farouk to reckon with.

2:40pm. Piper's Son arrives at Belfast Airport. He is picked up by a police car and is taken to RUC H.Q. where he meets with Sir Robert Norton, the inspector-general.

3:00pm. The Garda District Office in Castlebar phones the Killbawn station. They have two Ward itinerants in a cooling-off cell. The Wards were picked up on the previous day for unruly behaviour resulting from a dispute over a card game. Tricks Ward had been entertaining in public, performing card tricks. An argument broke out over a card game in which a man claimed to have been conned out of two shillings and sixpence. After some shouting and pushing, the offending parties were taken into custody to cool off. Today, the effects of alcohol have worn off and heads have cooled down. No charges were laid. Instead, a caution was issued, and Chief Superintendent David Fox agrees to release them. But first he needs to check if these two Wards are connected to the missing Paddy Lamp Ward. They could be of interest to Inspector Murphy in his murder investigation. On Fox's instructions, the duty officer contacts Killbawn Garda Station to inform Inspector Murphy that they are holding Francie Ward and Tricks Ward and that they will be released without charges at 6:00pm. Murf responds. He requests transfer of the two Wards to Killbawn for questioning.

4:00pm. Castlebar District Office delivers Francie Ward and Collie Tricks Ward to the Killbawn Garda Station. Murf has Francie placed in the holding cell and directs Tricks into the interview room. Garda O'Reilly joins them and takes notes to record the interview.

"So...tell me, Tricks, what were you doing in Castlebar?"

"We are on our way from the Reek to Donegal. Going through Castlebar is how you go. There was a horse-jumping event and dog trials in the convent grounds next to the army barracks. They have it every year on the Sunday of the long weekend, the first weekend of Lunasa. Y'see, school starts up again next week and this is..."

"I know all about the school year and the events of the August bank holiday. What were YOU doing in Castlebar, Tricks?"

"Well, y'know. With all the people there, sure some entertainment would not go amiss." Tricks is wearing his coat and cap and he is uncomfortably warm in the Garda station. He removes his paddy cap and stuffs it in his coat pocket. His greatcoat is unfastened as usual. He opens it wide and spreads it out from his shoulders. He declines to remove it. He trusts no one. Once he lets go of his coat it might be his no longer.

"And your entertainment is in card tricks?"

"And in dancing."

"I know. But the guards did not take you in for dancing in the street. Now did they? Perhaps you were playing 'find-the-lady' and the 'mark' got upset."

"Ah no, Guard Murphy. It wasn't like that at all...."

Murf waves his hands to silence him and asks, "What were you doing on Ireland's Holy Mountain?"

"That's one of Francie's portals for 'the memory'. He has to connect to 'the memory' every year at all four portals, y'know like. We're finished there now, and we're going to Donegal."

Murf doesn't know anything about 'portals' or 'the memory'. "Where's Paddy Lamp? Was he with you at your 'portal'?"

"Paddy Lamp? The last I saw of Paddy Lamp was on the Ballycorry Road outside Killbawn here, across from the creamery."

"When was that?"

"That would have been before noon on Thursday."

"Thursday, four days ago?"

"Aye. Four days ago. He went his way and we went our way."

"And which way did Paddy go?"

"And sure how would anyone know where Paddy Lamp goes?"

Murf realises that Tricks is not going to disclose the whereabouts of Paddy Lamp. Very likely Tricks does not know the current location of Paddy Ward, but if Doctor McBratt knows Paddy Lamp's schedule, then so too must Tricks.

"Kimmid, perhaps?"

"Och. Aye. But Kimmid in not for another week yet. And sure what would you be wantin' with Paddy Lamp anyways? Are you looking to buy a lamp?"

"I ask the questions, Tricks."

"Sorry, Me Honour sir."

"Was anything or anyone with him when you last saw him?"

Tricks blinks and looks sideways. "The whole clan and three horses, and a dog...."

Murf notices Tricks's uneasiness. Did Tricks wince at the mention of 'anyone'? "Anything he wouldn't want me to see? Any outsiders, Tricks?" Murf takes a stab at why Paddy Lamp Ward may have disappeared unexpectedly.

"I can't rightly mind. An outsider, you say?"

"An outsider, Tricks. One who is not a Ward."

"Ah, yes. Now that you mention it. Peter Oldthorpe was with him when I last saw him."

"Peter Oldthorpe?"

"Aye."

It is a struggle to get information out of Collie Tricks Ward. Eventually, Murf succeeds in ascertaining that Tricks and Francie had been with Peter Oldthorpe since the July new moon right up to four days ago, a journey that commenced in the centre of Cheshire and terminated in north Mayo. This Peter Oldthorpe sounds a lot like the elusive John Cross. What could they have learned from Peter Oldthorpe that might lead to his current or intended whereabouts? A family connection? A friend's name?

"So Tricks. Tell me about Peter Oldthorpe."

"Ask Francie. He was his minder."

Murf decides to take a rest from questioning Tricks. Perhaps Tricks is right to suggest questioning Francie. It can't be any more difficult than questioning Tricks.

5:00pm. Murf and O'Reilly reconvene in the interview room. This time with Francie Clé Ward.

"Francie, I hear you were Peter Oldthorpe's minder from Cheshire to Killbawn. Is that so?"

"Aye."

No denial. No evasion. This is uncharacteristic of a Ward itinerant traveller. "Are you unwell, Francie?"

"I passed a room just now. I thought it spoke to me."

"Which room?"

"The one with the candlestick and the key and the coin."

Murf and O'Reilly look at each other. These objects are on Murf's desk. But the door to Murf's office is closed. "Okay, Francie. Focus on my questions. What do you know about Peter Oldthorpe?"

"You want to know about Peter Oldthorpe? The answer is in the key and the coin."

Murf remembers saying exactly the same thing to himself on Friday. "Tell us about Peter Oldthorpe."

"You want answers on Peter Oldthorpe? Then ask the questions where the answers lie."

O'Reilly asks sarcastically, "What? You'll provide the answers with the key and the coin?"

"Aye. But I need Collie with me."

Murf stands up and says, "If it helps, then let's go into my office."

O'Reilly makes a face to denote disagreement. He takes his writing pad and follows Murf and Francie into Murf's office. Murf instructs O'Reilly to summon Garda Caldwell. Caldwell comes to the office. Murf instructs him. "Caldwell, fetch Tricks from the cell. I want him in here; and you too."

Murf's office has one available chair. His own chair is stacked with boxes. There are torn sheets of paper strewn on the floor. Murf stands leaning against the wall, the wall festooned with papers and threads. O'Reilly stands next to the desk within reach of pencils and writing pads. Caldwell and Tricks stand inside the doorway. Francie sits in the sole available chair. He sits facing Murf's desk and looks intently at the three objects thereon, positioned in a triangle as if on an altar – the bloodied candlestick in the centre, flanked by the coin and the key.

O'Reilly passes a pencil and notepad to Francie and says, "Why don't you write it all down for us. Everything you know about Peter Oldthorpe?"

Francie removes his cap and places it in his pocket. His long black hair falls in front of his face. He flings it back with a throw of his hand, and grabs the notepad and pencil from O'Reilly. Francie draws strange shapes on the pad and hands it back to O'Reilly.

"What's this? Some joke? It's just triangles and spirals and scribbles."

"Guard O'Reilly, if I were to read all this aloud, it would take me more than an hour."

Murf is frantically signalling to O'Reilly and mouths the word 'illiterate'.

"Okay, Francie. Why don't I write down all that you say."

Francie reaches out both his hands to the object on the desk.

"Don't touch the evidence, Francie." Murf cautions him.

Francie bows his head, and his hair falls forward concealing his face. Francie begins to speak. He sounds strange. His voice is different. And his voice changes as if he were more than one person. Murf signals to O'Reilly to write down everything, just like a court recording clerk. They can read it back later and extract relevant information.

Francie is speaking. "John Cross. You see; you hear. That which is, cannot not be. You are still John Cross, are you not?"

O'Reilly mouths to Murf, 'Do I write all this down?' Murf makes a writing motion with his hand and O'Reilly commences writing in his pad.

Murf turns to Tricks and whispers, "Do you know what Francie is doing?"

"He is having a 'memory'."

"A 'memory'? What's a 'memory'?"

"He sees things through portals, things that are sent to him. He relives events as if they are happening before his eyes, even things from hundreds and thousands of years ago."

"What do you mean 'through a portal'?"

"I don't know for sure. That is where the memories flow through to him. The three objects on your desk must have created a portal to John Cross."

Murf signals to O'Reilly to keep writing. O'Reilly breaks a pencil and grabs another one from Murf's desk. He struggles to keep up with Francie's low voice and he adjusts his ear to the changes in pitch and accent. He no longer attempts to make sense of Francie's account. O'Reilly concentrates on writing down the entire commentary.

After an hour, Francie keels over and collapses on the floor. Doctor McBratt is summoned. Francie quickly revives. Doctor McBratt arrives and determines that Francie has not suffered any ill-effects. Doctor McBratt counsels rest for Francie. Murf suggests a night in the holding cell to afford a dry bed for Francie and Tricks. This is agreeable.

7:00pm. Murf and O'Reilly are back in Murf's office. Murf has borrowed an extra chair from Sergeant Hughes' room. They sit side by side. Murf thumbs through O'Reilly's writing pad in an attempt to read Francie's account. "O'Reilly. I am unable to decipher your writing. Write me a second copy, a legible copy."

O'Reilly commences rewriting the entire commentary, transcribing from his scribbled writing to a neat legible rendering. As he completes each page, he tears it out and passes it to Murf.

O'Reilly complains that this is a futile exercise. "This whole account is wild ramblings with no foundation in fact. If we are to find Peter Oldthorpe or John Cross, we must deal in facts, in hard evidence. Isn't this what you always say, Murf?"

"O'Reilly. You are correct. Let's just finish this and call it a night. Tomorrow is another day."

O'Reilly applies himself to completing the assignment quickly so that he can go home. He is quiet for the remainder of the task.

Murf lifts page one and commences to read.

PART 2 – THE QUEST FOR JOHN CROSS

CHAPTER TWELVE

HIGH EXPLOSIVE RESEARCH

Wednesday 12 July 1950
Cheshire, England

1950 is an anxious year for John Cross. He is sitting in his living room, chain-smoking at 11:35pm, staring out the rear window at nothing. He checks off in his mind the things that are gnawing at him, and keeps count by knocking ash into the ashtray on the arm of the chair.

Thinking aloud, "In January, Klaus Fuchs confessed. He was sentenced to 14 years. He had worked at the Atomic Energy Research Establishment down at Harwell. Why do the Russians still want data on the development of Atomic weapons? They successfully detonated their own test bomb almost a year ago – in August last year. We, in Britain, are still years away from achieving this." 'Tap', he knocks a section of ash off his cigarette. "Harwell is a long way from Risley, 166 miles. But in terms of the work that is being done, and the interrelationship of colleagues, it may as well be 166 feet." 'Tap', he taps his cigarette again, but not enough ash has accumulated to dislodge. "Sonia has gone quiet. And I have a stash of Photostat copies in the cabinet under the wireless. If tomorrow Sonia fails to communicate and there is no request for a delivery, I will destroy them. Lord, if these are found in the house, I could go the same way as Fuchs." 'Tap'. "Maybe I should destroy them now."

John Cross moves to get up but decides otherwise. He sits back down and drags deeply on his cigarette. "Lighting a fire in midsummer? No. Tomorrow, if I do not hear anything,

I will burn them with the garden weeds. Everyone is burning garden weeds; there is nothing suspicious in that." This time, he forgets to tap his forefinger on the cigarette and a section of ash falls on the armrest. He looks at it, blows it away and determines that the cigarette has burned down too small. He stubs it out and selects a fresh one from the cigarette box on the side table. This is a familiar action. His hand chooses a cigarette and finds the lighter, all without the benefit of visual contact. He places the flame to the cigarette, draws on it and blows a cloud of smoke upwards. Placing the lighter back on the side table, he idly watches the dissipating smoke at the ceiling.

"How did it start?"

John Cross is 37 years old. Born in Lanarkshire, Scotland. He received his D.Sc from the University of Edinburgh. When war broke out in 1939 he worked in 'Royal Ordnance'. His work was mostly in theoretical calculations for the improvement and efficiency of weapons.

But that's not when 'it' started. Churchill agreed with Stalin to share weaponry to improve the Red Army in accordance with the terms of 'Lend Lease' enacted on 11 March 1941. Prudently, Stalin did not trust Churchill. Stalin sought, and obtained, independent confirmation of weaponry advancements through Soviet agents in Britain. John Cross had no hesitation in accommodating the Allied Powers against Nazi Germany. A friend from his college days, one of those intellectual communists found at every university in pre-war England, set up the introduction. And so 'it' started. Assisting allies against a common enemy. It was the right thing to do.

Throughout the war, at official levels, information and assistance were pledged. But in reality, information was frequently suppressed, hidden from and denied to the participating allies. As a consequence of the inter-ally suppression of information, all the allies engaged in espionage against each other at the 'unofficial level'.

In 1941, John Cross was transferred to 'Tube Alloys', the British atomic bomb project. In 1943, as the result of the Quebec Agreement, he was sent to work on the 'Manhattan Project' in the U.S., in the Theoretical Physics Division at the Los Alamos Laboratory, New Mexico. This period was frustrating. He was kept in the dark about what he was actually doing. The Americans were secretive and withheld information from the British scientists. Cooperation broke down between the U.S. and Britain and in 1945, at the conclusion of the war, Britain resumed its independent research, 'Tube Alloys', and commenced the project 'High Explosive Research'. John Cross was relocated to Risley in Lancashire in January 1946. In 1948, 'Modus Vivendi' allowed for consultation and limited sharing of technical information between the U.S, Britain and Canada. But by 1949 it was clear that cooperation on atomic weapons would be impossible to achieve.

Throughout all this, John Cross supplied the Soviets with information. At first he justified this by acknowledging that the USSR is an ally. Now, in 1950, and since the end of WWII, his justification is in contributing to the 'Balance of Power' as a way to ensure peace. Now that the Russians have the bomb too, and Britain is close to it, the balance of power appears to be in equilibrium. This should ensure peace, a peace that John Cross has contributed to.

John Cross and many hundreds participated in supplying the Soviets with information. Commencing in

1943, the 'Venona Project' intercepted and identified encrypted messages transmitted by the intelligence agencies of the Soviet Union. The project identified 349 covert relationships with Soviet intelligence. Of all the cables that were intercepted, 49% were decrypted in 1944, only 1.5% in 1945, and 0% in the following years. In 1948 Russian encryption became totally unreadable. Notwithstanding this astounding revelation, only a handful of spies were identified from their code-names.

John Cross lights another cigarette. It is past midnight now. It is 13 July, a new day. He resolves to start this day by withdrawing his services of providing information to the Soviets. He fears that the net is closing in since Fuchs's arrest and confession. If Sonia contacts him today, he will inform her (him? them?) of his decision, and deliver his final package. If, on the other hand, Sonia fails to make contact, then it's over. John Cross stubs out his cigarette. Now that he has made this decision, he feels much better. He yawns and stretches. He can sleep contentedly tonight.

Thursday 13 July. At 7:30am John Cross awakens bright and cheery. A quick visit to the bathroom and a shave, and he dresses in his usual light grey trousers, white shirt, blue tie (badly knotted), navy-blue blazer and black oxfords (in need of polish). Scientists are not noted for their attention to attire. He runs down the stairs of his modest semi-detached suburban house, opens the front door, brings in the milk bottle, and goes to the kitchen. He grabs a bowl from the cupboard, and the sugar bowl, and snatches the packet of cornflakes off the counter beside the sink. Together with his bottle of fresh milk he has breakfast. He spills some cornflakes into the bowl, followed by a generous spoonful of sugar. He tips the milk bottle gently to capture the cream that has settled on top, grabs a spoon from the drawer, and consumes his breakfast standing up. Placing the used bowl and spoon in the sink, he glances out the window to admire his back garden. There is nothing admirable at all in his garden, John Cross just feels good today. Seeing the raked weeds and garden waste bundled at the bottom of the garden reminds him of something. He rushes into the living room, gets his 'Sonia package' from the wireless cabinet, runs out the back door and conceals the package deep within the bundle of garden waste. He'll set this alight when he returns home. And if Sonia contacts him today...well, there is no harm done. He can still retrieve the package and make the delivery.

John Cross goes through the rest of his morning routine: he secures all windows and doors, gets his briefcase and keys from the hallstand, goes out the front door which he pulls shut behind him, and makes his way to the street where he has parked his modest Morris Minor. The drive from No. 4 Eve Street in Middlethorpe to the Royal Ordnance in Risley is 45 minutes. The route is so familiar that the car finds its own way. What a beautiful day, he thinks.

At 8:50am, John parks his Morris Minor at the Royal Ordnance building. There is no name on the building anymore, and it is no longer 'Royal Ordnance', but that's what it is called by everyone here. The correct title is 'High Explosive Research Building' or 'HER' but, since that's a secret, the old title is conveniently used. John Cross hops out of his car lightly, his briefcase slung casually over his shoulder, and makes his way to the entrance singing "*If you were the only girl in the world....*"

John Cross is not perturbed by the lingering mist in the parking lot. Normally, he would regard it as a damper on bright spirits. After all, it is because of the high prevalence of mist here that this location was chosen. The facility is close to major road and rail arteries, and has access to ample power, and being prone to mist it is not conducive to human habitation. All these combine to make it the ideal location for high explosive research. But the overriding factor in choosing this location is that the mist conceals the facility from aerial observation.

Once inside the building, John Cross stops singing, not because it's frowned upon, but because he senses a coldness that he has not experienced since Los Alamos. People are standing around in silence. The familiar sounds of the usual activity are absent. Tentatively, John Cross ascends the stairs to his office. He looks inside at his desk and sees that it is secured with security tape. He drops his briefcase and cautiously walks past the other offices and to the typing pool. Every desk is secured in the same way. There are unfamiliar men standing around in ominous stance. Special Branch? Counter-intelligence? Some government security service? The strange men are not identified. One steps forward, the man in charge presumably, and announces, "This is a routine security inspection. No one here is under suspicion of any wrongdoing. However, each of you will permit one of my officers to examine the contents of your desk, in your presence. You will not remove tape or attempt access to your desks until you get clearance. This also applies to any briefcases, portfolios, pouches or other conveyances of papers or files. Any questions?" The unnamed government man understood that there would be no questions. As soon as he finished speaking, well, he was finished speaking.

John Cross addresses himself silently. "Stay calm. Stay calm. Think now, John Cross. What is in your briefcase? What is in your desk? I handed in my projects-in-progress last night as required. So the only thing in the desk is an incomplete crossword from 'The Times'. And the briefcase? Today's 'Manchester Guardian' and 20 Players Navy Cut cigarettes. There is nothing for Sonia in either place." He needs to conceal his shaking hand, and he urgently wants a smoke. He could always ask 'the man' if it is okay to smoke. He DID say 'any questions?' He finds this thought amusing under the circumstances and stifles a nervous laugh.

One of 'the men' approaches John Cross and addresses him. "So, you think this is funny?"

This is intended to intimidate him but, on John Cross, it has the opposite effect. It emboldens him. His hand stops shaking. His desire for a smoke dissipates. He attacks the unidentified security man with a verbal barrage, reaming off his rights under Common Law and Statute Law starting with the 'Magna Carta'. The security man is momentarily taken aback, but recovers quickly and places handcuffs on John Cross. And does this quieten John Cross? Not at all. His gift of oratory soars higher than any soapbox in Hyde Park's Speakers' Corner. John Cross is marched to his office where the search there is given special attention by a team of officers. His briefcase is cut apart. His desk is opened; each drawer is removed and smashed in a vain attempt to find hidden areas. The ceiling is prodded, the walls are poked. Finally, after nearly wrecking his office, the officers concede that there is nothing untoward unearthed. At this point the senior security man enters Cross's office. He looks around at the mess, and at the fatigued John Cross, now too hoarse to continue his verbal barrage.

'Senior man' addresses the team slowly and softly. "Find anything?"

"No, sir! Nothing."

"Hmm, a bit extreme, would you not say?" eyeing the mess.

"Yes, sir! But it was..."

'Senior man' holds up a finger, and there is instant silence. "That's all right, officer. I'll take it from here. Undo the cuffs."

"Yes, sir!"

John Cross notices that 'Senior man's' finger, the one he held up, the one now pointing at the cuffs, is heavily stained by nicotine. The mark of a heavy smoker.

'Senior man' addresses John Cross. "John Cross, is it not?"

"Yes. I'm John Cross."

"Well, John, I think we should go outside to cool off. I could do with a smoke in a quiet place. Do you have any cigarettes?" Both John and 'Senior man' look at the shredded tobacco on the floor, the remains of the 20 Players Navy Cut.

"No, sir. Not anymore."

"Ah. Then you'll have one of mine. Come."

'Senior man' walks down the stairs calmly and casually, as if on a Sunday stroll. John Cross wonders if this is an arrest, or detention, or if he will be 'held for questioning'. They go out the main door, cross the parking lot and 'Senior man' sits on the wall. "Sit down," he says invitingly. There is nothing threatening in his manner.

He is the same age as John Cross, 37. He speaks with an educated voice, like a diplomat. He is slightly taller than John Cross, but not by much, perhaps 5'10". He is thin and hollow-cheeked, with dark-ringed bloodshot eyes. These are the signs of a man who drinks too much and smokes too much and obtains insufficient sleep. John Cross sits down beside him.

'Senior man' takes a gold cigarette case from his inside pocket, snaps it open and offers it to John. John selects a cigarette, so does 'Senior man'. He takes a gold lighter from his other pocket and tenders the flame to John's cigarette, and then to his own. Both men take a few drags. Both inhale deeply.

"John Cross."

"Yes?"

"Do you know who I am?"

"No, sir."

"No idea at all? Any guess? Speculation?"

"Sir, I have absolutely no idea who you are or why you, or we, are here."

"Good." He inhales again, and turns to look into John Cross's face. "You see the mist?"

"Yes."

"The mist shields us from spy planes."

"I know that."

"But the Russians don't need planes to spy on us. Do they, Pyotr?" He said 'Pyotr' in perfect Russian.

John Cross's entire body freezes. Even his eyes stop blinking, his heart stops beating, and his lungs stop breathing. This state of petrification seems to last for ten minutes. But it is just a sensation of fear and helplessness. And it lasts but for a brief second.

'Senior man' returns his gaze to the parking lot, and continues to smoke. "John Cross, here is what you will do. And you will do it EXACTLY as I tell you. First, you should know that we have discovered a security leak in HER. It is an agent, code-named 'Pyotr'. You are a suspect. So are a few others. You are under constant surveillance. You are followed everywhere, 24 hours a day. Your office is bugged, your car is bugged, your house is bugged, your phone is tapped.... I won't go on. You get the picture. One move of yours that confirms our suspicion and you are picked up, detained, arrested, and so on...."

'Senior man' moves his smouldering cigarette in a circle to illustrate the unnamed things that might happen. John Cross has visions of interrogation and torture. These people, whoever they are, operate for the government, but outside the law. "But there are no bugs out here, other than nature's bugs. So we can talk." Another drag on his cigarette and he continues. "You see, John, all this here today, I arranged for your sole benefit. But I alone know that. And now, so do you."

"This is for my benefit? How can..."

"Shut up, John. I'm speaking." He says this not threateningly, but with impatience, as if to a scatter-brained child. 'Senior man' takes another drag of his cigarette, inhales deeply and continues. "The Americans sent me information. Something they intercepted in 1944 from Russian intelligence, but have just recently decrypted. It makes reference to 'Pyotr', and lists what he did. Let me tell you, John, when I look at what information was passed to the Russians, and in what manner, and in what time span, and through which Russian medium, I can deduce the following. 'Pyotr' was part of the British team at Los Alamos in 1944," he hesitates, "and 'Pyotr' is the current leak at HER. There is only one person here at HER who was also at Los Alamos in 1944. Only one possible person."

Another drag on the cigarette, and he continues. "The American file is on my desk. At 8:00am Monday morning I will give the contents of this file to my operatives. I will point out the connection. At one minute past 8:00am on Monday morning, your door will be broken open and you will be taken into custody. Should you decide to run or hide, you will be arrested that much sooner. Any attempt to contact your Russian agent or the Russian Embassy will result in your immediate arrest. Don't dream of going to 44 Wellington Street, Manchester, letterbox 44D, in the common hallway of the apartment building."

John Cross is shocked even further. 'Senior man' knows the drop-off location of his deliveries. He moans aloud, "I'm...I'm..."

"Shut up, John. I'M talking. YOU will listen; and will do what you are told." His cigarette is almost burned down. "Tonight, you will walk – it's important that you WALK. You will walk from your house to the oak tree at the centre of Cheshire. You will time it to arrive there at 12:00 midnight. One minute earlier, or one minute later, and you will fail."

John wants to ask 'fail what?' but continues to listen and commit to memory.

"There, you will receive instructions. Follow them EXACTLY." 'Senior man' stands up, throws his cigarette butt on the ground and stubs it out with his sole. "Okay, John. Let's go back to your office and see what state it's in."

Back at John Cross's office, 'Senior man' summons the director of the facility to view the disorder. It will take a couple of days to get a new desk for John Cross and to clean up his office and repair the damage.

The director complains, "I don't know where we'll put Doctor Cross until then."

'Senior man' offers a solution, "So it seems that John Cross will spend today and tomorrow at home?"

"I suppose so," and turning to John, "Doctor Cross, you may take two days off. But don't take any work home with you." Clearly, the director is unhappy. But is this what 'Senior man' engineered?

An hour later, John Cross is sitting in his living room, looking out the rear window towards the garden. He looks sideways to the mantle clock. It is almost 11:00am. It's going to be a long day until midnight. He reaches his hand out to the cigarette box on the side table, and is surprised that his hand fails to connect. "That's funny," he thinks aloud. "I don't remember moving the chair, or moving the..." John Cross jumps up in panic and rushes out to the garden. He takes a rake and pretends to work, making his way to the rubbish pile. He prods at it and is relieved to see that Sonia's package is still in among the brambles. He throws a few more random twigs on the heap and sets it alight. "There. That was close. Could they have found anything untoward in the house? Well, nothing of interest, surely. Thank God I moved that package last night." John Cross is aware of the change in himself. He is an atheist and never says 'Thank God'. That is, not until today. Now he is hopeful that there IS a God. For if there is no God, whose hand will protect John Cross?

John Cross waits for the fire to burn down. Then he douses the hot ashes with a pail of water to extinguish all sparks. Satisfied with his work in the garden, he returns to the house. He needs to plan his visit to the oak tree. That is his immediate priority. He addresses himself aloud. "Okay. So where is this bloody oak tree? I know that it is close, but where exactly?" It is early afternoon now. John Cross decides on his course of action. He visits the library on Lewin Street.

12:35pm on a Thursday in summer, the library is quiet and empty of people. The librarian is eager to be of help. John Cross looks 'bookish' and she has no other clients. John Cross requests help. "I'm looking for walking paths, local walking paths that are not too strenuous."

"Of course. But keep your voice down," she whispers. "What have you in mind?" She can tell by John's mode of dress that he is not likely to be an avid hiker. "There are nice walks along the canal that are not too difficult. And you can always stop at a pub or teahouse during the walk. Would that interest you?"

John adopts the level of whisper appropriate to a library. "I was thinking of the oak tree that is at the centre of Cheshire."

"Now, that's a three-mile walk. But mostly on level ground. From here it would take you about an hour to walk. But from Eve Street it is a bit less, more like 50 minutes."

John Cross raises his eyebrows in surprise. How could the librarian know where he lives?

The librarian suddenly realises that she had crossed the line of acceptable library decorum by suggesting that she is knowledgeable of the client's personal life. She blushes, extracts a handkerchief from her sleeve and idiosyncratically dabs at her eye. "Oh, I'm so sorry, sir. I did not intend to get personal. I was just trying to be of help."

John looks at her nameplate so that he can address her by name, but the nameplate bears the word 'SILENCE'. "No offence, Miss, Miss...it's just a surprise to me that anyone would know me. Miss, Miss..."

"My name is 'Daisy'. And I'm really sorry..."

"Daisy, I'm grateful for your assistance. Please continue. You were saying that from Eve Street to the oak tree is a 50-minute walk?"

"Yes. I can show you on the map, Mr..."

"John Cross. That's my name."

"Ah, yes, Mr. John Cross."

"It's just 'John'. No 'Mister'"

Daisy produces a folded map from a pigeonhole in her desk and unfolds it. "I can show you on the map, (cough) John." Daisy dabs her eyes again and regains her composure. "Go to the A533. There is a sidewalk from Eve Street. See here, I'll mark it for you. From there you follow the dotted line. Follow the A533 to Bostock Green. There is no name on the road in Bostock Green. And here..." she places an 'X' in the square on the map and encircles it, "...is the oak tree. There is a sidewalk all the way, except for this length of the A533. You can walk along the pedestrian trail, if you like. Here it is on the map. See, it follows the Trent & Mersey canal to here. And then along the Dane river to here. And then across this field along a lane to the farmhouse next to the oak tree, here. Of course, the A533 is shorter and flatter, but watch out for traffic."

Daisy hands the map to John, still in the open position. John studies it. Daisy coughs again and enquires of John Cross. "John. I don't mean to pry. But have you a reason to walk to the oak tree?"

"Oh. Just for good luck."

"Ah. I thought so."

John Cross wonders what Daisy could have thought. Maybe it's just a figure of speech she uses to continue talking.

"Then I must tell you about the 'good luck' part. The good luck is strongest at the full moon, but that's a fortnight away. The next best time is at the new moon, and that's tomorrow night. Do you know how to do it? The good luck part?"

John Cross has no clue as to what she is referring. But she is undoubtedly continuing to talk. "The 'good luck' part?"

"Of course. You must do it right. You must walk – the good luck only works if the pilgrim walks; you must arrive at the sacred oak at midnight – not a minute too early, or a minute too late; you must walk around the tree three times clockwise. Don't walk counter-clockwise. Some people walk counter-clockwise, and they get no luck at all."

John Cross is thrown off balance by these instructions. This is similar to 'Senior man's' instructions. Is there a connection? Is Daisy something other than a librarian? John Cross folds the map as he ponders this.

Before he can leave, Daisy whispers, "John. Forgive me if I am being presumptuous. But here is something else you may be interested in." Daisy takes a folded information leaflet from another pigeonhole. She opens it and makes a mark in pencil. She refolds it and hands it to John Cross. "It's just something...something...well, you can read it."

"Thanks, Daisy. I'll be sure to read it." John Cross places the folded map and the folded leaflet in his inside pocket and he goes to the exit door. As he swings open the glass door he momentarily sees the reflection of a figure standing at a bookshelf. He turns as he goes through the doorway, glancing back. There is no one in sight other than Daisy. She gives him a faint wave. He smiles and waves back, and then he departs.

"Okay, John Cross," he says to himself. "What now?" John Cross needs a few minutes to think. He sees the 'Crowing Cock' across the street and two doors up. He crosses the street, enters the pub, and finds a private cubicle far away from the bar and out of sight of windows. He places his palms against his forehead and leans on his elbows with eyes shut. He thinks, "Daisy said 'I thought so'. She knows where I live. She gave me instructions similar to what I received from 'Senior man'. What all does she know? And was there someone observing us in the library? If there was, he was certainly out of earshot – Daisy insisted on whispering."

"So what will it be?"

The unexpected voice brings John Cross back to his surroundings. Being deep in thought, he had forgotten where he is.

"Sorry. Did I startle you? My name is 'Bess'. I am your waitress. Are you here to drink or eat?"

"Well, both actually. And smoke. Is that all right?"

"Of course. Do you need a moment?"

"No, no. Could I have 20 Players Medium, a pint of bitter and...? What is your 'special' today?"

"The same as every day – shepherd's pie, steak & kidney pie, fish 'n' chips."

"...and shepherd's pie, please."

"Ah. A gentleman. For saying 'please' you get an extra helping." Bess smiles at John Cross as she says this. He realises that she is being friendly to him. He smiles back. He is unaccustomed to this. Bess goes off to place his order.

John Cross pulls out the map and leaflet from his pocket and spreads both on the table. He reads the information on the oak tree.

'The oak is a symbol of strength and firmness. In ancient times, at pivotal points in the lunar cycle, men would circle the oak to restore lost prowess. Women would conduct a similar ritual for fertility. There is the custom of a man and a woman performing the ritual hand-in-hand to ensure a fruitful union.' John Cross casts his eyes to the leaflet. It is entitled *'Ancient Cures and Remedies'*. He flips it over to page four and sees a recipe for oak bark tea. *'Oak bark tea is a strong astringent for the treatment of throat and mouth infections,'* He runs his eyes down to where Daisy marked with her pencil *'...and to enhance male performance.'*

John Cross replays in his mind the conversation he had with Daisy. He had misled Daisy in his enquiry, and she was being helpful. John Cross thinks back. When was anyone helpful to him before? Once, a long time ago, back in Lanarkshire. The people in High Explosive Research? They are professionally polite and courteous at best, but usually a pain. But friendly? Never. In HER it's all about performance, results, try again, more results, better results. He berates himself. "John Cross. Fifteen years of your life spent with instruments of death." John Cross is aware of moisture at his eyes. He puts his hand in his pocket to take out a handkerchief, but there isn't one there. A paper serviette is thrust into his hand.

"Is everything all right, sir?" Bess places the pint of bitter and the cigarettes on the table.

"I ah, I ah...hay fever." John Cross is embarrassed.

Bess takes the pack of cigarettes, opens it and pushes a cigarette half-way out. John Cross takes it, puts it in his mouth. Bess strikes a match and puts it to the cigarette. John Cross draws deeply. "Your shepherd's pie will be another few minutes," she says.

"Thanks. Okay. Bess?"

"That's right. It's Bess," she says, pointing to her name badge.

"Thanks, Bess."

Bess goes off and John Cross is alone again. "For God's sake, John Cross. Pull yourself together," he scolds himself. "Good God. That's twice today I've said 'God'. Now it's three times."

Bess returns with the pie and a glass of hot toddy. "The hot toddy is from George. No charge. George says you look like you need a pick-me-up."

"Who is George?"

"George is the landlord. He's behind the bar."

John Cross looks towards the bar. George is polishing glasses. He stops and gives John a brief salute. George goes back to his polishing.

"Shall I write up your bill now? You can pay George at the bar when you are finished." Bess is writing in her pad. She keeps up a conversation. "I haven't seen you in before. Have I?"

"No. You haven't."

"But I've seen you around."

"Indeed?"

"You drive one of those Morris Minors. Right?"

John swallows a lump of potato, "Well, yes..."

"That's what I thought." And she places the bill on the table. "Here you go. And if you require anything else, give me a wave. I can add it to the bill. Enjoy the shepherd's pie." Bess goes off and sits at the bar talking to George.

John Cross is worried again. "How come these strangers know me? First it was Daisy, now Bess. They can't all be government agents. 'Senior man' back at HER warned me that I am being watched 24 hours a day. Are they watching me, Daisy and Bess?" John Cross consumes his meal, drains his drinks, and lights up another cigarette. He grabs his bill and makes his way zigzag through the pub patrons to the bar. George is pumping pints.

"Was everything to your satisfaction, sir?"

"More than I could have hoped for. Thank you." John Cross places the bill with his cash, including a generous tip, on the counter. He pushes it towards George, who segregates the coins into the cash drawer, takes the pencil from atop his ear, makes a mark on the bill, and skewers it on a dangerous-looking spike beside the till. George slides the pencil back along his ear.

"Anything else?"

"No thanks." John hesitates and stubs out his cigarette in the ashtray. "Well, actually, there IS something."

"Yes?" George is pouring, polishing and serving while having this conversation with John Cross. He even manages to exchange words with other customers at the bar. He is juggling four conversations all at the same time quite effortlessly.

"I get the feeling that people know me – people I have never met before...."

"Like Bess?" glancing to the other side of the saloon where Bess is busy.

"Yes. Like Bess. And Daisy at the library."

George chuckles. "It's a small village." George reads the puzzled look on John's face and demonstrates an explanation. Without taking his eyes off John Cross, George raises his voice loud enough to be heard at the end of the bar counter. "Fred!"

'Fred', who is leaning on the counter sharing a joke with one of his mates, looks up at George. He slides his drink, a pint of bitter, along the counter and approaches. "Hey, George! And what's up?"

"Fred. Who is this gentleman here?" he says, looking at John Cross.

"Why, Mr. Cross, of course."

"And where does Mr. Cross live?"

"No. 4 Eve Street." Fred takes a swallow from his glass, changes his mind, and chugs down the remaining contents until his glass is drained. "Aah! Another pint of bitter, George. And get one for Mr. Cross here."

"Not yet, Fred. One more question. What make of car does Mr. Cross drive?"

"Morris Minor. Get us the pint, George."

George smiles an 'I-told-you-so' look at John Cross, who is still trying to figure it out, and he goes to pump the pints.

John Cross is intensely curious. He cannot help but enquire of Fred. "So, Fred..."

"Yes, Mr. Cross?" Fred is looking at the pints being pumped, impatiently waiting.

"So, how do you know this, Fred?"

"What? Where you live and all? Well, it would be funny if I didn't know, considering that I place a pint of milk on your doorstep each morning before six. 'Drinka pinta milka day'. That's my slogan written on the milk cart. One pint for one person. Right? Lord, I've been coming to you for nigh on four year now."

Fred is distracted by the arrival of the two pints. "Thanks, George.

"Oh. And Mr. Cross. Don't forget to put the money under the empty bottle tonight. You forgot last Friday." He gives John Cross a friendly thump on the back and slides his glass along the counter to rejoin his mates.

John Cross shouts after him, "Oh, Right! And thanks for the..." He was about to say 'pint', but Fred may regard it as a lame joke.

George smiles at John Cross. "See?"

"And Daisy and Bess?"

"Villagers. Every young single lady here knows who you are. You are single, thirty-something, a house and a car. What do you expect? Where are you from anyhow that you don't know this?"

"Lanarkshire."

"And is it not like that in Lanarkshire?"

"You know, George, it is exactly the same. I had forgotten."

"And how could you forget.... Ah, Bess. This gentleman was talking about you." Bess has returned to the bar.

"Mr. Cross, the gentleman with the Morris Minor? Well, I hope he was saying nice things about me." She looks at John Cross with pretend annoyance.

She directs her attention back to George to talk business. Changing from her cheery voice to her serious voice, she says, "George, the out-of-towner back there."

"The one who talks like the 'six o'clock news'?"

"Yes, him. He bought one glass of lager over an hour ago, and he hasn't touched a drop of it."

"Is that right? And when did he come in?"

"Oh, the same time as Mr. Cross here."

"That's strange."

John Cross follows their gaze to get a glimpse of the 'six o'clock news man'.

"Well, he's not there now," says George. "He must have left."

"And his drink is still untouched."

John Cross is looking at an empty table at the far side of the room, an empty table with a full glass of lager. Once more, a cold shiver ripples over him.

Time for John Cross to leave too.

CHAPTER THIRTEEN

THE OAK

Thursday 13 July 1950
Cheshire, England

10:00pm. John Cross is anxious. 10:01, 10:02... It is too soon to leave the house. He sits smoking. He stubs out his cigarette and stretches his hand out in his usual manner to obtain another one. "Blast," he says suddenly, as he realises that the cigarette box is empty. He has smoked the last of his cigarettes. As with most people who live alone, he frequently speaks aloud to himself. This is one of those times. "I will get more at the garage at the crossroads of the A533. There is a petrol station there and they have a little shop that sells cigarettes and polo mints." He sits fidgety for a few minutes. But John Cross cannot sit still. "I must do something. I could go early, walk past the oak tree, and then turn back to be there at 12:00 midnight. No, I was told to do 'exactly' as instructed. I know. I'll go to the garage shop, purchase cigarettes and thumb through the maps and magazines for a while."

Having come to this decision, John Cross leaves by the front door. He reaches the street and stops. "What does one wear on a one-hour walk at night?" He goes back inside and puts on an overcoat and fedora. He walks down to the street again. He stops a second time. He realises that it is the middle of July. He will be too hot in a winter coat. John Cross looks up and down the street looking for inspiration. Old Mr. Jones from No. 8 goes by walking his dog. Mr. Jones walks every night, and Mr. Jones is wearing a black mac and is jauntily swinging a walking stick. John Cross returns to his house and finally decides that an ankle-length black mac and a fedora is the appropriate attire. He foregoes the walking stick because he has none. Black oxfords are his only shoes. No need to delay in choosing footwear.

At last John Cross is stepping along Eve Street and down to the A533. He glances at his wristwatch. It is 10:45. "This is perfect. I can adjust my walking speed, slow down for a smoke, or whatever, and time my arrival at the oak tree for 12:00 midnight." The night is dark – of course, it is the new moon tomorrow. Not pitch dark, however. There is a glow in the summer night sky. It is a civilised part of the country. There are roadside lights at intervals, and John Cross sets a rhythm to his stride.

Upon reaching the A533, John Cross is disappointed at seeing the garage in darkness. He walks to the entrance door and reads 'Open from 7:00am to 10:00pm Monday to Friday'. "Blast! Blast! Blast!" Through the glass door John Cross perceives a shelf full of cigarettes inside the shop. He looks at his watch. 10:52pm. It would take over ten minutes to walk back into Middlethorpe, to the Crowing Cock, to get cigarettes. And from the centre of Middlethorpe the walk to the oak is one hour, more or less. In his case probably more. No choice, but to continue, sans cigarettes.

John consults his map. He identifies landmarks along the way and determines that he is making good time. The footpath at the roadside terminates. He continues on the roadway. The A533 turns sharp left, but the map indicates that he should proceed straight ahead. The signpost has an arrow pointing left, to the west, with writing 'NORTHORPE 5 MILES'. John Cross proceeds straight ahead onto the unmarked road of the estate. The road is small but well paved. It also has a wide footpath. It is well lit and is straight. He encounters a spring in a little cave at the roadside. It is spilling water into a catch basin where horses and cattle can drink. Using his hand, John Cross spoons some water from the spilling fountain, and drinks. Refreshed, he resumes his walk.

John Cross observes a few houses in the near distance. He consults the map once more and is able to identify them. He has walked two miles and has one more mile to go. The map gives the estimated walking time, 20 minutes to reach the spot – the square on the map in which Daisy had placed the 'X' and a circle. He consults his watch. It is 23 minutes to midnight. John Cross could walk faster, or walk slower, whichever is required to time his arrival at the oak at precisely 12:00 midnight. He is confident that he will succeed.

There are a few people out walking, mostly walking back towards Middlethorpe. John Cross sees one person ahead walking in the same direction. He glances about. There is no sign of his Russian contact or of Special Branch agents. There are no cars on the road, neither parked nor moving. The road is lined with mature trees. Could someone be hiding in the trees, watching him? There is a curve ahead. He loses sight of the solitary walker ahead because of the bend. He glances back. There is no one in sight. If he is being watched or followed, as 'Senior man' warned, they are well hidden. Rounding the curve he catches sight of the walker again. Up ahead the line of trees terminates. According to the map, there are three farmhouses ahead and nine single-storey houses. There are two other walkers coming south towards him. John Cross will likely overtake the solitary walker and meet the oncoming walkers before reaching the oak.

Nearing the solitary walker, John Cross sees that it is a roly-poly little fat man out walking his terrier. The man's cheeks are red. Red from the effort of walking, or naturally red, John Cross cannot tell. He hears the man wheezing as he walks. He is in his late sixties and is not at all fit. He waddles as he walks and the terrier is impatiently pulling on the leash to encourage greater speed. John Cross peers ahead in an attempt to locate the oak. There is no sign on the path that indicates its location, certainly no flashing lights. Maybe he should ask the man. John Cross passes a large house on the right. He confirms this on the map. There are three small houses in a cluster ahead, and then he should be at the oak. Ninety yards. Why can't he see the oak? He slows his pace so that he can examine his surroundings accurately. Sixty yards. There is a copse of trees in front. But which one is the oak? Thirty yards. It is too dark to distinguish one tree from another.

In his effort to identify his destination, John Cross fails to notice how close he is to the wheezing man and trips over the terrier's leash. He stumbles off the edge of the footpath and pirouettes twice before regaining his balance. The terrier regards John Cross's performance as a threat. It runs at him and grips him by the leg of his trousers. The roly-poly man is upset and apologetic. John Cross is struggling in a tug-o-war with the terrier. Roly-poly man is pulling on the leash to haul the dog off to no avail. Now John Cross is struggling to limp, drag and hop his way for the last ten yards, while roly-poly and the terrier are pulling him back the way he came. The two walkers from the opposite direction stop briefly to laugh at the situation and then continue southwards at a leisurely pace. John Cross cannot see his watch but reckons that it must be midnight. With supreme effort he inches forward, dragging along the dog and roly-poly man. He holds on to the wooden fence at the side of the footpath and pulls himself along. Suddenly the trousers rip and the terrier lets go with a piece of John Cross's trousers still in his mouth. The counterbalance of dog and man thus gone, John Cross stumbles over the fence and lands on his back. He is winded and exhausted.

"What time is it?" he shouts at the man.

Roly-poly man interrupts his apology to consult his pocket watch. "Why, it's just gone 12 o'clock. Actually, it is one minute past 12...Now!" He snaps his watch shut. "It's an old railway watch, a stationmaster's watch. It's the most accurate watch you'll ever see. And why do you need to know the time, anyhow?"

"The oak. Where's the oak? The sacred oak. Where is it?"

At this roly-poly man laughs. Actually, he wheezes and laughs, and pants and laughs, being so much out of breath from the exertion of the tug-o-war. "Look up! You're such a silly man. Why you're lying under it."

John Cross glances up. Yes indeed, he is lying on his back looking up at the limbs and branches of a huge oak tree. The map, he remembers, indicated the location of the oak as a square. The square is actually the fence of the enclosure that surrounds the location of the oak tree. And over at the trunk there is a smaller square wooden fence, which also serves as a bench, and protects the tree from damage.

Roly-poly man makes his way into the enclosure through the appropriate opening in the fence. He hands John Cross his fedora. "I hope Towser hasn't done you any harm. Your hat seems okay from the look of it. But you? How do you feel? Are you able to get up?"

John Cross doesn't know whether to laugh or cry. He gets up, shakes himself and walks to the bench. He sits relieved with his back to the tree trunk. Towser is shaking the piece of torn trouser leg as if he were killing a rat.

Roly-poly man comes over to sit next to him. Roly-poly is still panting and sweating, his face ever so red. "I'm so sorry about all this. Oh, by the way, my name is Egbert." He extends a hand.

John accepts the handshake and introduces himself simply as 'John'.

"John, could you do me a favour. I'm so winded; I must rest for a moment. Could you take Towser over there to the bushes to do his business? Over there at the back, out of sight of the footpath. Then I'll be out of your way, and you can meet your friend."

"What friend?"

"Oh, I misunderstood. When you enquired about the time, I understood that you may have a romantic rendezvous."

John Cross tenders no explanation. He takes the leash and leads Towser to the rear bushes. He is anxious to be rid of the troublesome little man. Egbert shifts around in the bench to the same side to observe Towser.

"Pyotr," Egbert whispers. "The two men walking by — keep them out of sight."

John Cross freezes.

Egbert continues, "When I rise from the bench here, you will find a piece of folded paper underneath. Read it. Memorise it. Burn it. It is 'spy paper' so it will smoulder without flaming. You are due for a smoke, are you not? Crush the ashes of the burnt note and scatter them in the breeze. Follow the instructions to the letter. And one more thing, the ankle-length loose-fitting mac you are wearing, and the black fedora. That will work. So next time dress the same."

Egbert waits for a reply. John Cross is silent. "Do you understand?"

"Yes. Oh, I have no cigarettes."

"Really. You need the glow of a cigarette to read the note. But you have matches?"

"Yes."

"I will leave you one of my cigarettes."

Egbert rises and resumes his jolly voice. "Come, Towser. Come, boy." He takes the leash and waddles off, crosses the road and enters a lane in the direction of two farmhouses. Two hundred yards away, there is a car parked in a farm laneway waiting for Egbert.

John Cross sits down. He takes Egbert's cigarette from the bench and places it between his lips. He feels underneath the bench and finds a folded paper stuck to the wood. It feels like soft paper, the kind used for wrapping pears. This paper is unsuitable for writing. It tears easily. It falls apart when wet, and that includes wet ink. If he pulls roughly, the paper will surely tear. His finger locates the little strip of cellotape that is holding it. He gingerly peels it off the wood. He places the piece of folded paper against his black mac and leans his hip against it. He strikes a match and shuts his eyes against the glare. When the sound of the flare subsides, he opens one eye and directs the flame to his cigarette. He draws on the flame and extinguishes the match. From the laneway of the neighbouring farmhouse the two MI6 agents observe John Cross having a smoke.

John Cross extracts the paper from the shelter of his hip and rests it on his belly inside his open mac, like placing it inside the opening of a tent. The paper unfolds silently. Inside the folded paper he discovers a rolodex card. Taking the cigarette from his mouth he casually rests his elbow on his knee and tilts his cigarette back in towards himself. He holds the glowing smouldering tip close to the paper to provide sufficient light to read. The rolodex card is a beaten-up library membership card in the name of Peter Oldthorpe of

244 Nelson Street, Manchester. As John Cross suspected, the accompanying paper is unsuitable for pen and ink. The writing is in blue pencil crayon, the kind used by auditors.

Read   Memorise   Destroy

Go to your bank and close all accounts
Retain enough cash for two weeks
Transfer the remainder to
Westminster Bank, 101 Shale Street, Manchester
Account no 10101055 in name of Donald Blunt

Destroy all identification in the name of John Cross –
drivers licence, membership cards; everything that
bears the name John Cross.

Meet here tomorrow night at the same time
at <u>precisely midnight</u>

Carry nothing except what you are wearing.
John Cross will cease to exist as of midnight
tomorrow.

You are now Pyotr Staryygorodsky
*Enter Russia as **Пётр Старийгородский***
*on **Аэрофлот**. The airline will board you in this name.*

Your English name is Peter Oldthorpe
Carry this identification only.

You will be brought to your next contact –
***Белый** at St. Bawn's*

John Cross feels a chill. What does it mean 'will cease to exist'? He reads it again. He shuts his eyes and recites it, and checks to make sure he has memorised it correctly. He touches his cigarette to the top of the sheet. Immediately a spark spreads across the top like a crawling worm. He reads the note one last time moving his eyes ahead of the creeping spark. As ash forms and curls, he crushes it between thumb and finger and flicks it to the breeze. He hears the faint sound of a car far away to the west, the direction in which Egbert went. The smouldering spark finishes its journey to the end of the piece of paper held between the fingernails of thumb and forefinger. John Cross lets go and watches the final spark consume the remaining paper and drift to the ground between his feet. The falling spark is indistinguishable from the spark of cigarette ash that John Cross dislodges. He bends down and rubs the last piece of ash with his thumb and brushes it away. All this takes place in the tented concealment of his open mac.

The hidden MI6 agents wait for John Cross to finish his smoke. He crushes the cigarette butt under his shoe, gets up from the bench, walks around to the front of the tree and makes his way out of the enclosure to the roadside footpath.

The Secret Intelligence Service, commonly known as MI6, is Britain's foreign intelligence service, and is tasked with the covert overseas collection and analysis of intelligence in support of national security. 'Pyotr' came to their attention as a result of foreign operations and shared information obtained via the American Department in the Foreign Office, and this operation falls within their mandate of counterproliferation.

The two MI6 agents in Bostock Green could take John Cross in for questioning, but they decide against it for two reasons. First, as of yet they have insufficient proof to detain him and his premature arrest could backfire and expose their operation to the domestic agency, Security Service MI5. And secondly, even if Cross is truly passing information to the Russians then he is only a low-level agent. MI6 suspects that there is an actual Russian spy ring in extensive operation, one that they are unable to penetrate. If they are patient and vigilant, Cross could lead them to 'Sonia', or even to the elusive 'Bélyy' – the Bélyy who is the primary objective of their current 'Code White' operation. The two agents wait for an opportune time and place.

And so John Cross fastens his black mac, secures his fedora firmly on his head, and walks back unchallenged to No. 4 Eve Street, Middlethorpe.

CHAPTER FOURTEEN

THE OAK AT MIDNIGHT

Friday 14 July 1950
Cheshire, England

John Cross has had a busy day. Everything is done as he was instructed. He has closed all his bank accounts and transferred the funds as directed, having retained two week's expense money. He could get by on £1, but £5 is more prudent. He finally decides that £10 would cover any unexpected expenses. John Cross pats his pocket and feels the bulge of ten £1 notes. His driver's licence is gone, his car insurance certificate is gone, all his certificates of education and achievements awards are gone. Everything that bears the name 'John Cross' is now just the dying wisps of smoke in the garden fire-pit. He walks out his front door, leaving his house keys and car keys behind him on the hall table. He checks his inside pocket for his sole piece of identification, the Manchester library rolodex card in the name of Peter Oldthorpe on which he has scribbled '*Белый at St. Bawn's*'. Satisfied that he is ready to leave, John Cross shuts his front door, and 'Peter Oldthorpe' steps his way along Eve Street and down to the A533. He is dressed the same as on the previous night: black oxfords, black mac and black fedora. He glances at his wristwatch. It is 10:45pm. This time he has an adequate supply of cigarettes. He lights a cigarette and says "Okay, Peter Oldthorpe. There is no turning back now."

Upon reaching the A533, Peter Oldthorpe (he is already adjusted to the new name) sees the closed garage and strides past it without giving it any attention. Tonight is the new moon. There are a few others out walking tonight. Peter Oldthorpe catches up with a couple. He strides past them and hears the young lady address him.

"Mr. Cross?"

He turns and looks back.

"It's Mr. Cross, isn't it? Mr. Cross who drives the Morris Minor?"

It is the waitress from the Crowing Cock, Bess. "Bess, I did not recognise you...."

"Because I'm not in an apron?" And to her male companion, "Charlie, George tells me that Mr. Cross here was talking about me in the pub yesterday. What do you think of that?"

To which Charlie replies, "Well, that depends on what he was saying. Doesn't it?"

Peter Oldthorpe (John Cross) is a bit embarrassed and attempts an explanation. "I was surprised that anyone could know me...."

Bess pretends not to hear and continues talking to Charlie. "Mr. Cross has been living here for four years, and he doesn't know ANYONE in Middlethorpe. And he is surprised that we all know about him. How about that?"

Oldthorpe/Cross is still attempting an explanation and apology. Charlie and Bess still pretend not to hear him. Charlie responds to Bess. "Knows nobody? Not at the pub? The church? Not anybody at all?" Oldthorpe/Cross now realises that they are taking the mickey. He falls in stride with them and plays along.

Bess is dressed in a navy-blue gabardine coat. Because it is night, it appears black, but he knows that it is the style of coat popular with schoolgirls. She is also wearing a beret and black walking shoes. Yes, she looks all the world like a teenage English schoolgirl. Charlie looks like he is still in his teens too. He is dressed in a blazer, a school blazer perhaps? Light grey trousers and white shirt and black oxfords, and sporting a dark grey herringbone flat cap. He may or may not be wearing a tie. Flung around his neck is a long muffler scarf trailing down his back. A college scarf, perhaps? He walks with both hands in his trouser pockets. Bess has linked his arm and playfully tugs or pushes it to knock him off stride.

Bess and Charlie continue with their ribbing. "You know, Charlie, Mr. Cross DOES know someone in Middlethorpe."

"He does? Who might that be?"

"I think Daisy has taken a shine to him."

"You mean Daisy Wright, the librarian? No!"

Bess turns to Peter Oldthorpe/Cross. "We're all going to the sacred oak. No? For the new moon ritual. Are we not?" Bess does not wait for a response. As far as she is concerned there is only one reason to be walking this route at this time. "How come you're not walking with Daisy then?" Bess talks so much, there is little room for a response. She continues, "No, I suppose not. Daisy is one of the druids. All the druids walk along the riverbank, along the Dane, and come out by a laneway at the house beside the oak. That's the way the druids of old made their way to the oak. You're not a druid then, Mr. Cross?" and she nudges Charlie, "I'm not even sure if he is an adherent."

"Ah, a non-believer?"

Peter Oldthorpe/Cross does a rapid mental calculation. Druids? That's two thousand years ago. The oak tree can't be more than 300 years old. "The oak tree can't be that old...."

"Of course it is," replies Bess.

"It's not the original oak," counters Charlie.

"Yes, it is."

This time Charlie interrupts Bess and continues with the explanation of the oak tree. "There was once an ancient oak tree in the same spot. I don't know how old it was, but everyone believed that it was from ancient times. During the civil war, in 1646, just before the Siege of Goodrich Castle, there was a battle here – the battle of Bostock Green. It was not a decisive battle, more of a skirmish. But one thing of significance was the appearance of a new cannon, the 'Roaring Meg', that the Parliamentarians wanted to test. The Roaring Meg fired a 2cwt hollow ball filled with gunpowder with devastating effect, but totally unsuitable for the battlefield. It was designed for siege warfare. At the battle of Bostock Green, the only fatality at the hands of the Puritans was the sacred oak. Roaring Meg destroyed the oak."

"No, it didn't! The sacred oak got DAMAGED."

Charlie continues, ignoring Bess's interruption. "Some years later, Lord Bostock planted a new oak tree in the same spot."

"No. That's not how it happened at all. The sacred oak was struck by lightning and burned to the ground. Everyone believed that to be the end of the oak, having survived from druid times. But a year later a new shoot appeared coming through the ground from the roots. You see, the oak was damaged, but the destruction was only above ground. The roots survived. And what you see today is the same oak that the druids revered long ago." And turning to Peter Oldthorpe/Cross, "Don't listen to Charlie here. He only knows what they are taught at college. If you want the true story, you must ask Daisy or one of the druids."

They continue straight where the A533 turns left. Peter Oldthorpe hears again the trickle of running water. Charlie and Bess stop to drink from the fountain. Peter Oldthorpe glances up and down and every which way. There is no sign

217

of any of the men that Egbert warned him about on the previous night. He lights another cigarette and checks the time. He is satisfied that they are on schedule. It is a 20-minute walk from here to the oak. And the time is 25 minutes to midnight. Having satisfied their thirst, Charlie and Bess rejoin him, and they continue in the direction of the oak.

Twelve minutes later they come to the bend in the road. It's a ten-minute walk from here, but at Bess and Charlie's pace, thirteen minutes is more likely. Peter Oldthorpe is confident of reaching the oak at precisely twelve o'clock. If necessary, he can speed up or slow down to get the timing right. Having rounded the bend, he is now within sight of the oak or, to be more accurate, within sight of the house beside the oak, a distance of three furlongs. He spots two men ahead, also walking in the direction of the oak. The men from last night? They might be, or might not. He never got a good look at either of them. At this pace, Peter Oldthorpe expects to catch up with them. But this in itself is not suspicious. If they are also headed to the oak for midnight, of course they would be walking more slowly, being so much closer.

Five minutes from the oak, and from up ahead, in the distance, Peter Oldthorpe hears flute music and drumming.

"Oh, no," exclaims Bess. "Not the Irish. The damn Irish are here with their tin whistles and stupid drums."

"So what's wrong with the Irish?" Peter Oldthorpe asks.

"They are loud, most likely drunk. And they don't observe the correct ritual. Not in the way the druids explained to us. And THEY know the ritual from ancient times." Clearly, Bess is upset at the intrusion of 'heretics' at the ritual.

Charlie laughs in amusement. "Mr. Cross, Bess here, and the local druids, are jealous of the Irish. You see, the Irish actually talk to the oak, and they claim that the oak communicates to them. None of the druids here can make such a claim. They are upset because the loud drunken Irish always manage to upstage them."

Peter Oldthorpe can make out the party of Irish approaching from the other side. Although it is a moonless night, it is not pitch dark. It is easy to make out figures, but not features. There are two lots of Irish. About six men are out in front. Two are playing tin whistles, and one is drumming on a mummer's hand drum. A group of women in black and tartan shawls are walking behind them. Peter Oldthorpe cannot make out their numbers because they are huddled together behind the men. There appears to be a couple of children too. He then realises that his view of the Irish group is not obstructed by any walkers ahead. What happened to the two men? Where did they go? Peter Oldthorpe begins to feel troubled. Egbert was right. He is being watched.

Bess is still complaining about the presence of the Irish. "Look at those cockamamie caps they wear."

"Flat caps," Charlie informs her.

"No, they're not. You're wearing a flat cap, Charlie. These Irish are wearing caps that stick up and come down to their eyes."

"No. Watch." Charlie takes off his flat cap and unclasps the peak. He puts it back on his head and says to Bess. "See? Now don't I look Irish?"

Bess can't help laughing. She pushes Charlie off the sidewalk onto the road, where he pretends to stagger drunkenly back to the pathway. "And look at those overcoats. Overcoats in summer? Do you know why they wear overcoats, unfastened, unbuttoned and unbelted?" As usual, Bess continues with the answer to her own question. "Bottles of black porter carried hidden inside. Their overcoats are their own portable bars."

Charlie rearranges his flat cap back to a flat cap shape. He makes a face as if to say "So what?"

Coming around the corner of the house beside the oak, from the laneway to the river, six figures emerge, completely enveloped in white hooded robes, all carrying burning candles. Their arrival at the roadside coincides with the party of Irish walking south. Bess, Charlie and Peter Oldthorpe, walking north, meet up with them at the entrance to the oak enclosure. It is twelve o'clock midnight.

They all troop in and encircle the oak. The druids are sombre and silent. Their faces are concealed. One hood shifts slightly and rights itself again. Peter Oldthorpe catches a glimpse of Daisy who gives him a momentary look of recognition.

The Irish musicians cease playing. They put their instruments inside their overcoats, which Bess is certain contain a stock of black porter. There are over twenty people assembled in the small space. An orderly inner circle forms, and an undefined outer circle forms. The six druids are in the inner circle. They place their burning candles on the bench surrounding the trunk. Bess and Charlie join them. Bess gestures to Peter Oldthorpe to come too. But he declines. He is about to step back to the outer circle when one of the druids grabs him by the elbow and pulls him in. Now he is in step with the other eight. With arms linked, they walk sideways around the oak, three times clockwise. Then they stop. Unlink arms. And approach the trunk close enough to lean a hand on the bark. Peter Oldthorpe does likewise. After a minute or so, they retreat back from the trunk and join the outer circle. The candles are still burning on the bench around the base of the tree.

The Irish musicians start up again. A group of Irish break from the outer circle and approach the oak. Three of the men and four of the women form a new inner circle. As before, Peter Oldthorpe steps back to the outer circle, but once again, he is grabbed and taken into the inner circle. This time they don't walk. The music is frantic. The group encircles the tree; they dance vigorously with knees flying high. Clockwise, and then counter-clockwise, and then...Peter Oldthorpe loses track, he loses his balance, and would undoubtedly fall over except for the tightness of the circle. The smell from the Irish is peculiar. Yes, there is the unmistakable smell of porter, but what is the strange smell of smoke?

Suddenly they stop. The musicians cease. All are motionless. Peter Oldthorpe expects to place his palm against the bark as before. But no. The group addresses the oak. Facing the trunk they chant up to its branches, "Dara! Dara! Dara!" After a moment's silence, they resume the chant. Peter Oldthorpe gets a dig in the ribs and interprets this as his invitation to join the chant. Peter and the Irish all chant up at the overhanging branches, "Dara! Dara! Dara!" One of the women from the outer circle breaks through to the oak. Her tartan shawl covers her head and her body all the way to the ground. The inner circle moves back to merge with the outer circle.

The Irish girl beside Peter Oldthorpe whispers to him. "Shh, Shanwar."

Peter realises that Daisy told him nothing of this. All observe silence, even the druids and disapproving Bess. It is so quiet now they hear the flames of the candles flickering in the breeze. The Irish are all looking up at the branches. The English are also caught up in the solemnity of the ritual. They are, for the moment, at one with the Irish. The flames flicker audibly and a breeze shakes the upper branches. One oak leaf flutters to the ground. Oak does not shed leaves in July. This is regarded as a portent.

"Where did it land?" someone whispers.

"Shh!"

"Is it shiny side up or dull side up?"

"Shh! Wait for Shanwar to speak."

"Who did it land at? Is it pointing to or away?"

A crying wailing voice, like a keen, emits from the mouth of Shanwar. "The Sacred Oak speaks. See the leaf, the oak's message. See how the leaf lies between two stones. Is the shiny side up? No. Is the dull side up? No. It is bent in a curve and the edge is to the ground. There is no luck – neither good luck nor bad luck. Empty of luck. It is bent, pointing away AND pointing toward one person. Heed this. This person has no past; this person has no future; this person can bring no joy to the marriage bed."

Shanwar is pointing to the leaf. She slowly raises her pointing finger. All eyes follow her finger as it rises from the ground to the person standing over the leaf. Her moving finger stops to point at Peter Oldthorpe, still known as John Cross.

Peter Oldthorpe to be, John Cross no more, experiences a cold shiver even though he is not superstitious. The music starts up again before he has time to dwell on the Shanwar's curse. This time it is more frantic. Peter Oldthorpe is lifted once more into the tight circle of dancers. Around and around he is spun. He stumbles and is righted. Peter Oldthorpe speaks aloud to himself attempting to hold himself together. "My hat. I've lost my hat. No. There it is, back again. No. That's not my hat; it too low down on my eyes. I'm stumbling again. Blast. I spun clear out of my coat. Wait? Someone's put it back on. The music has stopped, but I am so dizzy I cannot stand. Thankfully I am being held up on both sides. Please, someone walk me to where I may lie down."

He hears the sound of a car. Then, thankfully, he is placed lying down. Peter Oldthorpe senses motion and hears the sound of a car accelerating. Speaking to no one in particular, he asks, "I am in a car? Am I going somewhere?"

To Bess and Charlie and Daisy, and to any observer, John Cross's experience is viewed with a different perspective. He is dancing with the drunken Irish, stumbling around the oak. It is somewhat amusing for the onlookers. The musicians cease playing, and the Irish dancers break formation and walk away from the oak, stumbling and staggering together. The druids retrieve their candles. John Cross extricates himself from the dancers and stands alone at the back of the enclosure. They know it must be John Cross. He is the only one here in a black mac and a fedora. They do not realise that this is not John Cross, but a John Cross decoy wearing his fedora and mac. They pay little attention to the three staggering Irish in their unclasped peaked Irish soft caps and unfastened overcoats, staggering towards the entrance of the enclosure. They are inattentive to the white van that drives slowly past the oak enclosure. Without actually stopping, the three staggering Irish are swished through the back doors of the van and taken off in the direction of Northorpe. If anyone notices, it is with relief at the removal of the drunken Irish. Isn't it always like this? Some of the Irish always get drunk and need to be removed and be transported away like bags of cement from a construction site.

The druids assemble for their walk back to Middlethorpe via the river Dane. The rest of the Irish walk north in the direction from whence they came. Bess and Charlie set off south along the roadway.

Daisy looks for John Cross. She sees him standing alone in the dark at the rear of the enclosure, but she fails to get his attention.

Bess turns around and shouts to him, "Mr. Cross! Do you want to walk back with us?"

John Cross makes no reply. He walks through the enclosure and continues straight across the road into Brick Kiln Lane.

"Don't go home by Brick Kiln Lane. It's the long way," Bess shouts.

Charlie nudges Bess. "He's gone to relieve himself."

"Oh, I believe you're right. I see him standing at the hedge in the lane."

Charlie and Bess walk slowly south in the direction of Middlethorpe, slow enough to allow John Cross to catch up.

The two MI6 agents, Andrews and Brady, standing in the shadow of the farmhouse lane, observe John Cross too. They had expected him to walk south past them within a few feet. They see the unmistakable fedora against the sky, and the shadow below, standing at the hedge in Brick Kiln Lane. They wait to see if he will return to Bostock Green and go back the way he came.

"It can't take him that long to relieve himself," remarks Andrews, the senior agent.

"I agree. Let's walk by him and see," responds Brady, his colleague. The agents casually walk up Brick Kiln Lane as if to go to one of the farmhouses. They walk past John Cross. He remains still.

"I'll go to the hedge as well to relieve myself too. That way I'll get a closer look."

"Okay."

Agent Andrews goes to the hedge, a short distance from John Cross. "Nice night."

No response. It is not polite to stare into the face of one who is thus engaged, so Agent Andrews glances down at John Cross's feet. He observes that there are no legs protruding from under the mac. He tugs hard at the mac and it slides off a tree branch, and the fedora falls to the ground. "He's gone! John Cross is gone!" he shouts to his colleague.

"We need to radio for backup. Damn, the radio is in the car."

"Right. And the car is a mile down the road."

"I'll search the field, you run to the car." Agent Andrews jumps through the hedge, but it is too dark to see anything of note in the field. "Damn you, Cross. Now I know why you walked."

Brady knows the procedure. Radio MI6, who will activate the emergency-measure protocols introduced during the war to coordinate appropriate agencies in the face of a threat to national security. MI6 (SIS) will immediately contact the Police Special Branch. The local police in Cheshire should be informed and engaged within minutes of Brady's radio call.

Five minutes have elapsed since Peter Oldthorpe was bundled into the back of a van. It would be another ten minutes before backup can be employed to seal off roads and commence a search.

CHAPTER FIFTEEN

THE ABDUCTION OF
PETER OLDTHORPE

Saturday 15 July 1950
Cheshire, England

It is 12:40am. Paddy Dhu Ward is driving a white unmarked van north along Bostock Green. He is driving slowly at 25mph, approaching the oak at the centre of Cheshire. In the back, out of sight, Paddy More Ward is sitting on two stacked bags of cement. Beside him are two crates each containing two dozen bottles of Murphy's Stout. Paddy More is dressed in Ward attire, except for the ganger's bent and battered gangster-style fedora he wears instead of the Irish soft cap.

"So, Paddy Dhu, you're sure O'Toole will not miss his van for a few hours?"

"Right now, O'Toole is too drunk to miss the ground even if he fell on it."

"You're right. And the van will be back at his yard long before he wakes up. He won't know it ever left."

"I see Paddy Beg Ward up ahead. Yes. There's the signal."

Paddy Beg is watching out for the van. He judges the speed of its approach to time the signal. The signal is to the musicians to stop playing at the oak and to usher the 'drunks' to the roadside. Three staggering men stumble off the kerb as the van draws alongside. They all look alike in Irish soft caps and big open flapping overcoats. The van slows, but does not come to a complete stop. Nevertheless, Paddy Beg expertly opens the rear doors and he and the musicians shove all three of the 'drunken' Irish into the back of the van like sacks of potatoes. Paddy Beg slams shut the doors, and the van resumes its modest speed of 25mph in the direction of Northorpe.

The two MI6 agents observe this. Agent Andrews nudges agent Brady. 'Typical Irish,' he communicates. Agent names are case-specific. Within MI6, 'Andrews' and 'Brady' refer to specific agents working on the John Cross assignment of the 'Code White' investigation, and is not their actual names. They note the registration number of the van – a local van, licence plate LMB 542.

12:41am. Andrews and Brady wait for John Cross to walk out of the oak enclosure and return home. So far, after a week of surveillance, John Cross has not led them to anything suspicious. If indeed he is leaking information to the Russians, they need him to lead to bigger fish. The chances that he is the leak in HER is one out of three. Those are good odds. Brady is inclined to nab him. Cross would probably break under interrogation. Andrews counsels him against it. First, it would warn the Russian contacts that they are moving in on them. The Russian contacts would simply go silent and disappear. Secondly, if Cross is not their man, his detention would surely warn the true mole and jeopardise the operation. It could also have serious repercussions for the agency. MI6 operates in complete secrecy. Its existence is concealed, even from MI5. A botch-up now with Cross could draw attention to their covert operation.

12:44am. The remaining people at the oak disperse. The Irish walk north in the direction of Northorpe; the druids go east to the River Dane, and the rest go south towards Middlethorpe. Except John Cross. He waits until he is alone. Then he walks west. That's unexpected. Taking Brick Kiln

Lane will take him to the A533. But that's the long way back to Middlethorpe, unless he intends to go further west to Moulthorpe. They observe him enter Brick Kiln Lane and stand at the hedge. Even though it is night, there is sufficient light to discern the figure at the hedge wearing a long mac and a fedora. They wait for him to move, to continue west on Brick Kiln Lane, or to return to walk south on Bostock Green.

12:47am. Unnoticed, a female figure, dressed completely in black, sneaks through the garden gate of the house on Brick Kiln Lane that backs onto Bostock Green. She enters Bostock Green at the place where the Druids leave the road to turn east towards the river, and where the cluster of Irish travelling women is walking north toward Northorpe. This figure slinks out of the garden and slides into a waiting shawl that covers her from head to toe. A wain is thrust into the crook of her arm inside the shawl. It is the same girl that danced around the oak with Peter Oldthorpe. Without breaking stride, the Irish travelling women continue walking north in the direction of Northorpe.

John Cross is still at the hedge in Brick Kiln Lane, standing motionless. This needs closer examination. Andrews and Brady investigate and discover the deception. 'Cross' is no more than an empty mac hanging from a tree branch. There is no sign of Cross in Brick Kiln lane, or on Bostock Green. There is no sign of him in the field through the hedge, but the shadowy hedgerow here could easily conceal a man. Andrews sends Brady to the car, parked a mile away hidden in a field beyond the bend in the road. From the car, Brady will radio for backup help. Andrews jumps through the hedge and examines the hedgerow and ditch, and searches the entire field but there is no trace of Cross. He wonders how Cross could have become so skilled in crafty rustic manoeuvres.

It is 12:50am. In the van, Peter Oldthorpe's head stops spinning and he is regaining clarity. Paddy More Ward addresses him. "Paddy, we will take you to St. Bawn's. Do you understand?"

Peter Oldthorpe realises that this must be the contact that will bring him to St. Bawn's and thence to Russia. "Yes. I understand. But my name is..."

"Everyone in my crew is 'Paddy Ward'. While you are with me, your name is 'Paddy Ward'. We'll call you 'English Paddy Ward'."

"I'm Scottish, actually..."

"You are what I say you are. You are 'English Paddy Ward'." And turning to the other two in the back of the van, "Isn't that so, Paddy Clé Ward and Paddy Tricks Ward?"

"Indeed it is too, Paddy More," they both respond.

"Now listen here, English Paddy. You were told to carry enough cash for expenses. How much are you carrying?"

"Just a few pounds here," patting his pocket.

"Show me."

Peter Oldthorpe removes the wad of notes to show to Paddy More. Paddy More grabs the wad out of Oldthorpe's hand and fans the notes.

"£10. That's enough to get you to St. Bawn's." Paddy More places the wad of notes inside his overcoat.

"And when will we reach St. Bawn's?"

"You reach it when you reach it."

"How will I know...?"

"Shut up, English Paddy. You talk too much!"

Peter Oldthorpe realises that he is now at the mercy of Paddy More. He has no identity, except for the Manchester

Library card. And he has no money. For the present he is a prisoner, and Paddy More Ward is his keeper.

12:48am. The van slows and comes to a smooth stop. Peter Oldthorpe enquires "Are we at St. Bawn's already?"

No response. Paddy Clé Ward opens the rear door with his left hand. He and Paddy Tricks lug the two crates of porter out of the van. Peter Oldthorpe follows at Paddy More's prompting. They all get out, except for Paddy Dhu, who drives off in the van.

A construction lorry is parked near them. The name on the side is 'Houlihan Construction'. The engine is idling. The two junior Paddies use the rear wheel for a toe-up and vault into the bed of the tipper, one at a time to accommodate the transfer of the porter crates. They lean back over the rim and assist Paddy More in doing the same. Then they lean over to 'English Paddy'. Peter Oldthorpe interprets this as an invitation to do likewise. He is hoisted up and into the bed of the tipper. Paddy More slaps the side panel and Houlihan, the driver, registers his understanding by engaging the gears and starting the lorry into motion. The two junior Paddies, Paddy Clé and Paddy Tricks, hold on to the rim of the side panel; Paddy More stands leaning back against the front panel on the cab side with hands thrust deep into his overcoat pockets. When the lorry moves, Peter Oldthorpe is thrown onto the bed of the tipper, onto the wet gravel that litters the floor. The two young Paddies laugh at him and slap the rim of the side panel to indicate to him to hold on. 'English Paddy' struggles to get his balance in the tipper; he manages to crawl with his hands up the side panel to join them. Rounding a corner, the lorry slows, and Paddy Dhu reappears. He hops onto the step of the cab of the moving lorry, opens the door and slips inside the cab beside Houlihan the driver.

12:50am. Just when Andrews and Brady are contending with an empty mac, four Paddies are travelling in the bed of a construction tipper on the A533, eastbound out of Northorpe in the direction of Manchester. At 1:00am, when MI6 is alerted to the disappearance of John Cross, Houlihan's construction tipper lorry is on the A559 passing Plumley. At 1:10am they are on the A56 passing Altrincham.

MI6 alerts local police who descend on Bostock Green to conduct a thorough search of the area. The police stop the walkers returning from the oak ceremony and question them about the disappearance of one of their participants.

The Irish are uncooperative. They know nothing, saw nothing. The druids are difficult to locate, being somewhere along the riverbank and inaccessible from the road. Charlie and Bess are cooperative and assist as best they can, but they have nothing to add to what the agents already know.

MI6 agents descend on No. 4 Eve Street, Middlethorpe, and commence an inspection of the house. Andrews and Brady speculate on how far a man can walk in 26 minutes, and consider that John Cross isn't very fit. Of course, he may have met up with a car or other vehicle. But there were no vehicles in Bostock Green since the disappearance. They arrange to have police check on all pedestrian and vehicular traffic in a 10-mile radius of Bostock Green. They also decide to trace the white van that drove by five minutes before the disappearance; maybe the driver saw something to help in the investigation. The owner of the white van LMB 542 is identified – Larry O'Toole Construction Company in Northorpe. The local constabulary knows that Larry O'Toole lives beside his supply yard on the south side of the town. His company has three vans registered. Police and agents decide to include O'Toole Construction in their enquiries.

1:45am. Houlihan's tipper lorry turns off Medlock Street into Nelson Street, Manchester. It stops long enough for twelve more 'Paddies' to hop aboard. Peter Oldthorpe recognises the name of the street. His library card shows his address as 244 Nelson Street, Manchester. He enquires of one of the newly-arrived Paddies, "Which one is number 244 Nelson Street?"

'Paddy' looks at him questioningly. "What do you mean 'which one is 244?' It's the men's hostel, of course, over there. That's where we've all come from."

Peter Oldthorpe realises that 244 Nelson Street is an address of convenience where men of no fixed abode can have post delivered for pickup whenever they are in Manchester. It is an address for one who has no permanent residential address.

The lorry drives off again. The Manchester stop takes less than a minute. Paddy More tosses a bottle of porter to each of the newcomers. They are all dressed alike, except for 'English Paddy' who is wearing oxfords instead of construction boots. And they are all in their twenties, except for 'English Paddy' who is 37, and Paddy More Ward who looks ageless like he was chiselled out of stone.

2:30am. The lorry passes Preston. The men are still mostly standing; a few are sitting or lying on tarpaulin. Peter Oldthorpe questions the Paddy next to him. "Preston? We are passing Preston? I thought we were to go south?"

"What is there in the south? The work that pays is up in Scotland in the hydro dams. Don't you know where you're going? Oh, and you can call me 'Paddy Finn'."

"Scotland? I know the name of the place where I am going, but not its location."

"What place?"

"St. Bawn's."

"No. Never heard of it. I think we're all going to the Grudie Bridge up by Loch Fannich. That's up past Inverness, near to Strathpeffer."

Peter Oldthorpe thinks back to his earlier life as John Cross in Lanarkshire. In the context of his knowledge of his home country, other than Inverness, he is not acquainted with the places named by Paddy Finn. And Inverness is a long way off, way up in the Highlands. However, he has heard of 'The Grudie Bridge' somewhere. After a moment of thought it registers with him, not in the context of Scottish geography, but in the context of energy and electricity. The Grudie Bridge Power Station is being built as part of the Conon Hydro-Electric Power Scheme started in 1946. The Grudie Bridge Power Station requires an underground water tunnel to bring water from a loch four miles away. The mass of rock beneath the loch requires blasting to complete the tunnel. The work must be dangerous and laborious. And is this where Paddy More Ward is headed?

4:00am. They are passing Carlisle. The men have arranged the tarpaulin to give some dry surface on which to sleep or sit. Paddy More addresses the men. "It will be daylight in an hour. That's when we stop. So hold everything for another hour. If any of you men do anything in the tipper, I will throw him out of the lorry. In an hour we'll get something to eat." After Carlisle, they enter Scotland. The lorry rumbles through Gretna on the A74.

5:00am. The lorry pulls off the main road onto the B7086 towards Boghead and Houlihan parks it near the primary school. The area here is all farmland. Three farmhouses are visible some distance apart, but well out of earshot. It is brightening in the pre-dawn day. Those that were asleep on the tarpaulin awaken and stretch.

Paddy More shouts, "Okay lads. This is your rest stop." All the Paddies jump out of the tipper to relieve themselves at the roadside. "Paddy Clé, Paddy Finn, Paddy Tricks! Jump into yon field and fetch turnips," shouts Paddy More, pointing to the vegetables growing in the fields next to where they are parked.

The three Paddies shortly return with arms full of white turnips which they throw to the others. They knock the dirt off and rub the turnips in the wet dewy grass of the roadside. Having thus cleaned the turnips, they produce pocket knives to peel them and commence eating. Paddy Tricks offers turnips to Peter Oldthorpe. But Peter declines to partake of the turnips, partly because he has no knife, but chiefly because he regards it as unhygienic to eat unwashed vegetables.

Paddy Finn observes English Paddy much better in the morning light. "English Paddy, are you not a bit old for this kind of work? And look at yah. You don't even have boots. You know your toes will get crushed by the rocks if you don't have boots."

Some of the other Paddies join him. Long Paddy remarks, "Lord, look at his hands. English Paddy has soft hands. Not suited to a pick and shovel."

"He'll bleed to death in half an hour with those hands," remarks one of the other Paddies.

Peter Oldthorpe sticks his hands into his coat pockets to hide them. Paddy More is watching and listening. Paddy Clé and Paddy Tricks remain quiet throughout the exchange.

"So what's this, Paddy More? Why do we have a softy in our crew? Are we expected to carry his load for him?" asks Long Paddy.

"Skills. That's what," Paddy More replies.

"And what skills has soft hands and no boots? Eh, Paddy More?"

"Explosives."

Everyone freezes to silence. No one is chewing or cutting turnips or horsing about now. 'Explosives' means 'blasting', which means overtime and danger money. If English Paddy is an 'explosive man', then he is highly valuable. Suddenly, English Paddy is someone they all want to know.

"Listen up!" Paddy More breaks the silence. "This crew is going to the Grudie Bridge to work on the 'Operation Bathplug'. Yes, you will be working with blasters; yes, you will get lots of overtime; and yes, you'll get danger money. You will earn more than four times what you could earn elsewhere. Just keep in mind, I'm the ganger. I get you the work, and I can get you off the work. For this, I get 12% of your wages, but you don't pay income tax. That's why there are 28 Paddy Wards all working in the same gang. If any of you don't like this, then you can walk from here to Glasgow and take the boat back to Derry."

"Oh, we're with you Paddy More!" they chorus.

"There's more. We're half an hour from Glasgow. That's where we'll pick up the rest of the gang coming off the boat from Derry – 16 more. The full gang will be 28. Now I know Paddy Finn here can add, and he's wondering how I come up the number of 28. Well, I'll tell ye. Paddy Clé, Paddy Tricks and English Paddy are off together to a different project. They will part from us in Glasgow."

Those who had previously ignored English Paddy and then, a moment ago, wanted to befriend him are disappointed that the 'explosive man' will be leaving them shortly.

"Everyone back in the tipper!"

This time Paddy More rides up front with Houlihan and Paddy Dhu. He directs Houlihan to the B7078, then to the A72, and lastly to the A749. At 5:30am, the lorry pulls up to the Burns & Laird dock in the Broomielaw next to the King George V Bridge in Glasgow.

5:30am. At Bostock Green there is sufficient light for Agent Andrews to examine the scene of Cross's disappearance more thoroughly. In the field, next to the location of the empty mac, Andrews observes footprints in the soft earth. He recognises his own prints, of course, where he landed from jumping through the hedge. And, as expected, he sees another set of prints. He knows that Cross was wearing oxfords. But these footprints are not oxford shoe prints. These prints were made by walking shoes or flat-soled boots, much smaller that Cross's shoe size. "A decoy." he mutters aloud. A decoy with a smaller shoe size, and approximately Cross's height, 5′8″? A woman's shoe prints. "It wasn't John Cross we watched leave the oak last night, but a woman decoy." Agent Andrews hammers his fist to his head. "Stupid, stupid!" How could he, an experienced agent, not see the switch to a decoy? When was the switch made, and by whom?

Agent Andrews replays the event in his mind. Cross came to the oak at midnight with Bess the waitress and her boyfriend Charlie. Shortly after Cross's disappearance, Bess and Charley were both seen and interviewed. No, neither of them is the decoy. But Bess, in naming all who were at the oak, informed them that John Cross was friendly with Daisy Wright, one of the druids. The significance of this hits Andrews – Daisy Wright, the librarian, is one of the druids. "The druids. Of course, the druids in their long white hooded cloaks are perfect for a covert person-exchange. And the druids left by way of the river." Andrews is talking aloud to himself.

Agent Brady, who is working alongside Andrews, enquires, "Are you talking to me or to yourself?"

"Both, actually. Brady, get on to all the druids from last night. The 'Cross' we observed at the hedge here was a decoy, a female decoy."

Andrews is pointing to the footprints. Brady instantly recognises the point that Andrews is making, and he concurs. Cross had changed places with a woman. Brady needs no explanation. The druids are the most likely abetters in Cross's disappearance. Brady goes off to get the local police to assist in identifying and interviewing all the druids. This will take some time. But one druid will be first on the list – Daisy Wright the librarian.

MI6, identified only as 'working with His Majesty's Special Branch', establishes a command post in the Middlethorpe Police Station in Queen Street. The Cheshire Constabulary provides full assistance and cooperation. The police agree to interview possible witnesses and report back to Andrews and Brady.

Since 6:00am, Brady has had them working at identifying the participants at the oak ritual. The librarian is the only known member of the druids. She should be able to identify the others. All will be questioned as soon as possible. Andrews adds a short list of people to assist in their enquiries – the patrons of the Crowing Cock who spoke with Cross on 12 July, and the driver of the white van that drove past the oak last night – Larry O'Toole. Brady sends Constable Manus McCann to question O'Toole.

6:00am. Larry O'Toole is an early riser. Even though he had been drinking the night before to midnight, Larry O'Toole is eager to get to work. He needs to set a good example for his workers. He leaves his house by the back door and walks across his backyard to the adjoining construction yard. In the yard is a caravan-office. Larry unlocks the door and goes inside.

Larry specialises in home renovations and landscaping. His foreman, Seamus O'Doherty, keeps the workers' noses to the grindstone. Seamus is due to arrive in the yard at 7:00am, and soon thereafter the workers will arrive. Larry's routine is to hand the clipboard of the day's work contracts to Seamus, who will assign the work teams. As soon as Seamus allocates the jobs, he sends the workers to their assigned job sites at 8:00am. Seamus will supervise the workers, going from one site to another throughout the course of the day. As soon as the workers depart, Larry hopes to grab an hour or two of sleep at his desk in his caravan-office. He will awaken if anyone drives into the gravel-surfaced yard, or if the phone rings. First, he puts on the kettle on the portable gas ring and sets about making a pot of strong tea. When the water boils, he wets the tea and waits for it to draw. He realises that he has no milk. Just then Seamus O'Doherty walks into the office.

"Hello, Larry! Rough night, eh? Shut your eyes so you won't bleed out."

"My eyes are bloodshot?"

"I'll say they are. And Larry, you forgot again."

"Forgot what?"

"Everything." Seamus slams a milk bottle down on Larry's desk. The thud disturbs him, but the welcome provision of milk is sufficient to forgive the intrusion. "You forgot to lock the yard again after you came back from your night out.”

“No. I did not forget. I remember locking the gate.” And then Larry adds faintly, “Or was that the previous night?”

“And you forgot to drive the van back into the yard. You left it out on the street overnight.”

Larry looks up at the corkboard inside the door. There are three hooks on it for the keys to his three vans. Only two hooks are occupied. Larry holds his head to think. “I remember driving the van into the yard and hanging the key up there,” pointing to the three hooks. And then adds in a low voice, “Or was that the previous night?”

“LMB 542 is out on the street.”

“I drove LMM 202 last night. Or was that the previous night?” Larry gets up from his chair. “Come on, Seamus. Let’s get the van into the yard. Damn! I don’t know where the spare keys are.”

“Well, let’s check the van. If it’s unlocked, we can push it in neutral into the yard.”

Larry and Seamus walk out of the yard onto the roadway and around the corner to where the van is parked. Looking inside, they see the key in the ignition and determine that the doors are unlocked.

“Okay,” says Larry with relief. “No harm done. I’ll just drive it into the yard.” Larry puts his hand on the door handle to open the door, but freezes in his movement when a gloved hand rests on his shoulder. In their anxiety to check the van they did not notice a policeman approach.

“Mr. O’Toole?” enquires Constable McCann.

Larry turns around. He knows that it is a policeman even before he turns. “I’m sorry about this, officer. I’ll move the van right away.”

"We'd like to ask you a few questions."

Larry mentally questions the logic of saying 'we' when there is only one policeman. This must be policeman language to indicate that it is a serious matter. "Of course, officer. My driver's licence is back there in my office."

"No. We don't need to see your driver's licence. We have questions pertaining to last night."

Larry swallows. What could it be? Driving impaired? Going through a stop sign?

"Where were you last night between the hours of midnight and 1:00am?"

"Around midnight I was on my way home. I don't know what time it was when I got home."

"And where were you coming from 'around midnight'?"

"From the Crowing Cock."

"In Middlethorpe?"

"Yes."

"Around midnight?"

"Or thereabouts. I didn't note the time."

"What route did you drive on your way home?"

"I always use the A530."

"Not the A533?"

"I don't rightly remember which road I took last night. Why do you ask?"

"Your van was spotted in Bostock Green at 12:41 last night."

"Well, then, it must have been the A533 I used last night, and I must have cut through Bostock Green. I could have sworn I used the A530, but maybe that was on a previous night. But what does it matter? It is equidistant whichever road I use."

"We are making enquiries into a possible abduction that occurred in Bostock Green between 12:00 and 1:00. What do you remember of your drive home? Did you see anything unusual?"

Larry O'Toole has no recollection of his drive home last night. He is no help to the policeman. After a few more questions, Constable McCann gives up. "Mr. O'Toole, we may have some more questions later on. And, in the meantime, should you recollect anything of note, anything at all, please contact us."

Larry is relieved at the policeman's departure. He was bracing himself for a charge of illegal parking or for a driving offence. Now he can breathe easy.

Seamus O'Doherty enters the van and inspects it for anything amiss. "Larry, do you know that there are two bags of cement in the back?"

"Oh, that must be the two bags I asked young Ward to collect from a job-site before it rained. It looks like he didn't bother to put them in the shed."

"Well, it's dry enough in the van, anyway."

"Seamus. Drive the van into the yard and store the bags of cement. I'm going back for that strong cup of tea."

CHAPTER SIXTEEN

THE SEARCH FOR JOHN CROSS

Saturday 15 July 1950
Broomielaw, Glasgow, Scotland

5:30am. Houlihan's lorry is parked at the Burns & Laird dock. Paddy More, standing on the step of the cab, addresses the men in the tipper. "Hey, Lads! Listen up! The Derry boat is due to dock here at six o'clock. As you can see, and feel, the rain is starting to fall. So while we are stopped here you'll rig up the tarpaulin to cover the tipper. When you move the tarpaulin, you'll find planks of wood stored underneath. You'll set up the planks of wood as makeshift benches inside the tipper. The tipper will need to hold 28 navvies for the five-hour drive to the Grudie Bridge. That's tight, but you'd better get used to tight, like when you'll be tunnelling under Loch Fannich on Monday. We pull out at six o'clock; that's in half an hour. So get to it!"

He jumps down from the step as the Paddy-navvies hook up the tarpaulin. "Paddy Clé and Paddy Tricks! Come with me!" Paddy More, Paddy Clé and Paddy Tricks walk away in the direction of the Burns & Laird office and disappear inside the building.

At ten minutes to six, the gang has completed the setup job in the tipper. They are standing smoking outside the shipping office waiting room, watching the Derry boat steam up the Clyde. It docks and the ropes are secured. Having thus secured the ship to the dock, the gangplank is lowered with a loud clang. A crewmember unlocks the chain to give access to the gangplank and the passengers disembark. The first to come streaming down to the dock are the 16 expected navvies for Paddy More's gang. They are instantly recognised in their distinctive Ward attire, just like all the others in the gang.

"Hi Paddy this. And Hi Paddy that," and so on, as greetings are shared.

"Okay, gang! Listen up!" Paddy More has returned with Paddy Clé and Paddy Tricks each carrying a large cardboard box which they place on the ground.

A waitress from the canteen is following close behind carrying a big teapot with two spouts. She is in her 50's; her brown hair is tied up in a bun and is held in place by a hairnet. Her apron is the wraparound kind you would expect to see in an institution, whitish grey with food stains. A cigarette is dangling from the corner of her mouth, its ash built up precariously. She blinks against the smoke that drifts into her eyes but is otherwise quite at ease with the smouldering cigarette.

"This box," says Paddy More pointing, "is hang sangwiches. And this one here is jam samwiches. Now line up for your tay."

Peter Oldthorpe has adjusted his ear to Paddy More's peculiar speech. Paddy More has provided ham sandwiches and jam sandwiches and tea for the gang.

All the Paddies produce tin mugs from their overcoats and, like inmates in a POW camp, they line up two by two. The waitress pours two cups simultaneously. The tea already contains sugar and milk and is steaming hot, close to boiling. As each Paddy obtains a full cup, he goes to one cardboard box and then to the other for his share of food.

Paddy More notices that Peter Oldthorpe is not in the queue. "What are you waiting for, English Paddy? Tea with lemon?"

"I don't have a mug."

"I thought so." He lobs an enamelled tin mug to Peter Oldthorpe, who catches it deftly, thanks to his cricket-playing skills. "Here. Use Houlihan's mug from the cab. He's in the canteen now drinking from a cup."

The last two in the queue are Paddy More and Peter Oldthorpe. Their mugs are filled and they obtain their share of sandwiches.

"So Paddy More, you're off to the Grudie Bridge? And I'm off to St. Bawn's now. Right?"

"Listen here, English Paddy. You were always on the way to St. Bawn's, and I was always on my way to the Grudie Bridge. We just shared the ride for a few hours."

"So how much closer am I to St. Bawn's now?"

"Well, you're closer in time, but farther in distance."

"What do you mean 'closer, but farther'?"

"At Bostock Green you were a lot closer than you are now. But this is the way you're going."

Peter Oldthorpe is confused. Isn't St. Bawn's in Scotland? Or does he now need to go back to England? "So tell me, when and where do I reach St. Bawn's?"

"You're asking the wrong man. Ask your minder."

"My minder? Who is...?"

"You thought I was your minder? No, English Paddy, I'm just a ganger who gave you a lift to Glasgow. Your minder hasn't left your side since midnight at Bostock Green."

Peter Oldthorpe looks sideways at Paddy Clé and Paddy Tricks, both of whom are standing in the morning drizzle silently looking at him. Paddy Clé is sporting a sly grin.

The drizzle turns to rain. Paddy More jumps up on the lorry, opens the cab door and hops in beside Houlihan and Paddy Dhu. Paddy Dhu is driving for the next leg of the journey. Houlihan intends to sleep for a few hours. The navvies in the tipper secure the tarpaulin, and the lorry departs the Broomielaw and Clyde Street and heads for the Grudie Bridge.

"So what now?" Peter Oldthorpe enquires of the two remaining Paddies.

"Now we get out of the rain. That's what."

Paddy Clé, Paddy Tricks and Peter Oldthorpe enter the Burns & Laird waiting room. Peter Oldthorpe places his hands deep into his overcoat pockets. He feels the presence of Houlihan's enamelled tin mug. He is satisfied that he is learning the ways of the road.

Sitting in the waiting-room canteen, Paddy Clé addresses Peter Oldthorpe. "Peter Oldthorpe, which is what I will call you. My name is Francie Ward. I go by the name 'Paddy Clé' over here. All Irish navvies are called 'Paddy' whether we like it or not. So we use 'Paddy' to our advantage. No one in Scotland or in England would know who Francie Ward is. I'm the left-handed Paddy – Paddy Clé. And this is my brother..."

"Collie Ward," interrupts Paddy Tricks. "No one calls me 'Collie', except another Ward. You'll call me 'Paddy Tricks', or just 'Tricks'."

"And you'll call me 'Francie'."

Peter Oldthorpe gathers from this information that he is with Francis Ward and Colm Ward. "But why call you 'Tricks'?" Peter Oldthorpe enquires of Paddy Tricks.

Paddy Tricks pulls out a deck of cards and fans them. "Pick a card. Any card."

"Put the cards away, Collie. There is a time for that, and soon too."

Peter Oldthorpe is anxious to know how he is going to get to Russia. Will he receive a message? And if he is going via St. Bawn's, where is St. Bawn's? "So, now what? We go to St. Bawn's?"

"First, we wait for the rain to stop. Then we earn our lunch. Then we set off again."

9:00am. The rain stops. Paddy Tricks retrieves the cardboard box that held the ham sandwiches, and he has found a white handkerchief. This is one of his tricks, 'finding' things. He sets up the box as a card table on the sidewalk in the shelter of the railway bridge beside the George V Bridge and invites the Saturday morning crowd to 'find the lady'. For a mere sixpence, one is invited to lay a bet to 'find the lady', the Queen of Hearts, in the cards spread face down on the table. Should the customer, 'the mark', succeed, Tricks will pay out two shillings and sixpence. Of course, Tricks has no winning card among the cards on the table, except when he himself turns a card face up using 'Mexican turnover' sleight-of-hand to reveal the location of 'the lady'. The winning card is always under Tricks's control. When the 'mark' chooses a losing card (he ALWAYS chooses a losing card), Tricks is able to show him that the Queen of Hearts is the card next to it.

Meanwhile, Francie is on the lookout for police, pronounced 'polis' in Glasgow. Francie is street-singing. As soon as he changes to 'Danny Boy', Tricks will know to conduct a quick disappearing trick. Francie also knows to shout 'polis' whenever a 'mark' gets suspicious of Tricks's trickery. Tricks will then pick up his box and 'disappear from the polis' and set up again elsewhere, or later, for a new 'mark'.

Tricks takes Peter Oldthorpe's overcoat and cap from him and hides it inside his box. He employs Peter Oldthorpe as a 'shill'. The purpose of the 'shill' is to encourage people to bet on the game. The 'shill' plays the game, makes the wager, and actually wins the bet. Peter Oldthorpe, the 'shill', by virtue of his dress and speech, appears to be unrelated to the dealer, and thus sets up innocent 'marks' to engage in what appears to be a sure bet. Peter Oldthorpe is learning more ways of the road. He has quickly graduated from fecking tin mugs to engaging in a confidence game. Thus, Peter, Francie and Collie do a fine business with the Saturday morning crowd.

At 1:00pm, all three are back in the canteen tucking into sausages beans and chips.

Middlethorpe Police Station in Queen Street. At 8:30am, Andrews and Brady are sifting through data and are directing police to collect information on all those whom John Cross has been in contact with in the past while. The list of contacts is small. John Cross has no friends and very few contacts in Middlethorpe. His pattern changed just two days ago after his encounter with MI6 at the Royal Ordnance. Since then, he met with a number of people, and this is where they will concentrate their enquiries.

They want the librarian/druid, Daisy Wright. And they want the Crowing Cock people that spoke with him. That would be Bess, the waitress; George, the barman; and Fred, the milkman. Cody, a third member of the unit, is in charge of the search of Cross's house. Cody is familiar with Cross's house, having been there a number of times to snoop around and to plant bugs. Cody is currently interviewing Cross's colleagues at the Royal Ordnance in Risley. Cody knows what Risley really is: 'High Explosive Research', meaning 'Atomic Bomb Research'. It is only two days since Thursday 13 July when he was in Cross's office there. Cody was one of the nameless 'security men' who descended on HER that day, and he was one of the team that conducted the thorough search of Cross's office.

Andrews is following the premise that the druids are the link to Cross's disappearance, and hence they are the link to his whereabouts. And the chief suspect is Daisy Wright. Andrews and Brady are standing together, bending over the desk, perusing their interview notes and leads, when they are interrupted by the arrival of 'a man'. He has the air of authority. And like the agents in MI6, he has no 'real' name. He is dressed like a London banker, pinstriped three-piece suit with bowler and umbrella. He places his hat and umbrella on a vacant chair and looks at Andrews and Brady.

"Piperson," is all he says by way of introduction. "And you would be Andrews, and you would be Brady," correctly identifying them both.

Andrews and Brady exchange looks, and look at the telephone. Andrews looks from the telephone and back to Brady to indicate that he needs to make a confidential phone call.

Brady attempts to guide 'Piperson' out of the office. "Do you mind stepping outside, please, Mr. Piperson?"

"Actually, I DO mind, and I won't. You need to make a secure call to confirm my authority here. So make the call."

There is a hesitation from Andrews and Brady. 'Piperson' continues, "If you have forgotten the number, it is 'Hounslow...'"

"No, we haven't forgotten."

"So go ahead. Oh, it's 'code white'."

Andrews goes through the various levels of passwords and responses as he progresses to his assignment director. 'Piperson' sits comfortably in a chair and fixes his trouser legs so as to avoid wrinkling or 'bagging' his knees. His feet are thrust out and his wrinkleless socks are clearly visible. He takes a gold cigarette case from his inside breast pocket and clicks it open. He selects a Black Russian in its distinctive black paper with a gold foil filter end, emblazoned with the Russian imperial eagle. Replacing the gold cigarette case, he draws out a gold lighter and strikes a flame, all in one smooth motion. He draws on the cigarette and replaces the lighter in his pocket. He blows the first puff of smoke towards Andrews and raises his eyebrows. His expression says 'So?' There is no need to say it aloud.

Andrews says, "Yes, sir." into the telephone, and puts the receiver back in the cradle. Brady is looking at him for an explanation. Andrews coughs. "'Piper's Son' is a senior member of 'Code White' and will be working with us in the Cross disappearance."

'Piper's Son' smiles and extends his hand. "You may call me 'Patrick Piperson' for the duration of our joint assignment. Actually, 'Patrick' is just fine. A pleasure working with you." They shake hands reluctantly and with apprehension.

Patrick Piperson continues, "Don't slow down for me. I'll keep out of your way. Just let me have access to your notes, and let me observe all interviews. I'll be like a fly on the wall."

Piperson does not know which department Andrews and Brady are working for. Nor do Andrews and Brady know which department Piperson is with. Such as it is in the various sections of the 'secret' Secret Service.

9:00am. Sergeant Morgan, the station officer, calls the meeting to order in the situation room. Sergeant Morgan is a gruff, honest and dedicated police officer. He is a Welsh church-going Methodist who disapproves of smoking and drinking. Nevertheless, he has the admiration and loyalty of all those who serve under him. "Men, we are working on a case here. This is a delicate and sensitive case. Officers Andrews and Brady are from the government department responsible for this investigation. We are happy to provide our assistance and full cooperation. Officer Andrews, as senior lead officer, will now address you."

Andrews gets to it without any small talk. "At 12:50am we learned that John Cross disappeared from Bostock Green. We are treating this as an abduction. Cross is one of Britain's scientists working on secure projects of national importance, projects that our enemies would like to have knowledge of. You understand that Cross has information that could be critical to the security of the realm. Our focus is to locate Cross, and to secure him." Andrews hesitates to weigh the quality of the men present. These are county policemen, not as sophisticated or experienced as MI6. But local knowledge is valuable at this stage of the investigation, and this is the local police's forte and home turf.

Andrews continues, "At Cross's house on Eve Street we discovered everything to be in place, as if he were still at home – his car is parked outside, his keys are in the hallstand, his clothes are all in place in wardrobes and presses. Everything is in place. Nothing is missing. Nothing to suggest that Cross has left. Except..." Andrews stops for dramatic effect. "...except that nothing in the house is identifiable as John Cross. There is nothing there that bears his name or identity. It's as if he does not exist. In the garden, in the ashpit, the ashes were still warm at 2:00am. It appears that Cross had been burning papers."

Andrews raises his voice for emphasis. "Cross could not disappear from Bostock Green without the involvement of a number of people. We believe he was switched with another person to trick us. He may have been complicit in his own disappearance, or he may have been forced. The latter is more likely; that is why I refer to it as an abduction."

This is misleading. Andrews is sure that Cross departed willingly, and did it while under his surveillance. But best not to draw attention to his own ineptitude.

He continues, "We examined footprints near the scene, footprints of the phoney decoy Cross, and we are certain that it was a female decoy. We also know that Cross befriended a local lady who was one of the hooded druids at Bostock Green last night. She was present at the time of Cross's disappearance. If we can identify the persons who assisted in the abduction, we will be able to make a connection, and ultimately lead to Cross's current location. Officer Brady is handing out assignments to you. You should recognise the persons of interest. They are all local and within a stone's throw of Middlethorpe Police Station here in Queen Street. I want a progress report in four hours. Any questions?"

A young constable raises his hand. Those near him snigger, "Trust 'Irish' to have a question."

"Constable Manus McCann. If I may."

"Yes, Constable McCann?"

Brady interrupts to inform Andrews, "Constable McCann is following up on Larry O'Toole and the white van."

McCann enquires, "You say that Cross was abducted. Are you considering any other possibilities? Such as suicide, or he just took off, or maybe he is just yanking our chain...?"

Andrews flinches slightly at the possibility that ransacking Cross's office two days ago may have unhinged him. It may have been the final straw to push him to commit some act of personal folly, or it may have been the very thing to drive him to defect to the Russians. "We are open to all possibilities. But regardless, we still need to locate him. Is that all?"

"Ah, no. One more thing. I understand that there were some non-locals at Bostock Green last night. Are we checking up on them too?"

"Again, we don't rule that out. But the focus of our inquiry is to where we are most likely to get the quickest results. And that is to the people that interacted with Cross in the past two days. These are the people with whom he had no connection hitherto. Think of it – two days ago he did not know any of them. He met them and engaged with them closely, and now he is gone. There has to be a connection."

"I see. You say that his house is completely intact, as if it is still occupied, with the exception that there is no apparent connection to John Cross? What is the status of his bank accounts? I don't see any banks listed on the assignment sheets."

"Besides the Cheshire Constabulary, we have other officers working this case. Be assured, we are covering all angles." This appears to satisfy Constable McCann. "Oh, McCann?"

"Sir?"

"What is your report on Larry O'Toole? Did you talk to him?"

"Inconclusive at this time, sir. O'Toole has three vans. He may, or may not, have been driving the one spotted at Bostock Green last night. I am working on establishing the identity of the actual driver, O'Toole himself, or a member of his crew."

"Okay, Constable. Carry on. And report back to me ASAP."

"Thank you, sir." Constable McCann departs on his assignment, to interview Fred Swanson the milkman, and to follow up on Larry O'Toole.

The officers depart to engage in their assignments. Andrews addresses the sergeant. "Sergeant Morgan. Could you have a constable bring in Daisy Wright for questioning?"

"I'll do it myself. The police station here in Queen Street backs on to the library on Lewin Street. The library is literally the closest building to us."

9:30am. Daisy Wright is assisting the police in their investigations. She is sitting in the interview room with officers Andrews and Brady. Morgan and Piperson are listening to the interview from the adjoining room via the intercom.

"Miss Wright, you are not under suspicion in any wrongdoing," Andrews lies. "We are trying to piece together the events of last night, events leading up to the disappearance and possible abduction of John Cross."

"John Cross was abducted? Who...? What...?" Daisy is very distraught. She is dabbing her wet eyes with her handkerchief. She is distressed, and now she is also puzzled.

"We will establish the 'who' and the 'what' when we collect all the information."

The interview progresses, or rather regresses. She is able to give them the names and addresses of the other druids, but nothing else. As they press for more information, Daisy gets increasingly upset. Andrews and Brady alternatively shoot questions at her quicker than she can form an answer. Sergeant Morgan is agitated and displeased at the way the interview is going.

It is clear that Daisy is unable to provide any information of substance. "He didn't have to go off suddenly like that, you know. I could have helped him. It was that Irish fortune-telling woman that upset him. Her and her talking to trees and stuff, and reading signs in leaves...."

Andrews and Brady are unable to make sense of Daisy's ramblings. They attempt to keep her on track but to no avail. After 30 minutes of pressure, Daisy is falling apart emotionally.

Sergeant Morgan shouts "Enough!" But he is inaudible in the interview room. He turns to Piperson, "Get in there and stop this interview. Do it now or I will. I don't care on whose authority you act. But NO ONE conducts an interview like this in my station."

"I agree. The interview is going nowhere; Daisy Wright doesn't know anything of value."

Piperson tears a page from his notepad and scribbles a hasty note. He hands it to the duty officer to deliver it immediately to the interview room. Momentarily, Morgan and Piperson hear Andrews stop the flow of questions, and then he recommences speaking. "Note the time. 10:40am. This interview is halted and will recommence in five minutes, at 10:45am."

Andrews and Brady enter the adjoining room. Both are visibly upset. Before either one can speak, Morgan barks, "My office. Now!" and strides off. Piperson gestures to Andrews and Brady to follow Morgan to his office. Once inside the sergeant's office, Morgan once again pre-empts Andrews' and Brady's attempt to protest the interruption of the interview.

"The interview is over. Daisy Wright is to be thanked for her valuable help and cooperation in our investigation, etc., etc. She is then released, free to go. Do you understand?"

Andrews is livid. "We had her cornered in there. We were about to get some important information – maybe the very lead we require to get John Cross...."

"You were getting nowhere, except to upset an innocent person and model citizen!"

Andrews approaches Morgan defiantly nose-to-nose and enquires, "And on whose authority do YOU, a county police sergeant, call a halt to two of His Majesty's..."

Andrews does not finish the sentence. He feels a punch to his solar plexus, his legs buckle, and he falls back, knocking his head on the wall. This is Morgan's skill, once expertly employed in Burma during the war against the Japanese. Brady pounces in to tackle Morgan, but not quickly enough. Piperson clearly sees where this is going and steps in between Morgan and Brady to prevent any further engagement.

Andrews recovers sufficiently to threaten Morgan with dismissal. "Interfering with His Majesty's Services..."

"Oh, do shut up, Andrews," Piperson quips. "You got what you deserve. If this incident is reported, you, Andrews, are more likely to be dismissed for the way you let Cross slip through your fingers. And now your follow-up is going nowhere. You have two hours until your next meeting. Now, change your shirt, take a shave, take a nap. You haven't slept all night, and your judgement is impaired."

Everyone calms down. Andrews relents. "You're right Piperson. I'm a bit wiped out."

Even Morgan warms up to Andrews. "Let us get Daisy on her way, with our thanks, of course. She is not likely to leave Middlethorpe; we can always check with her later if needs be. And I'll arrange a couple of rooms for you two boys with George over at the Crowing Cock. The Crowing Cock is just outside our back door, across from the library and two doors up. I'll send over fresh shirts and socks and stuff. What neck size are you...?"

And so things settle down. They settle down for Daisy, for Sergeant Morgan and for His Majesty's Secret Intelligence Service officers. At least for the next two hours.

12:30pm. Constable McCann returns to the station. He is prepared to report his progress. And since Andrews and Brady are not present, he reports to Sergeant Morgan. "Sergeant, I have learned a few things which may have a bearing on the investigation."

"Well, hold on. I'll bring in Piperson."

Piperson, who is all ears, hears his name mentioned, and approaches the sergeant's office.

"Come in, Piperson. Constable McCann has something to report."

"Very well. Let's hear it, Constable."

"First, I went to the Crowing Cock. I know that Fred the milkman goes there after his rounds."

"And was Fred there? And if so what did Fred tell you?"

"Fred was there all right. And he said that Cross paid him his bill in full, and cancelled his milk delivery."

"For how long? A week? A fortnight?"

"For good."

"Really?"

"There's more. I enquired from George if O'Toole was there as usual last night. George confirmed that he was. So I asked him if he saw which vehicle O'Toole drove away in. It was one of his white vans, he said, but George doesn't know which one. But here's a thing. George noticed that O'Toole scraped a bollard at the parking spot as he pulled out. He remembers that, and the red scrape on the front bumper."

"And did you check it out?"

"Yes. But something else significant first. As I left the Crowing Cock, the bank manager came in for lunch. The bank closes at 12:00 on a Saturday...."

"Yes, yes. We know that."

"The manager asked me how the investigation is going, Mr. Cross and all. Word is going around that something is up with John Cross, what with the presence of a police investigation team at his house and all. So I told him that I am not at liberty to comment on an ongoing investigation. And then he informed me that Mr. Cross closed his account yesterday. So I asked him for details, and he said something about client confidentiality and said no more about it. Strange that Cross cancelled his milk delivery and closed his bank account on the same day?"

Piperson is all attentive to McCann. "What else did you find out?"

"So I went to O'Toole in Northorpe. He was in his office and only one van was parked there."

"Yes?"

"LMM 202. With a red scratch on the front bumper."

"Not LMB 542?"

"Not LMB 542. And the other two vans are out on jobs today. Here is a list of addresses." McCann shows them his notepad, and continues. "O'Toole is not working any big jobs today. He is doing some cleaning up at a number of locations. It's hard to say where any of the vans are right now. The vans will all be back in his yard by 5:00pm."

"Good work, Constable."

"But wait. The worst is yet to come. Coming in here from the parking lot just now, I pop into the Crowing Cock for a cup of tea. And Bess lights into me about Daisy and all. 'And why don't we question the drunken Irish?' she says."

"Your account of Bess and the Irish will have to wait. Here comes Andrews and Brady for the 1:00pm meeting. You can report it all to them."

Sergeant Morgan is thinking. This is certainly not an abduction. Cross's disappearance has the marks of a defection. Andrews and Brady and even Piperson know a lot more than they are disclosing. John Cross's profile, the little he knows of it, is similar to Klaus Fuchs. Fuchs also worked at an Ordnance facility, and he was arrested just six months earlier, and is currently serving 14 years for spying for the Russians. Fuchs confessed. Was Cross also feeding information to the Russians? And has he decided to defect before he is caught? Sergeant Morgan may never learn the truth.

1:15pm. Constable McCann is concluding his report. "...and then Bess tells me about the Irish travellers that were there at the oak. The two tin-whistle players, the bodhrán player..."

"What's a bowran?" enquires Brady.

"A mummer's hand drum," Piperson informs him.

McCann continues "...and the dancers. Sure it's clear how Cross disappeared. It's one of Paddy Tricks's tricks. I've seen it three times or more."

Andrews jumps in as if stung by a wasp, "What do you mean 'it's clear how Cross disappeared'? A paddy-tricks-tricks? What on earth are you talking about? Enlighten us."

"Well, at the Renaissance Fair in Bostock Green, back on midsummer's day, I was sent out to check on illicit activities at the fair. 'Find-the-lady' was on top of the list. So I find the Irish travellers at the fair. Fortune telling and perhaps 'find-the-lady'. But with the police presence, any 'find-the-lady' activity ceased. Some do-gooder wanted to put a stop to these things."

Morgan interrupts, "I was the do-gooder who wanted to put a stop to the gambling and fortune telling."

Andrews is impatient. "Is this going somewhere?"

"I'm coming to it. There was this group of Irish traveller entertainers, two tin whistles, a bodhrán, and four dancers. Now the dancers, two young men and two young women, were dressed all in black in the usual big floppy overcoats many sizes too large, down to the ankles, and with the cloth caps unclasped so that they were pulled down low on the heads over the ears. That would be the two men. Now the two women were also all in black down to their ankles, and they had these big shawls covering them from head to toe. Well, they danced frantically, clockwise and counter-clockwise and back again, their heads and shoulders bunched together and their legs kicking out wildly. Then they stopped and stood in a straight line, and one of them says, 'Where's the ladies?' At this, they opened their overcoats and shawls, and there they were, changed. The men were in the shawls and the women were in the overcoats. I don't know how they did it, but an hour later, they did the same trick again. It was introduced by one of the dancers. 'Paddy Tricks' is his name and he claims to be able to defy logic and bend free will. Three times I watched Paddy Tricks do the changing-dancers trick, and I could not see the change occur during the dance."

"And you believe that Paddy Tricks was at the oak last night?"

"And in the dark."

"And did the same trick with John Cross as one of the dancers?"

"And with more accomplices."

It is clear to Andrews and Brady that they had focused their inquiry in the wrong direction. This does not bode well for them. First, they let Cross slip away while he was under their concentrated surveillance. And then, they had failed to widen their inquiry to all possibilities.

This new information puts the time of Cross's disappearance some nine minutes earlier than previously estimated. Andrews is silently cursing himself. Cross disappeared BEFORE the white van passed by. Andrews curses again. Three Irish travellers were bundled into the van as it passed by the oak. Cross must have been one of the 'drunken Irish'. And it is worse for Andrews. Because they had failed to pinpoint the time of Cross's disappearance, they miscalculated the location of the police checkpoints. At an average speed of 30mph, the van or a replacement vehicle would be outside the 10-mile radius by the time the checkpoints were in place. Andrews is aware of Piperson looking disapprovingly at him. "Damn! Damn!" he mutters silently as he clenches his fists so tightly that his fingernails draw blood.

"Okay. The focus of our attention is now on the Irish travellers, and on O'Toole's work gang. I want the Irish brought in, all those that were at the oak last night. And I want O'Toole and every member of his gang questioned. Brady will assign teams with Sergeant Morgan. I have another line of attack to engage in. I'll be in my office."

Andrews goes into his command-centre office. He needs to contact Cody. Has Cody learned anything? And he'll need Cody to arrange forensic experts to go through O'Toole's vans, and pay a visit to the oak in case they missed some key evidence. They will need to look into Cross's bank account. When he closed his account, did he draw out only cash; or did he obtain a bank draft which can be traced? Cody knows to follow the money. But, damn, the banks are closed until Monday, and Cross's trail is getting cold. MI6 will need to watch all known Russian points of exit – via the embassy,

Russian ships and Russian carriers. Cross has slipped out of his grasp, but they can still prevent Cross from leaving the country. Britain is an island, surely they can contain Cross here by securing all points of exit.

Andrews is pounding his head with his hand when he is aware of Piperson sitting watching him.

Piperson offers to help. "I'll look after the points of exit and Russian contacts. I know who to engage, and what measures to execute. You, Andrews, should go after Cross while the trail is still warm. I will remain and work locally with the police here."

"The van is the first step. I need to find the driver of the van. And next, where the van took Cross. And so on." Andrews is getting focused. He succeeds in contacting Cody by telephone, and then quickly narrates a complete account of the status of the investigation and explains what is required of him. Piperson does not regard it at all strange that Cody, one very active member of the investigation team, is never seen.

2:45pm. Andrews checks the status of the assignments with Brady. Piperson interrupts them. "If you lads haven't had lunch yet, you'd better hurry. The Crowing Cock stops serving at 3:00pm."

"You're right, Piperson. Come on Brady, we can talk over beans and chips."

2:59pm. Andrews and Brady are digging in to sausages, beans and chips at the Crowing Cock.

3:00pm. The Burns & Laird waiting room in Glasgow. Francie, Tricks and Oldthorpe have finished their sausages, beans and chips. They have also finished three cups of tea and three cigarettes. This is the first money Peter Oldthorpe has earned since he ceased being John Cross. He is feeling good.

His cap is balanced jauntily on the back of his head, and his coat is confidently thrown fully open like a cloak spread out from his shoulders. He thinks back to when he was John Cross. It seems like a long time ago. He shudders himself back to the reality of his situation. It was just yesterday that he was John Cross. He reminds himself that now he is a defecting fugitive. Two days ago his office was trashed by the Special Branch (or whoever) and up to fourteen hours ago he was under constant surveillance.

Realising how exposed he is, Peter Oldthorpe hunches his shoulders and turns his collar up so that his coat and cap connect. He pulls his coat closed and tries to make himself small inside the overly-large overcoat. That is not difficult to do, but invisibility is preferable. He hopes that he is adequately hidden inside his cap and coat. After all, the people hunting for him might be searching places like this – boat docks or train stations or airports. He peers out from beneath the flopped-down peak of his cap to observe the people arriving at the waiting room. More and more people are coming in, mostly male and female Irish seasonal workers and casual labourers. And he sees two gangers. He knows what a ganger is now. And they all wear a gangster-style battered fedora, the mark of their status.

Peter Oldthorpe is anxious. He wonders if he is being watched. He laughs inwardly at the foolishness of the thought. Of course he isn't being watched. The Special Branch – or counter-intelligence – is past watching him now. If he is located by them he will be instantly nabbed; or worse, he could be shot. He looks at Francie and Tricks, both apparently oblivious to his state of anxiety. His fate is currently in the hands of an itinerant confidence trickster and a street singer. And he is not rightly clear where he is going; he surely isn't any closer to Russia. Huddled in a winter overcoat in July, Peter Oldthorpe feels a cold wave wash over his body, and he shivers.

"The ticket office is now open." Peter Oldthorpe is jolted by the sudden intrusion of a harsh barker voice. There is a man standing at one side of the waiting room. He is dressed like a railway porter, except that he is wearing a marine jacket. He continues, "You may board the ship for Londonderry at four o'clock. The ship sails at six." He disappears and reappears again when he slides open a section of wall at the ticket wicket.

Peter Oldthorpe rises out of his chair concurrently with Francie and Tricks. Francie hands him a Burns & Laird ticket.

"So, we are going to board the ship?"

"Yes. But first go the wicket and exchange the ticket for a sailing ticket."

"A sailing ticket?"

"Yes. The ticket doesn't say which sailing you are going on. It is good for any day, or even for Belfast or Dublin. You need the sailing ticket so that you can board the right ship. You're going to Derry, Peter Oldthorpe."

Oldthorpe joins the queue with Francie and Tricks. He wonders how going to Ireland will get him to Russia. He seems to be going farther in the wrong direction.

4:00pm, Cheshire. As Peter Oldthorpe steps up the gangway of the Derry boat in Glasgow, the centre of Cheshire is abuzz with police activity. O'Toole's vans are located. The vans are directed to return to the yard where they are checked for fingerprints. O'Toole and all his workers are fingerprinted and the prints are compared to the samples found in the vans. The forensic experts quickly determine that some recent fingerprints are not matching.

"Mr. O'Toole." Andrews is addressing Larry O'Toole in his caravan office. "Is any member of your work gang absent?"

"No. They're all here. And they'd all prefer to be off home and all. Why do you ask?"

"We found a set of prints in your van there, recent prints that don't match yours or any of your workers here. Van with registration LMB 542."

"Oh yeah. The van you said I was driving last night when I said I wasn't; the van you later said I wasn't driving...."

"Mr. O'Toole, I caution you to be cooperative...."

O'Toole ignores the caution and continues to talk, clearly miffed by the whole police intrusion. "...and if I tell you, will you believe me this time? It's probably Paddy Ward."

Andrews expects O'Toole to continue speaking. But O'Toole takes his kettle off the gas ring and goes out to fill it at the tap in the yard. "O'Toole, I didn't say you could leave...."

"I'm not leaving!" O'Toole shouts. "I'm making a pot of tea. Is that allowed, or will you arrest me for it?"

"Mr. O'Toole, this is a serious matter that requires your full attention and cooperation."

"So ask your questions while I boil the kettle."

"Where's Paddy Ward now?"

"I don't know where Paddy Ward is now."

"You don't? He's one of your gang, is he not?"

"Not anymore. He finished up here yesterday and went off."

"Went off where?"

"I don't know. I heard talk that he was going off with Houlihan."

"Houlihan? And who is 'Houlihan'?"

"Who is Houlihan, you ask? Well, Houlihan is Houlihan, that's who he is. Why don't you get one of those smart constables to ask the questions? Maybe they'll understand the answers."

Andrews is getting annoyed at O'Toole's attitude, but concedes that here in Cheshire they don't take warmly to Londoners.

Brady steps in with advice. "Constable McCann is out there in the yard. Perhaps he should join us."

"Yes, Brady. Get him in here."

O'Toole is making his tea. He checks that there is some of O'Doherty's milk remaining in the bottle. He is stirring his cup vigorously when they are joined by Brady and McCann. O'Toole pours tea into a second mug and passes it to McCann, deliberately omitting Andrews and Brady. McCann helps himself to sugar and milk, hiding his amusement at the disapproving looks from Andrews and Brady. Both O'Toole and McCann are noisily stirring their tea.

"Who is Houlihan?" Andrews shouts over the din.

"He owns and drives a tipper. He sub-contracts out to builders and construction companies and such like." McCann offers the information as if it were widely known.

"And you say that Paddy Ward is with Houlihan?" Andrews directs the question to O'Toole.

"I don't know where Paddy Ward is. All I'm saying is that's the talk."

Brady fires a question. "Do have anything with his fingerprints? A mug or some of his personal things?"

"Something with Paddy Ward's fingerprints? Well, let me think. Ah, yes. The shovel. He was shovelling gravel on Wednesday. The shovel is hanging in the tool shed. No one has used it since. That should have Paddy Ward's fingerprints and some of his spit too."

Was it one of O'Toole's men who drove the van last night? Probably. One whose fingerprints are in the van. Brady is checking the owners of the matching fingerprints and is assigning police to question the men and to confirm alibis. Now he can also confirm Paddy Ward's presence in the van and add him to the list. But how will they question him and confirm his whereabouts for last night? Brady states the obvious. "We need to question Paddy Ward."

Andrews agrees. "But how do we get in touch with him?"

McCann offers a suggestion. "Well, if he's gone off with Houlihan, Mrs. Houlihan should know where he is."

"Houlihan's wife?"

"No. His mother. She lives on Lime Avenue, just off the London Road in Lefthorpe, near to where the Dane joins the Weaver."

O'Toole smirks at Andrews. "Now that's smart thinking."

McCann continues, "It's not far from here."

Andrews is making for the door. "Then let's get over there. You take us, Constable, you know the way. And leave the mug of tea."

McCann takes one last gulp. "Yes, sir." And follows Andrews to the car.

6:00pm, Glasgow, Scotland. Peter Oldthorpe leans on the deck rail and watches the ropes slip and the gangplank pull up. The opening in the deck rail is closed, chained and secured. The ship draws away from the dock. Oldthorpe is taken by surprise at the unexpected sway and roll. He grips the rail for support. If the ship is this unsteady in the calm waters of the Clyde, he wonders how rough a voyage he can expect when they get to sea. He swallows and grips the rail more tightly; the motion of the ship reminds him of his apprehension of the sea. They'll be out in the Atlantic before reaching Derry at 6:00am the following morning. Twelve hours. How can it take so long? He looks around. He is the only one on deck. No one is waving or throwing flowers as they do in Southampton. It is a dull, rainy Glasgow evening. He goes inside, careful to hold on to bulwarks for support. The deck hatch is small and watertight. He turns the dog on the inside to secure the hatch and wonders where Francie and Tricks have gone.

He goes in search of the saloon. He has no trouble finding it. The ship is small and most passageways have 'no entry' signs. The saloon is one of the few accessible compartments on the deck, and it is noisy and smoke-filled. The passengers are congregated here – men, women and children. There are only about 20 passengers in all. There is no moveable furniture, just a bench secured to the bulkheads, and a blank area at the hull with a single porthole. There is a short curtain hanging over the porthole, swaying like a pendulum with the motion of the ship. One young mother is sitting on the bench and has a wain in a go-car which she is soothing by rolling the go-car smoothly back and forth. She is wearing a salmon-coloured 'A'-line coat over a black skirt and fawn pullover. For shoes she is wearing not-so-white gutties. Her head-covering is a picture headscarf. It has slipped down to her collar, and Peter is unable to discern what picture is displayed on it. Clearly, she obtains her clothes from second-hand thrift shops and is unconcerned about fashion. Peter Oldthorpe observes that she has her hand on the go-car, but it is the motion of the ship that is rolling it to and fro.

The men are congregated at the open doorway of an adjoining compartment. Through the doorway, Oldthorpe observes crewmen working a bar/galley, serving drinks and sandwiches through the doorway to the saloon. The men are already drinking porter and are smoking. Except the two gangers. The gangers are talking loudly and are drinking whiskey, and they are also smoking. Everyone is smoking except the two children and the wain. The little boy and little girl are sitting on the bench swinging their legs back and forth and are eating crisps. The wain is asleep. Peter Oldthorpe decides that the wain made the best choice. He finds an unoccupied section of bench and settles down to sleep.

Sometime later, Peter Oldthorpe is awakened by a lurch and hears a thud on the hull. He opens his eyes enquiringly.

The mother beside him says, with cigarette firmly held in her mouth, "Greenock." She pauses to remove the cigarette and knock off the ash away from the wain. "We stop at Greenock to pick up passengers. There might be some of the cattlemen getting on here."

"Cattlemen?" he enquires.

"Well, it IS a cattle boat you're on. The main traffic is cattle. But the cattle all come from Ireland. There won't be any going back. Just the cattlemen."

"Then we're still in Scotland?"

She laughs. "Sure we're still on the Clyde."

"Oh, sorry. I was asleep and lost track of time."

"Well, it's about seven, and we are at Greenock." Just as she says that they hear the scrape of the gangplank retracting, and feel the lurch of the ship disengaging from the dock.

The mother continues, "We are leaving Greenock now. Soon we'll be out on the firth, and after that it's the wild Atlantic. With no cargo as ballast, you can expect the ship to pitch and roll a lot. The next stop will be Queen's Quay (pronounced 'kay'), Derry."

6:00pm, Cheshire. Constable Manus McCann knocks at the door of Mrs. Houlihan's house on Lime Avenue, Lefthorpe.

Andrews asks, "Are you sure this is the house? How do you know if you don't know the number?"

"I know it from the flowers in the garden."

"This is a garden? It's a wilderness."

"It's a wild-flower garden, native plants, a bees' paradise. But the neighbours agree with you. That is how I know the house – from the neighbours' complaints."

"Well, you wouldn't see the likes of this in..."

Mrs. Houlihan opens the door and Andrews' attention is brought back to the case. McCann identifies himself and introduces Andrews. "Mrs. Houlihan, we need to ask you a few questions, if we may."

"What? Is it about Seáneen? Well, you'd better come in."

In the parlour, Mrs. Houlihan offers to make tea.

"No, no, Mrs. Houlihan. No need to do that."

"Is Seáneen in trouble?"

"No trouble. Actually, it's not about your son, but about Paddy Ward who might be travelling with him. We need to contact Paddy Ward."

"If you mean Paddy Dhu, yes, he went off with Seáneen last night or early this morning. Seáneen says that driving a long distance is much easier at night. He usually sets off around two in the morning."

"So your son, Shawneen..."

"No. He's not 'Seáneen' to you. He's John Houlihan to you."

"My apologies, Mrs. Houlihan. Now your son, John, went off somewhere early this morning with Paddy Ward?"

"They were talking about it all of last week. Seáneen got a hauling job with his tipper up at the Grudie Bridge. You know they work 'round the clock up there. With Paddy Dhu, the two of them will be able to work the tipper 24 hours a day taking turns driving and make a fortune."

"And that's where they went this morning?"

"Aye. And to pay for the trip up there, Seáneen transported a work gang and all."

"What? In a tipper lorry?"

"And with Paddy Dhu as relief driver, they made the journey in under 10 hours."

"How do you know that? Did he phone you?"

"Fred the milkman told me. And he was told by George at the Crowing Cock who got the phone call. He gave me a contact number for Seáneen. I'll get it for you. I have it writ down."

Mrs. Houlihan goes off to get the contact number. Andrews gives a thumbs-up sign to McCann and mouths, "We have Paddy Ward. We're one step closer to John Cross."

Mrs. Houlihan comes back with the note.

McCann and Andrews copy the information into their notebooks. "This is an Inverness exchange. Is this where he is staying?"

"No, it's not where he's staying. He doesn't know yet. This is where you leave a message for him. And it's not in

Inverness. It's way past Inverness by an hour or more. Way up there in Scotland y'hear."

"Thank you, Mrs. Houlihan. This is a great help. We'll find our own way out. Good night to you."

Outside, Andrews smiles for the first time since he smirked at the 'drunken Irish' stumbling into O'Toole's van at 12:41am. "Okay. We get on to the Inverness police to track down this number, and so to Houlihan, and Paddy Ward, and then to John Cross."

Andrews neglects to make note of Paddy Ward's nickname, 'Dhu'.

"Well, Constable. It looks like we're off to Inverness."

"We? I'm not going, surely?"

"If Cross is disguised as an itinerant and hiding with your traveller friends...what's their names?"

"Paddy Tricks and Paddy Clé."

"Yes. Paddy Tricks and Paddy Clay. If Cross is hiding with them, we need you to identify them. That would be the final step to apprehending Cross. Who else do you know would be able to recognise Tricks and Clay?"

"Sir. You said 'apprehend'. Not 'rescue'?"

"Regardless, we nab him."

"I don't know if Sergeant Morgan will release me to this assignment...."

"Don't worry about that. A crime of abduction was committed in his patch. This is an extension of the investigation. He'll authorise the assignment."

At Middlethorpe Police Station, Andrews arranges the detail with Sergeant Morgan regarding Constable McCann. He contacts the Inverness police to commence tracking down Houlihan and Paddy Ward. Brady arranges airline passage for four with BEA out of Manchester Ringway to Inverness Airport *Port-adhair Inbhir Nis* at Dalcross.

Piperson checks in with Andrews to give a progress report. Andrews asks, "Anything else I should know?"

"Yes. The newspapers are hounding us for a comment. The police tape at Cross's house is hard to miss. They have learned of Cross's disappearance. And they have been talking to Bess and George, and to others at the Crowing Cock and elsewhere. If it's okay with you, Sergeant Morgan will make a comment to the press on Monday morning."

"Can we trust him to be circumspect?"

"Don't worry. I'll brief him, and I will be close by."

"And which papers, may I ask?"

"So far, The Mirror, The Express and the Empire News."

"Well, that's not unexpected. Okay, I'll leave it to you and Morgan to look after that."

The three MI6 agents and Constable McCann are scheduled to depart Manchester at 8:30am on the following day, Sunday, and to arrive in Inverness at 10:00am. McCann wonders if he'll get to see the invisible Cody tomorrow. Andrews looks at the clock on the wall. It is 7:00pm. He relaxes and suddenly feels tired. Tomorrow he will be refreshed and ready to nab John Cross.

7:00pm, The Firth of Clyde. Peter Oldthorpe tries to relax. He is relieved that he has departed Scotland. He has evaded the SIS (posing as Special Branch) and has eluded the police, and he is gone from them. He falls to sleep again before he considers that Derry is in the United Kingdom. Peter Oldthorpe may be gone from Scotland, but not necessarily out of reach of the long arm of His Majesty's Secret Intelligence Service.

CHAPTER SEVENTEEN

PETER OLDTHORPE AT SEA

Saturday 15 July 1950
Firth of Clyde, Scotland

Peter Oldthorpe, sleeping on the bench in the saloon, moves with the motion of the ship and bumps his head on the bulkhead. Thus awakened, he sits up to observe his surroundings. He remembers that he is on a ship en route from Glasgow to Derry. He is still in the saloon. It is noisier now, and the air is thick with tobacco smoke. He could do with some food, but he has no money to purchase anything from the galley.

There are three newcomers in the saloon since he last surveyed it. Judging from their attire, these must be cattle dealers that boarded at Greenock. All three are dressed in high-quality heavy tan trench coats, worn loose and unfastened. Like the gangers, they also wear gangster-style fedoras, only the cattlemen's fedoras are brown, stiff-brimmed and firm. Their boots are similar, except for the one wearing wellington boots. But the overriding unique feature of their attire is the drover's stick that each of them wields. They slap their sticks against their thighs as they speak; they tap their boots with them; they scratch their noses with them; and they point them hither and thither to emphasise a point in their discourse. When they require two hands for eating and drinking, the drover sticks are held in place by the armpits like a swagger stick. The cattlemen and the gangers are arguing about the merits of smuggling and the unfairness of rationing. And everyone is drinking.

Paddy Tricks is entertaining some of the company with card tricks. But he foregoes his profitable con game, 'find-the-lady'. If he were to upset any of these Irish seasonal workers or cattlemen, he has nowhere to hide. No money changes hands in the course of his card tricks. The company is happy to reward him with an occasional sandwich or a drink from the galley.

Francie Ward notices Peter Oldthorpe studying the cattlemen. Francie looks at Peter, pats his pockets and tilts his head towards the cattlemen. Peter understands this to mean that the cattlemen are loaded and plush with money. Francie begins to sing *'The Green Glens of Antrim'*. The drovers and gangers cease their debate to listen. At the end of the song they complement him and treat him to food and drink. The cattlemen are quite generous in their appreciation.

Francie looks at Peter and winks at him to indicate "You're next."

Peter sings *'Annie Laurie'*. At the conclusion of which, he gets a 'well done', but no offers of food or drink.

Francie signals to him to observe; and Francie commences another song, *'The Rose of Aranmore'*. Again, he gets the same generous appreciation.

Francie pauses to consume his drink and whispers to Peter, "Sing something they know, something that they can join in with."

Peter thinks. He knows hymns and school songs from his youth, back when he was John Cross, but not much else. Then he remembers his college days and starts to sing *'If You Were the Only Girl in the World'*. The smoking mother on the bench joins in. She and Peter ham it up as a duet.

The cattlemen enjoy it and offer to treat them both to sandwiches and drink. "What'll ye have?" "How about another song?"

Peter begins *'Indian Love Call'*, and the smoking mother plays along. She places one hand on Peter's arm, still clutching the smouldering cigarette, and she holds on securely to the handle of the go-car with her other hand. The baby laughs as the go-car is pushed to and fro to the rhythm of the song. The gangers make a big fuss over the two singers singing a Broadway-style popular song, and when they have ascertained their names, they announce to the crowd that Peter and Maura were the singers. There is appreciation from all present. The cattlemen order drinks for them at the bar – 'the best whiskey'. There is only one whiskey available, but it sounds so much better to order 'the best whiskey'.

"Whiskey, a man's drink, for Peter here. And what do you have for the lady?"

"Whiskey with a splash of white lemonade."

"There ye go Peter, the best whiskey in the house. And here's for Maura, the best whiskey with a splash of lemonade."

Francie, who knows all the songs, takes over the singing. Peter is content with his sandwiches and whiskey and lets Francie have centre stage. He resumes his seat next to Maura, the poor mother. Maura starts on another cigarette. She checks on the two children and shares her sandwiches with them. She turns her attention to the wain, a wee lad just old enough for solid food. She finger-feeds him bits of an egg-salad sandwich. She holds the cigarette in her mouth to free up both hands while she feeds him. Between bites, she removes the smouldering cigarette and holds it in her fingers. Bits of egg salad are stuck to her fingers, which she inadvertently transfers to the smoking cigarette. Peter is curious. A poor mother travelling with three young children. Where is the father?

"Pardon me, Maura, are you travelling alone? I mean, travelling alone with three children?"

She resumes pushing egg salad into the wain's mouth. "Oh, I am," she says through her partially closed mouth which is once again gripping the cigarette. She removes the cigarette, flicks off the ash away from the baby, and continues, "Me man went off to work at the Grudie Bridge. There's no place for weemen up there, so I'm going back to me ma until his work up there is done."

The cigarette goes back in her mouth and she breaks off another section of sandwich for the wain. Peter wonders if there is as much tobacco on the sandwich as there is egg salad on the cigarette.

"So how about yourself, Peter? I see you're dressed like a traveller, but you don't sound like one. And I noticed when we were singing together that you have soft hands. No one on this ship has soft hands, except for the wain here. Why are you travelling with the Wards anyways?"

"Well, it's funny that you mention the Grudie Bridge. I was on my way there with Paddy More Ward..."

"You're with Paddy More Ward's gang? Now NOBODY is in Ward's gang unless they are from the clan, or at least well in with them – either kith or kin." Maura looks at Peter Oldthorpe, and looks over at Francie and Tricks. "I can see that you are travelling with two of the Wards. But..." Maura shakes her head in disbelief and continues puffing on the cigarette and pushing the go-car.

Peter turns to face her and asks, "What time is it now, Maura?"

"It's about a half past eight. Sure we are not right started yet. We're still in the firth. Do you know any more songs?" And in this vein the night progresses.

Sometime later, Peter notices a significant difference in the ship's motion. The degree to which she pitches and rolls is disquieting. The people in the saloon are unable to stand erect. They lean against the bulkheads or against each other like a house of cards. Some sit on the bench or on the floor. The curtain is swinging at the porthole like a pendulum. Peter is perturbed that it is swinging more than 180°. He is unable to judge the degree to which the curtain is actually swinging against the degree to which the ship is rolling. Peter has lost all concept of horizontal plane. The galley stops preparing hot food. Only pre-prepared sandwiches are being served now. The bar is still serving drinks. Peter would be apprehensive of the ship's unfamiliar motion except that all the other occupants of the saloon are unperturbed by it. This gives him some assurance.

But as the sea gets rougher, and the pitching and rolling gets more pronounced, Peter feels compelled to go up to the upper deck to observe the true state of the ship in the water. If he can re-establish his sense of vertical and horizontal balance, he may be able to alleviate his fears and restore his tenuous sense of security. How much can a ship pitch and roll anyway? It can't possibly be as severe as it appears down here in the saloon.

Peter gets up from the bench, and promptly sits down again, unable to keep his balance. On his second attempt, he leans heavily against the hull and bulkheads, making his way slowly around the perimeter of the saloon, and proceeds out through the doorway. In the passageway, he continues to walk in the same awkward fashion. He makes his way to the ladder and climbs up to the upper deck level. Locating the hatch to the outer deck, he turns the dog handle on the watertight door, and swings open the hatch. He is immediately blinded by wind and rain. Taking care to step over the lip of the hatchway, he steps outside and grasps the deck rail firmly. With one hand secure on the rail, he leans back to close the hatch, making sure to turn the dogs to render the hatch watertight.

It is not yet night. But it may as well be. Peter Oldthorpe squints through the blowing rain and sea spray to view his surroundings. He peers out horizontally, but he is unable to perceive anything at first. On all sides it is dark – actually a very dark green. In a sudden jolt of realisation he grips the rail in terror. The dark green that he perceives on all sides is water. It is only in looking upwards that he is able to see above the water. The wall of dark green is coming towards him. He braces for when the wall of water falls onto the ship to engulf it. Why is it taking so long to actually spill over the ship? He sees the approaching wall of water clearly now, and the seaweed and kelp and wrack floating just below the surface. As the wall of water approaches, the seaweed rises upwards.

Peter relaxes somewhat in understanding the movement of the floating seaweed. Although the wall of water is approaching the ship, the seaweed is maintaining a constant distance. The water itself is not coming towards the ship at all. It is the force of the swell that is approaching the ship. The water, and all that is floating on top, is being forced upwards by the energy of the swell. Just as the seaweed is floating upwards, so too is the ship. He is able to confirm this by observing the crest of the swell. It is no longer towering over the ship. He actually feels the ship rise up and up and up. Looking out horizontally, Peter Oldthorpe now discerns the skyline. He laughs in relief at his own naivety.

He decides to observe a full cycle of rising and falling – up the crests and down the troughs. After which, he will return to the saloon, content is his understanding of a ship's motion. His fear is dispelled by his new-found understanding of a ship's motion at sea, and the novelty of the experience thrills him. "John Cross," addressing himself by his previous name, "you are one of Britain's leading scientists. Don't you understand energy, and buoyancy, and motion? Of course, the ship is designed for these conditions, riding and falling through the ocean swells, and all the while moving steadily to its destination port."

The ship crests the swell and, for a short moment, the propeller is free of the water. The ship gives an unexpected yaw, and she is then corrected back on course as the propeller and rudder re-engage. Leaning over the rail, Peter Oldthorpe strains to get a glimpse of the water again. The trough of the swell is deep down in the ocean. The ship begins its slow descent. Peter holds his breath. Will it slide down like a toboggan on a hill? No, of course not.

The ship's descent is just as slow as its previous ascent, but in reverse. Peter is on the starboard side of the ship. The port side is where the wall of water will reappear, moving away from the ship. Cautiously holding firmly to the rail, he shifts his position to get a view of the bow. Looking forward, he sees the length of the trough, and the ship falling slowly downwards. And throughout all this, the ship is moving at a regulated speed to its destination. This is as thrilling as a child's first experience on a roller coaster. Peter is soaked from the rain and spray, but he is determined to view at least one cycle of the ship's rising and falling. Then he will return to the saloon with much relief in his understanding of the ship's behaviour at sea.

The ship reaches the bottom of the trough. Peter braces for the expected change in motion. The ship should alter from falling to rising along with the accompanying appropriate pitching and rolling. Unexpectedly, the ship continues to fall. Peter grips the rail in alarm. She sinks deeper into the water. She is going down, down. The water is almost at the lower deck level. The ship continues to sink. The bow is completely submerged and seawater is flooding over the gunwales onto the lower deck. Fear grips him. What has gone wrong? Has the strain opened the watertight hatches and is water now flooding the ship? The ship shudders. The stern sinks backwards further into the sea. The bow rises up, throwing a huge surge of water back along the deck. The entire lower deck is flushed by the rushing water. Nothing could withstand the force of this gush of water. Had Peter Oldthorpe decided to observe the sea from the lower deck, he would now be washed out to sea. Even so, seawater is thrown upwards onto the upper deck drenching and blinding Peter Oldthorpe. It runs along the deck and spills over onto the lower deck.

The ship shudders again as she rights herself from the reverse surge and she pitches fiercely. She settles and commences floating upward on the wall of the next swell. In this period of relative calm, Peter plucks up courage motivated by near panic, and re-enters the ship. He is particularly attentive to securing the door of the watertight hatch. This recent experience fills him with bleak fear. He understands energy and metal stress. This stress on the ship is too demanding. How many more times can the ship withstand this punishment before she breaks apart? Maybe even in the next swell. Peter Oldthorpe's fear of the sea has returned, but this time it is more intense than before. He is filled with a deep dread.

Peter is totally saturated when he returns to the saloon. With all the drinking and smoking and singing, and all the falling around, no one gives him any notice. Peter Oldthorpe is convinced that he will perish on this voyage. He has no belief in God, or in the afterlife, so he seeks comfort in inebriation. He does not want to be around when he dies, at least not consciously aware of his dying. Without money to purchase drink, Peter resumes singing.

He discovers a new talent – singing songs he doesn't know. All he needs to do is sing the first line, and then wave his hand for all to join in. *'Roamin' in the Gloamin'*, *'The Northern Lights of Old Aberdeen'*. As he is plied with more and more whiskey, he also needs to drink and swallow, while waving his hand for the singing to continue. *'Marie's Wedding'* followed by *'Westering Home'*.

Peter continues with opening lines, hand waving and downing whiskeys. The ship continues to pitch and roll, and Peter feels her spinning around and around. He holds onto the bulkhead for support. The saloon deck slowly tilts up. He leans on the bulkhead; he leans on the rising deck floor. The deck floor continues to rise until it is vertical. Peter rests his cheek against it, holding on to it with both hands. The ship is spinning faster and faster. Peter doggedly attempts to continue singing –

> *"Three times 'round, spun our gallant ship;*
> *Three times 'round spun she.*
> *Three times 'round spun our gallant ship;*
> *Then she...*
>   *sank...*
>   *to the bottom of the..."*

CHAPTER EIGHTEEN

SCOTLAND

Sunday 16 July 1950
Ringway Airport
Manchester, England

8:00am. Officer Andrews is awaiting the arrival of Constable Manus McCann. He sees him walking from the car park. Brady and Cody have already checked in separately. McCann sees him. Andrews signals him not to greet him. Andrew slips McCann his ticket and walks away towards the departure gate without a word. McCann goes to the ticket counter to check in and get his boarding pass. He is informed that he will fly on a 24-seat Viscount turboprop for his flight to Dalcross, Inverness, departing at 08:40, arriving in Dalcross at 10:10. Andrews has deliberately arranged separate check-ins so that they are not seen as a group. And McCann is unsure which of the other passengers is Cody, or even if Cody is on the same flight.

On board, McCann accepts a copy of the Manchester Guardian. Andrews, in another section of the cabin, accepts the complimentary glass of whisky and a cigarette from the hostess. Brady sleeps through the bacon and sausage breakfast. McCann attempts to get a look at the other passengers. There are four empty seats. Although Inverness is in the Highlands and on the seacoast, none of the passengers look like fishermen or hunters. They appear to be businessmen, many of whom are working with briefcases on their laps or are in serious discussion with a co-passenger.

The passenger next to McCann greets him. "I haven't seen you on this flight before. Are you new with Conon?"

"Conon?"

"I'm sorry. I thought you were one of the new engineers or surveyors with Conon. You know the Conon Hydro-Electric Power Scheme? Oh, I'm Frank Hanna, one of the civil engineers on the Loch Fannich project – 'Operation Bathplug' as we call it."

"Manus McCann. And I'm not with the Hydro-Electric Scheme. I'm a policeman, actually."

"Stationed in Inverness?"

"No. Visiting, actually."

Hanna deduces that the visit is not recreational. McCann is dressed in a suit and is carrying a briefcase. "So, Manus, are you familiar with 'Operation Bathplug'?"

For the next hour Hanna describes the difficulties they have encountered in tunnelling under Loch Fannich. Loch Fannich was dammed and its water level raised. An underground water tunnel is required from the loch to the Grudie Bridge Power Station, a distance of 6.5kms. A final mass of rock is proving to be difficult. This requires sophisticated blasting skills and plenty of good old muscle power to work in a cramped and dangerous environment to get the project back on target.

"How are you getting into Inverness from the airport? You are welcome to use the Conon bus if you like." Hanna continues talking and offering help. "You know it will be raining when we land. It's always raining in the Highlands. But then, it's because of the water that we have all these hydro dams."

A few seats forward, Andrews is on his second whisky. Why, he ponders, would Cross go to Inverness? Surely this couldn't bring him closer to Russia. What is in the Scottish

Highlands that has a Russian connection? Agitated, he flips the pages of the in-flight magazine. It welcomes travellers to the Highlands and suggests sightseeing for visitors. 'Russian'. What was that? He stops the page flipping. Somewhere in the pages flipping past he saw the word 'Russian'. Andrews starts flipping the pages again, but this time slowly. Did he just imagine seeing the word? After all, 'Russia' is on his mind. There it is again. The page is headed 'Kinlochbervie'.

Kinlochbervie is a town about 100 miles from Inverness. Travelling time is two and a half hours. Kinlochbervie is a small fishing town, but because of its location so far north, trawlers plying the northern waters frequently use it to unload their catches. Foreign trawlers use the port as a shelter during stormy weather, and the town frequently accommodates Icelandic and Russian trawlers in the shelter of the harbour.

"Fishing trawlers," Andrews utters aloud, disturbing his co-traveller who is busy with mathematical formulae on his workbook. This is a lead Andrews must investigate as soon as he lands. He needs to contact Piperson to tell him to include fishing ports in the list of possible exit points to be monitored. Andrews considers the likelihood of Cross getting access to Russia via a Russian fishing trawler.

Brady, sitting a few seats away, opens one eye to look out the window of the plane. All he can see is thick cloud. They should be landing soon. The seatbelt sign is on. Why are we still up in the clouds? Then he feels the bump and hears the sound of the plane landing. They have landed, not in a cloud, but in pouring rain. All the regular travellers get out of their seats and put on raincoats. Even McCann has a fold-up mac and cap that he takes out of his hand luggage. It is a long walk across the tarmac to the terminal in a downpour.

Brady hadn't thought to bring any rainwear, but he has some satisfaction in seeing that Andrews has no raincoat either.

It is not unusual for a passenger to arrive in Inverness without a raincoat or umbrella. The hostess at the exit door provides a golf umbrella for Andrews and Brady to share on the walk to the terminal building.

Inside the building, there is a member of the Scottish police to meet them and provide transportation. "Officers Andrews, Brady and Cody? I am Constable Callum MacPherson. I will take you to Dingwall."

"Thank you, Constable. But Officer Cody is renting a car for his visit to the Highlands. I'm Andrews, this is Brady, and this is Constable McCann from the Cheshire County Police."

"Okay, then. Welcome to the Hielands."

"Constable, you said 'Dingwall'. Are we not going to Garve? Or maybe based in Inverness?"

"Och, Aye. But Garve is an area, not a town. It is served by Dingwall. Inverness is the DHQ (Divisional Headquarters). There is a Loch Garve; and four miles from that is a wee village called Garve with a school and a railway station, but no poileas station. Dingwall is 10 miles from the loch. The Conon people refer to the whole area as 'Garve' because of the location of their project up at Loch Fannich. But Dingwall is where you'll find them. And that's where we're headed now."

"Ah. I see."

"Here, follow me to the Land Rover. Oh, don't worry about the rain; I'm parked at the kerb."

They quickly settle into the Land Rover. Three passengers fit comfortably with hand baggage, but not so if the extra person Cody had been included. Andrews sits in front.

MacPherson makes friendly conversation. "The drive from Dalcross to Dingwall is 35 minutes. I'm afraid you'll not see much scenery on the way today with all the rain."

Andrews is uninterested in scenery. "I've a favour to ask, Constable MacPherson."

"And what is it?"

"I need to make an urgent phone call, a secure call. Could we stop at the Inverness Police Station en route?"

"Ay! That's nae problem. It's on our way. It's only 100 yards off the A9 on Longman Road. We'll be there in less than 15 minutes."

A short time later, the Land Rover pulls into the police station's car park at 6 Burnett Road. It is at the T-junction of Burnett Road and Longman Road, but it is a dead end with only pedestrian access from Longman Road. Vehicular traffic must use Harbour Road to Burnett Street to the dead end for access to the police station.

Andrews jumps out of the Land Rover as it comes to a halt. "I won't be a jiffy." And he runs into the station. Within a few minutes he is back in the Land Rover.

"Well?" asks Brady.

"Oh, I got through right away."

"And did you talk to Piperson?"

"No. I spoke with our own people on the 'Code White' file. They already have a watch on fishing ports. It appears that Piperson has covered all points of exit from the country just as he said he would."

"Okay, then? We're off to Dingwall?" enquires Constable Callum MacPherson. He engages the gears and sets off with more speed than necessary; up Burnett Road, right onto Harbour Road past the Rescue Service; left onto Longman Road at the Harbour Road Roundabout; three blocks farther on and a left at the Longman Road

Roundabout; and they are on the A9 and speeding to Dingwall. Passing over the Beauly Firth Bridge, MacPherson informs them, "Less than twenty minutes from here," and drives faster.

Five minutes later, the Land Rover turns left off the A9 at Tore – a little too fast, tires squealing in protest, and travels west on the A835. The A835 swings north and in another ten minutes they are skirting Conon Bridge. Just another five minutes to Dingwall. Passing Conon Bridge, the A835 swings west and south again.

Constable MacPherson points ahead. "Loch Garve is a few miles up yonder."

The three passengers stare ahead as if they could confirm MacPherson's statement, and are thrown off balance as the Land Rover makes another sharp turn, right this time onto the A862.

Constable MacPherson maintains his informative commentary. "We are on Station Road now, on the outskirts of Dingwall. Just a few minutes more to the poileas station. Here, the A862 becomes Greenhill Street." The passengers take his word for it. They don't know where they are. "And if we keep going, we are on Newton Road. Only we turn here...' and once more the Land Rover makes an unexpected turn. "...left onto Burn Lane. And here we are." Not quite 'here we are'. The Land Rover turns again, right onto Bridaig Avenue, and comes to an abrupt stop. There it is – the police station.

Constable MacPherson is still speaking. "And Garve is 14 miles from here. And the Grudie Bridge project is another 14 miles beyond that. There is no real road into the Grudie Bridge. If you need to go there you will require a Land Rover or a big-wheeled lorry. And it will take you almost an hour."

Andrews, Brady and McCann are relieved that the journey from Dalcross to Dingwall is over. They follow Constable Callum MacPherson into the police station.

MacPherson turns back to inform them, "The Sergeant is Colin Blake. You'll like him. He gets down to business without unnecessary small talk."

Inside, the sergeant is standing waiting for them. "It's 10:55, Constable. You are cutting it fine. Don't bother with the introductions. Look after the bags." And to the three visitors, "I'm Sergeant Colin Blake. Which one of you is Andrews?"

Andrews begins to speak. Blake nods and cuts him off. "Then this other one must be Brady."

Brady nods.

"But no Cody."

This time Andrews manages to speak. "Officer Cody is here, but elsewhere..."

"Ah, the undercovered part of an undercover operation? So who is th'aen one?"

"Constable Manus McCann, sir!" McCann boldly introduces himself.

"What? Not a Sassenach?"

"No, sir. I'm Irish, a constable with the Cheshire police."

"A constable from a county constabulary is assisting the Special Branch? Is this to give me confidence in the capability of the Special Branch?"

Andrews is irked at this. He begins to speak "We're..." and bites his tongue.

"You're what, Officer Andrews?"

Andrews carefully reforms his sentence. "Yes. We're working with Special Branch."

Blake notices a slight emphasis on 'with'. He determines that these officers are not Special Branch at all. They have spoken for less than a minute. But Andrews and Brady already sense that there is no love for the English here.

Sergeant Blake points at the clock on the wall. "My office at 11:00. I have the information that you requested. And we need to set the order of cooperation that you require."

Blake goes into his office. It is four minutes to eleven. Andrews gestures to McCann indicating that he is excluded from the meeting. The reason McCann is invited along is to point out Paddy Ward and Houlihan when they catch up with them. There is no need for a lowly constable to be privy to matters of sensitive national security.

Sergeant Blake's office, 11:00am. Sergeant Blake looks at Andrews and Brady. He glances at the clock on the wall. "Where's McCann?"

"Constable McCann is not part of the team. He will not be joining the meeting."

"Very well. Sit."

Blake moves a sheet of paper to the centre of his desk. "Cody left a message. He has been instructed to go to Kinlochbervie. He is to contact Inspector Malcolm MacDonald at Rhiconich." (So Blake knew that Cody was not with them when they arrived.) Blake continues, "I have been asked to track down some newcomers to the Grudie Bridge that arrived here yesterday – John Houlihan with a construction tipper, and one Paddy Ward. We know the whereabouts of Houlihan. We tracked him from the phone number we were given. We have not approached him, just as we have been advised, just keeping him in our sights."

"Good. But what about Paddy Ward? He's the one we need to question."

"Aye, but which Paddy Ward would that be?"

"What do you mean 'which Paddy Ward'? The Paddy Ward that came with Houlihan." Andrews displays impatience. Brady kicks him in the ankle to warn him not to get on the wrong side of the local police.

"Aye, and which one of the Paddy Wards that came with Houlihan?"

"How many Paddy Wards could there have been in Houlihan's tipper?"

"Thirty," Blake says in abrupt response.

Andrews looks at him in disbelief. "You want me to believe that thirty Paddy Wards came to Garve in Houlihan's tipper?"

Blake speaks slowly so as to penetrate the Sassenach's brain. "Thirty Paddy Wards came in Houlihan's tipper yesterday. All Irish navvies are called 'Paddy'. Right? And all the Paddies in Big Paddy Ward's gang are referred to as 'Paddy Ward'. Translation: 'Paddy Ward' – any Irish navvy in Paddy Ward's work gang. They never go by their real names. I need a nickname to distinguish which one you are looking for."

"Hold on. I spoke with Houlihan's mother. She said that Paddy Ward is Houlihan's relief driver. She referred to him as 'Paddy do', as in 'do this' or 'do that'. I thought she meant that Paddy Ward was a doer, like a worker."

"I think what you heard was not 'do' but 'dubh'. Paddy Dhu Ward. Paddy Ward of the black hair. I was hoping that it would not be the ganger himself that you wanted – Paddy More Ward. That's Paddy Mór, Big Paddy Ward. Upsetting the ganger upsets the gang, which upsets the work – work which is behind schedule."

Andrews and Brady detect that the Highland police would not take kindly to any English interference in the operation of the Conon Project. Andrews and Brady had better have good reason for their enquiries here in the Highlands. Brady decides to bring Sergeant Blake into their confidence. Not to tell all, but enough to ensure his cooperation.

"Sergeant, early yesterday morning, just after midnight, John Cross disappeared from a country lane in Cheshire. We don't know if he was abducted or if he disappeared intentionally."

"And why is he of interest to Special Branch?"

"John Cross is employed at the Royal Ordnance Facility in Risley. We have reason to believe that the abduction/disappearance was accommodated by a van driven by Paddy Doo Ward."

Blake nods in understanding. He even overlooks Brady's mispronunciation of 'Dhu'. "So you are looking for this John Cross? And Paddy Dhu will lead you to him?"

"That's the trail we are following. And it brings us to you and to your help. It's a matter of national security."

"John Cross, John Cross. I saw that name somewhere today." Blake goes to his office door and shouts out, "Bring me a copy of today's Sunday Mirror!"

Andrews and Brady look at each other. Brady mouths "the Sunday Mirror?" The duty officer brings in a copy of the newspaper.

Blake quickly thumbs through it to an inside page. "Here it is. The Mirror followed up on a crime scene, with no crime in evidence, in Cheshire on Saturday morning. *'Interviewing staff and patrons of the Crowing Cock...'* Here is the bit that's interesting: *'...disappearance of John Cross who works at Risley. Could we be looking at a defecting British scientist in the aftermath of Klaus Fuchs's arrest and sentencing? The Fuchs case revealed that Soviet espionage agents are active in Britain'"*

Blake slaps the paper and looks squarely at Andrews and Brady. "Is this the case you are working on?"

Andrews and Brady are taken aback by the Mirror's report. "That's not news," exclaims Andrews. "That's just cheap sensationalism and speculation!"

"Aye, but maybe close to the truth. Eh? And there are police alerts at all the fishing ports in Scotland. 'Watch out for any contact with Russian trawlers' Yes? And Cody's on his way to Kinlochbervie? Well, let me tell you, if Cross is on his way to Russia, willingly or unwillingly, he will not succeed via the Hielands."

"So let's find out. The trail leads to Paddy Doo Ward. We need to question Paddy Doo. Can you locate him, Sergeant? And we need McCann with us. McCann can identify him."

Andrews and Brady go into the outer office and shout "Constable McCann!"

The duty officer informs them, "Constable McCann went off with Constable MacPherson."

"Went off where? When's he returning?"

"They went to the kirk. Callum said that he could catch Mass at St. Lawrence's on Castle Street at eleven. So he drove him there."

"Good God. And who goes to church at a time like this?"

The duty officer looks at Andrews with puzzlement. From behind, Andrews hears Blake's voice bellowing from out his office. "We do. We all go to the kirk here. I don't know what you lads do in London."

"And when will they be back?"

"I don't know."

Andrews and Brady debate whether to wait for McCann, go fetch him at the church, or proceed to find Paddy

Dhu without him. In the course of this debate they hear the Land Rover arrive back.

The duty officer informs them, "And here they are now."

The two constables enter and are immediately subjected to verbal reproof. "McCann, time is of the essence. Jump to it. We are off to get Paddy Doo and question him."

Andrews is not too sure where he is actually going. He looks back at Blake for guidance. Blake signals to MacPherson to join them.

"Don't you want John Cross?" McCann asks.

Andrews looks at McCann as if he had asked the stupidest question of the day. "Of course we want John Bloody Cross. Why do you think we need to question Paddy Doo Ward?"

"He's in Glasgow." Everyone is walking towards the door. They stop and look at McCann. "John Cross is in Glasgow," says McCann to clarify his remark.

Andrews' patience is exhausted. "And how do you know that, Constable McCann?"

"From Paddy Finn and Long Paddy."

Blake comes to the rescue. "Gentlemen, my office." He walks back into his office and waits for Andrews, Brady and McCann to enter.

Inside the office, Brady, who is calmer than Andrews, questions McCann. "So, Constable, why do you say that John Cross is in Glasgow?"

"I went to Mass..."

"Yes, we know that."

"...and there, I met a lot of Irish lads. So I ask if any of them had arrived with Houlihan. I got to talking with Paddy Finn Ward and Long Paddy Ward. They told me about an 'English Paddy' that came from Manchester on Saturday morning – a softy with smooth hands and no boots. When they asked why, they were told that he is not a labourer, he is an explosives man. They take that to mean a blasting expert for the tunnel at Loch Fannich. Except that English Paddy left them at Glasgow."

"And what makes you think that 'English Paddy' is John Cross?"

"The driver was Houlihan, and the relief driver was Paddy Dhu Ward. And there was no other 'softy' in the gang. All the others were Irish navvies known to Paddy Finn and to Long Paddy. You say that Paddy Dhu Ward will lead you to John Cross? Well, there you are – Paddy Dhu Ward transported 'English Paddy' to Glasgow. And John Cross hopped off the tipper there."

Andrews and Brady speak at the same time. "Was he alone when he hopped off?"

"Where exactly in Glasgow did he get off from Houlihan's tipper?"

"What's the fastest way to Glasgow?"

Blake reaches out and shakes McCann's hand. "Good work, Constable. Don't let the Sassenaigh get to you."

Both Andrews and Brady are cognisant that Blake never shook hands with either of them since their arrival in Dingwall.

McCann attempts to answer the questions. "He hopped off with Paddy Tricks and Paddy Clé at the place where they picked up additional workers for the work gang – at the Derry boat at the Broomielaw."

Andrews and Brady are uncertain that they fully understand what McCann is saying. Is McCann speaking in English?

Blake, on the other hand, comprehends exactly. "What this smart constable is saying is that John Cross got off the tipper at the Burns & Laird dock in Glasgow, along with Paddy Tricks Ward and Paddy Clé/Lefty Ward." In anticipation of the next question, he continues, "And the quickest way to Glasgow is by the A9. I'll arrange a ride for you to the Pitlochrie poileas and have you meet up with the Glasgow poileas there. You'll be in Glasgow within four hours."

"Wait!" says Andrews to McCann. "Did you say Paddy Tricks Ward and Paddy Clay Ward?"

"That's right. John Cross and Paddy Tricks and Paddy Clé..."

"It looks like the..." Andrews interrupts McCann.

"...like the itinerants from the Bostock Green oak ritual are back in the picture." Brady finishes the sentence, coming to the same conclusion as Andrews.

"Are STILL in the picture," Andrews deduces smugly. "They have been together all along."

Brady reminds Andrews. "And Constable McCann is needed to identify either of those two Ward itinerants."

Constable MacPherson is tossing the Land Rover keys in the air in anticipation of another run.

"What about flying to Glasgow?" Andrews asks Blake.

"There are no flights from here to Glasgow. Take the A9."

"A connection. Are there any flights today that will connect to Glasgow?"

"There's one to London later today that connects to Glasgow. Go that way, and you'll be there tomorrow. Take the A9, man." What does he need to do to convince these Sassenaigh that the quickest way from Dingwall to Glasgow is by car on the A9?

Constable MacPherson is already loading the overnight bags into the Land Rover. The Secret Service men are not going to overnight in the highlands on this visit.

Andrews and Brady nod to each other in assent. "Okay. We're off to Glasgow by road." They address Blake in turn to thank him for his assistance.

"Don't thank me. It's Constable McCann you need to thank."

Blake returns to his office to resume his duties, without a farewell or handshake. Andrews and Brady, who feel upstaged by Constable McCann, neglect to acknowledge the constable's contribution. All three follow Constable MacPherson into the Land Rover and brace for another perilous ride. Andrews and Brady are no closer to John Cross than when they first started to track him; except that now they have a confirmed sighting and are confident that they will close in on him shortly.

13:00 hours. Speeding south on the A9 through intermittent drizzle and sunshine, they feel positive for the first time in 36 hours. It feels much longer than that from when they first lost visual contact of John Cross at Bostock Green. Their slip-up there will be forgotten if they can seize Cross within the next 24 hours. They are anxious to reach Glasgow.

17:00 hours. Andrews, Brady and McCann are in the Glasgow Police Station in Stewart Street, late on Sunday afternoon. The police station affords them access to telephones so that they are able to report on their progress and adjust to any change in orders. They are informed by London that Cody has been assigned to another aspect of the case. They are not enlightened as to what precisely that might be, except that Cody is off the team, but not off the case.

Four constables who are familiar with the Broomielaw/Clyde Street area of Glasgow are assigned to assist them. They meet at 6:00pm. Andrews and Brady bring them up to speed in their hunt for John Cross. McCann contributes his information on the Wards and how they feature in Cross's flight.

According to a reliable source, the two Wards and John Cross were together at the Burns and Laird dock last night. The local constables are familiar with the area and the operations of the shipping line. The cattle boats only regularly operate Mondays to Fridays. Any departures on a Saturday night would have been passengers only, or for a special demand. They explain that regular departures are to Dublin, Belfast and Derry. However, if there is a request, ships will call to other ports en route, frequently Greenock. The shipping line offers additional sailings to Sligo and Westport upon request. The Shipping office is closed today. Tomorrow they will question the Burns & Laird staff and the locals. They need to establish if the three men actually boarded a ship. Or if they remained behind in Scotland.

Monday 17 July 1950, 8:00am, Glasgow, Scotland. The four constables certainly know the area. They quickly learn that an Irish traveller was spotted under the George V Bridge playing 'find-the-lady' on Saturday. The Burns & Laird canteen manageress informs them that three Irish travellers boarded the Derry Boat, one of whom was earlier observed executing card tricks in the canteen.

"Tricks. That is Paddy Tricks Ward," McCann remarks. "He is the one who orchestrated the theatrical act that concealed Cross's getaway."

Next, they have the shipping office confirm that no one disembarked when the ship docked at Greenock. All passengers who boarded at Broomielaw could only have disembarked at Queen's Quay Londonderry at 6:00am Sunday morning, just 28 hours ago.

Andrews checks the time. It is now 10:20am. John Cross is getting farther away. "What's the quickest way to Londonderry from here? And don't tell me it's by car."

One of the helpful constables has the answer instantly. "The ferry from Stranraer. From here to Stranraer is one hour and forty-five minutes. You'll reach Stranraer just after noon. You'll miss the 10:30 sailing, of course. But you'll be in time for the 13:30 sailing. That means you would be in Larne in Ireland at 15:30, and you're only an hour and a half from Derry. You could be in Derry by 17:00, that's five o'clock pm. That's provided you leave now...."

"...by car. Somehow, I knew it would be by car."

"We'll get you a ride to the ferry at Stranraer, but you'll need to make arrangements with your own people for transportation from Larne."

Brady is calculating. John Cross arrived in Derry, presumably at 6:00am Sunday. He and Andrews expect to arrive in Derry at 5:00pm on Monday, a day later. Cross's lead is now a day and a half. And to think, on Saturday morning, just two days ago, Cross's lead was less than an hour. This does not bode well for them. Brady is aware that Andrews is fretting about his diminishing chances of apprehending Cross. Brady is losing his trust in Andrews' judgement and efficiency. If Andrews falls down on this job, Brady is in danger of being dragged down with him. A novice officer would have been able to hunt Cross down in a matter of hours. Here are two of Britain's elite MI6 officers, fumbling and stumbling, outwitted by illiterate Irish travellers. Brady hopes to make a report, independent of Andrews' report, at the next opportunity, hopefully at the police station in Stranraer, prior to boarding.

"Constable Mac..." Brady struggles to remember the constable's name.

"We're not all Macs, you know. Toombe is the name."

"Sorry, Constable Toombe. I believe your advice is prudent. We will avail of it. One thing in addition, could you send word ahead to the constabulary in Stranraer to provide us with a telephone link to London? We need to submit a further report arising out of this new information."

"Consider it done."

Andrews looks unhappy, but he makes no objection or comment. Brady suspects that Andrews might prefer to hold back on reporting on their progress, until some actual positive progress can be reported.

12:15pm. Piper's Son receives a telephone call. He had requested that the next time the Andrews/Brady team phones in, he wants to be informed and have the call transferred. The call has already gone through the required levels of security passwords, so when Piper's Son lifts the receiver he asks, "Which code?"

This is answered with the expected "Code White".

"Andrews?"

"No, it's Brady, sir."

"How close are you to apprehending Cross?"

"48 hours or thereabouts."

"Really."

"Cross has gone to Ireland."

"You are sure?"

"We are sure. He arrived in Londonderry by cattle boat on Sunday morning at 06:00 hours. We ascertained that information with the assistance of the Glasgow police a few hours ago."

"Cattle crossing the sea on a Sunday?"

"No, sir. No cargo. Just passengers."

"And Londonderry is at the border with Éire. Isn't that so?"

"I believe that is the case."

"So you are reporting that John Cross may already be in the Republic of Ireland. That is outside your jurisdiction as an officer of His Majesty."

"If in fact he did cross into Éire."

"Where are you now?"

"Andrews and I are in Stranraer about to board a ferry to Northern Ireland. Do you have any contrary orders to that?"

"Brady, I don't know who you work for, and I have no authority to give you orders. Your superiors and my superiors have deemed it appropriate that we work together on this. Unless you hear to the contrary, I suggest you continue to tail Cross. You may come up with information that will be useful in locating him. You may even be fortunate enough to corner him in Northern Ireland and detain him without drawing attention. Activities in Éire come under the Foreign Office and our cooperation with friendly governments. This could be sticky. So far, Cross has not been charged with an offence. There is no warrant issued against him to justify detaining him – although that could change very quickly. As of this moment, if he entered Éire voluntarily we have no reason to request his extradition. Do you understand?"

"Of course."

"If you are required to change tactics, you will be advised when you make your daily reports. In the meantime, I agree that you should continue on your present course of action and be close at hand when events turn to our favour."

"Yes, sir. I concur."

"If you are in Stranraer, then you are on your way to Larne. I will arrange to have a car available for you there. Now, goodbye." Piper's Son hangs up.

He immediately lifts the receiver and summons the in-house operator. "Contact Cody for me. I need to speak with him." He hangs up and waits. Cody was left hanging in the north of Scotland when Andrews and Brady took off for Glasgow. Cody is waiting for further instructions. They are about to come.

12:50 hours. Piper's Son receives the expected call. "Where are you now, Cody?"

"Inverness Police Station, awaiting further instructions."

"Cody, get to Dublin. Go to 15 Prince of Wales Terrace, Ballsbridge – a four-minute walk from the British Embassy."

"I understand. I can get a flight from here to London and connect to Dublin same day. Anything I need to know?"

"Cody, here's all you need to know for now. Wait in Dublin. You will be told your next move."

"Will the Éire police be advised?"

"Of the true purpose of your presence in Ireland? No. Advised of John Cross? Yes. There is no way we can continue to search for Cross in Ireland without the involvement of the Special Detective Unit, the SDU. We frequently work with them on matters of intelligence and counter-espionage. Although the reason given to locate Cross is 'Missing Person', it will be obvious to the SDU that this is a case of a fugitive spy in the process of defecting."

"Can we trust them to keep this quiet from the Americans?"

"Alas, no. It is only a matter of time, a week perhaps, and we will need to come public with charges against Cross. Then, the whole world will know."

"And I am to work in secret?"

"As usual, Cody. You are not part of the official team, so the Éire police will not be informed of your true purpose."

"Sir, if Cross is in Éire, and the police there find him before us, it could be bad for us."

"Of course. We both know that. Is there a reason for you to say that?"

"The best thing is to entice him into Northern Ireland and take him into custody there, quietly. The worst thing would be for him to find a way to Russia via Ireland."

"No, Cody. You are wrong. Cross getting to Russia is not the worst thing that could happen. In that case, there is no more damage he can do. If the Éire police detain Cross, undoubtedly the Americans will learn of his attempted defection and surmise correctly that he is, and has been, a Russian agent. How long do you think it will take them to associate Cross to the British team that worked on the Manhattan Project? The worst thing that could happen is for the Americans to stick their noses into this. The Americans warned us of this. Or maybe you haven't yet learned of the communiqué issued to all agents this morning at 08:00 hours?"

"A communiqué on Cross?"

"The Americans fingered him, and we identified him. And now we have lost him. The Americans will laugh at us and regard us as incompetent, or even untrustworthy. Relations with the Americans are currently...let's say, less than favourable. We can't afford any further deterioration."

"Well, then, it would be better if John Cross were not found at all, not by anyone."

"Cody, you have a perfect grasp of the situation."

"So I wait in Dublin for further instructions."

"Goodbye, Cody. And read your communiqués."

CHAPTER NINETEEN

PETER OLDTHORPE AT DERRY

Sunday 16 July 1950
Derry, Ireland

6:00 am. Peter Oldthorpe feels a kick on the sole of his shoe. Followed by another kick, and then another. How can he feel someone kicking and him dead? Peter Oldthorpe does not believe in the afterlife. So how come he feels this? He is aware that he is lying on the floor with hands clawed firmly to the ground. His body feels like a wad of wet blotting paper stuck to the ceiling, only he is on the floor. So this is what it is like to be dead? Then he remembers. There is no afterlife. Peter opens one eye; the other eye is pressed to the ground and cannot open. He sees, a few inches away, the face of Francie Ward staring at him. Francie is sporting a red welt on his cheek shaped like the end of a drover's stick. Why is Francie here? Is Francie dead too? He reminds himself a second time, there is no afterlife.

"Get up, Peter. We're in Derry. It's time to get off the ship."

'Derry'? 'Ship'? Where did he hear that before? Peter Oldthorpe raises his head in an attempt to raise his body. A sudden stab of pain runs through his head, and he sees flashing lights. He shuts his eyes in agony and tries to visualise the source of the pain. Inside his head he pictures a green soup. The soup is still, except when he moves. Then it sloshes around. There are things floating in the soup. Of particular note is the big lead ball floating there. Outside, in the world governed by physics, lead balls are unable to float in soup. But inside his head things are different.

Peter Oldthorpe moves. The lead ball stirs and bumps against the pain receptors encircling his head. The pain receptors are strung like a rosary at the perimeter of the soup. The lead ball cannot miss. As the lead ball bumps each pain receptor, lights flash and a stab of pain courses through his head. He once saw something like this in a pinball machine at a seaside arcade. He bites his lip to counteract the pain in his head. He would like to speak, but his tongue is dry and swollen. Peter rises slowly with assistance from Francie Ward. It takes great skill to move without disturbing the floating lead ball. Peter does not have the requisite skill. The pain stabs, the lights flash, and he bites firmly into his lower lip. He keeps his eyes tightly shut to avoid the flashing lights. But it is futile. The lights are inside his head. Eventually, he is standing upright. Now to walk and not move his head.

Every step sends a wobble through his body that disturbs the floating lead ball. Every step is a stab of pain and a flash of light. The only consolation is in the rhythm of his steps coinciding with the timing of the stabs of pain. He is able to anticipate each flashing pain, and he bites firmly down on his lip with each step. The ladder in the ship proves to be a hurting challenge. This is followed by the narrow gangplank. Throughout all this he permits Francie to lead him like a blind man off the ship and onto solid ground at Queen's Quay.

Here, the ground is level, and his movement is steady. Now he also hears bells in his head. He is still unable to speak. He bites his tongue to generate a flow of saliva. His mouth moistens and he attempts to speak. With eyes tightly shut and with hands covering his ears, he mumbles, "Bells. I hear bells."

Francie laughs. "Of course you hear bells. It's Sunday. That's St. Eugene's Cathedral you hear."

Tramp, tramp, tramp; pain, pain, pain; bite, bite, bite. They stop. Peter Oldthorpe stands still. Not moving. The stabbing pain is replaced by a throbbing pain. He risks opening his eyes. A stone wall. He sees a stone wall inches from his face. He turns his head slowly, very slowly so as not to disturb the floating lead ball. He is standing at a church. Francie and Collie are standing beside him, and they are looking in through the door of the church. Their noses are actually inside the church. There they are, standing with caps clutched in front in both hands. Their bare heads are bowed and their faces are screened by their long hair falling down in front. Whatever ritual is being conducted inside the church, it is concealed from Peter Oldthorpe. He sees only the stonework in front of his face. So he listens.

"Dominus vobiscum."

Maybe he is in another world where he is unable to understand his new environment. The afterlife? No. Peter Oldthorpe has no belief in the afterlife.

"...et in secula seculorum."

Ah. That is something he recognises. So now there should be an 'Amen' and it's over. He hears the 'Amen', but the unfamiliar prayers start up again. Sometimes bells are added. He listens for an 'Amen' to signal 'the end', but he hears countless amens and the drone keeps on going.

"Ita missa est."

"C'mon," says Francie, flinging his hair back and placing his unclasped cap on his head. "We're leaving."

Peter still cannot get an understanding of what is happening. "No. We can't leave until he says 'Amen'."

Collie also flings his hair back and secures his cap in place. He grips Peter's arm and says into his ear, "Amen. Now let's go."

As he leads him, Peter experiences a return of the stabbing pain. He counts as he walks. Surely if he engages his brain it will bring some distraction. And so he counts, multiplying by two – '2, 4, 8, 16, 32, 64...' He reaches 131,072 when he stumbles, bites his lip against the stab of pain, and needs to start all over again. The next time, he reaches 524,288. Peter Oldthorpe does not believe in God; he does not believe in Heaven or Hell. So if he is in an otherworld afterlife, one that he refuses to acknowledge, is he damned to walk like this for all eternity?

The sounds of the city fade away, replaced by the sounds of the countryside. They stop at a roadside water pump and drink. Peter drinks, and drinks some more. He feels relief coursing through his body. He was dehydrated. The pain is subsiding. He leans on the pump and looks at Francie and Collie. He speaks intelligently for the first time since leaving the ship.

"Am I dead?" he enquires.

"No. But you have one hell of a hangover."

"A hangover? And what happened to your face, Francie?"

Francie fingers the welt on his cheek, "Ah, just a friendly argument with one of the cattlemen last night. It was a great time, wasn't it?"

Peter leans back on the pump and bends his head down to drink some more of the spouting water. Two vows he makes. He dabs his head with water as in a solemn ritual "I promise never to go to sea again, and I promise never to drink again under pain of death; so help me God."

He looks about. "So where are we now?"

"The A2."

"The A to where?"

"To Limavady."

"On the way to Russia at last?"

"You are on your way. You will be where you need to be, when you need to be. Now we walk."

They turn off the A2 and walk on the Carmoney Road, through the village of Eglinton, on to Killylane Road and back on to Clooney Road/A2. Some hours later, after passing through Greysteel, they turn right off the A2, and walk four furlongs along a side road. They pass stables and reach a woodland area. They stop at a stone humped-back bridge.

"Okay," says Francie. "Let's go down here."

Peter, mystified, nevertheless follows Francie and Collie over the wall and down the bank and into the cavernous space under the arch of the bridge. There is a level ledge on each side of the running brook. Peter and Collie remove their clothes. They hang their greatcoats on the stone abutments and kneel naked in the stream. There, they use gravel and pebbles to wash their bodies. They rub wet gravel through their long hair and rinse thoroughly in the flowing stream.

"What's keeping you, Peter?" Collie shouts. "You smell like a wet dog." Peter is still wet from the previous night's sea spray. His heavy woollen coat is saturated. Peter engages in the same exercise. With no soap available, he uses the abrasive action of gravel and sand to rub his body clean. "Wash your hair too," instructs Collie.

Peter observes Francie and Collie scrubbing their clothes in the stream and rinsing out the sand and gravel and beating the items of clothing against the smooth rocks. So Peter does likewise. When satisfied that his clothes are clean, he wonders how to wear them while dripping wet. He observes Francie and Collie wandering about wearing their overcoats, but wearing nothing else. Peter Oldthorpe watches. What are they about? They start a fire under the arch and feed it with whin. They then stand naked over the lazy oily smoke, rubbing it over their bodies. They toss their long hair over the fire and whin smoke. When they are thus finished, they invite Peter to do likewise. Peter is hesitant about smoking himself over the pungent burning whin.

"You need to do this to get rid of mousies (fly larvae) and creepies."

Peter understands that this is a cleansing exercise against fleas and ticks and lice infestation. He braces for the initial sensation of the heavy oily pungent smoke. He is pleasantly surprised at the therapeutic sensation of the smoke. Like he saw the Wards do, he rubs the oily smoke into his skin. He notices that his hangover is gone. This is the best he has felt since burning Sonia's papers with his garden waste.

"Don't forget your hair."

When finished, Collie throws more whin on the fire. It blazes up. Then they hold their wet clothes over the fire to dry. In drying, the clothes absorb the smell of the whin smoke, permeating every fibre and thread. Whin smoke is the distinctive smell of the traveller. Afterwards, all three hold Peter's overcoat over the fire to dry.

"Wool repels water. But when it is wringing wet like this, it will stink and rot."

This is indeed a world that Peter Oldthorpe did not previously know existed. If this is the 'other world', maybe it's not so bad after all.

Peter adjusts his thoughts back to the purpose of his undertaking. He reminds himself that he is on his way to Russia. It was just two days ago that he ceased to be John Cross, one of Britain's research scientists. He needs to get back in touch with the real world, and focus on where he is headed and to what is happening in the world. First chance he gets, he will obtain a newspaper.

The two Wards crouch by the dying fire, and dig out sandwiches from their coat pockets. Peter had not thought to save any food from the ship. He looks at the Wards. Francie lobs half a sandwich at him.

"Peter, you need to fend for yourself. This is all you'll get today. From now on, earn your food, and ration your food."

Prudently, Peter eats only half of the half-sandwich, and stores the remainder in his coat. The Wards splash water from the brook onto the fire to quench it, and the walk starts again. They retrace their steps to Clooney Road/A2, and continue east.

Peter tries to calculate how long they have been walking. But his awareness of the first few hours is vague. His legs are beginning to tire. They must be close to St. Bawn's, surely. They pass through Ballykelly and turn right on Kings Lane to the hospital. At the hospital, they cross Kings Lane and continue walking east on Tully Road. Tully Road is by no means a straight road. It serves as access to the farms in the area. Peter follows the Ward brothers.

Shortly, they cross Baranailt Road and reach the end of the road at a T-junction but, instead of turning right or left, the Wards continue straight on through the hedge and onto well-trimmed grass. Peter sees that they have entered a golf course. Surely entry into the golf course is not permitted, at least not in this manner of access.

The Wards continue to a hill, not a large hill, more a mound of uneven ground located in the middle of the well-manicured golf course. The mound is not as neat as the rest of the golf course. The grass here is rough and there are a few whin bushes growing among the rocks. There are golfers playing their way around the perimeter, in the golf course proper. This is not surprising for a Sunday afternoon in mid-July. Thankfully, the golfers ignore them. And the Wards ignore the golfers. Francie goes to the mound and sits on a rock staring at the centre. Collie stands back a bit, and then sits on his hunkers. He plucks a blade of grass and chews on it. Peter looks from one to the other. Collie appears to be waiting for Francie to do something. Francie is immobile, staring intently at the centre of the mound.

"Tricks, what is Francie doing here?"

"Remembering."

"What is he trying to remember? Has he forgotten the way?"

"He's not TRYING to remember. He IS remembering."

"Remembering what?"

"Not remembering 'what', remembering the memory."

This is nonsense to Peter Oldthorpe.

"Sit down, Peter."

Peter sits beside Collie on the rough grass beside the whins. Collie continues, "Francie has 'The Memory'. See his face. He is in 'The Memory' now."

Sure enough, Francie appears to be in some kind of trance. "Would it disturb him if I go over to him?"

"Don't touch him. But go. You may hear him talk."

Peter steps over the clumps of grass and walks to Francie. He crosses through Francie's line of sight. Francie is staring ahead. He looks at Peter and through him at the same time. This is unnerving. Francie is speaking in a low voice, hardly audible. Peter gets closer to observe him, and he strains to hear him.

"Drumceatt"

Peter, who is unfamiliar with 'Drumceatt', hears 'drum cat'. He strives to understand. Is Francie referring to a cat that plays on a drum? Or is it a type of drum?

"There he is now. I see Colmcille. He is seated with his back to the door. See. Sods from Alba are fastened to his feet. He has moved the blindfold up to his forehead."

To Peter Oldthorpe, this is getting more peculiar. There is a cat and a drum? And who did Colum kill? With sods tied to his feet?

"He speaks to the Ard-Rí, Aedh. The Ard-Rí considers the holy abbot's appeal. The Ard-Rí speaks. He proclaims that the bards will not be abolished. Instead, from henceforth, the number of bards is reduced; their powers are removed, placing them subject to their regional king or lord. No longer are the bards permitted to wander the country demanding hospitality for themselves and their entourage. A king is henceforth permitted to limit the number of bards in his kingdom to one single bard, if he so decrees."

Peter attempts to piece together what Francie is saying. 'Alba'. He said 'Alba'. No one says 'Alba' anymore, except the Gaelic speakers in the Highlands. And he said 'holy abbot'. Surely he is not referring to Columba, Abbot of Iona? If so, that would explain 'Columbkille', whom the Irish refer to as 'Colmcille'. Peter comes to the realisation that Francie is describing an event from the sixth century. Peter strains to hear more. But Francie's voice fades. He is speaking softly. Peter catches very little of what he says.

"...Eoghan Rua Mac an Bhaird, left with O'Neill and O'Donnell.... He wrote the lament 'Emer's Farewell to Cuchullan'. He wrote it for O'Neill. But for us MacanWards, he wrote it before he departed from his clan. He left. We are still here. The last of the vanishing bards."

After that, Francie's voice fades to silence. His mouth still forms words, but Peter is unable to catch any more of what he says. Peter is disturbed by this incident with Francie. What else is he remembering? Is it relevant to him or to his clan? Is it sound memory, or just remembered folklore? Peter returns to Collie, and waits for Francie to return to himself.

Francie plucks a blade of grass and carefully places it between the thumbs of his hands. He forms a hollow with his clasped hands and presses his thumbs to his mouth. He blows. He produces a reedy oboe-like sound that hangs in the air and fills the surrounding area.

"It's 'Danny Boy'," exclaims Peter.

"No, it's not. Listen to it."

The golfers hear the mournful lament and stop their game. The entire valley becomes still and silent, except for Francie Ward's tune. Peter is familiar with 'Danny Boy' but in this context it is quite different. The B natural is rendered as C flat. There is no discernible time signature, each phrase standing apart. The underlying pulse is in triple time rather than in the familiar common time. His ear may hear the air as before, but his brain perceives it in a totally new context. Francie comes to a low slow finale. He lets go of the blade of grass and watches it flutter away.

The golfers resume their game. Francie rises from the rock and strides past Collie and Peter as if nothing unusual had happened. "Now to Claudy."

Collie and Peter rise and follow him. They retrace their steps to Baranailt Road. This time they turn left and walk on Baranailt Road, and walk, and walk. Peter Oldthorpe's legs are aching and his heels are blistered. He enquires of Francie where they are headed.

"Now we walk to Claudy. We will sleep in the woods there. There are no towns between here and Claudy."

Peter removes his shoes and walks barefooted on the grass verge. Each step aches more than the previous and he wonders how long he will be able to endure the walking. He digs in his pocket and finds the remains of his earlier sandwich. He eats it to gather strength.

Some hours later, they stop. There is nothing significant to notice. Since leaving the hill of Drumceatt they have been walking through farmland.

Collie sniffs the air. So does Francie.

"Do you smell that?" asks Collie.

"Soda bread," answers Francie. They nod in agreement. Francie looks at Collie. "We need your tricks here."

Collie gives him a wink and disappears up a laneway to a farmhouse. To be accurate, Collie disappears along a hedge that borders a laneway to a farmhouse.

Peter takes advantage of the rest and sits down on the grass verge. He dips both feet into the sheugh, into the drainage water flowing from the fields, and sighs with relief.

"Get up, Peter Oldthorpe. Tie your stuff together and be prepared to run. Now!"

Peter, still barefooted, stands up and secures his shoes to his belt. He is startled by Collie who jumps through the hedge and runs down the Baranailt Road with Francie at his heels. Peter follows as close as possible, aware that he is running barefooted on a tarred roadway. Francie and Collie jump over the roadside sheugh and through the hedge and land in a tilled field, closely followed by Peter. All three sit leaning back against the hedge, hidden from the road and hidden from the farmhouse. In the distance they hear a dog barking. They listen. The barking is not coming any closer. Then they breathe loudly and laugh. It is only then that Peter sees the hot scone. Now he understands. The bread was cooling outside the farmhouse. That's what the Ward brothers smelled. The scone is scored with a big 'X' that makes it easy to divide it into four farls. Collie tosses a farl each to Francie and Peter, and places one inside his coat. They rest and eat.

Francie looks at Peter's blistered feet. "Come with me," he says. Peter follows him, walking through the tilled field to a wooded copse. Francie chooses a big old tree with moss growing up the side. He tears off clumps of moss and turns back to Peter. "Here. Stuff your socks with this, and put your shoes back on."

Peter does so. His shoes are now a tight fit, so he accommodates the new size in lacing them loosely. After a few steps, the moss adjusts to the shape of his ankles and feet. He readjusts the laces and is ready to resume walking. His muscles still ache, but the pain is tolerable.

Some hours later, they enter Claudy, the first village they have encountered since leaving Drumceatt. They walk through the village to Glenhane Road crossroads. The signpost points to the right to St. Colmcille School, to St. Patrick's and to St. Brigid's College. They continue walking, crossing over Glenhane Road onto Church Street. Church Street is short, about 80 yards to the bridge over the Faughan River, then right onto on Cumber Road, and left onto an unmarked dead-end road.

Having walked a mile from Claudy they reach the wood. Francie and Collie walk into the wood with familiar ease. Peter trails behind. Presently, they stop at a sheltered dry area. Francie sits on a fallen tree trunk. He fastens his overcoat and fans it outwards from his body like a tent. He scrunches down inside and draws his arms in from his sleeves. He tucks his head down inside his upturned collar and his cap collapses to fill the space. Francie is now totally contained inside his coat as in a cocoon. Then he slowly keels over to lie on the ferns and leaves.

Collie is preparing to do the same. He says to Peter, "This is where we spend the night. Scrunch yourself up inside your coat and go to sleep."

Collie makes himself into a similar cocoon. Peter attempts it, but fails. He tries to sleep, but he tosses and turns and shifts his coat cover off. Whenever he lies still he hears things moving around in the wood. And he wonders if there are ants or spiders that could crawl up his clothes. Thinking this causes him to scratch and turn. After much adjusting, he finally gets comfortable and feels sleep approaching at last. At this point, Francie kicks him on the sole of his exposed shoe. "We're off to Drumskinny."

It is Monday 17 July 1950. The entire day is spent walking. This time, Peter Oldthorpe finds it less arduous. His muscles are acquainting to the new regime, and he is learning the skills necessary to walk the laneways like a traveller. They pass through villages and towns, singing or fecking to obtain food. It rains and it shines, and he has learned how to keep dry. So far, he has been unsuccessful in obtaining a newspaper. It feels like a long time since he last read the news. He thinks back. He read the news last Friday, just three days ago.

It seems like a lot of trouble to get to Russia. However, he admits that the route he is taking – roadways, laneways and pathways through woods and heath – would surely confound any Special Branch officer or police unit intent on tracking him down. He still has not reached St. Bawn's, the location of his next contact. Had he known from the outset that getting to St. Bawn's would take a week, he would have considered it reasonable and prudent to conduct his flight in this manner, with all its appropriate concealments and precautions. Peter Oldthorpe is feeling optimistic.

Towards the end of the day they reach Drumskinny. It is located between bogland and farmland and is unproductive land. Coarse bog grass grows in patches between rushes and whins. Peter views the site. It is roughly square and is about the size of four tennis courts. Standing upright are thirty-nine stones, varying from knee-high to chest-high. Most of the stones form a circle. There is an adjacent cairn with eighteen standing stones running east therefrom in alignment. Peter is not surprised that Francie sits on a stone and commences another 'memory'.

"Tricks," he asks. "How often do you come here?"

"Every year."

"You come here every year? How long have you been coming?"

"Since before the Éireannach."

"Before the Irish? What do you mean; you have been coming since before the Irish? Sure the Irish have been here for over 2,000 years."

"So count back to when the Éireannach came, and then count back further the same amount. That's when we first came to Drumskinny."

"That's not possible. You, or your forebears, have been coming here every year for over 4,000 years?"

"That's what Francie remembers."

"What else does he 'remember'?"

"We were here before the Éireannach. Earlier peoples disappeared, but us bards were accepted and held in high esteem by the conquerors. They wanted poems and songs to praise them and to remember them to succeeding generations. We became Irish, but always remained a little bit different. We lived in the west back then, and travelled to all the kings of Leath Cuinn, that's Connacht and the north. When the Normans came we moved to Northern Uí Néill. And here we are, always travelling, yet always here. It takes us one year to walk the whole journey, year after year..."

"...for over 4,000 years." Peter isn't sure if this is historically true or even possible, but it is the myth and legend that the travelling Wards remember.

Francie stands up and walks back towards Collie and Peter. "It's been a long day. We are a couple of hours from Kimmid. We'll get there before nightfall. There will be no sleeping on the ground this night."

Downhill a little ways, Peter sees one solitary house with a Guinness sign on the wall. There are no other houses around, and this one house is a pub? The Wards, however, do not continue onward on the Castlederg road as expected. They walk back uphill a few yards to the crossroads and turn left onto the Drumskinney Road. The road is straight but not level. It rises and dips with the hills and ridges.

Two hours later, two hours walking on the Drumskinney Road, followed by the Corlave Road, followed by the Procklis Road, the Wards turn sharp right, and they walk along the Bollawater Road. Shortly, Peter sees a village in the distance.

Francie informs him, "This is Termon. To enter the town we must pass two customs checkpoints. The customs officers will question us and check for smuggling. Peter, you may look like a traveller, but you don't sound like one. The water-rat officers, for sure, will take good note of you. We need to cross the river but avoid the customs officers. The approved way to enter Termon is by the Termon Road and over the bridge to Station Street. This road here, the Bollawater Road, takes us to the Inisclin Road. It is an unapproved road. It is for the locals only. And so we cross the river by way of the Mill Street Bridge on the outskirts of the town."

They come to a bridge situated upriver from the town. Francie sidles off the road and into a copse of trees at the riverbank. He signals Peter to follow. Collie walks casually across the bridge and is immediately surrounded by customs officers. He is made to empty his pockets and is questioned and released.

The officers are satisfied that Collie is not carrying contraband. One officer begins to lecture him on the correct crossing protocol, and quickly gives up. Travellers don't respect the border, and this traveller is not likely to give any heed to rules and regulations pertaining to approved border crossing points. Collie slowly refills his pockets and walks away. The older officers smile at the young enthusiastic officer's futile attempt to enlighten a traveller on border crossing protocols.

Inside the copse Francie remarks, "As I suspected. The water rats are out searching for smugglers. It's no problem, though. We walk upstream past the mill, past the dam and past the millpond. It's shallow up there but the water is rapid. That's where we will cross the river."

Fifty yards uphill from the bridge Francie stops. "Take off your shoes and roll up your trousers." They cross the river without incident and meet up with Collie. Then they walk through the Bircog farmlands. "Kimmid is just around the corner now."

In less than half a mile Peter hears children and voices, and sees smoke. There is the distinctive smell of burning whin. They round a bend and behold a traveller encampment. There are over twenty travellers here, with horses and carts and wagons and food and shelter. Children encircle them, shouting and tugging at their coats to lead them to the campfire.

"Tonight, Peter, you sleep in a wagon, or maybe a cart. But first, let's see if Maura Clishta has any stew for us."

At the campfire, Peter Oldthorpe slurps hot stew. He is unable to identify the meat, but it is the best stew he has ever tasted. After eating, he lies down on straw in the bed of a cart; he pulls a sheet of tarpaulin over his tired body and instantly falls asleep.

CHAPTER TWENTY

NORTHERN IRELAND

Monday 17 July 1950 15:30
Larne, Northern Ireland

"Welcome to Norlin Arlan." Two RUC constables greet the newly-arrived Andrews, Brady and McCann. Andrews winces in visible displeasure at yet another unfamiliar idiom of the English language. He leaves it to Brady and McCann to get through the introductions, making it clear that he is impatient to get on the road to Londonderry. They are shown to their car, a 2.5L (2443cc) RMB Riley. Andrews is pleased at the choice of car, large enough and powerful enough for his needs, and a lot better than he was expecting. The constables inform them that the RUC has been alerted to the missing person case, and are available to assist them anywhere in Northern Ireland. Brady thanks them and obtains the car keys.

"McCann? Do you know the fastest way to Londonderry?"

"Of course. A8 to A6. It will take an hour and a half."

Brady tosses him the keys. "Okay, McCann. You drive."

The Riley is a powerful car, but it burns petrol fast. 15 minutes before reaching Derry, McCann taps the petrol gauge. "Less than half a tank. We should fill up at the next petrol station."

"Okay. Turn off at the next town."

"Here's a crossroad. It's the Baranailt Road. We are a half mile from Claudy. I know it, and I know where the closest petrol station is located." McCann turns left and speeds into the town and pulls up at the petrol station. As he waits for the attendant to fill the tank, an RUC constable walks up to them.

"Do you realise how fast you were going in a residential area? So tell me now. What's the emergency?"

Brady jumps out of the car and produces identification to the constable. The constable looks at it and at Andrews, Brady and McCann.

"Ah, I know who you are. We were told this morning about you, a special unit is here from England attempting to locate a missing person. It must be a very important missing person. So who might it be?"

"A British research scientist travelling with two itinerants. He may be a little disturbed – burned out from overwork. He is privy to sensitive information which must be protected. We need to locate him before he comes to harm."

"Ah." The constable says 'Ah' to mean that he understands that there may be a lot more to this than the explanation he received from Brady. "Now here's something that might interest you. Late yesterday, three itinerant travellers passed through here. I know that because we received a complaint that three itinerants stole a loaf of bread from a farmhouse not far from here. I can show you where."

At this Andrews perks up and steps out of the car. "How far away?"

"Lyttle's farmhouse. About ten minutes from here."

"Let's take a look. Can you take us there?"

Fifteen minutes later, Andrews and Brady are examining the spot where the three travellers were spotted running away from the farmhouse. It does not take them long to locate the field where Francie, Collie and Peter hid to consume their ill-gotten bread. They observe two sets of boot prints and one set of bare-foot prints. And where the footprints return to the road they observe that there are two sets of boot prints and one set of shoe prints of the size and type of John Cross's shoe prints.

"It's Cross!" Andrews exclaims, filled with enthusiasm again. "This road? Where does it lead after it passes through Claudy?"

"It continues south."

"To Éire?"

"Eventually. Actually, considering that they are walking, they could take unapproved roads and cross and recross the border numerous times as they travel south."

"So Cross could be in Éire as we speak?"

"Yes. But if they travelled through any towns or villages, they would have been observed. I suggest that we go to the RUC station in Claudy and phone the neighbouring stations."

Brady and Andrews concur with this suggestion.

It is 5:45pm when they arrive at the RUC station in Claudy. Sergeant Tipping and the entire station assist in contacting the neighbouring stations. The first positive lead is from Strabane. At 11:00am today, three itinerants were observed street-singing and performing card tricks.

"That's them," exclaims Andrews. "There is no doubt. The singer and the trickster. And is Cross now singing too? How far to Strabane?"

"By car, half an hour. But a word of caution, Strabane is a border town. They could have crossed into Éire and out of our jurisdiction."

"Another constable at the station raises his hand. He is still speaking into the phone. "They were spotted in Castlederg an hour and a half ago."

"And Castlederg is how far?" enquires Andrews.

"Forty-five minutes from here."

Andrews cannot believe his luck. Cross is less than two and a half hours away. "Tell Castlederg that we are on our way. We will need their help when we arrive. Come on Brady, McCann. Let's go!"

Brady is finishing a very brief updating phone call to London. He passes the phone to a constable. "Here. Update them on where we are and where we're going." And he rushes off with Andrews and McCann. They are optimistic that they will apprehend Cross before the day is out.

It is 6:45pm in Castlederg when an anxious Andrews, Brady and McCann enter the RUC station. They are tired but newly-enthused at the prospect of imminently apprehending Cross. They introduce themselves to Sergeant Phillips who is expecting them. He assigns helpful constables to bring them to the town's Diamond where the itinerant trio was spotted earlier that day. This is where the commerce of the town is conducted and contains the community's main shopping area. As it is after 6:00pm on a Monday, the shops are closed for the evening, except for the two pubs. This is no obstacle to interviewing the shopkeepers. The local constables know where they live, mostly either above or beside their respective places of business, or nearby.

The constabulary quickly learns some helpful information from the shopkeepers. From approximately 4:00pm to 4:30pm, two itinerants were street-singing door to door for money. And one itinerant was performing card tricks for wagers. They did not linger, probably to avoid coming to the attention of the police for begging in public, or for engaging in a commercial activity without a licence.

"How were they travelling?" Andrews asks.

"Well, walking, of course. How else do siúlers travel?" The grocery-shop owner looks from Andrews to the constables with an enquiring look as if to ask 'what ayjit is this?'

Sergeant Phillips, who is supervising the door-to-door interviews, comes to Andrews' rescue. "The three itinerant travellers are on foot. They can't be far away."

"It is now 7:30pm. So they have a three-hour head start on foot, and we are in a Riley. That is good odds in our favour. So, if we follow the same road, where does it lead?"

"Let's see. They entered the town by the Lurganboy road. And they continued through the Diamond to the Main Street. Well, that takes them to the bridge over the Derg."

"And where does the Main Street lead after the bridge?"

"The Castlegore Road."

"So we take the Castlegore Road."

"Wait. The Castlegore Road follows the B72 for just a short distance. Once across the Derg, there are numerous roads, laneways and dirt tracks branching off hither and thither. They could have taken any of those on foot."

"So can you arrange roadblocks in a radius of 15 miles?" Andrews wants to avoid a repeat of the roadblocks in Cheshire where he originally failed to catch John Cross. This time he is certain that the travellers are walking, and a 15-mile radius is more than a walker could travel in four hours, leaving a cushion for error of almost an hour.

"A roadblock? Are you joking? There are hundreds upon hundreds of highways and byways and walking trails within that radius. Even with ten times the manpower we could not block every single road. Secondly, the travellers are walking. These travelling people are very cunning. They could spot a roadblock and bypass it unseen via fields and woods and hedgerows. No. Roadblocks will not catch itinerant travellers."

"So, we..."

"So, we use local knowledge. I'll contact the neighbouring RUC stations within a 15-mile radius and inform them of the situation."

"And we continue to pursue on the most likely road."

"If you like. It's your decision. I'll give you a constable to help you search the local area."

"Thanks, Sergeant. I appreciate your assistance."

"Constable Humphreys! You're joining these men in searching for John Cross."

"Yes, sir!"

The team, now Andrews, Brady, McCann and Humphreys, drive off south across the Derg. Humphreys is driving. Andrews is in the front passenger seat. "First we'll follow the B72," Humphreys informs them. "That takes us to Ederney."

"Okay."

Andrews and Brady check the time. It is now 7:40pm. Humphreys takes the B72, drives for 15 minutes and comes to a halt at a fork in the road.

"We can continue on the B72 to Ederney, or take the Castlederg-Montiaghroe Road here to Kesh."

"Stay on the B72 for a few more minutes."

It is 7:55pm. This decision by Andrews costs him dearly. They are a mere three minutes away from encountering Francie, Collie and Peter who, at that moment, are at the Drumskinny Stone Circle, at the crossroads of the Castlederg-Montiaghroe Road and Drumskinney Road.

At 8:00pm the itinerant trio leaves the stone circle site and walks back north on the Castlederg-Montiaghroe Road. At 8:03 they turn left at the crossroads of the Drumskinney Road and walk west. In another two minutes they crest the brae and walk out of sight of the Castlederg Road, concealed by a dip in the road.

Andrews and his team reach the termination of the B72 at the Castlederg Road in Ederney. It is 8:00pm.

"Where to now?" enquires Humphreys. "There is no way they could have walked this far."

"I agree. Can you take us back by another road to Castlederg?"

"Of course. Here I'll turn right and take the Letterboy road to Kesh and Letterkeen, and return to Castlederg by the Castlederg Road."

"Isn't this the Castlederg Road? Shouldn't we return by a different road?"

"We'll return by another Castlederg Road, the Castlederg-Montiaghroe Road from Letterkeen."

"Okay."

Five minutes later, driving on the Castlederg road, Humphreys points out the historic landmark. "See. There is the Drumskinny Stone Circle."

Disinterested, Andrews responds, "Is Cross there?"

"No, sir. There is no one there."

Andrews exhales a sigh of disinterest. "So who gives a hoot?"

They continue north without slowing, crossing the Drumskinney Road and they continue in the direction of Castlederg. A mere 200 yards away, Francie, Collie and John Cross are walking west on the Drumskinney Road.

"Sir we are coming up to the B72 again. If you look over to the left you can see Scraghey Road. I suggest taking a look there."

"Okay. Let's take a look."

A minute later, Humphreys turns sharp left on to Scraghey Road. "This is an unapproved road. I can only drive as far as the border."

"Why? Is the road blocked?"

"No, sir. I am prohibited from crossing into Éire in uniform."

"Oh?"

"I will go as far as I can. I believe we may get information there."

A minute or so later they see a group of six police officers standing abreast on the road to block traffic. They are armed with sidearms and Lee-Enfield rifles and appear ominous.

"B-Specials," Humphreys informs the team. "They are the 'B-Special' auxiliary police force operating to secure the border from IRA incursions." Humphreys brings the Riley to a halt. The auxiliaries recognise the RUC uniform and salute.

Humphreys addresses them. "Good evening, officers. We are looking for three itinerants that left Castlederg at 4:30pm. Did you see them come this way?"

"We have been here since noon the day. Only local farmers and the Catholic curate have come by since then. No. No itinerants."

"Thanks, Officer."

"It's a quarter after eight. Let's return to the RUC station. There might be some news awaiting us." Andrews' earlier optimism is waning.

8:30pm. Andrews, Brady, McCann and Humphreys are back in the RUC station in Castlederg. The constables are waiting to give their reports. They name all the towns and villages within a 15-mile radius that have been checked.

"We checked with the RUC in Kesh, Ederney, Tullyhaugh, Lack, Drumquin, Killeter...."

Andrews blocks his ears and interrupts. "You are telling me that you checked every town and village within a 15-mile radius and there was no sighting of Cross or of three travellers?"

Sergeant Phillips informs him, "If three itinerant travellers passed through any of those towns, someone would have seen them. People are suspicious of travellers. Travellers cannot pass through a town unnoticed."

"So what does this mean?"

"Three possibilities: One, they are still in the vicinity of Castlederg; two, they travelled off-road to avoid observation; or three, they crossed into the Free State unobserved."

Andrews phones in his daily report to London. He is instructed by London to keep searching in the area and to set up a temporary base in Enniskillen RUC station.

"How far is Enniskillen from here?"

"Forty-five minutes," replies Phillips.

"Why do you ask?" enquires Brady.

"We have been provided with a temporary base in Enniskillen. We are to work out of there until instructed otherwise." It is 10:30pm. Andrews, Brady and McCann drive to Enniskillen.

Tuesday 18 July, Enniskillen. No break, and no leads. Andrews is crestfallen. Yesterday he was sure that he would catch up with John Cross and succeed in apprehending him. Once again, Cross has managed to evade him and disappear without a trace.

Wednesday 19 July, Enniskillen. Andrews has taken to drinking and neglects to shave. Brady files the daily report with London.

A week goes by. Monday 24 July. London has news for them. London has intercepted a number of coded radio messages. They are to 'Bélyy', or from 'Bélyy'. The Americans have been advised of the Cross defection and they are now also involved. The Americans are working on decoding the radio messages with the British. The radio activity would suggest that Cross has not yet made it into Russia. Otherwise 'Bélyy' would have no need to communicate at this degree of high activity. Ireland has also been informed. And British/Irish cooperation on counter-intelligence permits the British agents to operate with the Irish Special Detective Unit. The Andrews/Brady team is to coordinate with the SDU in Sligo. Thus they are now able to operate cross-border and throughout the entire island of Ireland jointly with the Irish police.

One last piece of information which may be important: Cross is believed to be at 'The Lamp'. If 'The Lamp' is code, then it is meaningless. However, there is a chance that it may refer to a location. And that location may be where to find John Cross.

Brady goes to Andrews, who is drinking at his desk. "Andrews, get a grip. We have a lead. And we are also working with the Irish SDU."

"A week has gone by, Brady. We had Cross in our hand. We were this close," holding up his thumb and index finger, "and we let him slip through our fingers. We failed."

"Not yet, Andrews. We are not finished yet. Cross is still in Ireland, somewhere in Ireland. And we have a lead. He is at 'The Lamp'."

Andrews shakes himself. "'The Lamp'? How many lamps are there in Ireland? Street lamps? Bicycle lamps? Wait. You said 'The Lamp', not 'A lamp'. Brady, we need to find a place called 'The Lamp'."

They search. There are a number of pubs called 'The Lamplight'. There is a religious cult with a publication called 'The Lamp'. They engage the RUC to inspect these places thoroughly. The SDU assists in locating any place within the Republic with a reference to 'The Lamp'. Every possible place with reference to 'The Lamp' is investigated.

By the end of the week Andrews and Brady are exhausted. It is Sunday 30 July and, so far, they have failed to locate John Cross. 'The Lamp' did not lead to any success. They conclude that 'The Lamp' is code and has some concealed indeciphcrable meaning. They reach out to London for any more news on decoding the radio messages. The news is the same. They have not succeeded in decoding the radio messages. 'Bélyy' is active. Hence, Cross is not with the Russians yet. If Cross had succeeded in defecting to Russia, 'Bélyy' would have returned to his previous silence of the past two years.

Andrews tries to regain his optimism. The British and the Irish and the Americans are all working together on this. Surely their combined effort can't be outwitted by illiterate itinerant travellers.

Monday 07 August is the Summer Bank Holiday.

Tuesday 08 August, 08:00am, RUC Station, Enniskillen. Brady enters the RUC station. Andrews is still at the hotel, lingering over breakfast. Brady suspects that Andrews is adding whiskey to his morning diet.

The duty officer greets him upon entering. "Good morning, Officer Brady. There is a message for you." And points to the pigeonhole where incoming telephone messages are placed for pickup. Brady sees a telephone message note dated 08/08/50, 07:07. The message reads:

08/08/50, 07:07
Urgent
Contact Tullyhaugh RUC ASAP
c/b John Cross

CHAPTER TWENTY-ONE

PETER OLDTHORPE IN IRELAND

Tuesday 18 July 1950 06:00
Donegal, Ireland

Peter Oldthorpe awakens. He opens his eyes and spends a few moments figuring out where he is. He is lying in the bed of a cart in a travellers' camp somewhere in Ireland en route to St. Bawn's, and thence to Russia. What woke him? Ah, the whispering and shuffling of children. Peter Oldthorpe raises his head and turns in the direction of the sounds. There are five pairs of eyes peering at him over the sideboards of the cart. Upon realising that he is awake, the children run away. Peter listens to them whispering and arguing about what they saw.

"Did you see his horns?"

"Yes, I did."

"No, you didn't. That's not horns, that's blisters from sunburn."

"No. That's from where he cut off his horns and filed them down. That's why he's blistered on his forehead."

"And did you see his feet?"

"He has no feet."

"Yes, he has. He has shoes, so he must have feet."

"Didn't you see the grass sticking out of his shoes, all torn and ripped at the side?"

"So?"

"So? He has no feet. That's so. He has hooves like a donkey. And his shoes would fall off if he didn't stuff them with moss and grass...."

Peter Oldthorpe is puzzled by the children's opinion of him. But he is also somewhat amused. A stranger is in their camp and the children are making up imaginative stories to explain his presence. He sits up and turns to face the back of the cart. And almost falls back down again. A man is standing at the foot of the cart staring silently at him.

"Peter Oldthorpe?"

"Ah, Yes?"

"From High Explosives?"

What a strange thing to ask. And how would he know? And what relevance is it to his here-and-now? Peter is cautious in answering. "Well, yeah..."

"The work of the divil."

Peter Oldthorpe is uneasy with the direction of the conversation. He is about to state that he was engaged in important government-sanctioned work, but keeps silent in consideration of his present situation. What would an illiterate itinerant traveller understand about his top-secret research?

The traveller continues, "And you are English? Right?"

Peter would like to respond that he is Scottish, not English. He is not sure where this is heading, so he simply answers "Yes."

"So you are a black-orange-Protestant?"

Peter has no idea what a 'black-orange-Protestant' could be, and looks blankly at the traveller.

The traveller is still talking. "So who do you pray to? Some black-orange-Protestant God, or to the real God?"

Peter would like to respond that if there is a God, the Protestant God and the 'real God' are one and the same. Again he declines to respond.

"I see you don't answer. That must be because you don't believe in any God at all."

Peter is about to argue that if he is the devil, then he surely must believe in God. But arguing the antithesis of good and evil would not serve him well in his present circumstances. He remains silent.

"We'll reach Killbawn in six days...."

"Not St. Bawn's?"

"St. Bawn's is IN Killbawn. We'll reach Killbawn in six days. We're not going straight there. We will not cross the border. Staying in the Free State is a longer road, but I don't want water rats snooping through our stuff and risk them finding you. Six days it will take. I have wares to trade along the way. You, Peter Oldthorpe, will stay out of the way. I don't want you putting heretic ideas into the heads of the childer. And I don't want you getting friendly with our clan. And I don't want you seen with us. You may walk behind us or travel in the cart. If anyone comes to us, guards or people trading wares, you will hide from them. In camp, you will stay a field or two away from us, hidden behind a hedge or a hillock. On the road, if we need to hide you, you will hide here." At this the traveller slides two of the boards in the cart bed to reveal a compartment underneath. "This is for smuggling. Today we are smuggling you." The traveller waits for this to sink in. Then he asks, "Do you understand all this?"

"Yes, of course, Mr...I'm sorry. I don't know your name."

"Paddy the Lamp Ward. And remember, you are not part of our camp. The sooner I am rid of you the better. So stay by yourself."

For six days Peter Oldthorpe travels with the travellers. He walks most of the time. His sunburn heals. His legs no longer ache. He sees Francie and Collie with their family, but they do not acknowledge him. No one talks to him. For company, Peter sings to himself in rhythm to his walking. He is now skilled in keeping dry in the rain and in sleeping on hard surfaces. He is fed very little, but enough. He is lean and hungry and alert. They camp each day on the outskirts of a town. And Paddy Lamp collects junk and sells some lamps and clocks. He mends pots and pans and then they go off to another town. And so it is, day one, day two...

Monday 24 July 1950, mid-afternoon. The Ward party of itinerants makes camp at a roadside patch of wasteland opposite a rural creamery.

"Peter Oldthorpe!" Peter is called aside. "Come with us."

Peter goes with Paddy the Lamp and Francie and Collie. They cross the road to the creamery yard and continue to the perimeter fence. The corner post is loose. Paddy tilts it and Francie squeezes through.

"You next, English heretic." Peter follows Francie. Paddy and Collie follow Peter through the fence. They walk down an embankment to a river.

Paddy points to the river. "See this river. It's the Blackwater. Why do suppose it is called 'Blackwater'?" he asks of Peter.

"Because the water is black?"

"Watch."

Paddy nods to Francie and Collie. They are standing next to a large white stone. They roll the stone down the embankment and over the riverbank. It rolls into the water with a splash.

"So, English heretic, can you see the stone?"

"Of course not. The water is too black."

"So listen. If you are a bother to us, I'll fling you into the Blackwater where you'll disappear. Now stay here out of sight until I tell you otherwise." With that Paddy strides off through the fence and back to the camp.

Francie looks at Peter and asks, "You don't look frightened. Why is that?"

"Because I'm of value. Paddy the Lamp trades in wares. He knows what I am worth. In the river, I am of no value to you. And anyway, I have learned the Wards' manner of speech. Paddy is not threatening me. He is merely expressing a worst case scenario if things don't work out. And I don't take him literally."

"Peter Oldthorpe, you have learned a lot in the past week. You are right. Paddy Lamp Ward is not likely to fling you into the Blackwater. But don't underestimate him either."

Collie ominously adds, "If Paddy Lamp Ward is to fling you into a river, it will be far away from here where it will not be connected to him."

"Oh, by the way, Francie? Where are we now? The name of this place?"

"Killbawn."

"So at last, I'm at St. Bawn's?"

"From here, you could walk there and back inside an hour."

Peter Oldthorpe adds silently to himself, "If things fall off the rails, I'll make off from here on my own. I know how to survive in the ditches now. I may still have some bargaining chips to play. To do that, I need access to a radio. And Bélyy, the contact at St. Bawn's, must have a radio. Peter Oldthorpe, it is time to formulate an insurance policy for the possible implementation of a 'Plan B' – something to fall back on, if things go awry."

Francie and Collie squeeze through the gap in the fence and into the creamery yard. Peter follows.

"Peter Oldthorpe, where do you think you're going?"

"To the loading dock to lie down. I'm not going to lie down on a wet riverbank."

"That's okay, I suppose. But be gone from here when the creamery opens the morrow."

"When tomorrow?"

"I don't know. Early."

"Early dark, or after sunrise?"

"After sunrise."

Peter Oldthorpe lies down on the ramp of the loading dock. He curls up inside his coat and falls asleep.

Tuesday 25 July, Killbawn Creamery. Peter Oldthorpe awakens before dawn. He stretches out his arms and legs from underneath his coat. He shakes the dew from his clothes and gets up. He goes to the river and washes the sleep from his eyes. Sometime later he hears the sounds of activity at the creamery. Lorries and carts arrive. Milk is unloaded, sucked up by a big hose. Later, at mid-day he estimates, a large milk tanker arrives. The milk is transferred to the tanker lorry from the creamery. A lot less is transferred to the tanker than was delivered. Peter deduces correctly that the creamery is a collection station that separates the milk. What is transferred to the tanker is high in butterfat to be churned into butter. A few of the farmers are waiting in the yard. When the tanker departs, they line up at the loading dock and the creamery refills their milk cans with skimmed milk. The remaining unwanted skimmed milk is pumped into the Blackwater. The creamery workers flush out the creamery equipment with fresh water and the creamery shuts down operation until the next day. The remaining farmers and the creamery workers depart, and the creamery falls silent.

Peter Oldthorpe returns to the creamery yard to resume his spot of comfort on the loading dock ramp. From here he hears once more the sounds of the itinerant children at play. He takes notice of the cars that drive up and stop to bargain for Paddy's wares. The voices carry to him and he pictures the bargaining that is being transacted at the roadside. It is past noon and no one has offered him any food yet. He considers going to the camp, but waits until the camp is quiet and empty of visitors.

Peter observes a car stop at the campsite. A well-dressed man gets out. Peter regards it as peculiar that in rural Ireland this man is dressed in Mediterranean-style clothes and walks with a military stride. It reminds him of a British Security officer they once had with the British Team in Los Alamos when he worked on the Manhattan Project. Paddy Lamp and Francie go to meet the military man. The man speaks. This is uncanny, Peter thinks. The man even speaks like British Security. This looks very interesting. He wonders if this is his contact, Bélyy, who will connect him to Russia.

Peter listens to what they are saying. It is a heated argument. Military man is saying, "A delivery. I was told to expect a delivery. Like a package, or a briefcase, or maybe even a single manila envelope. You tell me you have a human being?"

Francie is arguing, "I have brought him, as agreed, from Bostock Green to St. Bawn's. I don't know what a cuemen bean is, or a malima envelope. But here is the delivery. He's back there behind the creamery."

"This isn't going to work. I need to contact my principal to get an explanation and find out what should be done."

"I don't care what you do after this. I'm making the delivery and I expect the payment. So pay up and take the delivery."

"Get real, Francie. Payment will be made 'when the delivery is successfully completed'. That means when I deliver the package to the next contact. And it's also to keep you in line until the package is off my hands."

"Hey! Are you trying to weasel out of...?"

"Shut up, Francie! You are not dealing in tin cans and junk here."

Francie and Paddy move threateningly closer to 'Military Man'. 'Military Man' snaps the button on his suit jacket and it opens. He moves his hand inside his jacket just enough to reveal a sidearm. Francie and Paddy move back and quieten down. They mutter in protest to regain some point in the argument.

"Okay! Okay! We understand the policy on payment. But we are sick and tired of dragging this English heretic divil about with us. Take him off our hands."

"And where am I to put him? Eh? He stays with you until I can make arrangements."

"And how long will that take?"

"Let's see. It's Tuesday. I need to contact..."

"How long?"

"Three or four days."

"Three or four days?"

Paddy advances on 'Bélyy' again. Francie tugs at Paddy's coat and drags him back.

Peter Oldthorpe is satisfied that this is Bélyy, his contact at St. Bawn's.

Bélyy speaks again. "Paddy, I know how you feel. But I don't want a live human being package either. The quicker I can arrange a satisfactory outcome, the better it is for all of us. Now smarten up and cooperate."

Peter Oldthorpe looks up and down the road. It is totally empty except for himself, the Wards and Bélyy. He holds up his index finger and confidently crosses the road to the arguing trio.

"If I may be of assistance to you in resolving the issue. You are overlooking an important element." The trio are struck silent by this unexpected interruption. Peter continues, "My trading value. I have a valuable asset. It is research data. It is bargaining leverage for you. Paddy Lamp Ward, you understand bargaining?"

Paddy Ward changes from argumentative to expressing concern. "Peter, get back to the creamery yard before you are seen." Peter Oldthorpe notices the change from 'English divil' to 'Peter'.

Back in the creamery yard Peter explains. "This unexpected situation necessitates an amendment to the agreement. An amendment to a more favourable settlement for both of you."

"Renegotiate the payment settlement?"

"Amongst other things – you require clarification on the delivery of a live package, do you not? And Bélyy, I need radio access to your contact, your principal contact."

"To do what?"

"I can't tell you that. But you can listen in as I communicate. I trust you have the encryption to encode a message."

Paddy the Lamp is not interested in the attributes of radio communication. He and Francie walk from the creamery yard back across the road and re-enter the camp. Peter and Bélyy remain in conversation.

"Communication with London is not always two-way. There can be a delay of a day. It could be a day or so before I have an answer."

"In the meantime, I need some things."

"Like what?"

"Soap, toothbrush and toothpaste, a shaving razor, and shoes."

"I'll come back later with these. But not the shoes. For shoes, you will wait until you reach Russia. Anything else?"

"Yes. I need some money for food. Paddy feeds me leftovers. Can you imagine what leftovers are in a travellers' camp?"

"Not much, I warrant."

"Not much, or some days none at all."

"You will not be able to go shopping for food, you know."

"I know that. I need to rely on the itinerants for that."

Bélyy pulls a few coins from his pocket. "Here is some money."

Peter remembers well the last time he gave money to a traveller. "Bélyy, I have learned that if I give money to a traveller, I don't necessarily receive a return. No. Give me a large coin. The enticement of a large coin will provide better results than piecemeal payments in small coins."

Bélyy understands this. It is the same reasoning he himself employs in paying Paddy. Entice him with money, but hold off payment until he delivers. Bélyy extracts a coin from his waistcoat pocket and hands it to Peter. It is a silver half-crown.

"Here, Peter. Show this to Paddy. But don't pay him until you finally part company on Tuesday. I'll be back in an hour with the stuff you requested."

"Bélyy, don't forget to pick me up from here to bring me to your radio when you have arranged the radio communication."

"Sure thing. And around here, no one calls me 'Bélyy'. I'm known as Thomas Farouk Gilban. 'Farouk' to distinguish me from four other Thomas Gilbans in the parish. But if you still prefer to call me 'Bélyy' in private, that's all right."

Peter is plotting inside his head. He is employing the same ploy of promise and enticement. Convince Bélyy and Paddy Lamp that he is a tradable commodity of commercial value. This is his insurance against the risk of either party reneging.

Bélyy returns to his car and drives off. Peter crosses the road and enters the itinerant camp. He makes sure that Paddy sees the half-crown. He spins it in the air before placing it in his trouser pocket. He pats his pocket for reassurance. This coin may prove to be his passport to better treatment from Paddy Lamp Ward.

"And when do I eat today?"

"How about right now?" Paddy is already warming up to Peter Oldthorpe's half-crown.

Friday 28 July 1950, St. Bawn's Church, Killbawn. It is 6:30pm. Jack Gilban has already left the church. The main doors are open. Thomas Farouk Gilban arrives and parks his car at the sidewalk kerb. He goes inside the church and determines that it is empty of people. He returns to the main door and stands on the top step from which he has an unobstructed view of the street. Paddy the Lamp's junk cart is slowly making its way down the street. It stops at the church. Farouk nods at Paddy. Paddy tugs at the tarpaulin in the cart and Peter Oldthorpe emerges therefrom. Peter enters the church unobserved. He follows Bélyy and closely observes Bélyy's actions and commits them to memory.

They walk through the narthex to the tower. Bélyy places his hand on the upper rail of the tower door. He locates the key. Taking the key, he unlocks the tower door and replaces the key back on the rail. Inside the tower, to the left of the door, is a candle secured in a candlestick, and beside it is a box of safety matches. Bélyy strikes a match and applies it to the candle. He shuts the tower door. Peter sees that the lock is exposed on the inside of the door. It is a simple up-down left-right latch and bolt. It can be manipulated to a locked or unlocked position from inside the tower without the need of a key.

Peter follows Bélyy up the winding stairs, past the choir loft and to an upper level. From the shape of the ceiling here, Peter realises that they are below the roof of the church. The winding staircase is interrupted by a locked door.

Bélyy says, "Here, Peter, hold the candle while I fish for the key."

Bélyy fumbles through his pockets. "Blast," he says. "That's the second time I have forgotten the key. It's in the glove compartment of the car. But don't worry; there should be a spare somewhere up here." He runs his hand along the rail above the door. "Ah, here it is."

Peter notices the make and brand of the lock – Yale. That is a very secure lock for an interior door. Bélyy opens the door and they go inside. He switches on a light at a desk lamp. It is a small circular room, clearly the inside of the tower. There is a metal ladder fixed to one of the walls ending at a trapdoor in the ceiling.

"What's up there?" Peter enquires.

"That is access to the belfry, and to the radio aerial antennas."

"And do you ever go up there?"

"Seldom. Only if we encounter a problem with the antennas."

"Or with the bell."

"Yes. Or with the bell."

"You have four radios?"

"That's to allow two transmitters and two receivers to operate simultaneously."

"So how long do we wait to contact your contact?"

"This contact is in England. We are scheduled for 18:52."

"Not 19:00?"

"Round numbers, like 19:00, are more likely to be intercepted. We will cease transmission not later than 18:59. What is your message? I have only fifteen minutes to encode it."

"Research data completed on a clean bomb."

"That's it?"

"Just say it's from me – Пётр Старийгородский."

"Pyotr Staryygorodsky? Of course, 'Peter Oldtown'. So that's what 'Oldthorpe' means."

"And request a revision of the payment. After the transmission, check for a response regarding any new instructions."

"While you are waiting, would you care for a whiskey? Or a cigarette?"

"No thanks. I was a drinker and a frequent smoker until the crossing to Derry. Now I don't smoke. I don't drink. And I will never go to sea ever again. I'll amuse myself by going up the ladder to the belfry."

"Go ahead. I need to concentrate on the message."

Up in the belfry the space is open to the evening air but covered on top. There are openings in the walls so that the sound of the bell rings out clearly and unimpeded to the town of Killbawn. One of the openings is large enough for Peter to pass through. He climbs out and stands on a ledge which is surrounded by a safety wall. There is another ladder here, an exterior ladder, going up higher. Peter looks up. He sees the aerial antennas and the lightning rod. And up at the very top of the tower is the cross. He looks over the safety wall to the ground below. He sees where the electrical wires enter the building from the utility pole in the street. And having satisfied his curiosity, he returns to the radio room.

Back inside, Bélyy has finished his transmission. He does not expect a response until 24 hours later.

"So, tell me, Peter, what is a 'clean bomb'?"

"It's better if you don't know." Peter feels that Paddy Lamp Ward may have hit the mark when he called him 'the divil'. "This I can tell you. The Americans don't have it. And the Russians don't have it. The Brits are two years away from having it. If the Americans get their hands on the data, they will have a clean bomb in three months. The Russians will take a bit longer, perhaps a year."

"So this is...my God, what research do you work in? Suddenly, you frighten me."

"Oh yes, it's frightening all right, Bélyy. You see, I work on developing newer and more efficient explosives in atomic bomb research. And they work me to death. All the work is about death and..." Peter leaves the sentence hanging.

Bélyy switches off the radios and whispers, "Let's get out of here. After all, we're in the house of God."

Peter mutters to himself, but audible to Bélyy, "And where is God?" They return down the circular stairs by candlelight to the storage room.

"Peter, it is not yet dark outside. Come. I'll take you out the back way to my car unseen."

Peter observes the modus operandi of navigating through the dim interior of the church. The nave of the church is the standard setup. Pews are spaced exactly one yard apart; the side aisle is 5′ wide; the altar rail is 6′ from the front pew. Peter and Bélyy go through the opening in the altar rail, clearly visible in the red light of the sanctuary lamp suspended over the chancel in front of the main altar. They continue up the three altar steps, and pass through the sanctuary to the sacristy. In the cramped sacristy, Peter runs the finger of his left hand along the edge of the island counter, taking care not to knock anything over. The counter contains water jugs, cruets, candlesticks and other articles used in the worship rituals. He stops momentarily at the end of the counter. At this point there is a sink on his right, followed by a chair situated next to the exit door. From the end of the sink to the door is an arm's length at shoulder height. The door opens on the inside by turning an oval-shaped knob for the latch to retract. It is another Yale lock. The door itself opens inwards. It self-locks when pulled shut. Peter commits all this to memory without effort.

Peter and Bélyy/Farouk walk the length of the passageway from the sacristy to the porch of the parochial house, and thence into the backyard. The porch contains an umbrella stand and a mat and a pair of wellington boots. The porch door has no lock in order to accommodate deliveries to the house. Peter observes that the house back door is fitted with a Yale lock similar to the sacristy door. One may freely enter the porch, but not have access to the house.

"Peter, stand out of sight behind the priest's garage. I'll drive around from the street and pick you up from there. It's best we keep you hidden at all times."

Sometime later, Thomas Farouk Gilban, code-named 'Bélyy', drops Peter off at the creamery yard. Then he drives to Shannon. Now that he has a live person to deliver, he needs to arrange a secure procedure with Malachy. There is no reason to wait for clarification. There can't be any mistake. A live package was delivered to him, so he is required to pass on this live package to the next contact at Shannon. Tonight he will perform a dry run of the operation in preparation for the scheduled delivery on the night of 01 August, actually for the early morning of 02 August.

Saturday 29 July. It is close to 6:00am when Farouk returns home. He is satisfied that the dry run for the delivery was rehearsed successfully in Shannon. In the afternoon he visits Paddy Lamp and Peter Oldthorpe to confirm that the delivery will go ahead as planned for the night of 01 August. Paddy Lamp enquires if there has been a response from England yet regarding a revised price for their services.

"Paddy, it was only last night that I sent the message. I will not receive a response until tonight. In the meantime, keep Peter Oldthorpe out of sight. I don't want him coming anywhere near the town or to the church. You know what prying eyes there are in Killbawn."

Later that evening in the belfry radio room, Farouk/Bélyy receives a message from London. He decodes it. It is brief and clear. 'Proceed as instructed. No change in arrangements. Shannon contact is ready. Take extra precautions – M is close.' Farouk understands. For the delivery to succeed, they must stick to the plan. There is no rearrangement of the proposed payment. And MI5 or MI6 is close. MI5 is engaged in countering domestic threats; MI6 is engaged in foreign operations. Either or both could be engaged in this situation – a defection of a British scientist to Russia via Ireland.

This can only mean that MI5/MI6 is already in Ireland and is working with the SDU. Shannon is most likely being watched. Farouk is thankful that Malachy will meet them at the bird sanctuary and enter the airport facility unseen and unchallenged via the dirt track to the perimeter road. Peter Oldthorpe will not go near the departure lounge or any public area of the airport. He will be handed over to his handler, Gregori, at a spot between the fuel storage tanks and the marine dock. From there, Gregori will steal him aboard his transportation to Russia. At least that's how they rehearsed it last night.

At 9:00pm, the church is locked for the night. Farouk waits until all is quiet. There is no problem for him if he is seen. But Father MacNamara will delay him and encourage him to spend some time socialising. At 9:10pm he slips out quietly and quickly through the sacristy door as he did on the previous night.

Five minutes later, Farouk stops his car at the itinerant camp. Paddy Lamp Ward is unhappy with the news. "What? No renegotiated payment? And I must keep this English heretic here for two more days?"

A heated argument ensues. Paddy eventually relents in recognition that there is no safe workable alternative. Peter is sent to the Blackwater to wait out his next two days.

"Paddy, in two days' time, on Monday night at midnight, bring Peter Oldthorpe to the old disused flour-mill. I will come by at 12:30am to pick up Peter from the rusty gate there. From there, I'll drive off with him to Shannon. Two days after that, if all goes well, the money will be released to the bank. I expect to withdraw the money from the bank in Sligo on Friday. So keep it together for just two more days, Paddy."

It rains on Sunday. Peter manages to stay dry in the creamery yard. There are pools of water throughout the yard. It is too wet to lie down, so Peter does not sleep on Sunday night. Paddy Lamp brings him food. He is tired, but not hungry. Peter has time to think about his situation. He regards Bélyy as his current contact and hence his minder until he reaches his next contact. His next contact will be the Russians. Why, he wonders, is he sleeping here in a wet creamery yard beside a river, when Bélyy should have provided him with a safe shelter?

Monday has intermittent drizzle with dry spots. Paddy supplies him with adequate portions of food. Peter huddles on the ramp of the loading dock all day and through the night.

On Tuesday morning, Paddy Lamp provides more food on condition he consumes it far away from the camp. Later, some of Paddy's children run across from the campsite pushing the cart. They enter the creamery yard and warn Peter of the presence of the guards. Peter observes a detective visiting the camp. He makes sure to get well out of sight. Sometime later, from his place of concealment, he overhears Doctor McBratt arrange with Paddy to deliver a clock to St. Bawn's. Paddy promises to deliver the clock before the Angelus bell ceases sounding.

Afterwards, when the coast is clear, Peter approaches Paddy. Peter sees an opportunity to get shelter from the rain, go to Bélyy earlier than the agreed time and shelter in the church.

"Paddy, you are going to St. Bawn's this evening? Sure there is no need for you to go into Killbawn twice. When you go, take me with you to St. Bawn's. I can hide in the belfry and catch some sleep there. When it gets dark, I'll simply walk to the old mill. And you'll be rid of me all that much sooner."

"That's a good suggestion, Peter. I think I'll do just that. You know, you can walk from St. Bawn's to the old mill by way of the footpath along the river. At night it will be dark, and it's right close too, only two hundred yards upstream."

Paddy Lamp knows that after the Angelus bell is rung, Jack Gilban the sacristan leaves St. Bawn's. As to Peter Oldthorpe hiding in the church, it's no secret to those who observe Jack's daily routine that the tower is accessible to anyone who knows where the key is located. And the tower has a number of secure hiding places. "Good," he thinks. "I'll be rid of this English divil at Angelus time on Monday. And I'll never have to set me eyes on him ever again."

CHAPTER TWENTY-TWO

PETER OLDTHORPE'S DEPARTURE

Tuesday 01 August 1950
Mayo, Ireland

6:35pm. Paddy Lamp Ward exits St. Bawn's Church carrying an elaborate sacristy lamp, his gift in exchange for the clock he delivered to Canon MacMorrow. Paddy is happy with the exchange. He delivered a mantle clock and in exchange he received the canon's old clock plus this fine elegant hanging lamp. In his cart, Paddy carefully covers the two newly acquired items with the tarpaulin. Also concealed under the tarpaulin is Peter Oldthorpe, the 'English devil'.

"Listen here, English divil, I'm going back into the church to check if it's clear for you to come in."

"Okay. I'll watch for your signal."

Paddy goes back inside the church and shortly reappears. He glances up and down the street, and satisfied that all is clear, he gives the nod to Peter Oldthorpe. Peter slips out of the cart and slinks into the church.

"Okay, Paddy. I'll make my way from here."

"Fine. So where's me half-crown?"

"Not yet, Paddy. Not until I'm out of here and on my way to Russia"

"That's not the deal...."

"Paddy, there is no deal. I will pay you the half-crown when I am finished here. Meet me at the old mill before Bélyy picks me up at half-past midnight."

"And I thought I'd seen the last of you. You have learned a lot in the past few weeks, English divil."

"Taught by the best, Paddy. Taught by the best."

Paddy does not press the point. He made a lot more than two shillings and sixpence on the deal with the canon. He is satisfied that his visit to St. Bawn's has been profitable. Paddy returns to his cart and makes his way back to the camp. A drizzle is starting to fall again, and the sky promises another rainy day to follow.

Peter Oldthorpe repeats the procedure that he observed and memorised from Bélyy. He goes to the tower, takes the key from the upper rail, and opens the tower door. He replaces the key back in its hiding spot and enters Jack Gilban's storage room. He finds the candle and the matches on the shelf beside the door. He lights the candle, shuts the door, and moves the bolt to its locked position. Prudently, he places the box of matches in his coat pocket so that he will be able to reignite the candle later.

He walks up the winding staircase, remarking inwardly at the lack of security in St. Bawn's. Perhaps in Mayo no one would violate a church by trespassing, but he, Peter Oldthorpe, is an 'English (Scottish, actually) devil'. At the upper level he encounters the door to the radio room. Peter quickly locates the key to the lock. He opens the door and walks inside. He quietly shuts the door and places the burning candle on the desk at the transmitter/receivers. The key is still in his hand. Lest he misplaces it, he puts it in his pocket with his half-crown.

There is a light switch on the desk lamp in the room. He declines to switch on the light. There are no windows in the tower wall, so light cannot leak to the outside. But he is not sure if the light would appear under the door and be visible in the storage room below. He listens for sounds of people in the church. He hears the swing doors open and shut a number of times. He concludes that there are worshippers in the church, so he decides to remain silent until the church is empty of people and locked for the night.

9:00pm. Peter Oldthorpe is impatiently waiting to hear the church doors being locked for the night, an indication that the church is empty of people.

9:06pm. He hears the sound of the doors closing and the sound of the key turning. He recognizes the sound of footsteps walking away from the main doors. But instead of fading into the distance, they come closer and into the tower. Peter listens. If this is Bélyy coming up to the radio room, he will need to come up with an explanation for his presence here in the church. A reasonable justification would be that he got worn down by living like an itinerant traveller in rainy weather, and he came here for secluded shelter. There, that's reasonable. However, if it is someone other than Bélyy who has entered the tower, Peter Oldthorpe may need to hide. He studies the trapdoor in the ceiling at the top of the ladder and prepares to make an exit up to the belfry if required. He hears the sound of voices coming from the storage room.

"Where is the candle? It should be right here." He recognises Bélyy's voice.

A second voice, "I must have put it elsewhere when I was here earlier with Paddy Ward." Peter is not familiar with Father Andrew MacNamara's voice.

"And do you get the odour of whin smoke in here?"

Peter has become so desensitised to whin smoke that he had forgotten the distinctiveness of its smell, the smell that clings to itinerant travellers, the smell that he himself now carries.

"Ah, yes. The Wards always manage to make their presence felt, even hours after they've left."

"Well, there is no shortage of candles or candlesticks here. There you go, light this one."

Peter realises that the missing candle is here with him in the radio room. Not only must he hide himself, he must also hide the candle, and he must get to where his smell is undetectable. He blows out the candle and slides it under the desk as far back as he can stretch. He feels his way to the ladder in the wall and swiftly ascends. The trapdoor opens easily. He lifts it gingerly so as to avoid squeaking the hinges. There is a rush of cool air, so he quickly pushes himself through and closes the trapdoor gently and quietly.

The belfry is open to the evening air drifting through, but it is dry and sheltered. He makes himself comfortable and waits for the occupants of the radio room to leave. After an hour or more, he hears them leave. And a few minutes afterwards he hears the sound of a car drive away. He assumes that it is Bélyy driving off. He re-enters the radio room, locates the candle and relights it. He decides to wait a while longer. He has lost track of time, but he knows that the entire town of Killbawn is thrown into darkness each night at midnight when the miller retires for the night. Through the open trapdoor he discerns the glow of the streetlights shining into the belfry.

He waits until the street lights are extinguished at midnight. Whereupon, Peter Oldthorpe secures the trapdoor and, taking the candle, he makes his way through the radio room. At no time did he get a suitable opportunity to use the radio. Nevertheless, he is grateful to have spent six hours dry for the first time in three days. He exits the room. The door self-locks when he pulls it shut. Quietly, he descends the stairs to the storeroom and places the candlestick on a shelf, a different shelf than the one on which he first found it. He has no trouble unlocking the tower door. He blows out the candle and exits the tower. He finds the tower door key and secures the lock, replacing the key back on the rail above the door.

Then he goes into the nave and feels his way along the side aisle, making his way to the sanctuary. How many minutes has this taken? Not more than five. There is no need to rush, but neither can Peter Oldthorpe afford to delay. He intends to reach the old disused mill ahead of 12:30am.

Walking along the dark aisle he unexpectedly bumps against an object knocking it over with a loud crash. He freezes and waits in silence. He breathes again. The noise does not appear to have attracted any attention. He continues up the sanctuary steps. Here, his way is illuminated by the faint glow of the burning sanctuary lamp. He sees the open door to the sacristy and makes his way to it. Eight more paces and he will be through the sacristy and out of the church.

In a few short hours he expects to be on his way to Russia. The past two weeks have been trying, and he is thankful that his ordeal is almost over. He is anxious to have these last few hours go without a hitch. He should reach the old mill in another five minutes or so. He considers jogging along the riverbank walkway rather than walking, just to be sure of reaching the rendezvous point ahead of time.

He secures the buttons on his coat in anticipation of his run to the old mill. In brushing his hand past his pocket he remembers that the key to the radio room is still in his pocket alongside his half-crown. He removes both and is undecided what to do with the key. Should he leave the key here in the sacristy, or throw it away when he exits the church?

Distracted by this decision, he stretches his hand to the sacristy door to where he expects to make contact with the doorknob. He is interrupted by a sudden and unexpected thump on his arm. "Bélyy?" he cries in surprise. He drops his half-crown and key. He braces himself to recover. He hears someone move but in the darkness he is unable to see who it is. And he hears the echo of the coin and the key strike the sanctuary floor, undoubtedly thrown by the unseen person. This cannot be Bélyy.

As the echoing sounds of the bouncing metal are still ringing through the quiet interior of the church, he punches out wildly in alarm in a defensive action. He makes contact. He hears the unseen person fall to the floor and the sound of a bone breaking. The person lies on the floor groaning, blocking Peter's access to the exit door. The matchbox in his pocket is rattling around due to his exuberant activity. Thus reminded, he quickly takes the box and strikes a light in order to weigh up the situation. In the matchlight he sees an old priest lying on the floor. Unfortunately, in the same light of the flaring match, the old priest also sees Peter Oldthorpe and recognises him as John Cross, the British research scientist who is defecting.

Too late, Peter Oldthorpe realises the folly of having lit the match. The priest points his finger accusingly up at Peter Oldthorpe, previously John Cross. Blindly, Peter grabs hold of the closest object at hand and swings it hard at the old priest striking him on the head. He drops the weapon and moves forward to unlatch the door. He tugs on it. The door is blocked by the slumped body of the priest. With an effort he pulls it open a few inches, enough to squeeze his way through and out to the passageway. The dead weight of the slumped body pushes the door shut behind him. Peter Oldthorpe reaches the end of the passageway and exits into the night.

Ten minutes later, Peter Oldthorpe is at the rendezvous point at the disused mill. Paddy Lamp is there waiting for him. Paddy wants his two shillings and sixpence. Peter explains that he dropped it in the dark. He lost it; he doesn't have it, and that's the end of it. Paddy gets threatening. They are interrupted by the arrival of Thomas Farouk Gilban. Farouk is impatient to be on his way. He pacifies Paddy with the promise of payment in two days' time from the completion of the delivery of Peter Oldthorpe to the next contact in Shannon. Why jeopardise it now for the sake of a paltry two shillings and sixpence? Paddy backs off but continues to protest.

It is now Wednesday 02 August. At 3:40am Thomas Farouk Gilban is driving by Ballycalla, past the Honk Bar, and on to Barley Harbour. He stops at the agreed meeting place at the marsh adjacent to Shannon Airport. He sees the momentary flash of car lights.

"Okay, Peter Oldthorpe, that's our signal. Get out. We walk from here."

They walk to the waiting Land Rover. They enter without speaking a word. Malachy Gilban starts the engine and drives to the airport's perimeter road via the dirt track. It is not an approved entrance to the facility, but it is a frequently used shortcut to the Honk Bar by a number of the airport staff. The Land Rover enters the facility, passing by the fuel tanks at the dock. The security guard recognises Malachy's Land Rover and permits it to enter unchallenged. Malachy parks the Land Rover in the parking area close to the dock.

He addresses Peter Oldthorpe. "Stay here. We are going to speak to someone."

Malachy and Farouk walk to the only other car in the lot. The occupant gets out and converses with Malachy and Farouk. Peter Oldthorpe rolls down the car window and attempts to listen to what is being said. He hears them clearly, but they are speaking in Russian. He picks up on the name 'Gregori', the name of the third man, but he is unable to follow the entire conversation. This third man, dressed in a two-piece charcoal black suit, must be his Russian contact. Gregori lights a cigarette and glances over at the Land Rover. All three are talking and nodding in agreement. They walk down to the dock where a rusty oil tanker is moored. Peter wonders if it is a wreck stuck in the sea marsh. But no, he hears Gregori hail the ship. A voice responds, but it is too dark for Peter to distinguish the speaker. The man on the ship and the three on the dock exchange words. Their voices carry in the still night air. They converse entirely in Russian. Peter's understanding of the conversation is spotty. His effort to follow what is being said is too onerous, so he gives up.

Shortly, Malachy, Farouk and Gregori return to the carpark and approach the Land Rover.

Gregori opens the rear door and addresses Peter, "Добро пожаловать, Питер!" which sounds like 'dobro pozhalovat, Pyotr!'

"Peter doesn't speak Russian," Farouk informs Gregori.

Gregori looks at Peter with disapproval. "You are coming to live in Russia, and you can't speak Russian?"

"Well, I...Меня зовут Пётр Старийгородский. Я рад познакомиться с вами." Peter struggles to introduce himself to Gregori.

The three men laugh. Gregori says, "At least he knows his name, 'Pyotr Staryygorodsky'."

"And he is pleased to make your acquaintance, Gregori," Farouk adds.

Gregori turns his attention back to Peter. "Don't worry about that now, Peter. We'll work on your Russian later." Gregori takes from his inside pocket a folded form and shows it to Peter. "This is your embarkation pass for your passage to Russia. Everything is in order. But we must meet down here away from the public area and out of sight of the departure lounge."

Malachy explains, "We suspect that the public areas of the airport are being watched. It is unwise to bring you into the departure lounge or to the departure gates. MI5 and SDU may be monitoring those areas."

Peter wonders who or what 'MI5' or 'SDU' are. Regardless of who they are, it would appear that these entities are hostile to this operation and should be avoided. He nods in agreement. He remembers that the Special Branch (or some other government security service) trashed his office in Risley – and that was a 'friendly' visit.

Gregori continues, "You will be taken directly from here, from this parking area, to board your passage to Russia."

"So, do I go now?"

"No. Not now. Here is your embarkation pass. Read it. It is all spelled out there."

Peter looks at the pass. It is in Russian. He is unable to make sense of it. He is not surprised. Even English boarding passes make little sense. He asks, "So, when do I board?"

Gregori throws away his cigarette and stubs it out with his foot. He blows smoke and answers, "Peter, you board as early as twelve midnight; but not any later than 04:00."

"As early as midnight? But it is already well past 3:00am."

"Look at the date on your pass. You board tomorrow night, at midnight."

Farouk clarifies to Peter. "Your passage is confirmed for departure at 04:00 on the morning of the 4th of August. You board at midnight tomorrow night, or soon thereafter. That is 45 hours from now. Meanwhile, you cannot stay here. You are coming back to Killbawn. We will return at 9:00pm tomorrow to arrive here just before midnight."

Peter is thinking about the priest left lying in St. Bawn's. "Can I not stay here? Surely I can be hidden here or somewhere in the marsh?"

Malachy laughs. "No. I will not permit you to hang around the airport. Even the dock area here will be busy all day. You stay with your minder until you board."

On the way back to Killbawn, Peter examines his embarkation pass. Studying the wording slowly, he is able to understand it. He quizzes Farouk for an interpretation of some of the words that puzzle him.

"What is this word here?"

"СВОБОДА. 'Svahbohdah'. It means 'Freedom' in English. Peter, you will be travelling on the 'Freedom' to Russia."

"The Russians gives names to their airplanes?"

"Yes, they do. But this is not an airplane. 'Svahbohdah' is a ship."

"A ship? What ship?" Peter has developed a fear of sea transportation after his frightening passage from Glasgow to Derry.

"You saw her docked at Shannon. 'Svahbohdah' is the Russian oil tanker that brings aviation fuel to the Russian planes at Shannon. She sails from the Baltic to Shannon and back every three weeks. On Friday morning, at 4:00am, she casts off to navigate out of the Shannon into the Atlantic, up over the Scottish coast and into the North Sea..."

"No. I am not going to sea again!"

"...to arrive at her home port of Ventspils, in Latvia U.S.S.R, on August tenth."

"No, no, no! I will not go to sea! I would sooner die than go to sea again!"

Farouk brings the car to a screeching halt. He engages the handbrake and turns to Peter. "You say that you would sooner die? Well, listen to your prophetic words, Peter Oldthorpe. If you fail to board your transportation vessel to Russia, you most probably WILL die. Do you think you can survive alone in Ireland? How long before you are spotted and reported? How long before MI5 catches up to you? And don't be so naive as to think that they will politely arrest you. When they catch up to you – and note that I say 'when', not 'if' – when they catch up to you, well...these are your options:

"Go to Northern Ireland and turn yourself in to the RUC. Hopefully, you will be escorted back to Britain alive;

"Die, probably, at the hands of MI5 if you attempt to flee, or;

"Endure a sea voyage in an oil tanker.

"Now shut up. I don't want to hear another word from you."

Peter shuts up. In his heart he knows that Farouk is right. Now he is wracked by multiple fears. Will he be connected to the assault on the old priest in Killbawn? What would be his fate if he turns himself in to the police? Should he turn back to Northern Ireland and contact the RUC? Will MI5 get to him? Or will he perish en route to Russia in a rusty unseaworthy oil tanker? A few hours ago, he was elated in the expectation of boarding a flight to Russia. Now he is despondent. They continue the journey to Killbawn in silence.

7:00am. Peter Oldthorpe is back at the Blackwater, behind the creamery at Killbawn. Paddy Lamp refuses to feed him or to have anything to do with him. But Paddy also knows that his payment is on condition of a successful delivery. Peter Oldthorpe needs to be watched and confined, that's all. Farouk promises to bring him food after he checks in at St. Bawn's at 9:00am. He has the month-end accounting to perform for July. He'll come up with an excuse to put it off for another day. He needs to catch up on sleep. Tomorrow night will be another late night.

9:30am. Farouk returns with a ham sandwich for Peter Oldthorpe. The creamery is now alive with activity. Farouk manages to slip the sandwich through the fence unnoticed. Farouk walks away, and Peter successfully gets hold of it. He grabs the sandwich and listens to Farouk speak with the farmers and workers in the creamery yard. He hears him relate the news of the morning's events at St. Bawn's. Canon MacMorrow is dead. It would seem that he had one of his weak turns and fell in the sacristy. He bumped his head and died from his injury. An unfortunate accident, alas, but not totally unexpected for a man in frail health. No, he didn't see the canon; Mrs. Friel relayed the news to him at the parochial house less than half an hour ago.

Peter Oldthorpe breathes a sigh of relief at hearing this. The old priest is dead. There is no mention of an attack or of an intruder. Peter Oldthorpe has dodged a bullet. The accepted premise appears to be that the feeble old canon accidentally fell and bumped his head. Peter braces to wait until 9:00pm the following evening. He hopes that Paddy Lamp's hostility is endurable for the next day and a half.

Thursday 03 August, 8:30am. Farouk brings Peter breakfast – slices of ham and hard-boiled eggs and a loaf of bread. "9:00pm tonight. I'll pick you up from the old mill. Be there."

Farouk is wary that Peter Oldthorpe's fear of the sea may cause him to back out and fail to keep his rendezvous. This could have dire consequences for Farouk and for Paddy Ward. Paddy Ward assures Farouk that, with the help of

Francie and Collie, Peter Oldthorpe will keep his appointment, like it or not.

"If Peter Oldthorpe is able to walk, he'll be there. Count on it. At the old mill at nine o'clock the night."

At the riverbank, Collie takes up a position a little ways upstream, and Francie sits some distance downstream, throwing sticks into the black flowing water. It is clear to Peter Oldthorpe that he is now a prisoner of Paddy Ward. Presently, the creamery accepts its last delivery of milk and completes its operation for the day.

11:00am. Inspector Murphy (Murf) pays a brief visit to the itinerants' camp. After Murf leaves, a small Ward boy in bare feet and with a running nose comes to the riverbank and speaks with Francie. Francie signals to Collie and addresses Peter Oldthorpe. "Paddy wants us back in the camp." Francie and Collie escort Peter from the river to the camp. Peter is aware of a restless activity in the camp. Paddy's merchandise is being wrapped up in canvas, and the horse is hitched to the cart. The women and children are busy packing and assembling their effects. Paddy has finished restoring a Tilley lamp which he is buffing to a shine. He holds it aloft by the handle and casts his eye up and down to admire his handiwork.

9:00pm. Farouk Gilban is at the old mill. At 9:10pm, Peter Oldthorpe has not yet arrived. Farouk is annoyed. The old mill is not all that far from the creamery and Paddy Ward's camp. Walking along the riverbank from the creamery is less than fifteen minutes to the old mill.

9:15pm. Farouk Gilban is anxious. He drives to Paddy Lamp's camp to enquire. Farouk is surprised to find the campsite cleared. There is no sign of Peter Oldthorpe, or of

Paddy Lamp and the Ward clan. The place is deserted. What could have occurred to cause Peter Oldthorpe's failure to keep his appointment? And why would Paddy Lamp leave before collecting his payment? If Peter Oldthorpe is not successfully delivered to his next contact, there will be no payment. It is not like Paddy Lamp to walk away from money.

Farouk drives around searching highways and byways and laneways in a vain attempt to locate Paddy Ward. He searches into nightfall. At 1:30am, he gives up. It is now too late to reach the Svahbohdah before she casts off. He drives to Killbawn intending to send a radio message reporting Peter Oldthorpe's failure to board his transportation vessel to Russia. Upon entering the town he sees that the street lights are dark. He realises that the town's electricity is turned off. He will not be able to transmit a message until 8:00am.

Where is Peter Oldthorpe?

PART 3 – THE QUEST IS LAID TO REST

CHAPTER TWENTY-THREE

KILLBAWN, 08 AUGUST 1950

7:00am. Killbawn Garda Station receives a telephone call. It is a message for the attention of Inspector Murphy advising that a Mr. Piperson is en route from London via Belfast, and is expected to arrive in Killbawn at 11:00am.

7:30am. Murf is walking to the Garda station. He pays no heed to the Mayo misty morning drizzle. He did not sleep well and his head is dull. He hopes that by walking to work by way of the riverbank he will clear his head. He is disturbed by Francie Ward's tall tale of last night. Francie's story cannot be considered a confession or a credible account. As an item of evidence it is worse than useless. Murf decides to keep it safe but separate from the case file. Francie's fantastic tale may have some elements of reality, but in a twisted far-fetched way.

Murf sits down on the pathway wall facing towards the river. His feet dangle over the current. He considers the strange anomaly of the Ward clan of travellers. Francie and Tricks and their cohorts engage in street entertainment. They sing, they dance, and they perform tricks. And they relate stories from folklore – stories about heroes and villains. That's what the Wards do, and have been doing it for hundreds of years. Murf tosses a pebble into the black swirling water. He continues to process his thoughts. And what the Wards do, they execute with the appropriate degree of theatre to make it convincing and entertaining to the audience. Murf himself has observed their dance routine in which the participants change position and attire undetected. He is always impressed by the Wards' entertainment skills.

Murf shifts his position on the wall. He realises, too late, that the wall is wet. The moisture has seeped through to his buttocks.

Last night Francie related a fanciful tale about John Cross a.k.a. Peter Oldthorpe. Was that theatre? The hair tossed forward to conceal his face? The arms stretched out to 'connect' to the 'portal'? The altered voices? And falling faint to the floor? Was this all Ward theatre? Murf flings another pebble into the river.

Granted, Francie concocts stories for the purpose of street entertainment, tales about heroes and villains and all. A story about an English fugitive evading the police is an ideal fit for his material. Murf spins a pebble high in the air and watches it arc and fall splashing far out in the current. How did Francie obtain the necessary information to have an understanding of the workings of British intelligence or counter-intelligence? Without this understanding he would not have been able to fabricate such a fanciful tale.

Murf pushes some loose pebbles into a row on the wall to form an abacus. He moves one pebble at a time, as he checks off information in his mind.

1) Francie Ward may be illiterate, but the same Francie Ward is smart. He is clever enough to have been entrusted to secretly escort and deliver a defecting scientist to the Russians – well, part way at least. This puts him on a par with Farouk Gilban, a trained security agent of the Foreign Office. Who could know him that well to entrust him on such a delicate stealthy assignment? And could Francie have surreptitiously elicited an understanding of the entity that engaged him?

2) He moves a second pebble and continues with his train of thought. John Cross a.k.a. Peter Oldthorpe spent two weeks with the Wards. During that time, did John Cross learn

anything of substance from the itinerant travellers? And in turn, did he open up his personal life to the canny Wards who read him like a book (metaphorically – they are illiterate)?

3) He moves a third pebble. Francie Ward's description of the attack on Canon MacMorrow is a plausible explanation. But if the assault was not actually witnessed by him, how was he able to describe it in such detail? Conjecture? Is he that smart? Or inventive?

Based on what he knows about the two Ward lads, and in the absence of any incriminating evidence, there is no reason to detain Francie Left-handed Ward or Collie Tricks Ward. The police in Britain may have cause to arrest them for offences in Britain. But unless they request their extradition, it is not Murf's concern. Murf's primary objective is to track down and arrest Peter Oldthorpe.

In the absence of Paddy Lamp Ward, the best hope of apprehending Peter Oldthorpe is through Thomas Farouk Gilban. Are John Cross and Peter Oldthorpe the same person, as indicated in Francie's fantastic tale? If he can establish this, he has a second route to catching Peter Oldthorpe the perpetrator – a promising route through the Brits who are attempting to apprehend the defecting John Cross. Murf tosses the three abacus pebbles into the river.

A voice addresses him from the pathway. "Are ye taking the day off today, Guard Murphy? Or are ye investigating where the Blackwater goes? It flows into the sea four mile from here. Don't ye know that at all, at all?"

Murf shifts his weight and turns around to face Mrs. Friel. "Ah, Mrs. Friel. It's such a nice day. I was admiring the soothing motion of the river."

"It's a nice day?" Mrs. Friel glances at the seat of Murf's trousers, "It's drizzling. And your arse is wet." Mrs. Friel continues on her way, shaking her head.

Murf springs off the wall and onto the pathway. His head is now clear. He resumes his walk to the Garda station. Francie and Tricks have been in custody without charges since late Sunday. Or to be more accurate – they have been in comfort in the Garda station since Sunday, eating good food and sleeping in a dry bed. He needs to release them.

7:55am. Murf arrives at the Garda station. O'Reilly is already in the station and is keenly awaiting Murf's arrival. He slaps the telephone message pad down on the front counter. "Murf. First thing. Read this."

Murf glances at the message and immediately perks up with enthusiasm. "O'Reilly, come into my office. Now, here's what we're going to do...."

9:45am. Francie and Collie Ward resume their journey to Donegal. They are much refreshed from their time in Killbawn Garda Station – well fed and well rested.

Murf, on the other hand, is in the bank in Killbawn. Opening time is 10:00am, but Murf arranged to have early access. He requests the manager to assist him in an inquiry. St. Bawn's cash lodgements, expected first thing after opening, could be of relevance. The manager instructs Jim Woods to put the St. Bawn's lodgements aside after accepting and receipting them.

At 10:00am the customers file into the bank. The bank has been closed for two days, since noon on Saturday. The customers are impatient. The first in line is Thomas Farouk Gilban. Murf peers out at him through the frosted glass door of the manager's office. Jim Woods counts the church's cash lodgements, stamps the receipts and hands the lodgement books back to Farouk. Having completed his transactions at the bank, Farouk returns to St. Bawn's with the lodgement books. Jim Woods brings the two cash lodgements into the manager's office with the accompanying lodgement slips. The manager takes the cash from the teller.

"Thanks, Jim." And turning to Murf, "So what is it that you want to see, Inspector? That the lodgements are in order?"

Murf confirms the receipted amounts, £7-16-9 from the funeral, and £2-1-7 from the Sunday Mass. He is satisfied that the amounts tally. Next he checks the make-up. There should be two half-crowns from the Saturday collection, and one half-crown from Sunday's. He is surprised to find that there are six half-crowns in all, five of which are Saorstát Éireann leath coróin in mint condition dated 1929

"I'll need to take those 1929 half-crowns."

"Why? We are meant to withdraw them from circulation and send them off to the Central Bank."

"Not these five coins." Murf takes a £1 note from his wallet. "Here. Give me the five 1929 half-crowns and the other one, plus five bob in silver. Your lodgements are still balanced."

"Well, if you insist."

"I strongly insist."

"Okay. Here you are, Inspector."

Murf departs the bank with £1 in silver jingling in his pocket. He walks to St. Bawn's and knocks at the back door of the parochial house. Mrs. Friel answers the door.

"Guard Murphy? And what do ye be wanting here? Do ye need to dry your arse? If it's for Father MacNamara you are, he's not in."

"Ah, no, Mrs. Friel. I'm here to see Thomas Gilban."

"Come right in. You'll find Thomas Gilban in the meeting room going over his books and figures. And wipe your feet on the mat as you come in. You cart in near as much dirt on your boots as Paddy Lamp."

Murf knows his way to the room. He sees Farouk with pen and pencil and ruler, comparing figures from a little red cash book to big full-size ledgers. Farouk looks up and sees Murf enter. He hurriedly snaps shut the little cash book.

"Murf, what brings you here?"

"Thomas, I've run into a slight conundrum and I'm looking for your input to help settle it for me."

Thomas places his pen on the open ledger and pushes it back. He stretches his arms and leans back in the chair. "Sure. Go ahead, Murf. Shoot."

"Well, it's like this. It is much easier to show you than to explain it to you. Why don't you walk over to the station with me and I'll show you?"

"What, now? I'm a bit busy at the moment, Murf. How about later?"

Murf remains silent and stares at Farouk. This bothers Farouk.

"Well, if it helps, Murf, I suppose I could take a break from this for a while."

10:30am. Farouk is shown into the interview room in the Garda station. "The interview room, Murf? You are bringing me into the interview room?"

"Thomas, my office is a mess. This room is much neater."

Farouk surveys the room. No windows, no wall decorations. Just a table and four hard chairs.

"Just give me a moment, Thomas. I need to get my file." Murf gets his file from his office. He employs Garda O'Reilly to observe the interview from the adjoining room. "O'Reilly, I want you to heed what is said and take notes.

There may even be another case resurfacing from twenty years ago."

"What case would...?"

"Just take notes. We'll weigh it up later."

Murf takes his time returning to the interview room. The wait should make Farouk uneasy. Murf enters the room and sits beside Farouk rather than opposite him. "Thomas, the canon's death. I can confirm to you that we are treating it as a homicide."

"So I understand. But what is the conundrum about it, and how I can help?"

"We are attempting to connect two items to their owners."

"And this is your riddle? What are these two items?"

"Items found at the scene, both bearing the fingerprints of the assailant."

"You have positive fingerprints of the assailant? Are you sure?"

"We are sure. There is no doubt. Now, as to the items. One is a key, a Yale key. Here is a picture of it." Murf flips a photograph from the file folder and shows it to Farouk Gilban. "I understand that you had a key cut recently, did you not?"

"Yes. I had a Yale key copied about two weeks ago. Mrs. Friel got it cut at Casey's. Are you suggesting that the key found at the scene, the one bearing the assailant's prints, might be that key?"

"Thomas, I am not suggesting. I am stating with certainty that the key found at the scene is your key, your extra key. This is the first part of my conundrum. Who would have your key? And why would he physically attack Canon MacMorrow?"

Farouk starts to answer, but he hesitates in order to form his response carefully. Then he decides not to comment.

Murf continues. "There is a second part to the conundrum. We also found a coin at the scene." Murf slides a second picture from the file.

"Like the key, this item also bears the assailant's prints. Now, this coin is unusual. It is a 1929 Saorstát Éireann leath coróin in mint condition. Unusual, but not rare. Now, here is where you can help. This morning you lodged the cash from St. Bawn's collections into the bank. The lodgements contained five similar coins, 1929 half-crowns in mint condition." Murf takes the silver from his pocket and spreads the coins on the table.

Farouk Gilban looks at the coins and is taken aback. "So some parishioners have money stashed away from twenty years ago, and they put some of it into the church collection. The coins could have come from anyone who attends St. Bawn's"

"Except that I counted the money, Thomas. When you prepared the lodgements after the funeral Mass, there were only two half-crowns, and only one was a 1929 coin. That one came from Granny McGrath. The Sunday collection contained one half-crown, an Éire half-crown. When you reached the bank this morning, four more 1929 Saorstát Éireann leath coróin in mint condition were included in the lodgement, substituted for other coins to the value of ten shillings. Thomas, you are substituting half-crowns from a stash of old coins."

"So what's wrong with that? The lodgements are deposited whole, and in the correct amount."

"Unless you are disposing of silver coins to avoid tracing them back to the source."

"What, laundering half-crowns? You can't be serious, Murf."

"The original source of the half-crowns is not my immediate concern."

"Oh, so what is your point?"

"You see, Thomas, I have a key and a coin, both bearing the prints of the killer, and when I look at where they come from, I am directed to you. Now do you see my conundrum?"

Thomas is drumming his fingers on the table in thought.

Murf looks at his watch. It is close to 10:50am. "Tell you what, Thomas. Take your time. I'll make a pot of tea and come back. Maybe by then you'll have a solution for me."

Murf takes his file and the silver coins and leaves the room. He joins Garda O'Reilly in the adjoining room. "O'Reilly. Make us a pot of tea. Be sure to heat the pot and have the water boiling."

"Are you not going to stay in there with Farouk?"

"No. Farouk can wait a spell. I intend to spring another surprise on him. Oh, and tell Caldwell to transfer any calls to me here. I'm expecting someone to arrive at any moment."

10:55am. The front desk rings the extension phone in the observation room. Murf picks it up. "What is it, Caldwell?"

"Inspector Murphy, there is a strange-looking man here at the front desk asking for you."

"How strange is he?"

"He is English by the sound of him. And he's dressed up like Sherlock Holmes gone fishing. His name is 'Piperson'."

"Ah, yes. That is Patrick Piperson from London. I'm expecting him. And yes, he is a bit strange."

Murf goes down to the front desk. He sees 'Piper's Son' whom he prefers to call 'Patrick Piperson'. Murf suppresses a laugh with much difficulty. Patrick is dressed in Harris Tweeds and is sporting a deerstalker hat and heavy brogues. The hat is pierced all around with fly fishhooks.

"My God, Patrick. Why are you dressed like that?"

"Hello, Murf. Nice to see you. I didn't want to stand out, dressed in a Savile Row suit. I thought that this manner of dress would blend into Mayo quite well."

"You look like George Bernard Shaw on a fishing holiday, without a fishing rod. And do you intend to stuff your fish into your briefcase?"

"It's that bad? Ah, maybe the hat is too much."

"The hat is fine. Remove the fishhooks. I have Thomas Gilban in the interview room. Do you want to be filled in and be brought up to speed?"

"No. Take me to him. From my perspective I know where I'm at."

Murf enters the interview room with a tray containing a teapot, milk and sugar, and three cups, and one other item, his manila file folder. "Thomas, here we are. A freshly-brewed pot of tea. And guess what? Mr. Patrick Piperson from London is joining us."

Farouk is taken aback by the appearance of the man in Harris tweeds. He searches his memory. He isn't sure, but he feels that he has seen him before, a long time ago. Piperson places his hat, now with the fishhooks removed, on a vacant chair.

He stretches his hand out to greet Thomas Farouk Gilban. "Bélyy! We meet at last. How many years has it been? Oh, I don't know. But here we are, and there is so much to talk about."

Farouk stands up and addresses Murf. "Murf, I need to leave now. Is that all right?"

"Of course you may leave, Thomas. You are not under arrest. But I was hoping that you could solve my conundrum." Farouk tentatively walks to the door. He expects his exit to be prevented, but Murf steps aside.

Murf speaks softly to him. "Thomas, consider who else might be out there searching for Bélyy."

Farouk hesitates. He suspects that Piperson is British Secret Service. They always travel in pairs or in teams. If Piperson is in here, who else is here, or close by? There is no point in Thomas Farouk Gilban denying that he is Bélyy. Piperson is here because he knows, or has good reason to suspect. Farouk concedes to himself that his cover is blown and that the Secret Service knows who he is. He returns to his chair. He decides to play a game of life-poker with the Secret Service. He hopes that the trump card he has been saving will be enough to win him a get-out-of-gaol free pass. He cautions himself not to play it prematurely.

"Are you going to read me my rights?"

Murf responds. "Why? Are you confessing to a crime? You are not under arrest here in Killbawn."

Patrick adds, "Let's see where this goes. Then we'll see."

"You want my help? My cooperation?"

"See. Already we have an understanding."

Murf offers to pour tea. Patrick indicates that he wants the milk poured into the cup first. Farouk accepts tea, but with the milk poured in last. Murf doesn't mind which is poured first. Sipping tea relaxes them and the cooperation begins.

"So tell me, Bélyy, you have been quiet for two years. What has brought you to life again?"

"I was asked to make a delivery."

"Like before?"

"No. Not like before. Way back during the war, authorised unofficial deliveries were frequently made."

"What do you mean by 'authorised unofficial'?"

"I was instructed to deliver packages in secret to the Russians during Allied talks."

"Instructed by whom?"

"I never knew. But it was someone, or maybe different persons at different times, but someone with clearance to top-level talks."

"Explain."

"Well, for example, there was the time when I was assigned to check the litter after meetings. We would all rush in to check the waste paper. Delegates could be careless in disposing of notes taken during a meeting. The Americans tried to snoop into everyone else's litter. Well, so did we, and the Russians too. My job was to retrieve British wastepaper notes and doodles before the Americans or Russians got to them. And then destroy them – the litter, that is – not the Americans and Russians."

"And..."

"At times I would find litter with a prearranged coded marking that was a directive to me to transfer the wastepaper to a Russian litter basket surreptitiously."

"And this could only come from a senior delegate at the meeting?"

"Precisely."

"And you complied?"

"Of course. This was the common modus operandi all throughout the war."

"And after the war?"

"After the war it became more complex."

"And you were at ease passing secrets to the Russians?"

"During the war, it was to help the Allies against Nazi Germany."

"But after the war?"

"I didn't question it. Was it information, or was it misinformation? I don't know. The directives came from high up in the Service. I was merely the delivery boy. I didn't question it until the Cairo debacle."

"And you questioned it in Cairo?"

"Yes. But nothing came to light. They concentrated on playing down an embarrassing incident rather than engage in uncovering what was really happening. I deliberated within myself. Were the secret deliveries, albeit irregular, properly authorised; or did they originate from a mole in the Service?"

"And what did you discover?"

"Nothing. I was uneasy, but I had insufficient grounds to make a complaint. Not knowing who might be the mole, I could not go to my superiors. Similarly, I could not trust anyone in Cairo with my suspicions. After the Cairo situation, when it blew up, we were recalled to London. This gave me the opportunity and excuse to extricate myself from the operation by citing health reasons."

"Or there could be another explanation. You were knowingly complicit all along, and the Cairo affair got too hot for you. You feared that things were coming to a head and that an investigation was closing in on the mole. You were in danger of being caught in the same net. Now, after two years, you consider the danger to have passed."

"You are winding me up. What I told you is how it was. Are you not in the Service? Surely you know how things are done." There is silence. Both men turn their attention to their tea.

After a few quiet sips of tea, Piper's Son continues questioning. "1950. So tell me about 1950."

"Two important things occurred in 1950. They occurred remotely from each other, but to connect them could blow the lid off every Russian spy investigation you have ever attempted."

"Really. And I am to believe you?"

"Really. And since when should I trust you?"

"Stalemate. Mutual distrust."

Another moment of tense silence.

Farouk Gilban breaks the silence. "Then let's move along. There must be some middle ground where we can meet."

"Bélyy, don't try to play me. Am I to believe that a lowly courier, such as you, could have any information of value? You are a lowly operative, and you have been found out. You are not even a 'spy' spy. You are, or were, a spy postman."

"Piperson, do you know about my recent delivery? It wasn't a piece of paper from a litter basket."

"No, it was to deliver John Cross to the Russians."

"Wrong. It was to secretly transfer Peter Oldthorpe to a prearranged passage to Russia, authorised and directed by a senior officer in the Service. Your senior officer, I suspect. The person I was to accommodate was Peter Oldthorpe, not John Cross."

"And did you?"

"Did I what?"

"Succeed in getting him to Russia?"

"No. He failed to show at his rendezvous point. He backed out when he learned that his passage to Russia was to be on an oil tanker."

"An oil tanker?"

"Yes. A Russian oil tanker from Shannon."

Piper's Son sips tea and considers this information. "Bélyy, let me understand you clearly. You met Peter Oldthorpe. You offered to bring him to a vessel that had arranged his passage to Russia. Peter Oldthorpe failed to show. Are you sure he failed to board the tanker?"

"I'm sure. I checked."

"So you are telling me that Peter Oldthorpe is still in Ireland?"

"Yes."

Murf slides a poster across the table to Farouk. It is the John Cross wanted poster with the top folded under. "Farouk, do you recognise this man?"

Farouk Gilban glances at the picture. "That's Peter Oldthorpe. How come you have his picture?" Murf unfolds the top part of the poster to display the name 'John Cross'.

Farouk lifts the poster and reads it through. "Peter Oldthorpe is John Cross?"

"Yes. A British research scientist defecting to the Soviet Union."

If Farouk is surprised, he doesn't show it. Secrets are what one expects when working with the Secret Service. Farouk could be desensitised to it.

Murf turns to Piper's Son. "Time to compare files, Patrick." Murf slides out from his folder a fingerprint sheet. Piper's Son does likewise from a file in his briefcase. They compare the sheets.

Murf addresses Farouk. "Thomas, this is interesting. Here is a sample of John Cross's fingerprints, and here is a sample of the prints we received from the murder weapon, and also from your key and from a 1929 mint-condition half-crown found at the incident scene. What, in your opinion, is the conclusion here?"

Farouk is sufficiently experienced to come to one undeniable conclusion. "John Cross killed Canon MacMorrow." He swallows and regains his voice. "But that's not possible. Peter Oldthorpe was gone from St. Bawn's on Lammas Day."

"He was at St. Bawn's? When?"

"He was in the radio room four days earlier, on the night of Friday 28th July. He wanted me to transmit a radio communication. But he was not there any time since then. He was securely under wraps in another location under close watch. On the night of Lammas Day, Father MacNamara and I were the last to leave the church. Peter Oldthorpe was not there at that time, and he had no way of gaining access once the church was locked."

"And where was he securely under wraps?"

"At Paddy Lamp Ward's camp."

"And Paddy Lamp is not around to collaborate this."

"I know. He's flitted."

"The Lamp!" Piperson unexpectedly exclaims. Murf and Farouk look at him in surprise. Piperson thumps his head with the heel of his hand and continues talking, presumably to himself. "'The Lamp' is not a place; it is a person."

Murf looks at him and tenders a clarification of the sudden remark. "Yes, Patrick. Paddy Lamp Ward is a person. He is..."

"...one of the itinerant Wards, a traveller. We had been going off in the wrong direction...." Piperson realises that his sudden unexpected remark requires some explanation. "Sorry, Murf. I just came to the realisation of where John Cross was hiding for the past week. You see, on July 24 we intercepted a radio communication in progress, transmitting from England to Russia. It made reference to 'Bélyy and to a 'delivery' and to a 'lamp'. We understood this to be a reference to John

Cross's location – at a place called 'The Lamp'. But no, he was travelling concealed with the Wards. He has been with the Wards all along, right from the moment he disappeared from Bostock Green."

"July 24, you say? Paddy Lamp Ward was encamped outside Killbawn on July 24. He remained here until he suddenly disappeared; that was on Thursday 03 August, a day of heavy continuous rain."

"Five days ago." Piperson turns his attention back to the interview. "So, where were we?"

Murf resumes speaking to Farouk. "Thomas, I questioned you previously about the events of August the first, and about the comings and goings in St. Bawn's. You didn't mention anything about a stranger in the church."

"Why would I? A stranger in the church four days earlier? Why would I make a connection? And when you questioned me it was not in the context of a homicide, now was it, Murf? No, Murf, don't pull that one on me. I didn't withhold information pertinent to your inquiry. This revelation here is a surprise to me. Delivering packages is one thing I did, but not covering up for a murder."

Murf and Piper's Son exchange looks. They are inclined to believe Farouk. Farouk continues. "Look, I want to catch Canon MacMorrow's killer as much you do. All three of us want to catch him, maybe not for the same reason, but to catch him nevertheless."

Murf remembers something. "No, not the three of us. The FOUR of us. Paddy Lamp said something like this too on the day he disappeared."

"Good Lord. Paddy Lamp is a jump ahead of us. If he..." Farouk is unable to complete his thought. Paddy Lamp is capable of many things.

"Bélyy, you stated that you could blow the lid off every Russian investigation we have ever attempted. If I am to believe you, to trust you, you must give me something to hang my hat on."

"Do I give you something you know, or something you don't know?"

"You don't know what I don't know. Try me."

"Okay. Two names – 'Gomer' and 'Shakespeare'."

Piper's Son visibly freezes for an instant, and then recomposes himself. "I've no idea what that means. Can you explain?"

"The directives I received, including this recent one, originated from 'Gomer'."

"I see. And who is this 'Gomer?" Piper's Son knows that 'Gomer' is the most senior and most elusive mole in Britain. They are unable to get close to him and have been unable to identify him. There is no way that lowly Bélyy would even know of his existence, and certainly not his identity. So how did Farouk Gilban come up with this name?

Farouk admits, "I don't know Gomer, or who he is, or anything about him. But Shakespeare knows all about him. And Shakespeare informed me that Oldthorpe's exile to Russia was instigated by Gomer. I had never heard of Gomer before that."

"Shakespeare knows all about Gomer? Why would that interest me?"

"Does it?" Each stares at the other in silence. Neither wants to flinch.

Piper's Son caves in first. "Okay. Let's play this game of make-believe, just for a moment."

Farouk congratulates himself silently: Gotcha! Piper's Son has swallowed the bait and is hooked. Now to play him. Farouk continues, "I never heard of Gomer until Shakespeare mentioned it. Shakespeare is my Russian contact. He has been for some time. Over the past two years we have kept in touch. We have become ham-radio pals sharing personal information. I believe I can induce Shakespeare to defect. I think that's what he is hinting at in mentioning Gomer. He must consider this to be valuable information to use as bargaining leverage. Shakespeare claims to know the identity of Gomer and four others. A group of five."

"A group of five? And Gomer is one of them?"

"Yes."

"And this Shakespeare trusts you?"

"So far. We have formed a relationship of sorts over the past seven years."

Piper's Son is calculating mentally. "We may never uncover the identity of Gomer. The elusive Gomer is so high up that his position is difficult to pinpoint. Some within the service fear that this 'Gomer' may even have access to Number 10 Downing Street. Unmasking the identity of Gomer is one of MI6's objectives of the highest priority. And now this 'Shakespeare' can finger him?" Thomas Farouk Gilban Bélyy has just earned himself a reprieve.

"Bélyy, we may have use for you after all."

1:07pm. Garda O'Reilly enters the interview room. "Mr. Piperson. There is a telephone call for you. And Sergeant Hughes says that you may take the call in his office." Piper's Son follows O'Reilly to take the call.

O'Reilly returns to the interview room. "Inspector, is there anything else I can do to assist?"

"Yes. I want you to join us. Our priority is to locate and apprehend John Cross, otherwise known as Peter Oldthorpe. When I say 'OUR priority', I include the British Intelligence and Counter-Intelligence Service, and Garda Special

Detective Unit. Contact Dublin and report to SDU what you have learned here this morning."

Piper's Son returns to the interview room. "Murf, I have been called to Enniskillen urgently. I must leave right away."

"You are leaving? What about John Cross?"

"This pertains directly to John Cross. The agents there have reported a confirmed sighting."

"A confirmed sighting in Enniskillen?"

"Actually, in a place called Tullyhaugh. I must leave right away." And turning to Thomas Gilban, "Thomas, you want to cooperate? Come with me to Enniskillen."

Thomas Gilban swallows. He knows that he must play this carefully. The conditions of the 'Official Secrets Act' are flashing through his head. And Enniskillen is in the U.K. This could be dire for him. But if he backs out, it could be worse. He considers his trump card, still an advantage in his favour, and decides to see this through. "Of course. We can continue our talk on the drive to Enniskillen."

"Hold on!" says Murf, who is unsettled at both Piper's Son's and Thomas Farouk Gilban's leaving at the same time. "I have a murder suspect to apprehend. If he is in Enniskillen or Tullyhaugh, I have reason to be there too."

"Murf, you have a murder suspect to apprehend. I have a defecting spy to apprehend. It looks like he has fallen into our jurisdiction, I'm afraid." Piper's Son and Farouk depart hurriedly.

Murf contacts Castlebar Divisional office to consult with Chief Superintendent Fox. RUC/Garda cooperation is required for Murf to pursue a suspect into Northern Ireland. He requests that this be arranged post-haste so that he may report to the RUC Station in Tullyhaugh.

1:22pm. Murf is waiting for Divisional Office to phone back. He decides to wait until 1:25pm. Then he is driving to Termon regardless. The information can be relayed to him at the Garda station there. Murf knows that Termon is a border town. The Northern Ireland part of Termon is identified as Tullyhaugh. If Murf gets permission to proceed to the RUC Station in Tullyhaugh, he could still get there well before Piper's Son arrives. It takes two and a half hours to reach Termon from Killbawn. To reach Tullyhaugh via Enniskillen adds another hour to the journey.

1:25pm. The phone rings. Murf shouts, "It's for me. I'm expecting this call." He rushes to the front counter and lifts the phone. Murf expects this to be Divisional Office. He is surprised that it is the Garda station in Termon.

"This is Inspector Murphy."

"This is Sergeant Mickey Hickey in Termon. Inspector Murphy, I'm pressed for time, so I'll come right out and ask. Does the name 'Peter Oldthorpe' mean anything to you?"

"It certainly does. He is a murder suspect I'm attempting to apprehend. What do you know about him?"

"Well, now he is a murder victim. The only identification we found on him is a Manchester library card in the name of Peter Oldthorpe. We checked the address on the card. It is a men's shelter in Manchester frequented by Irish seasonal workers. Written on the card is 'St. Bawn's'. Now that's the name of your parish church in Killbawn, isn't it? That's why we phoned you."

"I'll be there in two hours."

"Yes. You need to come right away. There's more. The body was discovered under the bridge at Mill Street. The RUC claim that it was lying in Northern Ireland, and that the crime was committed in Northern Ireland on a British subject.

They are demanding that we hand over the body and the investigation to them."

"And are you?"

"Lord, no. But there is a big row brewing. Belfast and Dublin are weighing in."

"It's not like the RUC not to cooperate."

"That's the funny thing. I don't believe that it stems from the RUC at all. Demands are being imposed upon them from higher up. It's getting nasty; particularly from the two men from London who claim to have been tracking this person from England since the middle of July. Get here as fast as you can. I need a strong argument to stand my ground, and your St. Bawn's murder connection strengthens my case. And I don't need some smart-ass Dublin unit like the SDU taking over from me either."

"I'm on my way. Hold tight, Hickey."

CHAPTER TWENTY-FOUR

TERMON, 08 AUGUST 1950

Enniskillen, 8:10am. Brady enters the hotel in search of Andrews. He sees him still sitting at the breakfast table staring blankly ahead with teacup raised, poised midway to his mouth.

"Andrews, get yourself together." Brady loudly slaps the telephone message pad on the table, rattling the tableware. Brady continues, "Here, read this."

Andrews focuses his eyes on the message and reads –

08/08/50, 07:07
Urgent
Contact Tullyhaugh RUC ASAP
c/b John Cross

The significance of the message hits him instantly. He stands up suddenly, pushing his chair back, scraping it loudly on the floor. "'Could be John Cross'. That's what it says. Brady, let's be absolutely sure of this before we report to London. Have you contacted Tullyhog yet?"

"No, not yet. You need to be totally in on this, Andrews. Get yourself into shape. You need a bath and a shave and a clean shirt. I'll contact Tullyhag, or Tullyhoff, and make arrangements to get there. Be at the RUC station in fifteen minutes."

Back at the RUC station, Brady asks the duty officer to connect him to RUC 'Tullyhoff'

"I'm putting you through now, sir. And it's pronounced 'Tullyhaugh', like 'Tully-haw'."

8:22am. Andrews, a much neater and alert Andrews, enters the Enniskillen RUC station. He is adjusting his necktie as he enters. "Okay, Brady. What have you learned?"

"The RUC in Tully-haw want us there ASAP."

"To identify John Cross?"

"Yes. But it's a bit complicated."

"How complicated is it to identify John Cross and haul him back to London?"

"First of all, he's dead."

"Dead? Cody got him, I'll warrant you. We haven't seen Cody since Scotland, but we know that he is operating undercover in Ireland. That's the sort of thing that Cody is good at."

"That's not the worst. The Tully-haw RUC don't actually have possession of the body. John Cross is 300 yards away on the other side of the river."

Andrews snorts a derisive laugh. "And they are afraid to cross a river?"

"It's not just a river. It's the border."

"Lord, nothing works right in Scotland or in Ireland..."

Brady interrupts him. "Be that as it may. We should get to Tully-haw as speedily as possible."

"Excuse me." It is Constable McCann. "Do you require me to accompany you to Tullyhaugh?"

Andrews looks at him. He had forgotten that McCann is still with them. "No, McCann. You can go back to Cheshire. We don't need you, now that we have located Cross, albeit a dead Cross."

"In that case would you sign this for me please?"

"Sign what?"

"My overtime and expense sheet."

Andrews grabs the sheet from McCann and, with no more than a cursory glance, he scribbles his signature and thrusts it back at him. The sheet is in triplicate. McCann tears off the back sheet, Andrews' copy, but Andrews ignores him. McCann places it on the duty officer's counter and leaves.

Andrews checks with the duty officer. "Which is the fastest way to Tully-haw?"

"It is 30 minutes from here. Turn left as you exit the police station. You are on the A32 here. Follow the A32 to a fork in the road. Take the left fork, the A47 to Kesh. From Kesh, follow the A35 all the way to Termon."

"And..."

"And what?"

"And how do we get to Tully-haw from Termon?"

"You don't. Tullyhaugh is in Termon. Tullyhaugh is that part of Termon which is in Northern Ireland. Most of Termon is on the other side of the river."

"And that is where John Cross is?"

Brady is impatient to leave. "Come on, Andrews. The RUC in Tully-haw will explain it to us when we get there. And the SDU will get us access to John Cross in Éire. We should get there by 09:00am. Let's get this John Cross thing settled and done, finally."

"Yes, Brady. Finally."

Tuesday afternoon, 08 August 1950, en route to Termon, County Donegal, Ireland. Murf turns off the N3 at Belleek and is in line at the customs post to cross the border. There are two cars in front of him. A customs officer is standing at the roadside inspecting all traffic crossing the border. As each car comes to a halt, its driver rolls down the side window and the officer waves him through. Murf and O'Reilly are both in plain clothes; otherwise they would be unable to cross into Northern Ireland. Murf flashes his Garda card and the customs officer waves him through on a rolling stop.

"Less than 20 minutes from here, O'Reilly. Through the town of Belleek and on to the Boa Island Road A47."

"Murf, back at the Garda station you said that there might be another case arising out of this? What did you mean?"

Murf takes an evidence envelope out of his jacket inside breast pocket and hands it to O'Reilly. Within it is a label from a bank's canvas coin bag. The label identifies the bag as the property of the Ulster Bank, dated and initialled by the teller on '17 December 1930 – SILVER £100'

O'Reilly reads it, and queries him. "Murf, has this to do with all those half-crowns you spoke about to Farouk?"

"Yes, O'Reilly, and a lot more, I suspect. When we get back to Killbawn, I want you to conduct a thorough search of Granny McGrath's property."

"What? To find more half-crowns?"

"Oh, you'll find more half-crowns all right, probably £99-17-6. But I expect you'll also find more interesting things."

"What stuff?"

"The rest of the stuff from the bank robbery."

"Are you talking about the Ulster Bank robbery in Westport in 1930?"

"In 1931. The McGraths and the Gilbans ran together back then."

"In the IRA?"

"In a splinter-IRA faction, one with strong socialist leanings and with Soviet Russian connections. It dissolved shortly after that."

"Murf, you are talking about the guns, aren't you? The guns that were never recovered from the splinter group."

"Attaboy, O'Reilly."

"It sure will disturb old Granny if I go poking about."

"Granny is dying. She may not last a week. I've been to see her with the doctor. Father MacNamara was there too. She is tired of living, O'Reilly."

"Ah. So in a few days..."

"Yes, O'Reilly. In a few days. Take note, the walls in her house are six feet thick. At intervals there are cubbyholes in the walls to store butter and cheese and for flour and cornmeal. The house was built in penal times..."

"...so there should be some hidden nooks in the walls."

On the B136 they pass the RUC barracks in Letter, the one haunted by a ghost that has come back to wreak vengeance. There is a lot of activity at the barracks and an unusual number of cars are parked there. The poor ghost must feel overlooked and neglected by this unusual activity. Seconds later, they recross the border a half mile from Termon.

"Look, Murf. Over there is a tinker camp up a side road on the left. I wonder if it could be the Wards."

"A travellers' camp, O'Reilly." And Murf entertains the same thought.

As they approach Termon they slow down. St. Mary's Church is on the left, at the edge of town. Parked there at the roadside is a 10hp Ford Prefect.

"Hey, Murf. There's a car just like yours, like this one." Murf slows down and glances inside. He sees Danny the Divil sitting in the driver's seat. Murf brings his car to a stop.

"O'Reilly, get out and enquire. Find out why the Divil is in Termon. Is Doctor McBratt here too? And which group of travellers is camped back there? Oldthorpe was last seen with Paddy Lamp Ward. And Doctor McBratt has some rapport with Paddy Lamp. Isn't it strange that all three are here in Termon at the same time? Check it out, O'Reilly. I'll be at the Garda station."

4:00pm. Murf enters the Garda station in Termon. It is a well-constructed stone building, previously the RIC barracks. Locally, it is still referred to as 'the barracks'. After partition, the RIC withdrew across the border and became the RUC. The previous RIC barracks became the Garda station. To avoid the confusion of two police stations in Termon, the new RUC station is identified as 'RUC Tullyhaugh'.

Station Sergeant Mickey Hickey greets Murf as he enters the Garda station. "Inspector Murphy? I'll bring you right away to the body."

"It's 'Murf'. And show me through."

Hickey dismisses the usual preamble and greeting. It is clear to Murf that Hickey has a pressing situation on his hands. As they pass by the station sergeant's office, Hickey hesitates and speaks through the doorway. "Chief, this is Inspector Murphy from Mayo. I told you about him."

Donegal District Chief Superintendent Eunan O'Boyle is utilising Sergeant Hickey's office during the current situation. He has the telephone receiver raised and is about to make a call. He replaces the receiver at Hickey's interruption. He looks from Hickey to Murf and addresses him. "Inspector Murphy?"

"Yes, sir."

"Give me a 10-second summary as to why you are here."

"August 02, in Killbawn, Canon MacMorrow succumbed to injuries sustained in an assault on his person on the previous night; we have a perfect set of prints on the murder weapon, an acolyte's candlestick; we have confirmation that these are the fingerprints of John Cross a.k.a. Peter Oldthorpe."

"That's what I wanted to hear." And addressing Sergeant Hickey, "Sergeant, give Inspector Murphy full cooperation in his investigation. I will not tolerate any interference or obstruction from outside interests."

"Sir, what about...?"

"I'm working on that. And if I had my way – which I don't – these RUC either cooperate with us in our case, or get to hell back to Northern Ireland. Meantime, stand your ground and assist Inspector Murphy. Carry on." Chief O'Boyle lifts the telephone receiver to continue with his work.

Thus dismissed, Hickey and Murf proceed to the station's meeting room. As they are about to enter, a man in a civilian three-piece suit exits the room and almost collides with them in the doorway. Hickey addresses him. "Sean, you're not leaving, are you?"

"Sergeant, there is no point in my staying. I am not permitted to have access to the body in there. When this jurisdictional dispute is settled, I'll arrange to have the body sent to Stranorlar for a proper forensic autopsy. In the meantime, I'm off."

"No, wait, Sean. First, tell us whatever you can."

"What? Before I conduct a proper examination on the body?"

"Anything?"

"Okay, Hickey. I can tell you this. Based on my external examination of the body at the scene, the body has been dead for at least three days, but not more than five. You notice the smell of decay from it. Stage one initial decay is complete and putrefaction is in its preliminary stage. There is a severe wound to the head caused by a blow from a blunt object."

"Could that be the cause of death?"

"I don't know for sure yet. But it is very likely."

"Could the wound have been caused by the fall into the river?"

"Absolutely not. He didn't die at the spot where he was found."

"He died, was killed, somewhere other than at the Mill Street Bridge? Where do you think...?"

"Hickey, I'm the Donegal County Medical Examiner, not a detective. I'm off. Get in touch with me when you are ready to release the body to me, and don't wait too long. A thorough external examination needs to be conducted as soon as possible." The medical examiner leaves and Hickey continues into the meeting room.

Inside the room, there is a body lying on a table, completely covered by a sheet. One guard is positioned at the head, and another at the foot of the table. They are standing with feet apart and arms held away from their bodies, like rugby footballers braced for a tackle. There are four additional men in the room. Two of them are young men standing facing the two guards. These two men look more puzzled than threatening, unsure of what mien to adopt. The final two men, standing facing each other, remain back against the wall. These last two display a nasty disdainful look. They are clearly impatient and critical of the situation. Hickey informs Murf that the two young men are RUC constables assigned to watch the body until a decision is rendered regarding the jurisdiction of the case. Hickey is not at all sure who the other two men are. They identified themselves as 'from London', assigned to apprehend John Cross, a defector, on a matter of national security. Whoever they are, the constables stand to attention when they address them. One is 'Andrews' and the other is 'Brady'. They are awaiting the arrival of the SDU. The SDU, they claim, will settle this misunderstanding and concede that the body should be handed over to 'His Majesty's Special Services'. They also claim that a representative of the Foreign Office should arrive here shortly to execute the diplomatic protocols. That's all Hickey knows about them.

"Murf, come with me. I'll show you where we found the body. And I'll fill you in on the situation as we go along."

"Don't you need to be here to meet people as they arrive? The SDU and the British Foreign Office and whoever else?"

"The chief is handling the brass as they arrive. Come, Murf. The Mill Street Bridge is just a few yards up the hill from here. It is within earshot. I will hear any car that drives into the barracks' yard."

They walk up Mill Street hill, past six houses, and reach the bridge.

"This, Murf, is the Mill Street Bridge. It is an unapproved road for cross-border traffic. There are two other bridges in Termon, the High Street Bridge, and the Station Street Bridge. Only the Station Street Bridge is approved for traffic."

"So, no one ever crosses this bridge here?"

"The locals walk across or cycle across. Vehicular traffic is not permitted, but some exceptions are tolerated. The priest crosses it in his car every Sunday morning to get to the chapel. Sometimes the schoolmaster goes to Mass there too. In the course of a week I would estimate that there are only about eight vehicular crossings here. The bridge is watched closely by the customs officers to ensure that proper exit and entry regulations are respected."

"And to catch smugglers, I'll bet."

"The jurisdictional disagreement we have back at the station stems from the location of where the body was discovered. The river is the border. Andrews and Brady claim that the centre point of the river is the border. We, and the RUC, understand that the entire river is in the Republic. In practical terms, we and the RUC cooperate on any crime that involves the interests of both jurisdictions."

The two men are walking across the bridge as they speak. At the end of the bridge, leaning casually on the bridge wall, there are two uniformed police officers guarding the crime scene. They are in conversation together. One is an RUC constable, and the other is a Garda. The Garda is smoking a cigarette. The RUC constable sees Hickey and Murf approach. He nudges the Garda. The Garda quickly tosses the cigarette over the bridge and assumes an official stance facing towards the Republic. The RUC constable stands back-to-back to him and faces the other way to study the non-existent traffic. Hickey pretends not to notice the lapse. He is sympathetic to the Garda's situation.

"Look down here, Murf. This is where the body lay." Murf peers over the bridge wall and looks down towards the river. They are at the end of the bridge, overlooking the riverbank.

"Hickey, I am unable to see the riverbed from here. The salley rods protruding from the bank obstruct the view; they are growing too densely to see through. How could you have discovered a body in that location down there?"

"Ah, come this way." They recross the bridge. Hickey leads him to an opening at the end of the bridge wall. It is an access path to the river. They enter and proceed down to the riverbank.

"Yesterday morning, Phonsey Connaghan came down this way with a donkey and cart. Not his own donkey and cart. Phonsey doesn't have a donkey and cart of his own. He borrows Breslin's. He dumped a load of swedes under the bridge and brought the donkey and cart back to Breslin. Then he returned here and spent the day washing the swedes in the river and slicing each one in half with a billhook. He says that he left at 'dinnertime'. Dinnertime for Phonsey could be anywhere between twelve noon and three o'clock."

Murf understands. Swedes are used as cattle fodder. The blue-till clay clings to root vegetables and is tedious to remove. The current of the river makes the cleaning task easier. And each swede is sliced in half to check for soundness. Standing under the bridge, Murf has a clear view of the river, all the way to the other bank.

"So Phonsey was here until early afternoon yesterday and did not notice any body lying over there?"

"Not until he returned this morning at 6:30am to load up the cart."

"And then?"

"That's when Phonsey first saw the body lying over there. We were immediately alerted, and so too was the RUC. The body was located lying on the rocks in the riverbed, but not in the water.

"The border is defined by mutual agreement with Britain. The river consists of the entire riverbed, including the dry part. Water reaches up to the riverbank in heavy rain. The border is actually the edge of riverbank on the other side. When we discussed the location of the body with the RUC, we considered the possibility that the body may have rolled over the riverbank and into the riverbed from the Tullyhaugh side. But we could not see any evidence of that.

"The RUC conceded that the body was found in our jurisdiction. They recognised the body as John Cross, wanted by the police in England. As required, they immediately reported back to their district RUC station that they had located him. They followed accepted protocols and we expected the usual inter-police cooperation. We prepared for a joint investigation, albeit in our jurisdiction. As per the required procedure is such cases, we contacted the county medical examiner, who conducted a preliminary examination of the body at the scene. Then we moved the body to the barracks.

"Murf, although the RUC constables identified the body as that of John Cross, the identification we subsequently found on him is in the name of 'Peter Oldthorpe'."

"Yes, that's correct. John Cross a.k.a. Peter Oldthorpe." Murf and Hickey walk back to the Garda station.

"So, tell me, Hickey. You say that inter-police cooperation is the norm. So with this case why is there a jurisdictional diplomatic standoff?"

"That all happened when Andrews and Brady arrived at 10:25am. They have been back and forth multiple times between here and the RUC station to contact the divil-knows-who. They are adamant that the body is to be surrendered to them and that there will be no joint investigation."

"On what grounds?"

"They confirm that the body is that of John Cross, a British subject wanted for breach of the Official Secrets Act, hence subject to British Law. They have been pursuing him for some time and have tracked him to here. They claim that he was killed in the U.K. and that the body was dumped here in the river on the U.K. side of the border. They are part of a joint operation with the SDU to apprehend John Cross and return him to the U.K."

"In the context of a defecting British spy, their argument may have substance. However, we have a homicide in Mayo and the evidence points undeniably to John Cross a.k.a. Peter Oldthorpe. And now we learn that the perpetrator of the murder is killed in turn. The murderer has in turn become a murder victim. Hickey, the death of Canon MacMorrow and the death of John Cross are undeniably related cases. Examination of the body here is pertinent to our homicide investigation."

"I totally agree. We retain the body here until we conclude our investigation."

"Exactly. The return of a defecting spy, in this case a deceased spy, will have to wait."

4:30pm. In the Garda station, Hickey catches up on developments. He learns that the Minister of Justice is sending a representative. The inspector-general of the RUC is open to a cooperative joint investigation and is on his way to the RUC station in Tullyhaugh. The police commissioner in Dublin advises courtesy to him should he arrive at the Garda station in Termon. The Garda Special Detective Unit is due to arrive. And a representative of the British Foreign Office is already en route from Enniskillen.

4:35pm. Two members of the SDU arrive. They are shown into the meeting room. They recognise Andrews and Brady. The four men form a huddle and converse in whispers. They compare notes, nod their heads, and scratch their chins, and frequently glance over at the prone body on the table. However, they make no attempt to approach the body, still guarded by two Garda officers.

4:56pm. Patrick Piperson arrives, accompanied by Thomas Farouk Gilban. Murf wonders what association

Farouk once had with the Foreign Office in the past, and if the current relationship is purely a progression to spycatcher. The meeting room is getting crowded and is filled with the buzz of multiple mini-meetings. Sergeant Hickey enters. The SDU officers inform him that they are directed to escort John Cross into the jurisdiction of the United Kingdom's Intelligence Services, represented here by officers Andrews and Brady.

"This is authorised by the Commissioner and you are required to comply, Sergeant."

Hickey does not acknowledge the SDU speaker directly. Instead, he addresses the room. "Gentlemen. And I address the visitors here. There appears to be some misunderstanding as to who is in charge here." He casts his eyes slowly around and lingers a moment to gaze at the four special officers at the back. He continues, "It is five o'clock. I ask you to vacate this room. We will reconvene here at six o'clock. In the meantime I suggest that we eat and refresh. This will give all parties a chance to discuss their respective positions and check with their superior authorities on the appropriate protocols. From our end, Chief O'Boyle has been talking to Phoenix Park. I hope that when we reconvene here at six there will be a consensus on cooperation." Hickey is tempted to add that in the event of a failure to cooperate, all visiting police and security officers will be directed to leave.

"One thing more. In Termon, we are in a busy pilgrimage season at St. Patrick's Purgatory until August the 15th. As a result, you will find many establishments well prepared to serve you with food and refreshments. The closest is Brennan's at the High Street Bridge. Thank you. And see you all in an hour."

On the way out, Murf encounters Garda O'Reilly speaking with the duty officer at the front counter. "O'Reilly, have you anything to report?"

"Oh. Hello, Murf. I was checking some details with the duty officer here. I have some information that will knock your socks off."

"Well, I'll hold on to my socks until I've eaten, O'Reilly. I don't believe you have eaten either since this morning. Let's walk down to the Diamond and choose a hotel." Murf decides to avoid pilgrim food. He walks past Brennan's that caters exclusively to pilgrims, and stops at the 'Angler's Hotel'.

"This place looks like it might have a more varied fare." They enter the hotel and make their way to the dining room. It is a bright room with clean white tablecloths. They choose a cheerful table at a window overlooking the Termon River. Murf relaxes and enjoys the sunshine. He hasn't noticed any sunshine since the canon's death; it has rained almost every day since then. Even the dry days were cloudy.

A waitress approaches their table. "You're a bit early. Trying to beat the rush, are we?"

"It's not too early to order, is it?"

"No, not at all. You don't look like pilgrims, so there is no point in offering you the pilgrim's menu. Are you here for plain tea or high tea?"

"High tea."

"I'll get you the high tea menu...."

"No need for the menu. I'll have a mixed grill with brown bread and a pot of tea."

"A mixed grill. What would you like in the grill?"

Murf enumerates the items. The waitress writes down each one in turn, "Sausages, black pudding, white pudding, fried potatoes, and eggs, a kidney, a lamb chop..."

The waitress tears off the sheet from the pad and crumples it. "Tell you what, why don't I write down 'everything'." And turning to O'Reilly, "And what about you, sir?"

"I'll have an 'everything grill' too, oh, and a pint of porter."

"You gentlemen are not pilgrims, and you are not fishermen, nor farmers."

"So what do you think we are?"

"You could only be customs men or guards. No, wait. I know. You are guards come here because of the Russian spy what was found kilt in the river up by the mill."

"Waitress, what is your name?"

"It's 'Bridget', sir."

"Well, Bridget, you are an excellent detective." Murf lowers his voice to a stage whisper. "Now tell me, Bridget, how were you able to figure that out?"

"Sure the whole town knows about the man in the river. But the Russian spy part? Aha!"

"You must be very skilled. So tell me."

"Well, it's like this." Bridget puts the pad into her apron pocket. She glances around the dining room. There are no other diners in the room yet. "I was at the barracks this morning...."

"At the Garda station?"

"No, at the police barracks in Tullyhaugh. I do the laundry there in the mornings, sheets and shirts and all. Well, this morning two English officers turn up. Now they don't know it, but I can listen through the wall of the scullery. The Englishmen were talking loudly, sort of excited. They spoke about Russians and secrets going to the Russians. That can only mean 'spy' stuff. Right?"

"Is that a fact? And do you know about spying, Bridget?"

"I'll tell you what I know. They said that Hoey must have caught him. That's what they said."

"Who is 'Hoey'?"

"I don't know. Maybe it was 'Louie'. I can only repeat what I heard, and I only half heard. And the bit I heard, I didn't understand the half of it."

"And Hoey or Louie caught whom?"

"The man what got kilt, I suppose." Bridget looks up as a group of priests enter the dining room. "I'll place your order with Cook. I have to attend to another table now."

O'Reilly looks at Murf and says, "What a load of baloney. Typical small-town gossip. Mrs. Casey would have a field day here. You can't take this seriously, Murf."

"You might be right, O'Reilly. Except that she said something that might explain why the British Special Branch wants to keep us out of the investigation – if indeed they are Special Branch. Farouk and Piperson mentioned a hitherto unspoken of 'Secret Service'. A Foreign Office Secret Service, something other than Special Branch or MI5? Whoever they are, they don't want us to discover that Cross was killed by one of their agents operating here in Ireland."

"Lord, Murf, that would be very serious. It would get the attention of..."

"Ministry of Justice, Internal Affairs, External Affairs. And then the British side, the Foreign Office, the PM's office, and a lot more."

Murf changes the subject and returns to O'Reilly's sock-knocking report. "So, O'Reilly, did you encounter Doctor McBratt at St. Mary's?"

"Yes, Murf. She was at a funeral there. One of the itinerant Wards – Michael Ward, a child. She left soon after I arrived, and she didn't even say 'hello'."

"That would be Wee Maechael. Ah, the poor sick cub died. How did she know to come here?"

"That's what I asked the priest, Father Macaward."

"A Ward? Is he related to the itinerant Wards?"

"He explained that. They both stem from the same clan, but they branched off and separated many years ago. Centuries ago, they were all itinerant bards. Today, the Wards are integrated into Irish society. Only a few Wards still cling to the nomadic life."

"Let's get back to Doctor McBratt. How did she know to come to the Ward child's funeral?"

"Doctor McBratt and Paddy Lamp Ward are first cousins."

"First cousins? I don't believe it. They are so different."

"Father Macaward explained it:

"Le Breton came from Brittany. He came to Ireland with the Norman mercenaries. After the success of the Norman invasion, honours were granted to them by the King of England, Henry II Plantagenet, himself a Norman. But Le Breton, not actually a Norman, was overlooked. So he decided to align with the Gaelic chieftains instead. He went to serve the Northern O'Neill. O'Neill granted him land in North Ulster and Le Breton changed his name to 'McBratt'.

"Later, in the Plantation of Ulster, Catholics lost their lands, including the McBratt family. In the War of the Three Kingdoms, a McBratt served with Sarsfield on the Jacobite side. After the Treaty of Limerick he joined the Williamite army. He served overseas with distinction, rising to the rank of Captain and earning the nickname 'Bully McBratt'.

"As a result of serving King Billy with distinction, he regained his land. McBratt may have been the only Catholic to succeed in regaining his land in North Ulster. The neighbouring Scottish planters accepted him, and the McBratt family successfully assimilated into the Ulster Scots farming community of North Ulster."

"What has this to do with the Wards?"

"A Ward served under McBratt during the Jacobite war and afterwards in the Williamite army. When McBratt regained his land, he engaged the Ward family as farmhands and seasonal workers. And so it continued from generation to generation. Then, sometime in the 1890s, a Ward servant girl became pregnant while working for Hugh McBratt and she gave birth to a boy. Hugh acknowledged the child as his and offered to foster him and raise him in the McBratt house. Instead, the Wards choose to raise the child in their itinerant tradition."

"That must have driven a wedge into the McBratt/Ward affiliation."

"Not at all. It cemented the relationship more strongly. As a result, the McBratts and the Wards look out for each other now."

"So Hugh McBratt is Paddy's Lamp's grandfather...."

"...and he is Doctor Antoinette McBratt's grandfather."

"That explains a lot. So, O'Reilly, did you find out anything about Paddy Lamp Ward?"

"Not really. The encampment outside town is Paddy Lamp's clan all right. They arrived here on Sunday. But there is no sign of Paddy Lamp."

"Sunday the 6th of August? Let's see, they left Killbawn on the 3rd of August. Three days to get from Killbawn to Termon. Three days in continuous rain. If the Wards travelled by backroads to avoid a direct route, they would not have had time to encamp. It is no surprise therefore that Wee Maechael did not survive the journey."

"On Tuesday, yesterday, the rain stopped. That's when they arranged the funeral with Father Macaward. The Wards dug the grave, supervised by the parish gravedigger. They placed flagstones at the bottom of the grave and built a stone wall out of limestone to form a stone sarcophagus. There was no coffin. When the child's body was interred today, they laid him down inside the sarcophagus on the flagstones, and placed a flagstone on top, and filled in the grave with earth.

"But back to yesterday. After they arranged the funeral with Father Macaward, the Wards took their horse and cart down Main Street to collect junk. They begged for junk at each house. And if they found anything of interest that was not nailed down, they simply took it. After Main Street they proceeded up Mill Street. At the top of Mill Street they crossed over the bridge and made their way to High Street."

Murf is drinking tea while waiting for his mixed grill. "High Street is in Tullyhaugh?"

"Yes, Murf. After High Street they crossed the river at Station Street Bridge."

"Back into the Republic?"

"Yes. They finished up at the railway station. Whatever junk they managed to collect, they took it all back to their camp."

"In Kimmid."

"Kimmid? I don't know anything about Kimmid."

"In Killbawn, Doctor McBratt said that the Wards would be in Kimmid next. At the time, I did not know the location of Kimmid. Back then, Doctor McBratt knew that the Wards would come here after Killbawn."

Bridget arrives with the plates of mixed grill. "Careful. The plates are hot."

"Bridget?"

"Yes?"

"The itinerant camp outside town. What's the name of the place?"

"What? The name of the place where they are camped? Kimmid, of course. Would you like more bread? I can add hot water to the teapot." Bridget leaves to attend to other tables. The dining room is filling up fast.

"What are you thinking, Murf?"

"At what time did the Wards cross the Mill Street Bridge yesterday?"

"That's what I was asking the duty officer. He told me that he heard their horse and cart go past the station shortly before four o'clock."

"Close to four o'clock? That's good work, O'Reilly. The events and circumstances of Cross's murder are falling into place. Finish up your meal. We are due back at the station at six."

"Hold on, Murf. With all the talking, I'm behind with my meal. We still have ten more minutes to six o'clock."

"Okay, then. Here's ten bob. Take your time, O'Reilly. There is no urgency for you to be back at six. When you are finished, settle up here. I'll see you later."

"At the station?"

"Yes."

Murf leaves. O'Reilly considers the ten shillings Murf left on the table and takes his time. He orders another pint.

6:00pm, Termon Garda Station meeting room. Murf notices that they are joined by Sir Robert Norton, Chief Constable of the RUC. Also present, and standing next to Sir Robert, is the Donegal District Chief Inspector, Eunan

O'Boyle. The Foreign Office Secret Service agents and the SDU officers are grouped together at the back wall. Murf thinks to himself 'birds of a feather'. Piper's Son a.k.a. Patrick Piperson, still dressed as Sherlock Holmes on a fishing trip, stands beside Thomas Farouk Gilban. Gilban is dressed in a lightweight white cotton suit and is wearing sunglasses indoors. Both these men stand together, but apart from the rest of the assembly. They also stand out from the rest of the group due to their unusual attire. There are two Garda officers in uniform and two RUC constables in plain clothes on the other side of the table. Station Sergeant Mickey Hickey, standing at the table, faces the assembled men. Murf sidles up to stand near him.

Hickey coughs in preparation of his announcement. Murf interrupts him. "Before we start the meeting, could we see the body? I would like to be sure that it truly is the body of Peter Oldthorpe a.k.a. John Cross."

"Excellent point". It is Sir Robert who speaks. "We have come all this way, so let's be certain that we have the right person here."

From the back, Andrews objects. "There is no need to do that. We agreed not to touch the body until we have agreement on the jurisdiction of the police inquiry. As to the identity of the corpse, I can confirm that it is John Cross."

Hickey nods to the two guards at the table. They remove the covering sheet from the body. Andrews suddenly steps forward. Sir Robert steps to the side to block him. There is a collision as Andrews bumps against Sir Robert.

Sir Robert turns around to Andrews, "Andrews, I believe you stumbled." And in a whisper, audible to all in the room, "The greatest secret in the Service is how an ass like you is allowed in the Service." One of the SDU officers opens his mouth to speak. A glare from O'Boyle shuts him up.

Murf address Hickey. "Sergeant, with your permission, I would like a closer look at the body." And turning to face Andrews, he continues, "and I give my assurance that I will not touch the body."

"That is a reasonable request. In fact, if anyone else wants to confirm the identity of the body, please come forward. When we are all satisfied, we will proceed with the meeting."

Piperson steps forward. "If you don't mind, I'll join Inspector Murphy in his examination." Sir Robert gives a nod of approval to him.

Murf and Piperson view the body together, commenting to each other on what they observe.

Murf asks him, "Patrick. Do you get that smell?"

"Yes. That's body decomposition. Putrefaction has started."

"No. Beneath that. There is another smell."

Piperson sniffs. "Yes, a smell of smoke."

"Whin smoke."

Sir Robert, attentive to their observations, says aloud, "Gorse smoke."

Piperson points to Cross's shoes. "He has burst through the stitching in his shoes, and the soles are worn through completely. See where he stuffed them with grass and moss. He must have walked a great deal since leaving Bostock Green."

"The moss here – this is tree-bark moss. Medicinal. It is applied as a wound dressing. Peter Oldthorpe has cuts and blisters on his feet, I'll warrant."

"Does this surprise you, Murf?"

"No. It confirms what I already knew – Oldthorpe travelled with itinerants. And Andrews must know this too if he has been tracking Cross all this time." All eyes look at Andrews.

Brady acknowledges Murf's finding. "Cross was travelling with itinerants. We followed him from Cheshire to Scotland, and from Scotland to Ireland. In County Londonderry we checked out a sighting at a farm where they nicked bread. The footprints found at the scene included bare feet. A short distance from there, the bare feet were replaced by shoe prints matching those of John Cross. That was in a copse where he would have applied the bark moss to his feet." Sir Robert smiles. Cooperation in the inquiry has begun.

Murf and Piperson pause to examine the bruise to Cross's brow. They look at it from above, from below, and from different angles.

"There is something written on the bruise. Can you make it out Patrick?"

"No. I need a torch. Can we have a torch, please?" Sergeant Hickey obtains a flashlight and gives it to Piperson. Piperson shines it on the bruise.

"Shine it at an angle, Patrick, Put the indentation into shadow."

"There. 'I' and 'T'. See Murf? It is 'IT'."

"I see it sure enough."

"Now why would a killer write on a wound? His initials, maybe? A message? Some killers leave their mark on a victim. IT?"

Murf stands up erect. He is stiff from holding a stooped position. He stretches his arms and back for relief. He addresses the room. "Rest assured, John Cross was not killed by a British agent, or by a Russian Agent. Not even by an American agent. Not by the SDU, or by any police or security agent." There are whispered grumblings of incredulity and some sniggering from the back of the room.

"Silence!" It is Sir Robert. "Inspector Murphy is one of the best detectives I have ever encountered. Listen, and attend."

Piperson adds, "I endorse that. We have worked with Inspector Murphy before. He cracked a seemingly impossible case for us two years ago."

And Hickey speaks, "Carry on, Inspector."

"I know how Cross was killed. And by whom. And where. And when. And why."

O'Boyle asks, "Can you explain that? And are you able to provide evidence to back it up?"

"Rather than explain it, I will bring you the evidence, conclusive evidence. Some of the evidence can be corroborated by Thomas Gilban who is standing here in this room." Thomas Gilban begins to protest. Murf cuts him off. "Thomas, I am not suggesting that you had a hand in Cross's murder. What I'm saying is that you can verify some of the evidence I present."

Sir Robert asks, "And when are you able to present this to us? Today? Tomorrow?"

"I need to go now while there is sufficient daylight. Shall we all meet here again tomorrow at 12:00 noon?" They are in agreement.

Murf continues, "I would like the assistance of a representative of the British investigation team. Perhaps Mr. Piperson would care to join me?"

"Gladly. Let's put this to bed quickly."

Sir Robert remarks, "It looks like we don't need a meeting now to determine cooperation or jurisdiction."

Murf and Piperson hit the road in Murf's car at 6:30pm. Murf looks over at Piperson and at his clothes. "Patrick, you are going to get dirt on your shoes."

"How come? Where are we going?"

"Killbawn. We need to get there while there is still daylight."

"That's almost three hours away. Do you think we'll make it?"

"It's two hours going this way. We'll cross the border twice. With a combination of your identification and my identification there will be no delays. Sunset is 8:15pm, full daylight until 8:45pm, and useable daylight until 10:00pm. After that it is twilight until darkness falls at 11:40pm."

"Murf, does that give you sufficient time for what you need to do?"

"With you helping me, I believe so. And one more thing I need, a case file from the Garda station. We'll overnight in Killbawn and be back in Termon by 10:00am tomorrow."

They drive in silence until they cross and recross the border back into the Republic.

"Patrick, you could have told me, you know."

"Yes?"

"You left Killbawn like a bat out of hell. You knew they had actually located John Cross, didn't you?"

"But you still got to Cross before me. So what? You need to understand, Murf, we are anxious to clear up the Cross episode quickly and quietly."

"Even if it means sweeping some things under the carpet?"

"Softening the truth, Murf, before the Mirror or the Daily Mail writes a speculative article about Russian spies active in Britain. That would be unsettling. We can't have people of Britain looking for spies under their beds."

"Ah. That's what you do: 'Softening the truth'."

Piperson mutters to himself, "And to whom does truth answer?"

"And what about your MI5 colleagues? Do they soften the truth?"

"You mean Andrews and Brady? I don't know who they work for...."

"Surely you must know if they are legitimate government agents."

"There is no doubt about that. I don't know which ministry they work for. All I know is that they were foisted on us by the powers above. I have encountered a similar thing before...."

"You mean, really secret Secret Service?"

"...when there was a perceived foreign threat."

8:30pm. Murf is driving through Killbawn. "Murf, are you not going to stop at the Garda station?"

"No. I'm driving through the town."

8:38pm. Murf drives into the creamery yard and skids to a halt. He jumps out of the car. "Come on, Patrick. Help me find it."

Patrick Piperson follows Murf across the road, jumping the ditch blindly to keep up with him.

"This, Patrick, is where the Wards were encamped the day that Oldthorpe/Cross failed to show for his rendezvous. It is also the day that the Wards broke camp and disappeared."

"Until they showed up in Termon?"

"...in Kimmid, outside Termon two days ago."

Murf is pacing to and fro in the deserted campsite. "Ah, here it is. The broken piece of wire."

"Slow down, Murf. What are we looking for? A piece of broken wire?"

"This is where I kicked a Tilley lamp, from here up over the salleys. I heard it land with a splash in the sheugh."

"Sheugh?"

"The drainage ditch separating the fields."

"You are looking for Paddy Lamp's lost Tilley lamp?"

"Yes. Help me find it. It's in the sheugh somewhere along here."

Piperson follows Murf through the salleys. The salley rods spring back as Murf passes through them, whacking Piperson on his upstretched arm raised to protect his face. Murf is through to the sheugh and steps into muddy green stagnant water disturbing the frogspawn floating on top. He realises, too late, that he has forgotten to change into his waterproof wellington boots. He is wet up to mid-calf. Piperson follows and suffers the same fate.

"We are both wet now, so let's take advantage of our plight. I'll paddle this way, and you paddle that way. By dragging our feet through the slime we should make contact with the lamp."

And so Piperson and Murf slosh through the sheugh. They find porter bottles and tin cans.

"Murf! I think I found it."

"Use your handkerchief to fish it out. I need it uncontaminated."

"Uncontaminated? You must be joking, Murf."

Piperson pushes the lamp with his shoe to dislodge it. He locates the handle and extracts the lamp from the mud and slime. He lays it on the bank. It topples over, and stagnant water and tadpoles pour out. Murf steps out of the sheugh and onto the bank. He kneels down to look closely at the lamp.

"Beautiful."

He extends his hand to Piperson and helps him up the bank. Piperson looks at what Murf referred to as 'beautiful'. Imprinted in large raised lettering is the brand name of the lamp – TILLEY. Piperson instantly sees that a blow from a Tilley lamp, like the one sustained by John Cross, would leave an imprint in retrograde as in a mirror. The first two letters TI would appear as IT.

"This is the murder weapon, Murf?"

"Yes."

"Now to match Cross's wound to the lamp. That should be an easy task for forensics."

"And to match the fingerprints on the lamp. I have a set of Paddy Lamp's prints in the MacMorrow case file back in the station. And Patrick, you have a tadpole swimming in your brogue."

Wednesday 09 August 1950, 12:00 noon, Termon. They are assembled in the Garda station as arranged. On this visit there is a strong smell of bleach in the meeting room. The body of John Cross/Peter Oldthorpe is absent from the table, a table which has been thoroughly scrubbed and cleaned. Station Sergeant Hickey informs them that on account of the stench, the body has been wrapped and stored under lock and key in the bicycle shed. All in attendance greatly appreciate this consideration. Station Sergeant Hickey is eager to get the meeting underway.

"I see we are missing Andrews."

Brady explains, "Andrews has been recalled to London. I'm replacing him."

"Okay. Let's begin."

Murf and Piperson give a full account, corroborated in pertinent places by Thomas Gilban. Paddy Lamp Ward killed Peter Oldthorpe, most likely in retribution for killing Canon MacMorrow. The RUC is invited to have an observer at the forensic autopsy of John Cross, and they will assist in providing forensic confirmation of the evidence to support a criminal case.

Paddy Lamp Ward is now wanted by the Garda Síochána and the RUC for the murder of a British subject, John Cross. Once caught and apprehended, Paddy Lamp Ward will be charged for the crime of murder. The crime was committed in the Republic of Ireland, and that is where he will be tried.

The duty officer informs Sergeant Hickey that he has some newspaper reporters in the front office asking for a comment. Some are from English newspapers. Hickey and Sir Robert come up with an agreed statement. They both go out to the reporters.

Hickey informs the reporters that a deceased body was found in the Termon River. Until an autopsy is performed and a coroner's report is completed by the county medical examiner, he cannot comment any further on an ongoing inquiry.

"Was it a suicide or accidental fall?"

"I cannot comment on an ongoing inquiry." Hickey continues to deflect questions until...

"Do you know the identity of the deceased?"

"Yes. We know the identity of the deceased. Sir Robert Norton and the RUC have joined us in this inquiry. Sir Robert here will answer the question."

"The deceased is Doctor John Cross, a prominent British Research Scientist who has devoted his entire adult life to the service of his country. He recently suffered a nervous breakdown due to stress and has suffered an unfortunate mishap. We regret that we were unable to intervene earlier to prevent this unfortunate incident. We are deeply grateful to Doctor Cross for his dedication to the benefit of his country and to the betterment of humanity. Thank you." Sir Robert walks off before any further questions are fielded.

Murf whispers after him, "Well played, Nobbie. No questions about spies or Russians, or even about murder." The only unanswered question pertained to 'accidental death' and 'suicide'.

Murf has solved a double homicide. Now to find the elusive Paddy Lamp Ward and charge him with murder. Only then can Murf bring a conclusion to the case. Paddy Ward will likely get the charge of murder reduced to voluntary manslaughter.

Voluntary manslaughter deals with what would otherwise be murder but where there is some excusing circumstance which reduces the offence from murder to manslaughter.

Usual sentence – 8 years with one year's suspension.

CHAPTER TWENTY-FIVE

KILLBAWN, 01 AUGUST 1951

Lá Lúnasa, Lammas Day
The First Day of Autumn
County Mayo, Ireland

Killbawn Garda Station is busy from early morning. Casey arrives, and so do a half-dozen farmers, to complain about the presence of 'tinkers'. Garda Seamus O'Reilly is at great pains to point out that the correct term is 'travelling people' or just 'travellers'. Garda O'Reilly states that unless the travellers have committed an offence, there are no grounds for a complaint. Garda O'Reilly has heard it all before. Just like last year on Lammas Day, the Ward clan of travellers has encamped on the outskirts of Killbawn.

Murf hears the cacophony of raised voices all the way to his office. He smiles at the familiarity of the discourse that occurs with predictability every Lammas Day in Killbawn. O'Reilly is now adept at handling these situations.

Murf looks at his newly-painted wall with a mixture of relief and loss. He had grown attached to the pockmarks from the drawing pins, and to the missing paint from frequently applying and removing cellotape. A fresh clean wall indicates that there is no pressing investigation in progress.

Today is Lammas Day. Murf thinks back to Lammas Day 1950. This calls to mind an open case, one that still irritates him – the murder of John Cross. He goes to the records room and retrieves the case file. Back in his office, Murf slowly flips through the file contents, reliving each stage of the investigation. He hesitates at the pathology report from the coroner. He reads it for the umpteenth time. John Cross was killed by a blunt force to the head. Undoubtedly the blow killed him, but not instantly. There was evidence of some healing around the edge of the wound. The injury was inflicted some six hours before the actual time of death. The description of John Cross's fatal wound and his subsequent death was uncannily similar to that in the coroner's report on Canon MacMorrow. Murf sighs. Yes, he solved the case. But it is still open until the fugitive Paddy Ward is apprehended and brought to justice.

Murf shuts the file and sits in silence. Well, not actually in silence. He hears Garda O'Reilly at the front counter addressing complaints against 'tinkers'. Murf slips out of his office and leaves the Garda station. Once out of earshot he admires the day. It is 10:00am, the time for banks and pubs to open for business. The sun is warm and the breeze is soft. He remembers what August days were like when he was a gossoon.

Approaching the square, he hears the melodic voice of a street singer, *"My thoughts today, 'though I'm far away..."* He identifies it as the voice of Francie Ward singing one of his signature songs, *'The Rose of Aranmore'*. Murf enters the square. He espies Collie Tricks Ward plying his skills, "Pick a card, any card..." Their accompanying ensemble is made up of four musicians and two cutty dancers. Francie finishes his song and refreshes his throat with porter. The musicians are warming up, or wetting up, their embouchures for smooth execution of their whistles and flageolet. The bodhrán drummer is shaking his wrists and stretching his fingers.

The musicians strike up a rhythmic jig in 12/8 time. The two itinerant girls break away from the group of musicians and proceed to dance on the flagstone sidewalk. The cutty-girls are wearing nail boots, and they strike the flags loudly in their stepdancing. They finish the dance and are joined by Francie and Collie. All four line up side by side.

The cutty-girls are wearing ankle-length black skirts and black pullovers. They wear dark-grey soft paddy caps to keep their hair in place. Loosely draped from their shoulders to their ankles are black shawls. Francie and Collie are dressed in similar nail boots, black trousers and black pullovers. They too are wearing dark-grey soft paddy caps to keep their hair in place. And over their clothes both Francie and Collie wear black overcoats many times too large, draped from their shoulders to their ankles. Murf is aware that it is too warm a day for long shawls and overcoats. But he also knows that these are props for their musical act.

The band strikes up a hectic reel. The four dancers, with hands linked, burl and twirl in a circle – outwards, inwards, now this-a-way, now that-a-way. Their boots strike the stone pavements shooting out sparks from their feet. At the end of the dance the four dancers line up as at the start. They remove their shawls and overcoats to reveal that the two cutties have finished up in the men's overcoats, and the two lads have finished up in the girls' shawls. Murf has seen it before and he is still enthralled by it. He is a detective, yet he is unable to spot the switch in clothing during the dance. The four dancers remove their caps and hold them out to accept pennies.

Murf calls out to Francie, "You don't have a performer's permit, so I am unable to pay you for your performance. However, please accept this gift in appreciation of your skills."

He spins a florin in the air in the direction of Francie, which Tricks intercepts and catches in his cap. Two shillings is double what they could expect for a dance performance. Of course, they would make a great deal more if they succeed in finding a safe spot for Tricks to engage in 'find-the-lady'.

Murf leaves the square and goes to his car. He drives out to the creamery to where the Wards are encamped. As usual, their wares are on display on the roadside. The selection of lamps and clocks is poor. Most of the wares are pots and pans and canisters. The fugitive Paddy Lamp is not in evidence.

Murf continues on past the camp and onto the straight mile. He passes by the old RIC barracks. The barracks is undergoing a cleanup. Mickey Travers recently bought the RIC barracks from the Department and is moving in. Mickey is going to open a pub, as if there are not enough pubs in Ireland at the minute. And with the Travers' move, that is one less household in Lough Corry Lower. Thinking about Lough Corry, Murf decides to drive there, to go the entire distance to Granny McGrath's old place. No one has been there in nearly a year.

Murf remembers the bumps in the road. He drives slowly, his head crouched down lest he knocks against the roof. A lot has happened in the past year. He enumerates them mentally.

O'Reilly found a cache of IRA weaponry from the 1930s at Granny McGrath's house.

Donald McLean, a British counsellor with the Foreign Office, defected to the USSR. At the time of his defection he was head of the American Department in the Foreign Office while also a Soviet agent with the cryptonym 'Homer', or 'Gomer' in Russian. He made his escape on 25 May 1951 with co-spy Guy Burgess, a diplomat with the Foreign Office, cryptonym 'Hicks'. There has been no word from the Russians confirming the defection, but it is generally accepted that Russia is where they went.

Thomas Farouk Gilban is still working with his radio transmitters and receivers. The British supply him with little tads of useless information to feed to the Soviets, just to keep the communication link active. So far, Farouk has not succeeded in coaxing any Soviet agent to defect, but the British are more anxious than ever for him to succeed. As long as this window of opportunity remains open, the Brits have a use for him and are unlikely to arrest him. Nevertheless, Farouk is closely watched and operates on a short leash.

Killbawn is now joined to the national electric power grid. There is electricity 24 hours a day, seven days a week, and it is reliable. The rural areas surrounding Killbawn are scheduled to join the national grid within a year.

A bump in the road brings Murf's attention back to the present. Although he is familiar with the road, it unexpectedly comes to an end in Glen Corry. The rhododendrons have overgrown the road. He stops the car and turns off the engine. He has come thus far. He decides to thrash his way through the foliage and continue the remainder of the journey on foot. It can't be more than two furlongs. The branches part easily, permitting him trouble-free passage, but it is much too narrow for a car. At intervals there are clearings in the roadway, and his progress is speedy.

Within a few minutes, Murf breaks free of the rhododendrons and finds himself standing a few feet from Granny McGrath's house. His jaw drops at the sight. What was once a pristine cottage is now a ruin. The effects of winter frost and constant moisture have rendered devastating damage to the cottage. The whitewash has run off the exterior walls, exposing the limestone. White circular blotches of efflorescence disfigure the walls. Devoid of the drying warmth of the fire, the roof thatch has succumbed to dampness, and thence to mildew and weeds. The roof is heavily saturated and appears to be spread with a substance resembling cow-manure. It is in danger of collapsing at any moment.

Murf reaches the half-door. It is hanging lopsided from a single hinge. He moves the door gently. It collapses to the ground and shatters. He peers inside. The tunnel-like entrance to the kitchen is interrupted by dislodged wall panels strewn on the floor. He sees where they had been wrenched out to reveal nooks in the walls, like vaults in a crypt. This is where O'Reilly found the cache of weaponry. Looking inside to the kitchen, he sees the pictures on the wall obscured by black mildew – like faceless black squares. There is the pervading smell of mould, rot and wet soot. Murf decides not to venture beyond the entrance. He predicts that in another year only the outer stone shell of the once cozy abode will remain. Two hundred years obliterated in two years. He turns and departs the depressing sight.

Murf is unsettled by his visit to Granny McGrath's house. He returns to his car, oblivious to the warm sunshine. He is unproductive for the remainder of the day.

At 5:30pm he decides to quit work and go home. He buys a bottle of Powers Gold Label on the way and plans to share it with Suey McBride next door. Suey should brighten up his day with her astrological predictions and news of all the goings-on in Casey's. It is warm in the car. He rolls down the car window. He hears the ringing of the Angelus bell. It is 6:00pm. The ringing bell reminds him that he is due to be at St. Bawn's for a meeting at 6:30pm. It had slipped his mind. Murf is annoyed. He is in no mood for a meeting. And now he has insufficient time for a meal.

6:30pm. Murf enters the meeting room in St. Bawn's parochial house. In attendance is Father Patrick Brennan, the parish priest, and Father James O'Mahoney, the new curate, along with Casey, Thomas Farouk Gilban, and Murf. Murf greets them and sits next to Farouk.

He speaks quietly, "So, Thomas, tell me. Are things still going okay?"

"Not quite. The new priest wants me to remove all the radio stuff out of the church."

"So, what'll you do?"

"I've purchased Mickey Travers' place...."

"In Lough Corry Lower?"

"...and I'm moving in."

"Are you taking up farming?"

"Ah, no. I didn't buy the farm, just the house. They are putting in electricity in the area in November. That's when I'm moving the radio transmitters and receivers."

"You'll need an antenna tower."

"No one will object to that out by Lough Corry."

Murf considers the history of Lough Corry. The people once hid there from the penal laws. And it was an IRA refuge until the thirties. And now it is to be used for spying?

The meeting comes to order. Murf has little interest in the agenda or in the proceedings. August 15th is a holy day and a holiday. This year they plan to have a marching-band competition and a girls' camogie match against the St. Joseph's convent girls from Castlebar. Murf asks, just to be troublesome, "Will the itinerant Wards' band be competing in the band competition?"

Casey responds, "The tinkers don't have a marching band, Murf."

"Well, they walk as they play. And they walk more than any of the other bands."

Father Brennan interjects, "Gentlemen, the itinerant group of musicians may be quite talented, but they don't qualify as a marching band. And anyway, which community would they represent?"

Murf mutters to himself, but audible to all, "Members of the human race, perhaps?"

Father Brennan ignores the comment and continues, "Let's move on to the final item on the agenda. The Killbawn Girls' camogie game. Casey, are the team uniforms completed and distributed?"

"Good old Casey," Murf thinks, "as always, he managed to make a sale out of the event." Murf has no interest in discussing girls' uniforms. He excuses himself and leaves the meeting.

Father Brennan enquires, "Are you leaving, Inspector Murphy, before the final prayer?"

"I'll stop into the church as I leave."

Murf leaves the room. He shuts the door and he hears the voices from inside.

"What's up with Murf tonight?"

"He's not himself at all, at all."

Murf walks towards the back door and out of earshot. Passing the kitchen, he encounters Mrs. Friel.

Mrs. Friel addresses him. "Guard Murphy. The doctor left word for you. After the meeting you are to go to the church. She is waiting for you there."

Murf thinks, "Will I ever get home tonight?"

"Will you go through the passageway? If you do, I'll need to get the key."

"No, Mrs. Friel. Don't bother. It's no trouble for me to go via the street and enter the church by the main doors."

Murf enters St. Bawn's church and proceeds to the nave. He sweeps his eyes around the interior. There are no hidden areas in the nave, not like last year on Lammas Day. Newly-installed electric lights illuminate the entire area, including the shaded side aisles. Murf spots a lone figure in the church. Doctor McBratt is seated in the front pew at the side altar to the Sacred Heart. This was once the preferred spot of Granny McGrath, and frequently occupied by Canon MacMorrow during his nightly prayers. Murf walks down the side aisle and sits next to Doctor McBratt. He stretches out his legs into the aisle, his hands jammed into his trouser pockets.

"Hello, Ant. You want to see me?"

Doctor McBratt crosses herself in completion of her prayers, and looks at Murf slouched unbecomingly in the pew, his legs protruding out into the aisle.

"I see you still wear spotty woollen socks."

"You didn't summon me here to discuss my socks."

"No, Murf. It is the anniversary of Canon MacMorrow's death...."

"Tomorrow. Tomorrow is the anniversary. Tonight is the eve..."

"Murf, you can be a pain sometimes. Now, as I was saying. It is the EVE of the anniversary of Canon MacMorrow's death. Looking over the past year, I need to ask about your progress on catching Paddy Lamp."

"He's still at large."

"And you are still looking?"

"Of course. And so are the RUC, and the English police, and all police forces in the U.K."

"How long will you go on looking for him?"

"Until he is apprehended."

"No, Murf. Realistically, how long will you go on looking for Paddy Lamp?"

"Well, priorities change over time. I don't believe that there is an intense search for him at this time. But we are alert to any sign of him. If there is a report of a sighting, an intense search will recommence."

"Will it ever stop? The search, that is?"

"When the case is 20 years old."

"Twenty years? Do you know how old Paddy Lamp will be in 20 years?"

"In 19 years. And I don't know how old Paddy Lamp is. Do you?"

"Well, he's a few years younger than me...."

"He's in his teens then?"

"...so in 19 years he will be dead. Itinerant travellers seldom live past their late fifties. And Paddy Lamp on-the-run is unlikely to reach the age of 60."

"The average life span of a traveller is 28." Murf considers it a blot on Irish society that it is unable to provide for the health and welfare of its own people.

"That's because of high infant mortality rate. Once past the age of five, the life expectancy is fifty-two."

"Now THAT'S a crime."

"So, Murf, say you caught Paddy Lamp. What would he be facing?"

"What charge? A charge of murder."

"And if he gave himself up?"

"Still a charge of murder. But it would go in his favour in sentencing."

"So would he hang?"

"No, not hang. The evidence we present would show extenuating circumstances. The trial judge, or the defence, would introduce voluntary manslaughter."

"What's the difference?"

"Voluntary manslaughter occurs when the defendant kills with mens rea, an intention to kill or cause grievous bodily harm, but with mitigating circumstances which reduce culpability."

"Or he could be found 'not guilty'?"

"Not guilty? Not likely. The evidence is too strong."

"So gaol time?"

"For Paddy Lamp, if he turns himself in, you are looking at eight years in prison with one year's suspension."

"So, Paddy Lamp, if he were to turn himself in, would go to prison and be out before the age of fifty?"

"Or remain on the run, and die on the run."

"Thanks, Murf. You have enlightened me. I'm off now. But one more thing, Murf." She places her hand on Murf's shoulder. Murf draws in his feet in readiness to stand. Doctor McBratt squeezes his shoulder and says, "It's the anniversary, Murf. Go to Canon MacMorrow's resting place and say a prayer for the repose of his soul."

Murf opens his mouth to speak. She squeezes his shoulder once more and says. "Please. It may bring peace to a lot of us."

Murf rises and steps into the aisle to permit Doctor McBratt to exit the pew. She stands beside him, waiting. Murf understands this to mean that he should proceed to the ambulatory space behind the altar, the location of the flagstone entrance to the crypt, the resting place of Canon MacMorrow.

He ascends the sanctuary steps to the altar and turns around to face the nave as it is momentarily washed in sunlight from the church doors opening and shutting at the departure of Doctor McBratt.

He continues to the ambulatory space. The area behind the altar is in shadow. Murf distinguishes a figure silhouetted against the sanctuary wall. It's not the recognisable shape of any statue in the church. The shadow sways. He realises that this is a person standing there. A nun perhaps? That's the shape of the figure, a person dressed in a long flowing robe with a veil covering the head. Probably a relative of Canon MacMorrow who has come for the anniversary Mass tomorrow. Not wishing to intrude, Murf stays back and waits. The dark figure sways again and, with a toss of the head, flings the veil back over the head like a horse flicking its tail. Murf realises that he is mistaken. What he took to be a veil is actually long hair. This is the idiosyncratic mannerism of tossing long hair back from the face.

This is the idiosyncratic mannerism of...

ACKNOWLEDGEMENTS:

Allied technological cooperation during World War II –
Wikipedia

Mac an Bhaird – Diarmuid Breathnach agus Máire Ní
Mhurchú (ainm.ie)

The Bretons – HouseofNames.com

Cambridge Five – Wikipedia

Donald Duart Maclean (spy) – Wikipedia

Drumceatt – *Drumceatt of Lore and Behold,* by Dr. Bob
Curran

Factors Affecting Human Decomposition – Hanna, J-A, &
Moyce, A. (2008), Queen's University Belfast

Fashion History – Women's Clothing of the 1950s – Bellatory

Flora of County Mayo – mayo-ireland.ie

Grudie Bridge and Loch Fannich – Wikipedia

Ham radio – Wikipedia

History of Shannon Airport – shannonairport.ie

Ideology of the post-civil war IRA and 1926-1936
marginalisation in the Free State – Wikipedia

Manhattan Project – Wikipedia

Nuclear Weapons of the United Kingdom – Wikipedia

Old Irish Coins – Central Bank of Ireland (centralbank.ie)

Translations – Google Translate

Traumatic Brain Injury – Wikipedia

Venona Project – Wikipedia

Walking distances – Google Maps

ABOUT THE AUTHOR

Fergus Patrick Egan was born in 1945 in Donegal in the northwest of Ireland. His childhood home was a small village at the Donegal / Fermanagh border between the Irish Free State (later the Republic of Ireland) and Northern Ireland. He spent summers with his paternal grandparents in Mayo. While employed as a banker he lived in ten different areas, where he observed and absorbed the cultural peculiarities of urban and rural communities in the Republic of Ireland and in Northern Ireland. He currently resides in Ontario, Canada.

Books Written by Fergus P Egan:

Black Donnelly, Rats and Pigs
The Coin and the Key
The Famine Field
Dorinda Trapper of Red Rapids
Field of Endeavour and Death
Lanta: Song of the Sea